Praise for *The Henna Artist*

"Fantastic, so evocative and beautiful and full of life and light…and deeply satisfying in its storytelling."
—Leah Franqui, author of *America for Beginners*

"Read this book slowly and savor it: Every page is rich with intricate pleasures for both the mind and the heart."
—Anita Amirrezvani, author of *The Blood of Flowers*

"An entertaining debut about an important theme—balancing family with personal ambition—that allows readers to escape into a fantasy teeming with sensory pleasure."
—*San Francisco Chronicle*

"Vibrant characters, evocative imagery, and sumptuous prose create an unforgettable tale."
—*Christian Science Monitor*

"Alka Joshi's debut novel exposes a society hobbled by a rigid caste system, misogyny, superstition and age-old traditions. The smell of sandalwood, cooking fires, and tropical flowers wafts through it all, but the injustice and poverty are all but inescapable."
—*BookTrib*

"Alka Joshi's debut novel is so evocative, so expressive and so exotic that it leads me to suggest she drop whatever else she is doing and write a second novel—like now."
—*Calgary Herald*

"A bold, ambitious, beautifully written novel about India…and about class, identity, love and deceit. The broad cast of characters will etch themselves into your psyche."
—Tom Barbash, author of *Stay Up with Me*

Also by Alka Joshi

THE HENNA ARTIST

The
SECRET
KEEPER
of
JAIPUR

ALKA JOSHI

mira

Recycling programs for this product may not exist in your area.

ISBN-13: 978-0-7783-1145-4

The Secret Keeper of Jaipur

Mira
22 Adelaide St. West, 40th Floor
Toronto, Ontario M5H 4E3, Canada
BookClubbish.com

Printed in U.S.A.

For Bradley, who encouraged me to write
For my readers, who fell in love with Malik

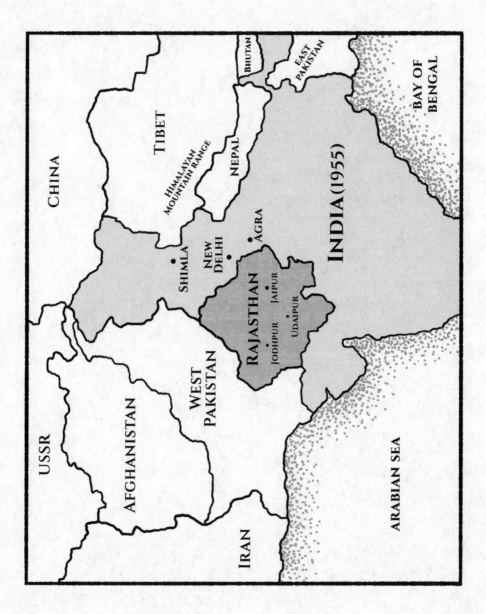

The good you do today may be forgotten tomorrow.
Do good anyway.
Honesty and transparency make you vulnerable.
Be honest and transparent anyway.
What you spend years building may be destroyed overnight.
Build anyway.
Give the world the best you have and you may get hurt.
Give the world your best anyway.

—MOTHER TERESA

If you want the rose, you must put up with the thorn.

—HINDU PROVERB

Be humble for you are made of earth
Be noble for you are made of stars.

—SERBIAN PROVERB

CHARACTERS WHO APPEAR

Malik: 20-year-old former ward of Lakshmi, graduate of Bishop Cotton School for Boys

Nimmi: 23-year-old tribal woman of the Himalayan hills, mother of Rekha (girl) and Chullu (boy)

Lakshmi Kumar: 42-year-old former henna artist, now director of Lady Bradley Healing Garden in Shimla, married to Dr. Jay Kumar

Jay Kumar: physician at Lady Bradley Hospital in Shimla, director of the Community Clinic, school chum of Samir Singh, married to Lakshmi

Radha: 25-year-old perfumer, Lakshmi's younger sister, lives in Paris with French architect husband and two daughters; had a baby out of wedlock with Ravi Singh twelve years ago; the baby was adopted by Kanta and Manu Agarwal

Samir Singh: 52-year-old architect and managing director of Singh-Sharma Construction, from a high-caste Rajput family related to the Jaipur royal family, husband of Parvati Singh and father of Ravi and Govind

Parvati Singh: 47-year-old society matron, wife of Samir Singh, mother of Ravi and Govind, distant relation of the Jaipur royal family

Ravi Singh: 29-year-old son of Parvati and Samir, architect in family firm Singh-Sharma Construction, married to Sheela

Sheela Singh: formerly Sheela Sharma, 27-year-old wife of Ravi Singh, mother of two small children, Rita and Baby

Manu Agarwal: 38-year-old facilities director for the Jaipur Palace, husband of Kanta

Kanta Agarwal: 38-year-old wife of Manu Agarwal, originally from a literary Calcutta family, mother of 12-year-old Niki, or Nikhil

Nikhil Agarwal: 12-year-old adopted son of Kanta and Manu; Lakshmi's sister, Radha, is his birth mother

Baju: an old family servant of Kanta and Manu Agarwal

Saas: means "mother-in-law" in Hindi. When Kanta refers to her *saas*, she is referring to Manu's mother, and when addressing a mother-in-law directly, a woman would call her by the respectful "Saasuji."

The Sharmas: parents of Sheela Singh, co-owners of the Singh-Sharma firm. Mr. Sharma, 80, is infirm. His wife hardly goes anywhere without him. So Samir Singh manages all operations for the company now.

Moti-Lal: prominent jeweler, owner of Moti-Lal Jewelers of Jaipur

Mohan: Moti-Lal's son-in-law and assistant at Moti-Lal Jewelers

Hakeem: accountant for the facilities office of the Jaipur Palace

Mr. Reddy: theater manager of the Royal Jewel Cinema

Maharani Indira: 74-year-old dowager queen, childless widow of a former maharaja of Jaipur, mother-in-law of the Maharani Latika, lives in the Maharanis' Palace

Maharani Latika: 43-year-old glamorous widow of the recently deceased maharaja of Jaipur and daughter-in-law of Maharani Indira, lives in the Maharanis' Palace, founded the Maharani School for Girls in Jaipur

Madho Singh: Alexandrine parakeet gifted to Malik by Maharani Indira

A glossary of Hindi and French terms is listed in the back.

PROLOGUE

MALIK

May 1969
Jaipur

It's opening night of the Royal Jewel Cinema, which shines as brilliantly as a gemstone. A thousand lights twinkle in the ceiling of the immense lobby. White marble steps leading to the upper balcony reflect the glow of a hundred wall sconces. A thick crimson carpet hushes the sound of thousands of footsteps. And inside the theater: every one of the eleven hundred mohair seats is occupied. Still more people stand, lining the walls of the theater for the premiere.

This is Ravi Singh's big moment. As lead architect on the prestigious project, commissioned by the Maharani Latika of Jaipur, the Royal Jewel Cinema stands as a testament to what modern ingenuity and a Western education can create. Ravi Singh has modeled it after the Pantages Theatre in Hollywood, eight thousand miles away. For this most celebrated of occasions, Ravi has arranged for the cinema house to show *Jewel Thief*, a film that was actually released two years ago. A few weeks ago, Ravi told me he picked the popular film because it reflects the name of the cinema house and features two of the most renowned Indian actors of the day. He knows that Indian audiences, crazy for films, are used to seeing the same movie multiple times; most cinemas only change their offerings every few months. So even if Jaipur residents saw the movie two years ago, they'll come see it again. Ravi also arranged for the film's stars Dev Anand and Vyjayanthimala, as well as one of the younger actresses, Dipti Kapoor, to be present for the grand opening. The press is also in attendance to write about the opening of the Royal Jewel Cinema, report on all of Jaipur high society in their bejeweled finery and gawk at the Bollywood glitterati.

Taking in the modern architecture, the plush red velvet curtains shielding the movie screen, the palpable air of anticipation, I'm impressed with what Ravi's accomplished—even if there are other things about him that make me uneasy.

My hosts, Manu and Kanta Agarwal, have been invited to sit with the Singhs and the Sharmas in the balcony, the most expensive seats in the house. I'm sitting with the Agarwals as their guest (otherwise, I'd be sitting in the cheaper seats down below, closer to the screen; I'm only a lowly apprentice at the Jaipur Palace, after all). Children are allowed up here on the balcony, but Kanta has left her son, Niki, at home with her *saas*. When I arrived at the Agarwals' earlier this evening to accompany them to the cinema opening, I could see just how devastated Niki was.

"It's the event of the century! Why can't I go? All my friends are going." Niki's face was flushed with anger. At twelve years old, he's able to charge his words with a strong sense of injustice.

Manu, ever calm in the face of his son's and his wife's explosive personalities, said, "Independence of our country was actually the event of the century, Nikhil."

"Well, I wasn't alive then, Papaji. But I'm alive now! And I don't see why I can't go." He looked to his mother for help.

Kanta met her husband's eyes as if to ask, *How much longer can we keep our son from social events where the Singhs are present? Niki is getting old enough to question why he's allowed to attend some social occasions and not others.* Kanta glanced at me as if to say, *Malik, what do you think?*

I'm flattered they feel comfortable having these conversations in front of me. I'm not related to them by blood but by the mere fact that my former guardian Lakshmi (or, as I call her, Auntie-Boss) is a close friend. I've known the Agarwals since I was a young boy, so I know about Niki's adoption, even if Niki himself doesn't. And I know that the moment the Singhs see those blue-green eyes of his—so uncommon in India—they'll be reminded of their own son's indiscretions; Auntie-Boss's sister, Radha, wasn't the first girl Ravi impregnated before his marriage to Sheela. Being aware of their son's shortcomings is one thing, but being confronted with it in the flesh would unnerve both Samir and Parvati Singh.

In the end, the Agarwals didn't need me to help decide the issue, which was a relief. Manu's mother, busy with her sandalwood rosary, settled the argument. "Because all that dancing and singing in films corrupts people! Come, Niki, help me up. We're going to my temple." Nikhil groaned. He was a polite child; an order from his grandmother was not up for debate.

Now, amid deafening applause inside the Royal Jewel Cinema, the Maharani Latika—the third and youngest wife, now widow—of the Maharaja of Jaipur, takes center stage to welcome all the moviegoers. This is the first major project she's headed since the death of her husband. She is Manu's boss; none of the other wives of the maharaja wanted to manage the finances. Manu is the director of facilities at the Jaipur Palace, shepherding building projects like these, and I've been sent by Auntie-Boss to learn his trade.

"Tonight, we celebrate the grandest movie house Rajasthan has ever known, the Royal Jewel Cinema." The maharani waits for the applause to die down before continuing. Her ruby-and-diamond earrings and the gold-embroidered *pallu* of her red silk Banarasi sari send a thousand sparkles out into the audience as she scans the packed house, a beatific smile on her face. "It's an historic occasion for Jaipur, home to world-renowned architecture, dazzling textiles and jewels, and, of course, Rajasthani *dal batti*!" The crowd erupts into delighted laughter at the mention of the famous local dish.

Her Highness acknowledges Manu's supervision of the project, compliments the fine work of Singh–Sharma architects and finishes her speech by welcoming the actors from the film onto the stage. Anand and Vyjayanthimala are followed by the kohl-eyed Kapoor in a sequined sari amid whistles and shouts of *Waa! Waa!* The audience showers all three with roses, frangipani and *chemali* and gives them a standing ovation. When we were growing up, Auntie-Boss's sister, Radha, was more of a film buff than I was. But tonight, even I'm caught up in the feverish excitement, the thunderous clapping and whistles from the audience.

Finally, the theater curtains part and a hush descends on the crowd as the film certificate and title credits begin rolling on the screen. Even the rickshaw-*wallas* and tailors in the cheap seats of the front rows are coaxed into silence.

Indian movies are long, lasting almost three, sometimes four, hours, broken by an intermission. At the break, we file out of the building—along with the majority of the audience—into the street for refreshments. The street vendors are prepared. They've arranged themselves along both sides of the street in front of the theater. The aroma of roasting chili peanuts, *panipuri*, onion *pakoras* and potato *samosas* is almost too much to resist. I buy small glasses of chai for everyone and pass them around. Samir buys a large plate of *kachori* and *aloo tikki* for our group.

It's May in Jaipur and already sweltering. The theater is air-conditioned, but the air outside is fresher than the odor of a thousand bodies pressed close together inside the theater. Ravi's wife, Sheela, refuses the chai and the food, claiming it's too hot to eat. Her baby daughter has fallen asleep on her shoulder, the warmth of her small body making Sheela squirm. Sheela puffs out her cheeks and walks over to a stall selling *khus-khus* fans. A bead of sweat glides down her throat and disappears into the low neckline of her fuchsia silk blouse. I force myself to look away.

Parvati is proudly showing off her four-year-old grand-daughter Rita to the society matrons who have come to say hello. *"Tumara naam batao, bheti."*

Kanta is chatting gaily with friends. Samir and Manu are being congratulated for their work on the cinema house by the Jaipur elite who have shown up for the gala affair. I look around for Ravi, who was with them earlier, and wonder why he would miss this opportunity to be in the limelight. It's not like him.

As always, I'm watching and listening, something Auntie-Boss taught me to do well. In my next letter to her and Nimmi in Shimla, I'll be able to tell them what the moviegoers thought of the leading lady's hairstyle or the color of her sari (I'll wager Nimmi has never seen a movie in her life!). I'll also be able to tell them that most of the ladies of Jaipur would marry the handsome Dev Anand given half a chance.

I see Sheela coming back to join our group, waving her fan in front of her face. Parvati reaches up to lift damp curls away from the sleeping baby's forehead. Sheela is looking past her mother-in-law. Suddenly, her face hardens. I follow her gaze to the corner of the cinema house. That's when I notice Ravi discreetly escorting the younger actress out the side door of the building. Sheela's eyes narrow as her husband and the starlet disappear in the darkness, away from the throng. I know there's a loading dock there. It's also where the drivers for the maharani and the actors are waiting to whisk them away. Perhaps he's taking her to her car.

We hear the bell announcing that intermission is almost over. The second half of the film is about to begin. I check my watch. It's now 9:30 p.m. Sheela's girls should be in bed, but Ravi had insisted that the family be present and seen by the public at his big moment. I'm sure Sheela fought him on it. She prefers to have the *ayah* look after the girls.

The crowd files back into the lobby and through the open doors of the theater. I hand the empty tea glasses to the chai-*wallas* making their rounds. Banana leaves on which *chaat* was sold litter the ground. A fragrance of food served and eaten—not wholly unpleasant—lingers in the air. I lift up Rita, Ravi's other daughter, whose eyes have started to droop, and hoist her onto my shoulder.

I follow the rest of the group inside the lobby.

Before we make it through the doors, we hear a yawning creak, then a complaining groan, and then suddenly the roar of a thousand pounds of cement, brick, rebar and drywall crashing down. Within seconds, the earsplitting sounds of a building collapsing, screams of agony and howls of pain are coming from inside the theater.

TWO MONTHS BEFORE
THE COLLAPSE

1

NIMMI

March 1969
Shimla, State of Himachal Pradesh, India

I stop walking to look at the mountains rising from their sleep. Winter in Shimla is coming to an end. The men and women wrap themselves in two, sometimes three, pashmina shawls, but the hills are casting off their blankets. I hear the plunk, plunk, plunk of melting snow hitting the hard ground as I make my way carefully to Lakshmi Kumar's house.

Yesterday, I saw the first pink anemones in the valley below us, brazenly pushing their noses through the thin air. In the distant hills to the north, I imagine my tribe herding their goats and sheep through the Kangra Valley to the village of Bharmour, in the upper Himalayas, as I would be doing were my husband,

Dev, still alive. It is hard to believe it's been a year since he's been gone. My daughter, Rekha, would be running beside her father, waving her tiny arms in an effort to help him shepherd the goats and sheep, while I carried our baby, Chullu, on my back. We would be accompanied by the other families of our tribe who had wintered in the lower Himalayas to secure food for their herds. As soon as the snows started melting in early spring, we always made our way back up the mountains to start cultivating our fields with the sheep manure that had matured into rich fertilizer over the winter months.

I haven't seen my family since I left my tribe last spring after Dev's fatal accident. They don't come down south as far as Shimla, but not a day goes by that I don't think about them with fondness.

As we walked, Old Suresh used to tell us jokes. *Did you hear the one about the flatulent goat and the shepherd without a nose?* No, tell us that one, we would laugh.

Grandmother Sushila, toothless, gray whiskers poking out of the triangular tattoo on her chin, would begin one of the folktales told to her by her grandmother. *So the king commanded the queen to weave a blanket for him from the finest wool, which he knew would take her the better part of ten years.* We all knew the story by heart and would finish the final sentence for her, at which point she would look at us with a frown. *Oh, you know that one already?*

Having sold the wool from our sheep in the lower Himalayas, we would be flush with our winter purchases: a factory-made sky-blue sweater, a Philips transistor radio, a squawking chicken bought at a hill-station market. A few families may have picked up a handsome spotted house goat or a young black bull we would all admire. My sister-in-law would be showing off a new winnowing tray; my older brother walking proudly by her side with his sons. We would wag our heads and agree that the tray could separate the husks from the rice grains much more quickly.

I smile now as I think about those treks through the Himalayan mountains. I feel happy, almost. What would make it complete is a letter from Malik, even if I have to share it with someone else, especially if that someone is Lakshmi. If only I could have attended school, I would not be subjected to the humiliation of having his letters to me sent to *her* to be read to *me*.

My goatskin boots make a satisfying squelching sound on the mushy gravel as I conjure ways I would like to stomp Lakshmi Kumar out of my life.

The day Lakshmi first came into my life, I was not in my right mind. I had been so delirious with fever and grief that I was not even aware of my son, Chullu, coming into this world, two months before his time. Earlier that same day, my husband Dev had tried to drag a young male goat, drunk on rhododendron leaves, back onto the narrow mountain trail. We'd been on our way to our summer homes in the upper Himalayas. Dev lost his footing, and both he and the goat hurtled hundreds of feet into a ravine. We all saw it happen, but there was nothing any of us could do. We have always known the Himalayas to be the home of the gods—Shiva, Ram and Kamla—all of whom are much more powerful than we are. If they want to take someone from us, that is their right, their privilege. Still, I was not ready to let my husband go. Over and over I cried, *Wasn't the goat we sacrificed at the start of our trip enough to protect us? Or was it an evil nazar?* That our sheep had produced so much wool the winter before may have aroused someone's jealousy.

I grabbed the shoulders of those near me, screeching into their startled faces, *Tell me you didn't give Dev the evil eye!* I screamed at Lord Shiva. I beat my fists on my distended belly, promising to give Shivaji the baby if he would just bring Dev back. My father-in-law and my brother had to pull my arms away from my stomach to keep me from hurting the life within. The women rubbed my temples, hands and feet with warm mustard oil until I finally sank into a stupor. Almost a week later, when I awakened as if from a long sleep, I saw little Rekha's face, pinched with worry, hovering at the edge of my bed and called my daughter to me. She was just three and didn't understand yet that she might never see her father again. It was then that my father-in-law told me about the doctor and *doctrini* who had come from Shimla to tend to me; my body had needed medicines stronger than our tribe carried. My husband's father spoke to me through a curtain that the women had erected to keep nursing mothers isolated for the eleven days after a baby's birth. I looked down and noticed for the first time a sleeping baby boy in the crook of my arm, his head slung away from my leaking breast, his rose-colored mouth drooling pale blue milk.

How could I ever have wished this baby away? In him Shiva had given me Dev's fine nostrils and wide forehead, the slight curl in his hair. I asked Rekha to climb onto the blanket with us and say hello to her brother Chullu.

The next time I met Lakshmi Kumar was also the day I met Malik, last June. I was selling flowers along the main walkway in Shimla. Rekha was three, a serious girl, and I had asked her to watch her three-month-old baby brother. That morning in the Shimla woods, I had picked roses, daises and buttercups for tourists and perennial visitors, and for the discerning buyer: peonies, yarrow and foxglove. Living as I had with my tribe, I knew how certain flowers could cure aches and coughs, ease monthly bleeding, lull fretful bodies to sleep.

At my stall, I removed the flowers from the large shallow basket I'd woven with fairy grass and arranged them on a horsehair blanket on the ground. When Chullu began fussing, I reached into my blouse, extracting a small rag from my leaking breasts to give to him. He began sucking on it and quieted down. Soon he would begin to teethe, and eventually I would have to stop suckling him, but for now I enjoyed feeling his warmth—Dev's warmth—next to my body.

The last thing I always unpacked was the silver statue of Shiva. I set it to one side after offering a silent prayer to him, to thank him for my Chullu. Then I put both my children in the empty basket. Like my mother before me and her mother before her, I had learned to tether my babies when I was busy boiling goat milk for the cheese, sewing a coat or gathering dung for the fire. Chullu watched as I tied the cloth rope around his wrist. When I kissed his cheeks, he squirmed to one side and rocked his head back. Rekha played with his hair. No sooner had she braided his curls than he shook his head and giggled, tossing the braid off, and she had to start over again.

I knew I looked different from the other vendors along the walkway, and this I saw as an advantage, particularly with tourists—honeymooning Indians, elders on spiritual retreats, Europeans fascinated by our tribal ways. Like other women of my tribe, I wore my flowered skirt in bright yellow cotton over my green *salwar kameez*. A silver medallion sat like a small cap on my hair, crowning the orange *chunni* draped over my head and around my shoulders. A rope made of sheep wool, boiled and dyed black, was tied twenty times around my waist. Then there were the telltale dots—three of them tattooed in a triangle onto my chin when I came of age—that always made visitors to Shimla stare. The only thing I'd stopped wearing was the elaborate nose ring—as large as a bracelet—given to me at my wedding; I realized it made me not just a curiosity but almost a sideshow, with visitors pointing it out to one another. They thought they were being discreet, but I found the fascination in their faces disturbing.

After Dev died in the gorge, I'd became adamant that my children would never suffer the same fate, migrating back and

forth with the tribe through the mountains, toes lost to frost-
bite, the threat of death always only a few paces away. I asked my
father-in-law to let me stay in Shimla. He would have liked me
to marry another bachelor from our tribe, but he was grieving
over his son's death, too, and agreed, reluctantly, on the condition that I would have to make my own way. His parting gift
to me was a large supply of dried meat and all the silver jewelry
from my dowry. As a woman, I had no right to property, not
even a sheep or a goat, but I knew I could sell my jewelry if we
fell on hard times.

To the left of my stall on the Shimla Mall, a balloon seller
was squeezing his air sausages into the shapes of elephants and
camels. My children watched, fascinated. Chullu reached for
one, but Rekha gently pulled his arm down. To my right was a
Coca-Cola stand whose owner had not yet arrived. It was a little
early in the day for people to ask for a cool drink. By afternoon,
visitors would be lining up for its exotic taste.

The clock at Christ Church struck eight times. On spring
mornings, early risers hiked to pray at the temples on Jakhu Hill,
Sankat Mochan or Tara Devi. The mildly religious slept in late;
there was no need for them to hurry about their day.

I spotted a young man and a woman in the distance walking purposefully in my direction. The woman wore a maroon
sari and a matching wool cloak, embroidered at the edges with
white flowers. She walked quickly, taking short strides. Her hair
was pinned neatly to the top of her head in a twist. The young
man was lean, a head taller than the woman, but his walk was
looser, as if he had all the time in the world. Still, he easily kept
pace with her. When they were closer to my stall, I noticed that
she was old enough to be his mother. Fine lines crisscrossed her
forehead and the corners of her mouth. The man looked to be no
more than twenty, perhaps a few years younger than me. He was
dressed in a white shirt, blue jumper and dark gray slacks. The

woman's eyes were focused on my flowers, while his, bouncing with amusement, were watching my children in the basket.

The woman reached for the peonies. "Where did you find these?" she asked.

I had to wrest my eyes away from the young man; he reminded me so much of my late husband. Dev's eyes, gentle and sharp-edged at the same time, much like this man's, had wooed me, loved me, made me feel safe.

When I turned to the woman, I was startled by her eyes, as well. She was a handsome woman made beautiful by those blue orbs, the color of the mountain sky after a night's rain. "In a ravine about a mile from here," I told her. "It plunges sharply from the cliff. There is a grove of them at the bottom." Revealing my find did not concern me. I was used to scaling steep slopes, and I was confident that no one so refined would follow me there. When our tribal elders called one another "old goats," they were referring to the way we trotted so easily up mountains alongside our herds.

Chullu cried out and the woman's attention fell on him. Her eyes flickered and her mouth opened slightly. I rubbed a finger along Chullu's aching gums to soothe him. The woman's face broke into a wondrous smile. "I see he has grown."

Did I know her? If I had met her before, I didn't remember her. She saw my confusion and nodded her chin toward Chullu. "Dr. Kumar and I helped you with his birth a few months ago." She glanced at the top of the ridge. "Several miles on the other side of that peak."

So this was the *doctrini* who had attended to me! She was responsible for saving my Chullu; I owed her a great deal. I brought my hands together and reached down to touch her feet. "Thank you, Doctor. If not for you—"

She bent to stop me, covering my hands with hers. That was when I noticed the finest henna work I had ever seen on a woman's hands. It looked like the elegant bead-and-sequin work on a wedding *chunni*—almost as if she were wearing gloves made of an intricately patterned chiffon fabric. It was with an effort that I tore my eyes away from her hands. She was speaking again.

"It is my husband, Dr. Kumar, you have to thank. Up at Lady Bradley Hospital," she said. "I'm not a doctor. I work with him to help ease the pain during and after childbirth. I'm glad to see you and the baby so healthy."

I noticed that she made no mention of my husband, for which I was grateful. The intense pain I had felt upon first losing Dev had narrowed now into a trickle of hurt, perceptible only at certain moments—like when my eyes fell upon the amulet of Shivaji that Dev used to wear around his neck and that I now draped around the statue of the god in my home.

Turning away from the woman and my thoughts of Dev, I began wrapping peonies in old newspaper. I heard the young man ask my children which creature they would like the balloon vendor to make for them. I glanced at him, crouched in front of the children's basket. Chullu stared, mesmerized.

"Please…it is not necessary," I said.

The man with my husband's eyes turned to me and said, "No, it is not necessary." He kept smiling at me until I had to turn away, my face flushed with heat.

I busied myself with the flowers. When the woman tried to pay me, I waved her money away. "I could never repay you enough, *Ji.*"

But the woman pressed money into my palm anyway and said, "You can repay me by feeding them well," pointing at the children, who were now playing with the elephant balloon the young man had bought for them.

The *doctrini* asked, "Will you make sure you have some peonies for me tomorrow, as well? And I should take some yarrow while I'm here."

As the couple began walking away with their purchases, I called after them, "MemSahib, may I know your name?"

Without breaking her stride, the woman with the blue eyes turned her head and grinned at me. "Mrs. Kumar. Lakshmi Kumar. And yours?"

"Nimmi."

She pointed to the young man, who had turned to face me and was now walking backward to keep pace with her. "This is Malik—Abbas Malik—who will pick up a regular order of flowers from you every few days."

Malik stopped to *salaam* me, grinned, and ran to catch up with her.

The next day I took more care than usual as I got ready, making sure my hair was pinned back. I wore my heavy silver earrings and necklace, the ones from my marriage. I told myself I had dressed for the tourists, but I waited eagerly for Malik. I wasn't sure he would come, but I had a feeling. When he did, he first said hello to Chullu and Rekha. Chullu grinned at him with pink gums, but Rekha studied him seriously, as is her way. Then Malik pulled a small jar from the cloth bag he was carrying and handed it to me.

Surprised, I took it from him and looked at the dense golden liquid inside. My hands were trembling. The last gift anyone had given me were the mirrored ties for the ends of my braids that Dev's sister had made for my wedding.

"For when he is teething," he explained.

I twisted the jar open and twirled some honey on my finger, holding it out to Chullu, who opened his mouth in response. I rubbed a little along his gums, and he started flicking his tiny tongue along his lips. Rekha wanted some honey, too, and so I gave her a fingerful to lick. I had not had the money to buy honey and was overcome with gratitude that such a thoughtful gift should come from a man not of my family.

"Thank you," I said, not taking my eyes off my children.

"It is I who am grateful to you for the peonies. Otherwise, Auntie-Boss would have made me scale the cliff to get them." His laugh was rich and deep.

I looked at him. "Auntie-Boss?"

"Mrs. Kumar. She's my boss, although she pretends she's not." He grinned.

"How did you know about the honey?" I asked.

"From *Omi*'s children—both hers and the ones she looked after in my old neighborhood. Someone was always teething. My mother—well, I call Omi my mother, but she's someone who took me in when I was little—rubbed honey on their gums." He grinned. "Wait till you see what I can do with hair. I helped with all my cousin-sisters' braids."

Before I could ask him what happened to his real mother or who this Omi was, Rekha cried out, "Do my hair!" She'd been listening to our exchange.

After that he arrived each day with something for the children: a bow for Rekha, a sack of sweet litchis, a green cricket for Chullu. From the start, I felt easy with him. I started harvesting the rarest of plants for him to take back to Mrs. Kumar. Rhododendron for the cure of swollen ankles. Roots of snowpeaks raspberry to stop bleeding when a woman's monthly flow becomes too heavy. I even gave him a bowl of *sik* one day, made from the dried fruit of the *neem* tree, browning it in *ghee* before adding sugar and water. It was what I ate during both of my pregnancies and what all women of the hills consume to keep their bodies healthy before and after delivery.

One fine August morning, when the mist had left the mountains and I felt the sun redden my cheeks, Malik showed up with a tiffin carrier. He said it was filled with corn and wheat *cha-*

pattis and a curry made from summer squash and sweet onions. "Today, we are buying everything you have and I am taking you on a picnic."

Rekha smiled—rare for her. Then she clapped and hopped out of the basket. I untethered the children and placed Chullu on my hip.

"Who is 'we'? You and your shadow?" I teased.

He began gathering my flowers and placing them gently into the now empty basket. "The Lady Bradley Hospital. Yesterday, the daughter of a financier gave birth to twin boys. I'd shared your *sik* with the nurses, who shared it with her. She said it was one of the best things she'd ever tasted and it made her feel better. Next thing you know, her father is gifting money for the new wing of the hospital! What do you think of that?" Malik tapped his forefinger on Chullu's nose, then Rekha's, and they giggled.

I covered the flower basket with the horsehair blanket and hauled it onto my back. Then I hoisted Chullu over my head, letting his head dangle over one shoulder while I grabbed his ankle over the other shoulder. I showed Malik how to carry Rekha that way, too. It is the way our tribe has always carried our small children for their comfort as well as ours.

Malik took to it as if he had been doing it all his life.

On a warm evening, a few weeks later, he showed up at the lodgings I rented for myself and my children in lower Shimla. The air in the room was thick with the fragrance of spicy potatoes I was preparing for the children, and I'd propped the door open to catch the breeze. Malik stood at my threshold, wearing that lazy smile of his. For a moment, I stood, staring, the spoon I'd been using frozen in my hand. Then I let go of the spoon, walked to the door and wrapped my arms around him, never even asking how he discovered where I lived.

My lodgings are nothing more than a covered area underneath

the overhang of a house—packed earth, walls made of wooden planks, one window with a curtain. It feels familiar—so much like the hut where Dev and I lived during the summers, high in the mountains. There, we layered long grasses over a wooden frame to construct the walls. Everyone in the tribe helped. Our windows had no coverings or glass, and we slept on bedrolls stuffed with grass.

My landlords here in Shimla, the Aroras, gave me a two-burner stove that took a little getting used to; I was accustomed to cooking over an open fire. The tap and outhouse were outside. The Aroras are in their sixties and have no children of their own. On the day they first saw me with my two, breaking camp on a hill overlooking their house, they invited us to breakfast with them. Mrs. Arora took Chullu from me and sniffed his hair, closing her eyes. Rekha hid in my skirts until Mr. Arora offered her a toffee. After learning of my situation, Mr. Arora offered to enclose the space underneath their house, directly below the cantilevered drawing room. They told me not to worry about the rent, but I try to give them as much as I can from what I make at the flower stall. For their part, the old couple are delighted to look after Chullu and Rekha in the mornings while I forage the forests.

In the seven months since Malik and I started sharing a bed, I have seen Lakshmi, his "Auntie-Boss," only a few times. She has left the buying of her medicinal herbs to Malik, coming with him only to see if I've harvested any new flowers since her last visit or to ask if there is another variety of Indian snakeroot that might be more potent for lowering blood pressure than the last batch Malik bought.

A few months earlier, she had come with Malik to the stall, and I thought she must be looking for a special herb. I stood up to greet them both. But she seemed distracted, cursorily eyeing my flowers and plants while Malik gathered the supplies he needed from my stall. I felt her studying me when I wasn't looking. My children cried out to play with Malik when he was finished. Rekha wanted him to engage in a hand-clapping game he had taught her, and Chullu wanted a ride on his back. Malik smiled at them but avoided me.

I glanced at Lakshmi, whose eyes were darting from Malik to me. I felt a flutter in my heart—the way I do when I'm troubled—and sensed the beginnings of an unease between us. I realized then that it embarrassed Malik to have Lakshmi know that we had more than a passing acquaintance.

2

LAKSHMI

Shimla

I love this season, the sharp air in my nostrils, the crunch of snow crystals beneath my boots and the anticipation of a new season ahead. Having lived the majority of my life in the dry heat of Rajasthan and Uttar Pradesh, I never thought I'd come to love the cooler weather of the Himalayan foothills.

As I round the last hill on my morning walk, I spot the roof and gables of my Victorian bungalow topped with the last of the snow, like an elaborate pastry decorated with cream. Off to one side of the house is a Himalayan cedar, its branches weighted with white powder. The scene always fills me with joy, and I wonder—as I often do—how I could capture its delicate beauty with a henna design.

Then I spot Nimmi waiting on my doorstep.

On the path, I hesitate.

In full tribal regalia, her slim figure is striking. Her skin is the color of wet bark, so dark that her eyes—small, deep set— shine like those of an energetic black-eyed *bulbul*. These and her hawkish nose make her seem severe. I chide myself for judging her. Haven't I taught myself to appear pleasant even when the situation doesn't call for it? It's a skill I mastered during a decade of tending to the whims of the ladies of Jaipur as I painted their hands with henna. Perhaps the women of Nimmi's tribe are raised not to temper their true emotions?

I find myself frowning. Does Nimmi make me uncomfortable because she holds me responsible for taking Malik away from her? Possibly. Maybe that's why I go out of my way to be polite, pleasant to her. I probably buy the majority of her flowers on the Shimla Mall. I have told Malik to pay more than she asks because I know she's a young widow struggling to make ends meet and care for her children. And yet, I sense hostility in her attitude toward me. Or is it wariness? As if she's waiting for me to disapprove or chasten or reprimand her? Am I? I have to admit she does remind me of those early years with my younger sister, Radha, who was so quick to discount anything I might say to her.

I force myself to smile as I mount the veranda steps. Nimmi takes an anxious step forward. That hungry look in her eyes is asking, *Is there a letter from Malik today?*

Her hair is covered with a *chunni*, and she is wearing the silver medallion over her hair that marks her as a nomad. She doesn't seem to feel the cold that I, wrapped in a light wool shawl over a cashmere sweater and a heavy sari, do. Malik tells me the weave and weft of Nimmi's homespun wool clothes keep her and her hill people warmer and drier than the yarn with which I knit sweaters for Jay and me.

I nod and murmur a welcome. I turn the key in the front door and hold it open for her. She takes a few steps inside and stops. The room glows orange and yellow from the fire Jay laid before he went to work this morning. Its flames make shadow puppets on the gleaming wood floor. Opposite the fireplace are a sofa and two armchairs covered in cream cotton.

I try to see the room as Nimmi sees it; she seems so uncomfortable. To her, a hill woman accustomed to sleeping in the open air on bedding quilts padded with scraps of old blankets, these two-story Shimla houses, built by the British, must seem obscenely luxurious.

"*Namaste! Bonjour!* Welcome!" squawks Madho Singh. Nimmi reacts, looking for the source of the sound—much as Malik had done all those years ago when he first saw the talking bird at the Maharanis' Palace in Jaipur. Madho Singh's cage stands by the fireplace (he likes to be warm; he's a tropical bird, after all, and Shimla is a little breezy for him). Malik had to leave him behind when he left for Jaipur (he somehow managed to keep the bird in his rooms at Bishop Cotton when he boarded there). I have to admit that I've grown used to the Alexandrine parakeet— would miss him, almost, if he weren't grumbling at me all day long, as he used to do to the Maharani Indira. So charmed was the dowager maharani by Malik and his fascination of Madho Singh that she gifted him her parakeet when we left Jaipur (although I also wonder if this wasn't just her way of getting rid of an old annoyance).

Now there's a ghost of a smile on Nimmi's lips; the bird amuses her.

I hang my cloak on a hook by the door. Jay's green wool cardigan, the one he wears at home, hangs there, as do our hats, umbrellas and coats. I see Nimmi's eyes go to the drawing room table where we take our morning tea. Beside the empty cups and saucers is an envelope, slit cleanly, with a silver letter opener beside it. Her eyes fasten on the envelope as if it were a precious jewel.

"Would you like some tea?" I ask her.

She shakes her head no, politely but impatiently. She can barely keep from commanding me to read the letter. It's the only reason she is here. Her tribe moves with the seasons, up and down the Himalayas, so most of its members have never attended school or learned to read. Malik made me promise that I would read aloud the letters he wrote to her.

"I made something special just for you. Let me get it." Before she can object, I walk into the kitchen and start the tea. She may not be feeling the cold, but my body is. As the milk and water come to a boil, I drop in cardamom seeds, a cinnamon stick and a few peppercorns before spooning in the tea leaves. The candied lemon slices and sugared rose petals I'd prepared earlier are sitting on a stainless steel plate. Nimmi has been grieving since Malik left a month ago, and I know the essences of fruits and flowers are a natural balm for sadness. My old *saas* had taught me that, and I've used the recipe to treat many a downhearted soul.

With the tray of tea and the candied fruit, I return to the drawing room to find Nimmi warming her hands at the fireplace. I indicate the armchairs opposite the hearth, and Nimmi lowers herself onto one, pushing her heavy skirt aside and perching on the edge, a skittish bird ready to fly the nest. I settle in the other. Between us is the drawing room table. I push the plate of sweet treats toward her and pour the chai into our porcelain cups. "How are your children?"

She picks up a lemon slice and examines it; perhaps her people don't eat candied fruit. "They are healthy," she replies in Hindi. Her native language is Pahari and her dialect is so different from what I know that I barely understand a word of it.

"That's wonderful to hear."

My husband, who is a doctor at the Community Clinic, told

me both her son and daughter had been suffering from ear infections the last time he attended to them.

Nimmi nods, absentmindedly, and takes a bite of the candied fruit. Her eyes widen. The sweet-and-sour taste takes her by surprise. She hides a small smile behind her teacup as she takes a sip.

I lower my eyes and drink my tea. "Before I read Malik's letter, there are some things I would like to say."

With an effort, she lifts her eyes. It's hard to tell what's in those deep orbs. Her features are sharp, lean, but there is beauty there. Her brows are prominent, as are her cheekbones. Years in the high sun, crisscrossing the Himalayan mountains with her family's tribe on their annual migrations, have toughened her skin. I'm not a tall woman, yet she stands a few inches shorter than me.

"Nimmi, I know Malik cares for you and is fond of you. I wish you no ill will. I only want what is best for him."

The words fly out of her mouth in anger. "You aren't his mother."

I take a breath before answering. "No," I say. "We may never know who his real mother was, but I've been looking out for him since he was a boy. And I was his legal guardian once we moved here until he came of age."

She may have heard this much from Malik, but I want her to hear it from me. And so I tell her how Malik, a shoeless, bedraggled child, had followed me around Jaipur and attached himself to me when I worked there as a henna artist. He had a pride in his bearing, but also hunger in his eyes. So I'd let him run small errands for a few *paise*. He'd done everything I asked of him so quickly and so well that, over time, I'd given him more responsibility—until he was purchasing supplies and delivering my aromatic oils and creams all over the city. He'd quickly become a part of my small family, as necessary to my life as the hands with which I painted henna on the bodies of my clients.

Together with my younger sister, Radha—who was nearing fourteen at the time and like a sister to him as well—the three of us had all come to Shimla twelve years ago so they could attend the excellent schools here while I worked at the hospital.

"We were so lucky that a benefactor from Jaipur financed Malik's education at the Bishop Cotton School for Boys. It was such a relief, Nimmi. I knew it would open doors for him anywhere he chose to go—"

"Could you please just read me the letter?" She's squeezing her hands so tightly that her knuckles have turned pale.

I reach for her hands. She seems surprised, but she lets me. They are a laborer's hands for one so young. Rough, scarred. I rub my thumbs over the evidence of her short, but hard-working, life: hoeing, planting, shearing, herding, milking. I turn her hands over, feeling for her pulse points between thumb and index finger, gently pressing them to relax her. I give her time to study the henna on my hands; I've noticed her curiosity about it. To me, henna is a way for a woman to find a piece of herself she might have mislaid.

When I used to apply henna for a living in Jaipur, it was so satisfying to watch the change in women after their skin had been oiled and massaged and decorated with a cooling henna paste, after they had whiled away a half hour telling me stories about their lives, after they'd seen the reddish glow of a custom imprint as the henna dried and flaked off. They emerged calmer, happier, more content.

I miss those intimate moments with my clients as much as I miss the joy of their transformations. I think that's why I paint henna on my own hands now. (In Jaipur, I would never have allowed my hands to upstage the work I did on my ladies; I merely oiled my hands smooth and kept my fingernails neat and trimmed.) But that precious feeling of serenity is missing from Nimmi's watchful countenance—I want to offer her that.

"Other than the time of your marriage, has anyone ever painted your hands with henna?"

She shakes her head, interested now.

"Would you like me to do it?" I turn my wrist to consult my watch. I have work to do, but this is more important. "I have two hours before I must start at the clinic. We have plenty of time."

She looks again, with wonder, at my hands, then at her own undecorated ones.

"Perhaps I can draw the wildflowers you harvest? Or something your children particularly love? How about that cricket Malik found for them?"

At the mention of Malik's name, Nimmi snatches her hands back. She rubs them together, as if I've scalded her.

She's not ready for this kind of comfort.

I pick up the envelope, remove the folded onionskin pages and smooth them out with the flat of one hand on my lap. I want so much to reach her. I know she's had a difficult life. I know how hard she's working, still, to put food in the mouths of her children. But I'd been thinking about Malik's future long before she arrived on the scene. I press my lips together, almost as if I'm trying to keep any harsh words from leaving my lips.

"I did not send Malik to Jaipur to keep him away from you, Nimmi. I merely wanted to keep him from getting into trouble here," I say. I'm searching for the right words. I don't want her to resent me; that would create a gulf between Malik and me, and I couldn't bear that. "He is an enterprising young man, and I'm sure he sees the money to be made across the Nepalese border. Surely your tribe has seen some of that activity in your treks up and down the mountains. The unrest along India's northern borders seems to have created many illegal businesses— gunrunning and drug trafficking among them." I watch Nimmi for signs that she's understanding what I'm saying. I think I see her nod slightly as she picks up another candied lemon. "Of course, I'm not suggesting Malik is actually doing any such thing. I sent him to Jaipur to work with our family friend Manu Agarwal because that seemed the best way to keep him safe and expose him to the professional world there. Manu is the director of facilities at the Jaipur Palace. He can introduce Malik to many people, people who can help shape his future."

To my own ears, I sound like an overinvolved mother. Is that how Nimmi sees me? I reach for my cup and drain my chai. Malik is twenty, a grown man. But in him I still see the eager, enterprising boy he used to be. He hasn't lost his taste for risk.

I know Nimmi is upset with me for sending him away, but I need to do what's in Malik's best interest. I gather the tea tray with the teapot and unused cups from the table and take it to the kitchen. Having been at the service of so many of the elite in Jaipur, I prefer to do my own tidying up rather than hiring a servant. Once a week, a local woman—Moni—comes to clean the house. Moni's husband clears our walkways in the winter.

When I reenter the room, Nimmi is gazing into the fire. Her hands are clasped under her chin, under her tribal tattoo, her elbows resting on her thighs. I sit down again.

"If Malik does not take to the work of construction and building, he will come back, Nimmi. But I want him to try it. Here in Shimla, he is at loose ends. And I fear he stays because of me." This draws a sharp look from her. *What about me*, I hear her thinking. *I know he is fond of me, as well.*

She says, "My children have grown used to him. They never stop asking about him."

I hear the sadness in her voice and want to press more candied fruit on her. There is no denying Malik's attachment to Nimmi and her children. I've seen the way his eyes caress her face and light up when he sees Rekha and Chullu. She's a strong woman, and he has always been drawn to strong women. I take a deep breath, remind myself what I need to accomplish.

I pull out the drawer on the side table next to me. Inside are my eyeglasses and a notebook. With my glasses on, I know I appear sterner, but I can't help it. I flip through the book, stopping at a page. *"March 8, 140 rupees, Nimmi. February 24, 80 rupees, Nimmi."* I turn back a few more pages. *"January 14, 90 rupees, Nimmi. December 1, 75 rupees."* I look at her.

Her eyes are blazing now. "What is that?" She points to the notebook in my hand.

"His bankbook. I opened an account for him when he started school here. It's part of what all smart young men must learn to do." I put the book back in the drawer.

Her nostrils flare. Her jaw tenses. "Malik offered to help me through the winter months, when there were not enough flowers to sell and not enough tourists to sell them to." She closes her eyes and clasps her hands together. "Would you just read the letter, Mrs. Kumar?"

I swallow my sigh. I pick up the onionskin pages and begin reading.

My Dear Nimmi,

Jaipur is lonely without you. Manu Uncle and Kanta Auntie have been extremely gracious in welcoming me to Jaipur. Their son, Nikhil, is only twelve years old and almost as tall as I am! They must be feeding him a lot of extra ghee!

Manu Uncle is keeping me busy. The civil engineers on his staff are teaching me about things like impact load and shear stress and beam-column joints till my head spins. Manu-ji takes me to important meetings with building-wallas and to construction sites (the palace has so many building projects going on!). I'm learning about stone and marble, when to use steel and when to use wood, and a lot of complicated formulas about the pressure a column and post can take. Most recently, he told me I would eventually be as-

sisting the palace accountant, Hakeem Sahib. So I will be adding up a lot of figures. Soon I will be bringing back knowledge that will prove how much smarter a man can be than a woman! (That was for you, Auntie-Boss, since I know you're reading this to Nimmi.)

March is starting to heat up. My shirt is sticking to my back as I write this. I have only been in Jaipur a month, and I have already forgotten how cool Shimla was when I left. Has the snow melted, or did you get one last storm?

Please give the little barrettes to Rekha. I thought they would look pretty in her hair. For Chullu, I have found the most beautiful marbles (which I'll hold on to for the time being, since he's liable to eat them). I will teach him how to become a sure shot when I see him next. Just think! By the time he's two, he'll be able to run his own marble gambling operation (joke, Auntie-Boss!).

I must get ready for my dinner at Samir Singh's house. (Did I tell you, Boss, that he has invited me? Not to worry; no one will remember me as the eight-year-old ruffian I once was, scurrying around after you in Jaipur.) Manu-ji has told Samir Sahib to make sure he refers to me as Abbas Malik. Besides, I'm fooling everyone with my English-gentleman act!

Nimmi, you would love the room I'm writing this letter in. It's the small Palace Guest House, which Manu Uncle was kind enough to arrange for me. I love this tiny bungalow because it comes with a tiny library. (Actually a set of bookshelves, but a man can dream. Auntie-Boss, why don't we have a library at our house in Shimla?)

Say hello to Madho Singh when you're at Auntie-Boss's house. And bring the children to meet him. Madho is pretty contrary, but he loves company even though he pretends not to.

I miss you, Nimmi. Not a day goes by that I don't think about you or Rekha or Chullu. I imagine us hiking up at Jakhu Hill and watching Chullu trying to catch the monkeys or walking along the Mall eating hot chili peanuts.

Now I really must go. Uncle and my stomach are both calling.
Yours,
Malik

At the sound of his own name, Madho Singh starts pacing back and forth on his perch. *"Drums sound better at a distance! Squawk!"* That clever bird has picked up proverbs that my husband, Jay, and I trade when we're teasing each other.

I set the letter down on the table and take off my glasses.

Nimmi frowns, as if there might be more that I have kept from her.

Gently, I say, "As you know, my husband is a doctor at the Lady Bradley Hospital here in Shimla. I'm sure Malik has told you that, long before we married, Jay—Dr. Kumar—asked me to establish an herb garden on the hospital grounds so the clinic could offer natural treatments for the local residents who don't trust manufactured medicine. Since we've been purchasing the flowers you harvest, I've been telling Dr. Kumar about you, how much you know about the mountain flora and fauna."

I glance at her to see if she's listening. She meets my gaze, looking puzzled.

"He thinks it would be a good idea if you could work with me on the Healing Garden. To see if there are more plants you know about that we should grow. Nimmi, you could have work all year around. Not just in the summer months."

Her eyebrows gather in a frown. "But…what about my stall on the Shimla Mall?"

"You can still run that in the summer months, as you do now. We could also hire a local woman to run the stall while you work in the garden. Spring will be our busiest time for planting in the Healing Garden."

"You would be my boss?"

I clear my throat. "You'll be working for the hospital, Nimmi. It's a way to feed your children, to provide for them, since you are no longer with your tribe."

She draws a sharp breath, and I regret reminding her of how alone she is. I want to tell her how I made an independent living from my henna designs back in Jaipur—that it was hard work, but it made me realize I could rely on myself, that I was strong enough, clever enough. And how good it felt to know that. But she might think I was bragging, so I merely say, "A job will let you stand on your own feet."

"You mean so Malik doesn't have to spend any more money on me?"

The words boil over, like hot milk spilling out of a pan before it can be removed from the flame.

I know she's frustrated, but I persist. "So you can be independent. Forever, Nimmi."

I stop short of telling her that her children are growing; they will need new boots, new clothes and new books for school. She knows these things—she's their mother, after all. Malik has described Nimmi's simple lodgings to me. Last winter must have been brutal on the earthen floor; those flimsy walls couldn't have kept them warm enough. If Nimmi could afford more comfortable lodgings, the children wouldn't suffer so many ear infections or runny noses.

"Please think it over," I say quietly.

Before she leaves, I hand her the barrettes that Malik sent for Rekha and bundle the candied lemons and rose petals along with some walnuts from my pantry in a cloth bag. She tries to resist taking it, but I fold her hand around the bag, keeping my hand on hers until she nods.

3

MALIK

Jaipur, State of Rajasthan, India

At Samir Singh's house, I'm greeted by an old gateman in a khaki uniform—not one I remember from before—who asks me to wait under the mango tree while he announces my arrival for dinner. I watch him totter down the gravel drive toward the stately house, his white turban bouncing lightly on his head. I've been in Jaipur for a month now. Before that, I hadn't visited the Pink City since I was eight years old. Back then, waiting outside houses like this one for Auntie-Boss to finish applying henna to one of her society ladies was a regular part of my day.

The Singh property is much as I remember it: freshly watered rosebushes, their deliciously scented blossoms large, dense and bloodred. The desert heat has not yet scorched Jaipur's gardens;

there will be ample time for that in the coming months. Even so, the Singh house—made of fine marble and stone and shaded by large neem trees—will stay cool. Frangipani vines, gracing each terrace of the two-story mansion, invite visitors to admire the fragrant flowers, their soft yellow centers spiraling into a fan of white petals.

The *chowkidar* returns and asks me to go straight through the house to the backyard.

As I approach the front veranda, I make note of the servant to one side of the house waxing a Mercedes sedan. Next to it stands a gleaming Rolls-Royce, which has been freshly washed and polished. The Singh-Sharma company must be doing very well indeed; the car I last saw Samir driving was a Hindustan Ambassador, a nod to post-independence made-in-India policy designed to promote the manufacturing of goods in India, including automobiles.

On the veranda, a neat array of shoes to one side of the front door reminds me that I must remove my own. I step out of my loafers, polished to a high shine, as I'd been taught to do at the Bishop Cotton School for Boys. Like my private-school classmates, I never wear socks. When I step through the wide front door into a quiet foyer, I stop a moment to take in my surroundings. I've never been *inside* a home as grand as this, though I spent many an afternoon outside homes I might have found to be as grand, or grander, had I been invited in. But at the time, I was just the boy who came with Lakshmi; the scrappy assistant, known only to the household's gatemen, gardeners and servants.

On the wall to my right hangs a large tiger skin, the spoils from one of Samir's shoots with the maharajas of Jaipur or Jodhpur or Bikaner. I wonder what Nimmi would think. She, who has guided sheep and goats through the Himalayan gorges with an eye out for predators like tigers, leopards and wild elephants, might think the killing of such animals for sport unnecessary, even cruel.

On the opposite wall, next to the wide staircase fashioned from pink Salumber marble, a large photo shows Nehru, the late prime minister, standing with Samir and Parvati and several others—official-looking men and women—in front of a government building. I know from Auntie-Boss that Parvati Singh is particularly proud of her past association with our government's effort to strengthen Indo-Soviet relations.

Would I want to live in a house as imposing as this? Dr. Jay and Auntie-Boss's bungalow in Shimla is comfortable, and welcoming. Walls and floors of wood, not marble. Cozy nooks where Lakshmi writes her letters or reads books that she borrows from the Shimla library. My next thought surprises me: Where would Nimmi and the children and I live?

Would that ever have occured to me before I came to Jaipur? A month of being separated and I'm thinking marriage? I have to shake my head to clear it.

I continue through the foyer, past the open French doors at the back of the house. I see an expansive green lawn and the many wrought-iron chairs and tables, dazzlingly white, placed in various configurations. The chairs are empty, all save one. A man in a fine linen shirt sits facing away from me. The thinning hair, graying now, tells me that the man is Samir Singh, surveying his domain. I call him Uncle, not because we are related, but from custom and respect. His arm is raised, his hand jiggling the half-full glass of ice and amber liquid.

"Welcome," he says. He doesn't turn around.

I drop into the chair beside his own and offer him my hand. He grasps it firmly.

"Uncle," I say.

I have always found his presence reassuring. He is not a handsome man, nor particularly tall, but people feel looked after in his presence, and protected. I would rather be in Shimla, staying close to Nimmi and her children, or reading by the fire with Auntie-Boss and Dr. Jay. But if I have to be in Jaipur, I'd just as soon be with Samir.

He looks tired, the pouches under his eyes more prominent, the creases along his mouth deeper than they were a dozen years ago.

"I trust you had a good trip from Shimla." He nods at his glass. "Join me?"

I smile. "Sure, why not?"

He calls to a servant in a white uniform and turban, who is watering the petunias and marigolds along the high stone wall at the back of the property. Light from the setting sun makes the shards of glass along the top of the wall sparkle like emeralds. The servant drops his hose and walks into the house.

Samir sips his drink and studies me with those striated brown eyes of his, so much like the marbles we used to play with on the street. "Has that boarding-school education finally turned you into a *Pukkah Sahib*?"

This is the reason I've accepted his invitation to come see him. For twelve years, Samir Singh paid my tuition at the Bishop Cotton School for Boys. My crisp white Oxford shirt, the long sleeves of which I roll upward from my wrists, my slim trousers, cuffed at the ankles, are evidence of that education. Unlike the shapeless half-sleeve shirts and baggy pants that other Indian men my age wear, I've adopted the more tailored look of a private-school uniform. I even sport a flat Swiss watch, a gift a wealthy schoolmate gave me in exchange for bourbon I was able to supply him for his birthday party.

Samir's reaction to me is similar to the one that Kanta Auntie and her husband, Manu Agarwal, had a month ago, upon my arrival from Shimla. When I showed up at their bungalow—far more modest than the Singh estate—Auntie's eyes went wide with admiration. She quickly brought me inside for a closer look. Manu, quieter and more reserved than Kanta, laughed at her speechlessness—so unlike her—and moved forward to shake my hand. I had not seen either of them in the twelve years since I'd been away. Kanta and Auntie-Boss sent photos and letters to each other every week or so and had long conspired to have Manu take me on as an apprentice before I ever learned of it. Lakshmi had hoped I would live with the Agarwals during my stay in Jaipur. But having boarded at an all-boys school where privacy was a scarce commodity, I wanted my own space. So Manu Uncle had kindly arranged for me to stay at the smaller of two guesthouses, separate buildings on the perimeter of the Rambagh Palace grounds.

Now, surveying Samir's lawn, I tug at the sharp crease along one of my pants legs and laugh. The grass is cool under my feet, and it feels good to stretch my toes. I notice Samir is also barefoot. The servant returns with a small tray, offering me a cut-glass tumbler of scotch and ice. As I take it, I say, "Think I can pass for an *angrezi*? With this?" I gesture to my face, the color of my skin not unlike an overcooked *chapatti*.

Samir chuckles as our glasses clink. His pale wheat complexion could pass for a Brit. He takes a long swallow.

It's more than the color of my skin that will keep me from the ranks of the privileged. Long used to serving rather than being served, I affect a deference in my bearing that's hard for me to shed. I suppose the upper classes might suss me out sooner or later, but that doesn't really bother me.

Samir lowers his voice so the servant in the yard cannot hear us. "I have strict orders to call you Abbas while you're here in Jaipur."

The memory of that day makes me smile. Auntie-Boss was filling out my school enrollment form shortly after we'd moved to Shimla. She had marked my age as eight, an age I preferred, though neither of us knew how old I really was. She asked me for my full name to put on the form.

"Malik," I said.

"First or last name?"

I had to think a moment. If I ever had a naming ceremony as a baby, I didn't remember it. I shrugged. "Only name."

She turned down the corners of her mouth as if considering this. "Let's pick a first name for you, then." She ran through an impressive list, rattling off the meaning of names like Aalim, Jawad and Rashid. I pretended to be embarrassed, but I was secretly pleased; no one had ever spent this much time thinking about my future. We finally settled on Abbas, which is Urdu for lion. I liked the sound of that: *Abbas Malik*. For days after, I practiced writing my new name over and over.

Like me, Samir is wearing a custom tailored shirt and raw-silk pants. He has loosened his tie—he must have just come from work—and it sits like the wilted stem of a plant on his chest. "Manu Agarwal told me you've come to Jaipur only at Lakshmi's request, and I think it a wise move. But then, Lakshmi has always been wise." He sounds wistful, and I wonder if he misses her. She has never talked to me about the two of them, and I have never asked. "The Maharani Latika trusts Manu Agarwal to manage the facilities department. It's a big job, and he's been doing it now for fifteen, sixteen years? I'm of course grateful he hires my firm to design and build the larger projects." Samir is not being entirely truthful; his blood relation to the royal family makes his work for the palace a foregone conclusion. Luckily, he has the talent to justify the nepotism. "You'll learn a lot about the construction business from Manu. After a time, you can decide whether the work suits you. It's what I tell my sons. Their career, their choice."

When Auntie-Boss and I left Jaipur in 1957, Samir had just merged his architectural firm with Sharma Construction, now

known as Singh-Sharma. Lakshmi had arranged the marriage
of Samir's son Ravi to Mr. Sharma's daughter Sheela, so the
business merger was inevitable. Ravi Singh, having completed
university at Oxford and architecture school at Yale, now works
alongside his father as an architect in Singh-Sharma. Samir's
younger son, Govind, is studying civil engineering in the United
States. Manu told me Samir is hoping both his sons will eventually take over the family business. Singh-Sharma is now the
biggest design-build firm in Rajasthan, constructing projects
throughout northern India.

"I heard Mr. Sharma had a stroke?"

Samir nods. "Five years ago. The good Mrs. Sharma looks
after him." He jiggles his glass and a servant comes forward
to pour more scotch into it. "None of his sons or his brothers
wanted to take over his part of the firm. Besides, they're scat-
tered over the globe."

"So it's all on your shoulders now?"

"Mine and Ravi's."

"Congratulations." I raise my glass and he taps his drink
against mine.

It makes me feel better to hear Samir say that my apprenticeship at the palace is a chance to see if I like the work. I've been
wondering if I should give this opportunity my all rather than
looking at it as a way to appease Auntie-Boss, who I know is
only looking out for my future.

Nimmi had a hard time understanding why I would want to
go four hundred miles away just when she and I were getting
close. I told her: Auntie-Boss made it possible for me to look
after Omi and her children. Without her, where would I be?
Hustling contraband cigarettes off the back of a truck? Serving
time for peddling pornographic films? I knew Nimmi was terribly lonely after the death of her husband, and that I had filled
a gap in her life, so the news about my internship in Jaipur came

as a blow to her no matter how many times I told her it was temporary. I think what hurt her the most is that my immediate loyalty is to Lakshmi; Boss is my *family*.

Would it be too much to hope that Nimmi and Auntie-Boss might become friends in my absence? Their relationship is important to me in a way it wasn't with any of the private-school girls I bedded. First, because Nimmi is older than me by two or three years. (We don't know for sure how far apart we are in age because she never had a birth certificate either, but we made a guess based on what she could remember about the time when India gained her independence. And the answer was: *nothing!* So she must still have been a baby.)

Moreover, in Nimmi's presence, I feel like a grown man— an adult—though I can't explain why. I do know I want to take care of her, and Rekha and Chullu. But I'm only twenty—too young to have a ready-made family. Here in Jaipur, I know many of the *cousin-brothers* I grew up with must already be fathers, but I never expected that to be my fate.

These thoughts are interrupted by a woman's scolding voice, which startles both Samir and me. "Ravi!"

We both turn around to see who is shouting.

There, on the veranda, stands a young woman in a yellow silk sari, a sleepy baby resting on her shoulder. A young girl, maybe five years old, is trying to conceal herself behind her mother. The girl is dressed in a pale pink tutu; she's crying. It's hard to understand what she is saying. The woman's dark curly hair is only long enough to reach her shoulders, as is the way of India's modern women. Her cheeks are flushed. And at the sight of me, her eyelids flutter. "Oh! I'm sorry. I thought you were my husband."

Samir Uncle looks amused. "Come and meet our guest, who will be joining us for dinner."

The woman hesitates, before hoisting the baby higher on her shoulder and coming down the steps. The little girl follows.

"Meet Abbas Malik," says Samir. "He's working with Manu Agarwal at the Jaipur Palace, and he's joining us for dinner tonight." Now he turns to me. "Abbas, this is my daughter-in-law, Sheela."

Instead of greeting me with a deferential *namaste*, Sheela steps forward and offers her hand for me to shake. Her fingers are long and carefully manicured, the nails are polished and catch the sun's light. She wears a slim gold watch, seed pearls surrounding the face. Her handshake is firm, warm.

She says, "How do you do?" Of course she has no reason to remember *me*, but I remember *her* as if I'd seen her only yesterday, when, in fact, I last saw her when she was fifteen, dressed in a pretty satin frock, telling Auntie-Boss she didn't want a Muslim decorating her *mandala*.

The girl in the tutu must be her daughter, who has now stopped crying and is staring at me. Sheela introduces her as Rita. "For now," she says, patting the baby's bottom, "the baby is just Baby."

Sheela turns to address Samir. I can see the infant now over her shoulder. Her kohl-lined eyes are trying to focus on me.

"Papaji, it is shameful," Sheela says. "Must I do everything myself? The nanny and housemaid should not have been allowed to take the same day off."

Whether or not Sheela is stamping her foot, underneath her sari, she might as well be.

Samir Uncle's eyes are smiling. "I hear you took second in the tennis match at the club today. *Shabash!*" He toasts her with his glass and smiles at little Rita, who scurries to hide behind her mother.

Sheela's expression softens slightly. "Let me tell you, it was no easy victory. Jodi Singh thinks that all she's there for is to stand on the court in a short skirt and smile. As usual, I had to do all the work!"

Now I know the rosy color of Sheela's cheeks is the result of exercise. She gives off an energy, an aura of vitality that is palpable. In fact, she makes me think of sleek young goats, charging up the Himalayan hills, their exertion producing a steaming heat. The image amuses me.

"Jodi does have nice legs," muses Uncle.

Sheela slaps him playfully on the shoulder. "Shame on you! Now, I need to put Baby down for a nap. And then feed Rita. When that lazy husband of mine comes home, tell him to come help me." She turns to me and smiles. "So nice to meet you," she says, then briskly turns and heads back into the house, followed by her daughter, who is clutching a handful of her mother's sari.

"E-man-ci-pa-ted," Samir Uncle whispers. He winks at me. "Modern generation."

"How long have Sheela and Ravi been married?"

Samir purses his lips. "Six years. They married after Ravi graduated with his architecture degree."

I nod. I'd been wary the week before, when Manu told me over dinner that Samir Singh wished to invite me for dinner. "Singh-Sharma is close to completing the work on the Royal Jewel Cinema, the palace's latest project," Manu said. "It's the first substantial building Ravi has managed on his own. It would do you well to reacquaint yourself with the Singhs. If you thought they were important all those years ago when you lived here, they're even more important now. Ten times what they were before."

Although Lakshmi never told me to stay away from the Singhs, I don't think she would be pleased that I'm spending the evening with them. The last time I remembered seeing Auntie-Boss and Samir together, in Jaipur, they had seemed tense—painful currents running between them. I don't think they parted on good terms. But a lot of time had passed since then, and I, for one, am all for letting bygones be bygones, especially where business is concerned. What the two of them once had between them is nothing to do with me now.

And Manu Uncle is like family. If Manu says that I should go somewhere, I go.

When the Singh's maid calls us inside for dinner, Samir invites me to join the others in the dining room while he takes a phone call.

Dinner turns out to be a seven-course affair that lasts two hours. Samir's wife, Parvati, presides. She scolds the servants as they're serving food. "You call this *dal*?" she says. "Who ever heard of putting potatoes in *dal*?" And, later, "Take back these *paranthas*. They've gone cold. Even *ghee* won't melt on them."

In the years since I last saw her, Parvati Singh has put on weight, but it has only added to her beauty. Her cheeks are plump, her bosom larger but still firm, and her full lips are painted with mulberry-colored lipstick. She has lively dark eyes and a lusty laugh. She stands almost as tall as her husband.

From her seat at one end of the long table, she is now overseeing the serving of hot *puris*, fresh from the stove. "Abbas," she says, "you are a *bilkul* mystery to us." She makes a gesture with her fingers, touching them to her thumbs, then opening her hands again, as if she were sprinkling salt on the table. "Samir told me only that a bright young man would be coming to dine with us. That's all he said, and nothing more."

"Yes," says Ravi, the couple's older son. "We've been wondering just who *is* this bright young man?" He flashes an engaging smile in my direction. It's hard not to like Ravi, whom I would have met already if he hadn't been out of town on business. Like his father, he seems to enjoy everything he does, which, as I've learned in the past half hour, includes playing polo, eating and talking.

Now Sheela chimes in. "Satisfy our curiosity," she says. "We want to know more!" I notice she has applied a coral lipstick since we shook hands on the lawn. The color suits her.

All eyes are now on me. "It's no use pumping a dry well," I say. "I am neither mysterious nor very bright, as you will soon find out." I smile.

"But that can't be true. Samir said you'd been to boarding school up north? Of course, both my sons attended Mayo College." Parvati beams proudly at her oldest. "Ravi continued to Eton, then went on to Oxford and Yale. And our younger son, Govind, is now in New York studying at Columbia. And you?"

"Nothing quite so grand," he says. "Your sons are definitely smarter. I was a Cottonian."

Parvati's face is frozen, halfway between a smile and a frown. "You went to Bishop Cotton School? In Shimla?" She pauses, seemingly to search her memory. "But that's where Samir went!" she says. "He didn't tell us."

I keep my expression blank and look at Ravi. "The English winters must be just as cold as those in Shimla. *Brrr!*" I wrap my arms around myself and mimic shivering to distract Mrs. Singh from whatever thoughts are now whirling in her head.

"Right enough!" says Ravi. "We used to have spitting contests to see whose spit could freeze before it hit the ground." He laughs.

Across the table, Sheela is giving him a stern look with her wide-set eyes. "Ravi!" she says. "Don't give the children ideas!" She tilts her head toward little Rita, sitting next to her, quietly eating her rice and *dal*.

Ignoring his wife, Ravi turns to me again. "No doubt we have stories to share—*after* dinner." He raises his eyebrows and wags his head in amusement.

Samir arrives and sits at the head of the table, opposite his wife. "*After* dinner?" he says. "Does that mean that everyone has gone ahead without me?" He shakes open his napkin, lays it on his lap and smiles. Everyone else around the table seems to breathe a sigh of relief.

When I was a boy working with Auntie-Boss, she used to lecture me about discretion. "We know things about people, Malik, because we go into their homes, the place where they are most vulnerable. That does not mean that we can divulge what we've have seen or heard to everyone we know. There's more power in keeping a secret than in betraying it."

I never thought Lakshmi meant that we should blackmail people using our knowledge, only that our clients would be loyal to us if we showed loyalty to them.

I look around the dinner table and consider what I know about this family—the Singhs.

I know Lakshmi helped to keep many of Samir's mistresses childless during the ten years she spent in Jaipur.

And I know that Samir Uncle once shared a bed with Auntie-Boss before she married Dr. Jay.

I also know that Auntie-Boss's younger sister, Radha, had a baby boy, and that Ravi Singh was the baby's father. Now that boy is twelve years old, and Ravi's never seen him. That's because Parvati Singh whisked Ravi away to England, where he could finish his studies without being touched by scandal.

I also know that Sheela Sharma—then fifteen and plump— didn't want a dirty street child like me to help with the *mandala* Lakshmi was designing for her *sangeet.*

But since that time, my face has filled out, and my hair is styled neatly. My style of dress is more appropriate to someone of her class; no wonder she doesn't recognize, or remember, me now, sitting opposite her at the dinner table.

Why would she? For Sheela I was nothing more than a blemish on an otherwise perfect afternoon that ended years ago.

But I have not forgotten how she looked at me that afternoon. I didn't need to know her, or anything about her, or her family, or what she must have thought of me—however worthy, or unworthy. It was enough to witness the expression on her face.

4

NIMMI

Shimla

Today, I've left my children with the Aroras while I make my way to the Lady Bradley Hospital. The Aroras, my landlords, would love nothing better than to care for (and spoil!) Rekha and Chullu every time I leave the house to tend my flower stall. But I would miss my children too much, and so I usually want them with me. As I go about my day, my daughter and son are learning our tribal rituals and knowledge the same way I learned them by staying close to, and observing, my mother.

When I woke at dawn this morning in our cramped lodgings, my children were pressed against me on our cot, one on either side. I smoothed the heavy cream blanket covering our bodies, a blanket I had woven from the wool of our sheep. A sharp bit of straw pricked my finger.

Rekha kicked one of her legs outside the blanket and Chullu clenched his little fist. I wondered what they dream about, my children. Do they dream about their father? Or their grandfather? Do they dream about the goats we left behind, the smell of summer corn being roasted? Do they ever dream of Malik? His joyful laugh, the gifts he brings for them? I let my hands rest on the blanket as they slept, for the comfort of it, to feel the gentle rise and fall of their breathing.

I thought about Lakshmi inviting me to help with the hospital garden. Rekha needed new shoes; already her feet had grown too large for the ones I'd made for her last year from a goat's hide. Soon she would be old enough to go to school. (Just think! I'd never had the chance, but my girl would get to go!) But she would need books and paper, pencils and erasers.

Chullu was growing, too. He needed a new sweater, but without our sheep, I had no wool to make one for him. My children needed these things now and would need more as they got older, and rather than find ways to get those things for them, my thoughts kept turning back to Malik, always Malik. The feel of him, the sharp angle of his jawline, the way he reassured me that I belonged here in Shimla. Then my thoughts turned to Lakshmi, and I felt my teeth clench. I didn't want Mrs. Kumar to plan his life for him. Was it jealousy I felt? Jealousy of her? Certainly, she held more sway over him than I did. Otherwise, why would he have left me and the children without a backward glance? Did he think so little of us? It would be for only a short while, he said, but if Lakshmi asked him to stay in Jaipur forever, would he?

I tucked Rekha's leg back inside the blanket. Was I being unfair to my children—putting my own needs ahead of theirs? Was it pride or selfishness, or both, that made me think about these things? What would Dev have wanted me to do? I sighed.

My husband would have wanted me to do what was best for his children.

So, later that day, I asked Mrs. Arora to watch Rekha and Chullu while I trudged up the hill to the Lady Bradley Hospital, where I knew I would find Lakshmi Kumar.

Now I stand in front of the hospital, a sprawling three-story building. Several times, while I was working at my flower stall on the Shimla Mall, and Malik worried that my children might have ear infections, he took them to the Community Clinic run by Mrs. Kumar's husband. I know the clinic must be near the hospital. And Lakshmi must be at the clinic.

A steady stream of people are going in and out through the glass doors of the main entrance. Each time the doors open, I see nurses dressed in white and nuns in wimples going about their business.

I've never been inside a hospital, never been this close to one. Even from here, twenty feet from the entrance, I detect a strong odor—foreign to me—but I don't know where it comes from, or what it is.

A young nurse who has just come through the door seems to sense I'm lost and asks if she can help me.

"Yes, please. Do you know where Mrs. Kumar works?"

She tells me that around the corner of the building, to the left, I'll see a door marked "Community Clinic," and points the way. She's assuming I can read, which makes me grateful to her, and I thank her for her help.

There are two doors on the left side of the building, but only one has writing on it. If not for the nurse, I wouldn't have known which door to try.

When I cross the threshold, I find myself in a room with walls painted the color of lichen. The four people sitting on chairs set against one wall are wearing vests and skirts and local headdresses. A pretty woman in a sari sits behind a desk writing something on a piece of paper. She wears black eyeglasses and pink lipstick. Her hair is styled in one long braid down her back.

When I step forward, she says, "May I help you?"

Before I can answer, Lakshmi Kumar steps through a white curtain covering the entrance to another room and calls out "Nimmi!" She has on a long white coat that's covering her sari. I can tell by her smile that she's pleased to see me. Suddenly, I feel self-conscious. In my finest dress, silver jewelry and the medallion on my forehead, I look so out of place. The hill people, the receptionist and Lakshmi are in their everyday clothes. But Lakshmi grins at me reassuringly.

"I'm so glad you've come," she says. "I'll be right with you."

She holds the curtain open to allow another woman to exit the room they were in. She's a hill woman, and the girl whose hand she's holding has a fresh white bandage on her arm. The woman and child go to the front desk, and Lakshmi follows. To the woman behind the desk, she says, "Please tell her to put ointment on the wound only after she has washed her hands with hot water and soap. Tell her it's important."

The receptionist repeats Lakshmi's instructions in another dialect, and the woman wags her head to indicate she understands. Lakshmi smiles at the child and fetches a red balloon made to look like a monkey from behind the desk. It looks just like the animal balloons the vendor next to my stall sells. That must be where Lakshmi buys them. That shouldn't surprise me, but it does.

Lakshmi, grinning, turns to me. "Tell me you're taking me up on my offer."

I wag my head, which can mean *yes*, or *no*, or *we'll see.*

Lakshmi grins as if I've said yes. She turns to the receptionist. "Sarita, this is Nimmi. You'll be seeing her more often."

Now Lakshmi takes me by the arm. "Come. I'll show you

the garden. But I must be quick because we have a few more patients waiting. Dr. Kumar is in the other exam room. When he's finished with his patient, I'll introduce you to him."

She leads me into a long corridor. A few steps farther and we've come out of the back of the building, where I see a neatly laid-out garden that's twice as large as the footprint of the clinic. It's surrounded by a wooden fence. Each row is carefully labeled, I imagine with Lakshmi's handwriting on a wooden stake. I can see the soil has been turned recently and some rows have been tilled but not yet planted. Off to one side are more mature trees, like *nag kesar*, whose leaves our tribe always uses to make a poultice for head colds. I spot a spindly tree, struggling to survive.

Mrs. Kumar sees where I'm looking, and laughs. "That's me being hopeful," she says. "The powder I make from a sandalwood tree is good for relieving headaches, but I haven't found the right place for it. I'll keep trying until I find it."

Three-foot shrubs are planted next to the trees. I recognize moonseed, *brahmi* and wild senna.

"I've set some rows aside where we can grow the flowers you provide for poultices and treatments."

Lakshmi talks as if I have already accepted her offer. When I nod, again, I realize I haven't said a word since I came into the clinic.

"In Jaipur I used herbal remedies made from native plants to heal women's ailments. I've been doing the same in Shimla, using plants that grow only here. Shimla's climate is so different from Jaipur's. I had to learn about the native herbs and flowers that grow in this soil, in these foothills." She pauses, looking at me. Maybe thinking that she's telling me too much? Or is she waiting for me to respond to what she's telling me or to ask a question? I'm not sure, so I say nothing. In a moment, she continues.

"There's so much more to learn. That *sik* dish you made from local fruit for one of our patients? If you can do that, just imagine how much more you can do with medicinal plants that grow in the higher elevations. You could help so many of the people who come to our clinic, Nimmi. Let's try growing those same plants in the Healing Garden and see what happens!"

Lakshmi's blue eyes are sparkling with excitement, and she bends down and grabs a handful of soil. "I've put different ingredients in the soil, trying to make it as rich as it can be—and also a little less acidic." She lets the dirt—moist, black, free of twigs, pebbles and leaves—fall through her fingers. "Mostly I've been using pulverized limestone—" She stops, turns to me and laughs. "I'm going on and on, aren't I?"

She rubs her hands together to get rid of the soil. "Shall we get started on the paperwork to see that you get paid on time?"

As always, Lakshmi exudes confidence. I have to wonder if she's ever failed at anything. If any of her many plans have not worked out. Is she so confident because things always go the way she means them to? Did she always know Malik would agree to go to Jaipur for his apprenticeship? Does she mean to keep him there…forever?

"After we've done the paperwork, I'll introduce you to the staff," she says, already on her way to the back door of the clinic. "We'll draw up a list of plants you think we'll need to fill out our garden. Our tools are in that shed. I use dung for fertilizer—cow or sheep or goat, depending. Bhagwan knows there's plenty of the stuff to go around, though certain of the staff complain about the odor of the sheep dung!"

The afternoon passes quickly. Given my dress and jewelry, most of the staff I'm introduced to would normally stare at me on the street, but here they're polite to my face, murmuring welcomes. I can tell by the way they defer to her that they obviously respect Mrs. Kumar. After we wash our hands—with more soap than I've ever used in life at one time—she introduces me to her husband. I've been curious to meet the man Malik has told me so much about. Dr. Jay, as Malik calls him, is tall, taller than anyone I've met. His black-and-white curls are in disarray over his forehead. He has gray eyes, both observant and kind. When he first sees me, his eyes flit to my silver medallion, my skirt, the overhead ceiling fan and his shoes. He's shy, like my Rekha. His smile reveals two overlapping front teeth. I find myself smiling back at him.

"So this is the mother of the charming Rekha and little Chullu! Pleased to meet you. If Sister out there weren't watching me, Rekha would be able to charm me out of the whole lot of animal balloons Mrs. Kumar stocks!" The skin around his eyes crinkles into small folds when he smiles.

Mrs. Kumar looks at him fondly. *"Arré!* The balloon seller has been able to remodel his whole house because of your generosity!"

I see now that my clothes are not right for gardening. The sisters are in white habits. Dr. Jay wears a white coat over his clothes. Mrs. Kumar and the woman at the front desk wear white coats over their saris. Should I ask for a white coat to keep my finest skirts from getting soiled? And what will I do about my jewelry?

As if Lakshmi Kumar has heard me ask the question, she says to the nun behind the front desk, "Sister, would you please give Nimmi-*ji* one of the gardening aprons and a set of gloves? Oh, and also that paperwork I filled out earlier for Nimmi-*ji*."

I feel a jolt up my spine. She knows I can't read Hindi or English. What will the other clinic staff think—the ones who can read and write? Is Lakshmi trying to humiliate me?

The nun hands the paperwork to Mrs. Kumar, who rolls it and puts it in her coat pocket. She glances at me. "Perhaps later this afternoon, you and I can go over it, *accha*? I must join Dr. Kumar now." With a reassuring smile at me, she parts the curtain, about to disappear into the area where she and the doctor work with patients. Where Malik must have taken Rekha and Chullu for their ear infections.

"Lakin…"

Mrs. Kumar turns her head around to look at me, inquiringly.

"It's just… My Chullu. I must feed him."

She looks down at my blouse, stricken, as if she's just remembered that I'm still breastfeeding.

"Oh, Nimmi. I'm sorry. Of course! Why not bring Chullu and Rekha to work from now on? Maybe we can get Rekha to help water the plants." She raises her brows. "But we would have to be careful around the clinic. Most of what the patients come in for isn't infectious, but we want your children to stay healthy, *hahn-nah*?"

I return to the clinic in an hour, Chullu on my back and Rekha at my side. At home I changed into a homespun skirt, and a sweater blouse my sister-in-law gave me. I've cinched the blouse with the wool belt where I keep my husband's knife. I've covered my head with a patterned shawl that holds my hair back.

Lakshmi comes with us to the garden carrying a clipboard, and we talk about the healing plants we need to sow. She makes notes and says she might forget unless she writes down what she's thinking. As I watch her write, I think about the vendor who twists balloons into the shape of animals. The letters formed in Hindi are something like that, except, instead of animals, they make swirls and dots, circles and slanted lines. Lakshmi's writing is even and neat, but what I find more beautiful is how her henna-decorated fingers move in rhythm with her pen. The henna's cinnamon color is richer today than it was yesterday, and the contrast of cinnamon against the white page is striking.

When she sees me watching her, I look away. From the corner of my eye, I see her tap her lips with her fountain pen.

"Since Rekha will be coming here so often, I'd like to teach her how to read. If that's all right with you. She's four now, isn't she? A perfect time to get her interested. We'll practice during breaks, and you can sit in if you'd like."

My daughter is drawing circles with her fingers in the loamy soil. I'm thinking of the possibilities. Might she become a *padha-likha*, or even a *doctrini* like Mrs. Kumar? Imagine! A tribal girl writing on paper, just like Lakshmi!

"Eventually, you'll need to make lists of plants and supplies. For now, you can draw what the leaves of the plants look like." With a few quick strokes, she draws a leaf on the edge of her clipboard. "Like this."

"Moonseed!" I grin.

"Quite right." She offers me the fountain pen.

I've never held a pen before. It's smooth. And slick. I clutch it in my fingers, trying to hold it the way she does. I push hard. There's a dark blot on the paper now, like a drop of blood. I look at Lakshmi, the way Rekha looks at me when she's done something wrong. Lakshmi puts her hand on mine and lifts my fingers ever so gently. "Not so hard," she says.

I ease up on the pressure. I draw a line, and the ink flows more smoothly. I draw another line, then another.

"Toothache plant?" she asks.

I nod.

"*Shabash!* You're going to get along just fine, Nimmi!"

I'm not used to compliments. My face is warm, whether from embarrassment or gratitude, I can't tell. She is being so kind. It's not what I expected. I feel my eyes get moist.

She looks away and removes the rolled-up papers from her coat. "Let's get this taken care of, shall we? But first, I want to check the fungus on that leaf."

Lakshmi stands and walks in the direction of the wild senna, leaving me time to wipe my eyes.

ONE MONTH BEFORE
THE COLLAPSE

5

LAKSHMI

Shimla

I snip a drying leaf off the burdock plant with my clippers and inspect it. Tiny holes perforate the center. I turn it over. There might be insect eggs, or larvae, but I can't see them; at forty-two, my eyes aren't as sharp as they used to be. I'll have to look at it, tomorrow, under the microscope. I put it in my basket and survey the Lady Bradley Healing Garden, a garden I started over a decade ago—the reason I came to Shimla in the first place. Would I have come if Jay hadn't offered me this lifeline, persuaded me to take it? After all, scandal had put a full stop to my life as a henna artist in Jaipur. And even though the accusations of thieving their jewelry weren't true, my clients, the wealthy ladies of Jaipur, weren't about to forgive—or forget—easily. In the end, I had to leave Jaipur in order to start over.

Nimmi is hoeing another row in the garden. In the few weeks she's been working with me, she has taught me so much about the plants that her tribe gathers in the Himalayan meadows between here and Kashmir. From the gaping monkshood, a three-foot shrub with blue flowers that we're planting today, we'll harvest the roots, pulverize them and mix them with geranium oil to make a sweet-smelling ointment for boils, abscesses and other skin irritations. In my time working with the hill people, I've learned that they don't trust medicines that smell like chemicals; they will only use remedies that smell of the earth, of the trees and flowers they know. That's one of the reasons our little clinic has become so popular with the locals. Wealthier patients, or foreign ones, prefer the Lady Bradley Hospital's more antiseptic environment, which tribal people like Nimmi don't like or trust.

I watch her now, making furrows only as wide as we absolutely need to lay the seeds of the monkshood. She works quickly and efficiently, wasting no energy on movements that don't help her get where she's going.

She must sense me watching her. Without breaking stride or looking my way, she says, "We're a little late getting this in the ground, but it might still take." She looks at the sky, then at me. "If the weather holds. Don't be surprised if this plant doesn't sprout for a year, though. It's touchy."

I nod. At times, I feel as if she and I have come to an understanding—a friendship of sorts. But sometimes, her tone is gruff, as if she resents being here at the clinic. She is earning enough to care for Rekha and Chullu—a salary that Jay and I pay out of our own pockets, although she doesn't need to know that. What she is teaching us is valuable enough, but until we can show the hospital board the results of her work, we won't be able to cover her wages from the hospital budget. The paperwork I had her sign the first day (after I showed her how to form her initials in Hindi) was a contract between Nimmi and Jay and me. We didn't need it at all. I just didn't want her thinking I'm offering charity—she would hate that—so I told her it was a contract with the Lady Bradley Hospital.

She's probably still trying to work out how she feels. Whether she can fit me into a slot between resentment and gratitude. I understand. It was the same with me in Jaipur: ladies of privilege to whom I automatically said *yes, Ji*, and *of course, Ji*, no matter how unreasonable their requests because they were paying me, giving me the money I needed to build my house. I swallowed my pride until the day I finally said *no, never again* to Parvati Singh. I close my eyes. That's all in the past now. *What's the use of crying when the birds ate the whole farm?*

Nimmi is missing Malik. I miss him, too. His easy way with people, making them feel comfortable—safe—around him. But he is miles away in the Rajasthani heat.

I shake my head and make some notes on my clipboard about how much fertilizer we need to purchase.

"Have you forgotten?" At the sound of Jay's voice, I turn around.

He's walking toward me from the back door of the hospital. His curly hair, which used to be merely threaded with gray, is now more silver than black. He's wearing his white doctor's coat, a stethoscope peeking out of one pocket. There's something about the way he looks at me that always makes me smile.

"Clinic starts in five. Tea first?" he asks when he reaches me. He removes a leaf from my hair where it must have caught on my bun.

I look at Nimmi. "Nimmi? Tea?"

She straightens and gives Jay one of her rare smiles. When she glances at me, her smile disappears, and she shakes her head. "I want to finish this."

Jay takes the gloves I'm removing from my hands and walks with me into the shed where we store tools and supplies. I'm putting the gardening sheers on their peg when I feel his fingers trail the back of my neck, starting at my hairline, down to the scalloped edge of my blouse. I close my eyes, feel that delicious tingle. His familiar scent of lime and sandalwood is so comforting. I turn to face him, raise my lips to his. "I thought you wanted to get to the clinic."

He laughs lightly, tapping my nose with his finger. "Ah, yes. So I did."

The Community Clinic was not doing well the first time I stepped through its doors twelve years ago. That was right around the time my sister, Radha, gave birth at the adjoining Lady Bradley Hospital. While we waited for Radha to recover, Jay—Dr. Kumar, as he was known to me then—suggested that I use what I knew about herbs and their healing properties to treat the local hill people. Without my henna business to support me, Radha and young Malik, I needed the work he was offering. True to his word, Jay secured the funds to start the Lady Bradley Healing Garden. He found a house for Radha, Malik and me on the periphery of the hospital grounds. It wasn't lush, but we weren't used to lush; the house I'd built in Jaipur was but a single room. I could afford to buy the small cottage Jay found; I had money from the sale of my Jaipur home.

From the beginning, Jay was respectful, kind; he listened to my ideas. We worked well together; he would help decipher the tribal languages of the patients so I could administer the appropriate poultice, lotion or food remedy. We got into the habit of having a glass of scotch in his office at the end of the workday (I'd started with chai but eventually switched to his Laphroaig when I discovered that I liked its smoky taste). We started to attend plays at the Gaiety Theater together, hike to Jakhu Temple with Radha and Malik, play cribbage (all four of us are competitive!), and cook together. At that time, Malik boarded at Bishop Cotton School for Boys nearby and Radha was at Auckland House School, both of which Samir Singh funded to atone for his son's indiscretion.

Then, six years ago, on a fine Sunday evening, Jay and I were returning from a long hike. Radha had moved to France the year before with her husband, Pierre, a French architect she met when she was nineteen and he was on holiday in Shimla. Malik was away, playing in a cricket match in Chandigarh, an overnight trip with his school.

On our walk, Jay and I had been trading proverbs—one of our favorite games—trying to best each other.

"Giving jewels to a donkey is as useless as—"

"—giving a eunuch to a woman," I said, laughing.

Jay raised his brows in surprise, then smiled, pleased. "Hmm. I was thinking *dancing for the blind*, but yours trumps mine." We were standing on the front veranda of his house, a tiny but comfortable bungalow his aunt and uncle had left him. They'd raised him in Shimla after his parents died.

"Cribbage?" I asked. We usually ended the evening with a game.

Instead of answering, he looked at me for a long moment. I felt my face flush. Then he turned, unlocked the front door and pushed it open, stepping back—just slightly—so that I had to brush against him to enter. When I did, I felt his fingers, as light as breath, on the back of my neck. I stood still, felt a jolt run down my spine, every tendon, every muscle in my body quivering. The last time I'd felt a sensation that intense was the night I'd succumbed to Samir Singh's charms in Jaipur—once and only once—six years before. That same year Samir had introduced Jay to me—quite by chance—and neither of us could have predicted what happened next.

Jay placed a warm hand on my hip, on the exposed flesh just above my sari. He drew me gently toward him so I could feel the heat of his chest against my back. I felt his lips graze that tender knob at the top of my spine. I let out a soft moan. I couldn't help myself—it had been so long since I'd been touched this way. So long since I'd trusted *any* man. My sister, Radha, had teased me for years: *Dr. Jay is smitten with you!* But I'd been wary. Having left a bad marriage at the age of seventeen and then finding that I was nothing more than a distraction for Samir Singh, I didn't want to be made vulnerable again.

Jay pulled on my earlobe with his teeth. "Lakshmi," he whispered, "we're not playing tonight."

No sooner had he ushered us inside the house than I whipped around and kissed him on the mouth, my tongue searching for his, my pelvis, aching, arching toward his. I pressed my breasts against his chest, clutched his buttocks through his trousers. I was surprised at the depth of my want, at the urgency of it. His hands found the hooks on the back of my blouse, undid them.

When Jay pulled away to free me from my blouse, he and I were breathing hard. A lazy smile played about his lips, as if to tell me he had always hoped that this would happen, known it would. And though he'd had to wait, it had. *Finally*—it had.

Finally. I put my lips against his mouth again, massaged his nipples through his shirt.

He whispered against my lips, "Rumors have been circulating for the past six years about us. Don't you think it's time we put an end to them?"

Before the week was out, we'd married, in a simple ceremony at the civil court in Shimla. Radha and Pierre came from France. Malik wore his best suit and his wing-tip shoes for the occasion. (In Jaipur, he had never owned a pair of closed-toed shoes, but private school had changed his tastes.)

Our marriage didn't change our working relationship. Jay continued as a physician at the Lady Bradley Hospital and remained director of the adjoining Community Clinic. I was in charge of the Healing Garden. Three afternoons a week, I worked with him at the clinic with a nurse and a few sisters, assisting with patients. We eventually sold our bungalows so we could buy a larger home together where Malik could stay when Bishop Cotton closed for holidays and, after he graduated, live with us, if he wished to.

Madho Singh, the Alexandrine parakeet gifted to Malik by the Maharani Indira of Jaipur, had pride of place in our new drawing room and kept watch on all comings and goings. Whatever Malik happened to be doing at the time, I made sure to share his latest news with Madho Singh.

Nimmi collects flowers early in the mornings to sell on the Shimla Mall immediately afterward. Then she comes to the Community Clinic with Rekha and Chullu. She stows her empty flower basket in the toolshed, and while she hoes or plants or waters seedlings, Chullu and Rekha play in the clearing next to the shed. The children are used to sitting quietly by themselves and keeping each other company. Nimmi is a calm, patient mother. If Chullu tries to eat the soil or Rekha starts to pull up shoots, a few soft words from her in their dialect makes them listen. When it's time for Nimmi to feed Chullu and for Rekha and me to start our Hindi lesson, Nimmi sits near us so she can also see the pages of the *Panchatantra* book. The stories are short and beautifully illustrated. Radha and I grew up with these very fables, and now Rekha and Chullu are growing up with them, too. (I wish Radha were here to see us! Like me, she loved teaching the small children at our father's village school in Ajar.)

Our first story is the tale of the monkey and the crocodile, who start out as friends. But the crocodile's wife decides she wants to eat the monkey's heart, so the crocodile invites his friend to dinner. The monkey readily hops onto the crocodile's back. But on the river, the crocodile confesses that he means to kill him, so his wife can eat his heart. The monkey tells the crocodile he always leaves his heart on his tree and they will have to go back to get it. Of course, as soon as they reach land, the monkey climbs his tree, saving himself, and the crocodile loses a friend.

When we get to the end of the story, I hear Nimmi cough. But when I look over at her, I realize she's laughing, the corners of her eyes creased with delight! More of a cackle, really, but no matter. It's the first time I've heard Nimmi laugh, and soon enough I'm laughing with her. She moves closer to us and says, "Read it again, *Ji.*"

Another first! Until this moment, she has never called me *Ji*—a term that's meant to show respect. Relief floods me. I'm pleased, as I know Malik will be, and smile at her to let her know it. But she's not looking at me. Chullu has fallen asleep, and she is fashioning a harness for him with her *chunni*. She slings him across her back.

I start again, at the beginning of the story. Rekha learns quickly. She and I sound out the words together and trace the written words with our fingers. Nimmi holds back, afraid of making a mistake, but her daughter helps her, and she joins us.

Already I'm thinking about the next book I'm going to check out of the Shimla library: a children's book of Himalayan flowers: blue poppies, purple water lilies, yellow irises. The drawings are colorful and large, and both Rekha and Nimmi are sure to recognize the flowers.

As we read out loud, Chullu continues to sleep on his mother's back, soothed by the sounds of his mother's and his sister's voices.

Now when Nimmi comes to my house to have me read Malik's letters, she brings the children. She even eats the treats I make for her. I can tell the sugared fruits I serve are lifting her spirits. The loneliness is leaving her, little by little. Sometimes she brings treats to share: a basket of wild ghingaroo berries or a handful of Indian figs or sweet Himalayan apples she's picked on her way here.

When I begin reading the latest letter from Malik, Rekha sidles up next to me to get a closer look. I think she's pretending that she's reading it along with me.

Dear Nimmi and Auntie-Boss,
Now I've seen everything! Manu asked Ravi Singh to show me the Royal Jewel Cinema. That's the big project Singh-Sharma has been building for the palace. Ravi says there's nothing else like it in all of Rajasthan. It's a two-story building that takes up the entire city block between two of the busiest streets in Jaipur. He told me he would have liked to model it after the Old Vic in Bristol (as if I've seen that!), but the Maharani Latika had just been to America and she wanted more of an art deco design like the Pantages (hope I spelled that right) Theatre in Los Angeles (that's in California). Architecture of the 1930s in America is still news here in India, I guess. (Boss, aren't you proud I learned something in my art history classes at Bishop Cotton?)
Here's what was happening the day we visited the cinema house: two men were installing the name of the theater over the entrance in three-foot high gold letters; others were painting the outside walls pink, like the color of the old city walls. Then there were masons creating the stone mandala *in the front of the building with a blue-and-green peacock at its center—not nearly as good,*

of course, as the mosaic you designed on the floor of your house in Jaipur, Auntie-Boss.

Then we entered the lobby... Waa! Waa! First, it goes on forever. Second, it's carpeted in plush red wool and silk. I bet Chullu would love to slobber all over that carpet (ha ha). I looked up at the ceiling and saw the largest chandeliers—different from anything we ever saw at the Maharanis' Palace—dangling from huge concave circles. Inside each circle are millions of tiny twinkling bulbs. It's like looking at a sky that's glittering with stars and planets and galaxies!

Then we walked inside the theater where the seats are. It's bloody brilliant! Ravi is really proud of the fact that he managed to squeeze in eleven hundred seats—it's that large! He designed the theater so the seats are tiered and keep rising as you get farther from the screen—like those Greek amphitheaters we also studied in art history class (and you thought I learned nothing there, Boss!).

There's a balcony (where the rich people sit) from which you can look down onto the stage and the seats below. The screen is almost as tall as the Hawa Mahal in Jaipur! And here's something I'd never heard of: surround sound. The Royal Jewel Cinema has it. Apparently, it was recently invented in America. So in this cinema house, everybody can hear and everybody gets a good seat.

I was imagining all of us in the theater together. How you would both marvel at this building! (Chullu would marvel at that carpet.) Rows and rows of stone arches carved into the walls of the theater and inlaid with flowers and leaves (don't ask me which flowers and which leaves—that's your department).

Have to go! My other boss is calling me. Give my best to Dr. Jay!
Yours,
Malik

6

MALIK

Jaipur

As part of my training, Manu asked some of the larger contractors of the Jaipur Palace to show me around their construction sites. It was Singh-Sharma's turn today. At the behest of his
father, Ravi Singh is showing me around the Royal Jewel Cinema.

The building is splendid, indeed an amazing accomplishment,
and I tell Ravi so. Drapes the color of the red hibiscus Nimmi
loves are being hoisted on both sides of the screen. Workmen
are bolting red mohair seats to the floor of the final row. Electricians are testing the recessed lights along the perimeter, which
turn the walls from yellow to green to orange periodically.

I whistle. "How long did it take to build all this?"

"Not as long as you would think. Would you believe that what was supposed to take us five years only took us three?"

"How did you manage that?"

He smiles at me. "Ah, old chap, that's the advantage Singh-Sharma Construction has over every other builder. It's why Manu keeps hiring us for these showcase projects." He taps his index finger against the side of his nose, meaning, *It's a secret*.

When he excuses himself to talk to the construction supervisor, I return to the grand lobby, imagining Nimmi and her two children here with me, marveling at how many people it takes to build something so monumental.

Then we head out for lunch at a nearby restaurant, where Ravi orders platters of fragrant lamb and chicken curry, steaming *basmati* rice with cashews, a bowl of *matar paneer*, and a stack of hot *aloo paranthas* with a dollop of *ghee*. Everyone at this restaurant seems to know Ravi. The proprietor greets us when we arrive, unfolds our napkins and places them on our laps. Two waiters help move our chairs closer toward the table and a third fills our water glasses.

Now a very pretty waitress in a white blouse and a slim black skirt arrives with tall glasses of Kingfisher beer. The proprietor beams at her and glances at Ravi to gauge his reaction. Ravi is watching the young woman with a bemused smile, his eyes roving the length of her figure. The restaurant owner smiles at Ravi, gives a slight bow and moves discreetly away.

"So what do you think of my house, the one my father designed?" Ravi asks.

Following that dinner at the Singhs' almost a month ago, Samir had taken me around the corner of his property to show me the house he'd built for Ravi and Sheela, his daughter-in-law, as a wedding gift. Thirteen years ago, when Auntie-Boss first proposed the marriage arrangement between the Singhs and the Sharmas, Sheela agreed only on the condition that she would not have to live in a joint family household where the eldest son and his wife live with his parents. So Lakshmi suggested that Samir build a separate house for Ravi and Sheela on the vast Singh property. Sheela didn't get exactly what she wanted, but Boss's creative solution sealed the deal.

I reach for a *parantha*. "Impressive," I say. "So modern inside. All that light." It reminds me of Kanta and Manu's house. Raised in a westernized family in Bengal, Kanta favors the modern design: clean lines, large plate-glass windows and minimal decoration. "What does Sheela think?"

Ravi chuckles. "Her majesty decided she liked it only after she realized how much bigger it is than her friends' houses."

I smile, remembering how difficult Sheela could be when she was a young girl.

Ravi continues. "Papaji did a good job with our house, mind you. But there's so much more we could be doing at the firm. Look at what Le Corbusier has done in Chandigarh." He fixes his dark eyes on mine, suddenly enthused. "Chandigarh inspired me. I wanted the Royal Jewel Cinema to stand out, to be different from any other building in Jaipur. This is how I'll make my mark—use it as a stepping stone to bigger and better things."

I take a sip from my beer glass. "Bigger and better things?" I help myself to another piece of lamb, so tender it falls off the bone. I suck on the marrow—the best part.

Ravi's grin is wolfish. "Bigger than Papaji has ever dreamed of." He spoons some chicken curry onto his plate. "My father believes in doing everything just as it's always been done. But now there are newer, better techniques, materials, processes." He raises one eyebrow. "For the time being, though, *What can't be cured must be endured*."

I laugh. "Your father doesn't agree with you? About your modern ideas?"

Ravi's face clouds for a fraction of a second. "I'm still working on him. We don't quite see eye to eye on some things."

The pretty waitress approaches with a basket of bread and a pair of tongs. "More *paranthas*, Sahib?"

Ravi turns to her, allows his gaze to linger. When she blushes and smiles at him, he nods. He watches her until she finishes serving both of us. When she walks away, he keeps his eyes on her, the movement of her buttocks.

Again, he turns to me, his gaze intense again. "Do you bat or bowl?"

This change of subject is so abrupt I look up from my lamb and stare at him. I've always loved cricket. Back when I lived in the bowels of the Pink City, I was always organizing games with the neighborhood boys, and we played hard and rough. At Bishop Cotton, where we played with official bats and wore spotless uniforms, I learned a more formal, refined version of the game.

Suddenly I'm wary, though I can't say why. "Both. Depending."

"On what?"

"On what's needed."

Ravi shows me a generous smile, and the dimple on his chin deepens. He picks up his beer glass and clinks it against mine. "Abbas Malik, allow me to welcome you to the All-Rounders Club. We will definitely have you out for a game, sometime soon."

While the busboys clear the dishes, Ravi excuses himself, stands and walks over to the far side of the room, where the young waitress is wiping wine glasses with a white cloth. He leans close and whispers something in her ear. She giggles and shrugs. Ravi looks at the proprietor, standing near the door, who nods. Ravi returns to the table and taps two fingers on its surface. "Listen here, old chap, I have to run an errand. My driver will take you back to your office."

He flashes one of his brilliant smiles at me, then grabs some sugared fennel seeds from a bowl on the table. He puts them in his mouth, to sweeten his breath, then winks at me and walks back to the waitress.

So far, Manu has rotated me through the engineering, design, and construction departments. Now he's assigned me to accounting so I can learn the financial side of the business.

Hakeem is the accountant for the palace facilities department. His domain is a stuffy, windowless office shoved into one corner of Manu's operation. At the far end of the floor are Manu's and the chief engineer's offices as well as a glass conference room. In between sit the secretaries, estimators, draftsmen, junior engineers.

I could have drawn a picture of Hakeem before I ever met him: a rotund man sitting behind his desk, wearing a neat black skullcap, white *kurta* and black vest. His glasses have thick black frames. I could have predicted that he would run a finger under his trim mustache when he's agitated, which is what he does the moment I step into his office.

"Uncle," I say, "I'm Abbas Malik. Mr. Manu asked me to avail myself of your good teaching." I smile humbly. "Thank you for taking me on."

Hakeem sits, a small Buddha, within the circle of his table lamp. He studies me through those thick glasses, his eyes as large as an owl's, and strokes his mustache. I look for a chair, but there is only one—Hakeem's—and he is sitting in it. The shelves lining the walls are filled with large cloth-covered ledgers, each neatly labeled along its spine. The shelves take up most of the space in the room and fill it with the smell of dust, musty fabric and old glue. On one spine I read "1924," which, given Hakeem's age—he must be in his sixties—might be the year he started working here. The old man makes a noncommittal noise and adjusts his glasses on his nose. "You will not eat in here. Yes?"

I fight the urge to smile. "Of course, Uncle."

"Or drink. Yes?" Was ending every sentence with *yes* another of his tics? I decided to follow suit.

"Yes."

"These books are important. They must be kept spotless. Yes?"

"Yes."

He scoots his chair to one side so the ledgers in the bookcase behind him become visible. "These are the most important ones. Yes? In this one," he says, pointing, "we keep records of the supplies we buy to remodel or construct a new project. And in this one," he says, pointing to an adjacent ledger, "we record all the monies we owe to suppliers and contractors. Accounts payable. The next one is a list of money owed to the palace. Say reimbursement for returned materials. Or rental of palace facilities by others. That's accounts receivable. The fourth is the account of what and how much we have already paid for the project. There are four ledgers per year."

I can't help myself. "Yes," I say.

He lowers his chin and looks at me over the top of his glasses. He strokes his mustache. Finally, he says, "Yes."

Hakeem has to stand to pull a hefty book off one shelf. He opens it and turns it so that I can read the entries. Pointing to one column of text written in Hindi, and another that contains only letters of the English alphabet, he says, "See this?" Pointing to the English column, he says "W-T S-N-D. Stands for white sand. Yes? A kind of shorthand for the item, which saves time. I created these abbreviations. If I had to write the full name of every shipment ordered or received, I would be doing nothing else, and I have many other responsibilities. Yes?" Again, he adjusts his glasses and looks at me as if I might be about to challenge him.

I nod. This is a man who takes pride in his work. I try to look impressed—I *am* impressed—and I decide, for now, it's better if I keep my mouth shut.

Hakeem tells me to spend the afternoon memorizing the abbreviations because I'll need them when I'm recording purchases.

Every time I go to dinner at Kanta and Manu's house, it's hard to believe that the twelve-year-old boy bending down to touch my feet is the same Nikhil I used to carry in my arms and whose tummy I used to tickle when he was a baby, back when I lived in Jaipur. When he straightens, I'm surprised that Niki is now only a few inches shorter than me and that he's going to be taller than either of his parents, who are standing behind him in the open doorway to their home. Kanta puts an arm around her son, smiling proudly, welcoming me to another dinner at their home, chatting happily about the latest test Niki has aced. Manu Uncle is more reserved. He waits until his wife has finished talking to acknowledge me and return my *namaste*. Out of respect for them and because they are like family to Auntie-Boss, I address them as Auntie and Uncle.

Their old servant Baju brings the tea tray. He and I trade a look; I know sharp-eyed Baju recognizes me from my days as Lakshmi's little helper, someone who could never hope to be invited to sit at the family dinner table. And that's how it would have been if not for my Bishop Cotton education.

Baju is followed by Manu Uncle's mother, waddling from side to side in her widow's starched white sari, sandalwood rosary beads dangling from one wrist. She's frowning at me, probably wondering how it is that Auntie and Uncle seem so happy to see me when she doesn't remember me at all. It's no wonder. Not many people recognize the scruffy boy behind my polished exterior.

With Kanta's mother-in-law in the room, we stay on safe subjects, chatting about Shimla's weather, how fresh the air is there, compared to here. Kanta's *saas* says she regrets not being able to get to the foothills of the Himalayas as often as they used to. Kanta and I exchange looks. I know the real reason she and Manu haven't visited Shimla in years: the stillborn baby boy she delivered at Lady Bradley Hospital. Not even their adoption of Radha's baby, whom they named Nikhil, could erase that painful memory.

Kanta talks about people we both know in Shimla—like the steadfast tandoori *roti* makers on the pedestrian mall—and one of Radha and Boss's favorite places, the Shimla library, an old haunt of Rudyard Kipling's.

Later, after Manu's mother leaves the room to do her evening *puja*, Kanta and I stand on the front veranda. Niki is practicing bowling for his cricket game in the yard. Manu is giving him pointers.

Kanta Auntie says, "He's perfect, isn't he?"

Niki looks over at us to make sure we're watching him. I wave and smile. I'm among the few who know that when he was a day old, she and Manu secretly adopted him. Even Kanta's *saas* doesn't know. She thinks Niki is the son Kanta delivered twelve years ago in Shimla. "Yes," I say. "He is."

Kanta lets a moment pass, then says, "Does Radha ever look at the photos of Niki I send to Lakshmi?"

I hesitate. "Auntie-Boss forwards your letters to Radha in France."

This is true, but Radha has never acknowledged receiving photos of Niki or the letters telling her what the boy is doing, how he's faring at school or at cricket. Even before she left for France, Radha never looked at Niki's photos, the ones Lakshmi would leave lying about on the dining room table. Radha told me that her baby ceased to exist the day she decided to leave him in Kanta's care. It had been so traumatic leaving him like that; she wanted no reminders of that time of her life. I often wonder if marrying Pierre and moving to France was a way of creating even more distance between herself, her son and her former friend Kanta. If so, I understood. Radha was fourteen when she had Niki—an unmarried girl on the cusp of becoming a woman. Parting with her baby was the hardest thing she'd ever had to do in her life. She'd also had to part with Ravi, whom she'd loved but who had hurt her deeply.

Kanta decides not to pursue the matter. "I miss Lakshmi, Malik. I wish she still lived here. I talk to her in my head all the time but, of course, it's not the same." She glances at me, her eyes crinkling. "Even if it's only in my head, I make sure it's a two-way conversation. She always has the best advice for me!" Kanta laughs.

Lakshmi doesn't talk about it often, but I know that she misses Kanta, too. They were easy with each other; I haven't seen Boss be that way with another female friend in Shimla.

We watch Niki wind up the ball and throw it to his father. I think it's clear to all of us that keeping the Agarwals and Lakshmi apart is best for everyone. Anyone who saw Niki with Lakshmi or Radha would almost certainly suspect Niki and the sisters were related. With his fair skin, and peacock-green eyes, so much like Radha's, he looks nothing like his adoptive parents.

Luckily, he's usurped the mannerisms of the mother and father who've raised him. He shrugs his shoulders up and down when he laughs, just like Kanta does. When listening intently, he stands with his head tilted to one side, his hands behind his back, a perfect copy of Manu.

I watch him pitch a ball, so gracefully for a boy so young. He's a natural athlete, like his birth father. I often wonder if Ravi Singh knows that the son he had by Radha lives only a few miles from him. Would he want to know? When his parents learned about Radha's pregnancy, they hustled Ravi to England

and kept him there for the remainder of his schooling. He was only seventeen at the time.

Kanta turns to me now. "I've seen him watching."

"Who?"

"Samir Singh."

"Samir is watching who?"

"Niki."

Well, of course, Samir would have occasion to run across Niki. For *sangeets* at the homes of mutual friends and community festivals—*unless* Kanta and Manu have deliberately stayed away from such events. Because it would make them so uncomfortable—all the questions they'd have to answer. The silent judgment. All at once, I realize what a burden it is for this family to keep Niki hidden, as it were. Does he realize the measures his parents have taken to keep the gossip-eaters at bay? But what choice do they have? *Bastard. Illegitimate.* They don't want his life to be tainted by labels. A wave of sadness passes over me.

Kanta sees the look on my face. "What I mean is—"

Just then, Niki calls to me. "Uncle, look!"

I turn to watch him pitch a perfect burner. Manu strokes his bat and misses.

Kanta claps and Niki raises both arms, declaring victory. He calls to me. "Now you try, Abbas Uncle!"

I look at Kanta. She presses her lips together and nods. "Go on," she says. "We'll talk later."

I head off across the manicured lawn to take the ball from Manu. For the next hour, Niki, Manu and I improvise a makeshift game. Of course, Niki is the winner.

Over dinner, I ask Niki about his school and the classes he's taking. He says English and history are the classes he likes best, and I fight back a smile. I can imagine a young Radha sitting with us at this table, telling us about her love of Shakespeare and her fascination with the Moghul Empire.

Eventually, our talk turns to the Royal Jewel Cinema project. Manu says, "You know that Maharani Latika is the driving force behind that project?"

I'm holding a piece of *chapatti* and eggplant *subji* in my hand. "Yes, I think Samir Uncle told me."

Manu smiles. "Her Highness took it upon herself to complete the building projects the maharaja had started before he died. We'd just finished His Highness's hotel remodel and broken ground on the cinema hall when he passed unexpectedly." Manu sips from his water glass. "So far, things are going smoothly. What did you think of the Royal Jewel Cinema?"

"Brilliant. Really impressive, Uncle."

Manu looks pleased and helps himself to more *subji*. "Completed in record time."

I sip some of Baju's excellent *moong dal*. "What's it like working for her, the maharani?"

"The most beautiful woman in the world." Niki chuckles. Those words appeared on the most recent cover of *Vogue* magazine, across a photo of the glamorous Jaipur queen.

Kanta slaps his arm, but she's grinning.

Manu smiles. "She's remarkable," he says. "Quick to catch on, eyes wide-open. Doesn't miss a thing. And don't forget she founded the Maharani School for Girls—" He cocks his head. "But of course, you would know all that, Malik. Lakshmi helped Her Highness through that rough period of her life, *hahn-nah*?"

I nod. That was twelve years ago. Maharani Latika had become despondent after her husband sent their firstborn son—and only child—to boarding school in England at a tender age. All because the maharaja's astrologer had warned His Highness not to trust his natural heir. So the maharaja adopted a boy from another Rajput family and anointed him crown prince.

I remember how Lakshmi gradually coaxed the young queen

out of mourning, using daily applications of henna and the sweets and savories she infused with healing herbs. When, a few months later, Her Highness overcame her depression and resumed her official duties, Maharani Latika was so grateful to Lakshmi that she offered Radha a scholarship at her prestigious school. And Lakshmi's business started exploding. What a heady time that was! The boom went on and on until the day everything came crashing down.

"Where's Her Highness's son now?" I ask.

Manu clears his throat. "He stays away from Jaipur. I imagine it's hard for him to come face-to-face with his replacement—although the adopted crown prince won't come of age for another few years." Manu takes a sip of his buttermilk. "Last I heard, Maharani Latika's son was living in Paris. At the apartment the dowager maharani keeps there."

The Dowager Maharani Indira! At eight years old, I was more awed by her talking parakeet than I was by her. At this very moment, Madho Singh is likely grumbling about some grievance or another from his perch in Shimla. Or repeating a proverb Dr. Jay and Auntie-Boss have been tossing around. *We are both queens, so who will hang out the laundry?*

After dinner, when I say my goodbyes, Kanta takes my arm and walks me to the front gate. "When Niki's finished with his game, we go to a stall near the cricket field and order *chaat*." She lowers her voice and whispers, as if we are conspiring. "Saasuji doesn't let us give him fried food, so Niki and I cheat when he's with me." A mischievous smile plays about her lips. "*Sev puri* is his favorite. Mine, too." We laugh.

We've reached the end of the long driveway.

Kanta takes a deep breath. "Several times, at Niki's cricket practice, I've seen Samir Singh in a Jeep parked opposite the grounds."

"You're sure it's Samir?"

She makes a face. "Not a hundred percent. The *peepal* trees on either side of the street shade the cars. And there are always people milling about. Cars going in and out."

"But if it's him?"

She lets out a sigh. It's dusk, and half her face is in shadow. Even so, I see from her expression, and the furrows on her brow, that this is serious. "I've never said a word to Manu," she says, "but I think about it all the time. Sometimes, the strain of keeping Niki separated from…all the vigilance…it's too much." Her voice is strained, and if she's crying, I can't see her tears because she has turned away from me. "I lie awake at night worrying that Samir will take Nikhil away from us," she whispers.

An alarm bell goes off in my head. Should I tell Boss about this? If it's true, Lakshmi would want to know. For now, I have to reassure Kanta. Niki means the world to her and Uncle. After the stillbirth twelve years ago, Kanta can no longer have children.

"Listen to me, Auntie. You and Manu are Niki's legal, adoptive parents. Samir Sahib can't touch you."

"But he might come to Niki and tell him that he was adopted. That his son is Niki's father. What do we do then?" She's twirling the end of her georgette sari around her finger as she talks, her voice a hush.

"Before long, Niki will be old enough that you can tell him yourself, if that's what you and Manu choose to do. But I doubt Samir will talk to Niki if you don't give him your consent." I'm speaking with a confidence I don't entirely feel.

Kanta bites her lip. "You don't think Samir Sahib would take the opportunity to start a conversation with his grandson on the cricket grounds?"

I'm wondering how Auntie-Boss would answer that, when

Kanta says, "It's why I go to every game. To keep an eye on Niki. And if I can't be there, Baju knows to bring my son directly home from practice." She sniffles, presses her sari to her nose.

"Listen to me, Auntie. First, the Singhs would have a lot to lose if word got out that Ravi is the father. Everyone would know Radha was underage when Ravi got her pregnant. Second, they took no responsibility, and hushed the matter up by sending Ravi thousands of miles away. It would be a scandal for them, and I doubt the Singhs would risk it." Another thought occurs to me, and I tap Auntie's arm. "By the way, Samir drives a Mercedes, not a Jeep."

She searches my face, then lets out an embarrassed laugh. "You're right! The problem might not be Samir—it might be my imagination!"

A new, disturbing, thought occurs to me. "Has Niki ever asked about this? Have any of the kids at school suggested he's adopted?" It's never made sense to me that while royal adoptions are public, private adoptions are considered shameful. No couple wants to admit they are sterile; it's considered a personal failing, a problem best solved by magical gems, amulets and alms to Ganesh.

The worry returns to Kanta's voice. "I don't know of any. Niki's never asked. We try to keep things as normal as possible." Her gaze drifts behind us, to the house. "I haven't noticed any changes in him."

Before she unlatches the gate, she says, "Thank you, Malik. I feel better now." When she shuts the gate behind me, another thought occurs to her. "You sure you don't want Baju to drive you home?"

The guesthouse is only twenty minutes on foot. I shake my head and tell her that I need to walk off that superb meal. I thank her for a wonderful time and ask her to give my thanks to Manu, as well. And then I head home, my head now swirling with anxieties about the boy his parents are determined to protect from the clutches of the Singhs.

7

NIMMI

Shimla

At night, after Rekha and Chullu have dropped off to sleep on either side of me, I look through the picture books Lakshmi has lent us. They are children's books, she said, that she borrows from the Shimla library. I never knew there was a place where you could go look at books, much less borrow them, then return them when you are through looking. Imagine! Something that precious! That's like borrowing a woman's bridal jewelry for your marriage and giving it back the next day. No one in their right mind would hand over something that valuable and expect to get it back!

I hold the book to my nose and inhale, trying to call up the scents of all the hands that have flipped the pages. But all I smell is something like the *atta* I make *chapattis* with. I turn the pages carefully. Our tribal elders may not know how to read, but they revere those who can. *Books contain magic*, they say. If we so much as stepped on a book or on a piece of paper, we were punished. I trace the letters with my finger, and mouth out the words in the book, just as Lakshmi taught us to do. She spends an hour reading with Rekha and me every afternoon. Sometimes Lakshmi shows us how to write the names of the foods we're eating. I now know that the word *chapatti* starts with a *c*.

Wait until I show Malik that I can write my name now! So can Rekha. Dev would be so proud of her! She learns so quickly; she thinks nothing of it. At four years old she's learning what I'm only learning at the age of twenty-two or twenty-three (I think that one of those is right!). I've always been able to do simple math in my head, but now I take great pride in writing out the *names* of numbers from one to ten *(ake, dho, theen, chaar!)*, and now that I'm learning to read, I can recognize the numbers by their names.

Lakshmi has given each of us a workbook so we can practice. Sometimes, when I'm in the garden, I copy the names of the plants that are written on labels in each row. Even if I don't know what the labels say, I want to find out, later, so I can remember them.

When I form the letter *M*, I think of Malik, and wonder if I might, someday, read the letters that he sends. When Lakshmi reads his words and thoughts to me, I feel embarrassed, ashamed even. Those messages should be a private thing, between Malik and me; I want to read the parts I like best by myself, or just take his letters with me when I go up on the ridge at night. I like to imagine his fingers tented on the corner of the thin paper, holding it steady, as he writes my name. I sometimes think how it would feel to have him write "Nimmi" on my palm, my back, my thigh!

I finally allowed Lakshmi to henna our hands—mine and Rekha's. Lakshmi is so practiced that it took her only minutes to create a new design for Rekha. Rekha was so good; she didn't move a muscle until the henna paste was dry enough that it could be removed.

On Rekha's palms, Lakshmi drew an elephant with its trunk stretching from one palm to the other. When Rekha brings her hands together, the elephant is complete, and she squeals in delight. She moves her hands, pretending that the elephant is raising its trunk and moving it about.

When Lakshmi tried to put some dots on Chullu's palms, he tried to lick the henna off, which made us laugh!

The first time Lakshmi asked me what design I wanted on my hands, I couldn't think of one. So she decided to draw peonies on one palm and roses on the other. When I bring my hands together, I have a bouquet that I can raise to my nose and breathe in the henna's clean and earthy smell. It reminds me of my wedding day, the only other time my hands and arms and feet were decorated.

Chullu is fussing and I rub his back until he falls asleep again. My boy. A year old already! He's walking and starting to talk. In a few years, Rekha will be able to teach him how to read and write his name. That would never have been possible if Dev hadn't died, and we hadn't left the mountains, and my people, to live in town. I would love for Dev to be with us now. I want him to see how his children are thriving. How I'm doing what I never thought possible: learning to live without our tribe, and without *him*. All at once, my eyes fill. How I loved those creases on the sides of his mouth, the rough feel of his palms, hardened by years of guiding his shepherd's crook, scaling trees to chop leaves and branches for the goats to feed on. How he loved his goats! I can almost hear him saying, *Never approach a goat from the front, a horse from the back, or a fool from the side!* Then he would laugh. Oh, how he would laugh, as if it was the first time he'd said it!

I trace one of Chullu's eyebrows. Dev is no longer in my life, and I have to show Rekha and Chullu that they can survive without him, too. I blink to clear my eyes. I glance at the picture book of wildflowers. I try to sound out the words below the photo. But I recognize only the letter at the beginning. I close the book. Will I ever be able to write a letter to Malik? If I could, what would I say?

My love,
After Dev died, I didn't know if I could love another man. Then you came along. You're like him but also different. And I miss you so much!

Let me tell you something that will make you happy. I'm enjoying working for your Auntie-Boss. Mostly because she leaves me alone. I decide what to plant, whether to use seeds or seedlings, when to fertilize and when to harvest.

She's made some mistakes—I can tell you that much. She's trying to grow a sandalwood tree, but it'll never take. I haven't seen another tree like that one here. But your Auntie-Boss never gives up, does she? She's always trying something new, mixing new things in the soil, moving that sandalwood sapling to different parts of the garden.

I've told her what she should substitute for the Rajasthani grasses she's used to using for her ointments. I hope I'm right. I've never been anywhere south of Shimla, and I don't know what Rajasthan is like or anything about the plants that grow there. Your Auntie-Boss says it's so dry in Rajasthan that the soil just turns to dust and flies away. I can't imagine that!

She lets me bring the children to work, and they love being out-

doors, near the garden. I used to fear that when I left Rekha and Chullu with the Aroras, who are as old as the Himalayas, the children got no exercise. Now my children breathe fresh air all day.

I brush a strand of hair away from Rekha's face. She sleeps so soundly.

What else would I write?

The Shimla Mall has become busier with tourists from all over. But it isn't the same when you're not around to surprise the children with your little presents. They're restless, always hoping you'll show up. Rekha says she's angry with you for not coming to see us. She wants you here so you can buy balloon animals for her from the vendor in the next stall. Chullu is gnawing everything in sight as his teeth come in, including the balloon creatures, so most of them are no more. (Rekha has shrouded them in scraps of cloth that Mrs. Arora gave her and given them a funeral.)

I remind Rekha that Lakshmi-ji and Dr. Jay always give her a balloon animal when she asks for one, but she says it's not the same as when you do it because she likes to hear you make the different noises of the animals you give to her. You've spoiled her!

Rekha released the green cricket you gave her somewhere in our room. His loud chirps, early in the morning, wake us up. She tries to catch him, but the cricket's faster. Still, she won't give up.

Chullu just cut another tooth! He's grouchy because it's hurting, but I rub that honey you gave us on his gums, which makes him very, very happy.

They'd both be happier if you were here. They want to know when you're coming home.

So Malik, when are you coming home?
Your Nimmi

TWO DAYS BEFORE
THE COLLAPSE

8

LAKSHMI

Shimla

It's late afternoon. I'm at the Community Clinic, washing my hands at the basin while my patient buttons up her blouse. Jay is at the hospital next door, seeing to an emergency delivery. He left an hour ago.

Like many of the people in this area, my patient speaks a mixture of Hindi, Punjabi, Urdu and her local dialect, but I didn't need to understand what she was saying to figure out why she had come to the clinic. Years of carrying firewood from the edge of the forest to her hearth has taken a toll on her right shoulder. Even while sitting on the exam table, she is listing to one side, leaning away from the weight of her invisible cargo.

The nun who is helping me today puts warm water compresses on the sore shoulder to relax the muscles before I apply a mixture of turmeric powder and coconut oil to the bruised skin. That should reduce the inflammation. I tell my patient to remove the ointment when it dries, in half an hour, then reapply the warm compress and rub on more of the lotion, which I'm sending home with her. I wish I could command her to stop hauling firewood until her shoulder heals, but she's a widow, and her children are too small to help her with the task.

Now I dry my hands and moisten them with lavender oil to prepare for the next patient; the scent relaxes patients who might be nervous about coming to the clinic. It relaxes me, as well. I breathe it in.

I hear the receptionist in the outer room say, "Wait! You can't go in there!"

A boy and girl—ten years old or thereabouts—burst through the curtain that separates the exam room from the clinic's waiting room. They're carrying a sheep—the boy holding the front end, the girl carrying the rear. The receptionist follows them, apologizing to me.

"*Theek hai,*" I tell her. *It's fine.*

She looks relieved and returns to her desk.

The sheep is bleeding from what appears to be a nasty gash on its right side. I can't understand what the girl is saying to me, so I turn to Sister and wait for her to translate. The foothills of the Himalayas are home to many indigenous tribes, and between the staff and me, we can usually manage to work out what our patients are telling us.

My patient with the swollen shoulder, now dressed, jumps down from the exam table. She points at the sheep and says something I don't understand. It's clear she's frightened.

I look for help from Sister, who shakes her head; she doesn't understand the woman's rapid-fire speech any better than I do.

The girl and boy stare at the patient, their mouths hanging open. The sheep bleats.

My patient grabs the bottle of turmeric ointment I mixed for her and flees the room as if the building is on fire.

Is she frightened of a wounded sheep?

I inspect the gash while the sheep struggles to escape the clutches of the children, but they hold on fast, and I get a good look at the area. The fleece appears to have a clean slit, like a welt pocket on a coat. The wound is underneath the fleece. How could that have happened?

Then I see a coarse thread hanging from the fleece. And uneven stitching at the edges of the slit. It's like a pocket that has been sewn shut. Working gingerly, with a pair of scissors, I cut the ragged stitching open and peel back the layer of fleece. And now I understand the problem. Underneath the wool, the skin is covered in sores, pus and blood oozing from an open wound.

I'm wondering who would shear a sheep's fleece in this way, then stitch it back together. Why not treat the wound? Why would a shepherd try to hide these sores? Sheep are as precious to the hill people as gold is to the matrons whose hands I used to paint with henna. No shepherd would leave an injured sheep on its own or, worse, abandon it.

If only Jay were here. Except for his time at Oxford, Jay has always lived in Shimla and speaks many of the local dialects. He could find out if the sheep belongs to the children, and if so, where is the rest of their flock? Where's the shepherd? Or, if the animal isn't theirs, where did they find it?

It occurs to me that Nimmi could help. Perhaps she speaks their language or could understand enough of it to clarify what happened. She's grown up with sheep and goats and might have some idea why this animal's wounds are so peculiar.

I indicate with gestures that the boy and girl should stay where they are.

In the Healing Garden, I find Nimmi on her haunches, patting down the soil where she must have just sown seeds.

"I need your help, Nimmi." I tell her. "In the clinic."

She knits her brows, and I know she must be thinking: *You need me at the clinic?*

"An injured sheep," I say. "Two children brought it in."

Nimmi stands. She still looks puzzled, but there's no time to explain. I take her hoe and spade from her and put them in the shed while she brushes dirt off her hands and goes to wash them at the outdoor tap.

Inside, the sister on duty is laying a fresh sheet on the exam table. Then she helps the boy and girl gently lift the animal onto the table.

The instant Nimmi sees the wounds on the sheep's shorn skin, she steps back with a shocked expression on her face. She glances, first, at me, then at the children. She says something to them in her dialect.

The boy just stares at Nimmi, but the girl responds and makes a gesture with her arm.

Switching to Hindi, Nimmi tells me, "I asked them if it is their sheep. The girl says no. She says they found the animal on the trail while they were collecting firewood on the mountain."

"Without a shepherd?" Having lived in Shimla for a decade, I know that the nomadic tribes would never leave an animal to die alone; it would be too cruel—and the animal too expensive to replace.

Nimmi turns to speak to the girl. The two of them are communicating both with words and gestures. Most of the tribes, whether from the Nepalese or the Kashmiri border, share some common words in Urdu, Hindi and Nepali. Like many North Indians, I speak mainly Hindi with some Urdu words thrown in—but the hill dialects make use of words I've never heard, and the sentence structure is entirely different.

"The only sheep they saw was this one," Nimmi says. "They could hear others farther up the mountain—but they wanted to help this one because she's hurt."

I ask Nimmi, "Do you know what might have caused the injury? Did someone do this deliberately?"

Nimmi moves closer to the animal, who is still lying on one side and breathing heavily. She leans forward with her elbow on the table and uses her forearm to hold the animal's neck and head still while she peels the hide back as far as it will go. She probes the cuts with her fingers, as the sheep jerks and flinches.

"Illness didn't cause these sores," Nimmi says. "These are abrasions. Something was irritating her skin, and so she rubbed herself against a tree trunk or a rock—some hard surface—to scratch herself...or soothe herself...or maybe..."

When Nimmi eases her hold on the sheep and starts to examine one of its ears, she suddenly pulls back, and gasps.

The hair on my arm stands up.

Suddenly the air feels heavy, tense.

The children feel it, too. They look at me, then at Nimmi.

I say. "What is it?"

She frowns, staring at the animal, her lips a thin line. There's something she doesn't want to say. What?

Finally, Nimmi takes a breath and sighs. She says something to the girl, her hand on the girl's shoulder. Again, they're using words and gestures to communicate, and when the girl responds, Nimmi nods.

Then the girl turns to the boy, takes him by the arm, and leads him from the room.

Nimmi turns to me. "I told them we will help the animal. They mustn't worry."

I still don't know what's going on, but the set of her mouth tells me that she's not going to tell me what she's thinking. A bubble of resentment rises in my chest. I'm used to being in control of my exam room, my patients, the Healing Garden. But now even Sister is looking at Nimmi for instructions about what to do next. Sometime in the last fifteen minutes, Nimmi seems to have taken charge of my exam room. But she works *for* us. She has no reason—or right—to hold anything back. My feelings are hurt; I can't help it.

I point my chin at the sheep. The words that come out of my mouth are as sharp as the needles Jay uses at the hospital. "Ask Sister to get you the supplies you'll need to dress the wound. She'll help you."

Before Nimmi has a chance to answer—to object or tell me that her only job is to tend the garden—I walk over to the basin, turn on the faucet and briskly begin washing my hands with soap.

She knows more about what's happened—but she's reluctant to share. I'll talk to Jay about it when I see him this evening.

My husband comes home later than usual; the delivery of the twins was fraught with complications. His days are longer now that he also has so many administrative responsibilities, fund-raising events, board meetings. When he returns from the hospital, he likes to have an hour to unwind together before dinner. He is settled in his favorite armchair in the drawing room with the *Times of India* and a glass of Laphroaig. I check on dinner—*masala lauki* and *dal*, simmering on low, and join him. He hands me my glass of whiskey and a section of the newspaper.

But I can't concentrate on the article about the ongoing battle between India and Pakistan over the Jammu/Kashmir area. We live over a hundred miles from there. And aside from Indian soldiers coming into Shimla for provisions or passing through on their way to the northeast provinces, we have little to do with the war. For Malik's sake, I want it to stay that way. Providing provisions for profit is one of his specialties.

I fold the newspaper and set it aside. I sip my scotch.

Jay turns down a corner of his paper to peer at me. "What is it?"

I smile. My husband can sense my mood so easily.

"A sheep. At the clinic today. Two tribal children brought it in."

"They brought in a sheep?"

"It was wounded."

He chuckles, setting the paper on the table beside him. "Ah, that explains everything, then." He drinks from his crystal tumbler, his eyes dancing.

I rise from the couch and sit on the arm of his chair. I love the salt-and-pepper curls that hang over his forehead; they grow too quickly and I'm forever brushing them away, as I do now.

"I called Nimmi to help. I thought she would be able to communicate better with the boy and girl."

"And?"

I tuck a curl behind his ear; it springs back again. "Jay, what's the reason someone would shear a sheep—halfway—and then sew the hide back on as if it hadn't been sheared?"

He raises his brows.

"The wounds were *under* the sheared wool," I say. "As if the animal had rubbed her raw skin against something abrasive. But how could she possibly have done that when the fleece was mostly still attached?"

"Still attached?"

"Exactly. Like a pocket someone tried to sew back on. The thread had come loose, so the flap of fleece was visible." I indicate the wound's size—maybe four inches by five inches—with my hands. "Just about this big."

Jay puts a hand on my arm. "Who brought the sheep into the clinic?" He says it quietly enough, but something in his tone alarms me.

"Two children. They came across her on a mountain trail while they were gathering firewood."

"Where's the sheep now?"

A shiver crawls up my spine. I can tell when he's trying to make something sound like nothing, like when he has to tell a patient they have cancer. "At the clinic. I asked Nimmi to take care of it."

"And where is Nimmi at this moment?"

I feel Jay's hand on my arm tense. Now I'm more afraid than worried. Jay knows something I don't, and I sense that he's about to tell me I've put Nimmi in some kind of danger.

"At her house, I would imagine, with her children. And the sheep," I say slowly.

Jay blinks. "You said the wound was only on one side of the animal. Did you check its other side?"

I shake my head.

He covers his mouth with his palm. The look on his face raises goose bumps on my arms.

"Why?" I ask. "What's happened?"

When we reach Nimmi's lean-to at the bottom of the hill, I can see the light of a kerosene lamp through the window. I don't want to wake her landlords on the floor above hers, so I tap lightly on the door, and Nimmi opens it a moment later. She looks surprised to see us.

She's carrying Chullu in a homemade sling strapped to her back. Behind her, I see Rekha, sitting on one of the many bolsters lining the walls of the room. She's eating a *chapatti*. Rekha sees me, smiles and looks at me as if she's hoping that I might have brought another book for her to read. I smile back.

Then I hear a bleat. I hadn't seen that the sheep was in the room as well, sitting on another grass-stuffed bolster, munching on thistle leaves.

Nimmi hasn't moved from the door. She looks from me to Jay. Baby Chullu regards us over her shoulder.

"Nimmi," I say, "Dr. Kumar thinks we need to take the sheep."

"Why?" she says. She sounds annoyed. "She's better now. She needed food and rest."

Jay steps forward. "Nimmi," he says, "the owner must be looking for it. May I check—"

Nimmi steps in front of him to block his way.

"I won't hurt her, Nimmi. I just need to see if—"

"I've already done it." Her voice is low. She looks down at her feet.

"Done what?"

Now she looks at Jay. A moment passes. "Checked her other side."

Jay steps back and nods. "And?"

Nimmi finally moves aside to let us in, then pulls the door closed.

When she turns to face us, she says, "Still intact. The gold." She sighs.

Jay nods, turns to me. He had explained it all to me earlier, before we left the house to see Nimmi. He showed me the article in the paper; more and more gold being smuggled through the mountains.

Nimmi reaches an arm behind her to pat Chullu, more to comfort herself than him, I think. "The gold moves on the same trails as our tribe. Two years ago, a man—a trafficker—told Dev there was a lot of money to be made if he agreed to help the smugglers, but Dev refused." She steals a glance at me. "I knew, this morning, when I saw the sheep had not been sheared. See, we always shear the sheep when we arrive here, in the foothills, for the winter. That way we can sell the wool before we make the trek back up the mountains in the spring. The tribes already sheared their sheep and left weeks ago to take their herds north for the summer."

My husband frowns. "Nimmi, it's not safe for you to have her here. Someone will come looking for her." He bites his lip and looks at me, then back at Nimmi. "The smugglers won't stop until they find what's theirs."

"You think I don't know that?" Nimmi turns away from us and squats in front of the wool blanket on which she has collected the family's few possessions. "They used to sneak it in their shoes, the lining of their coats—gold ingots the size of those candied lemon slices you make." She flicks another glance my way. "But now they're using our sheep. Hiding it under their fleece. And for that, they need a shepherd." She knots the ends of the cloth together tightly and sets the bundle on a padded quilt laid out on the floor. Then she stands and turns to look at us. "I have to go. I have to find his flock—and him. They'll kill his family if the gold is not delivered."

I put a hand on Nimmi's arm. "Find who? *Whose* family is in danger?"

She turns away, her shoulders tense. I can almost smell her fear. She stares down at the quilt. "My brother. Vinay."

Now she looks at the sheep quietly munching in the corner. "The markings on her ear. That's my brother's flock."

When she turns to us, I see desperation in her eyes. "I have to find him. The only reason one of his sheep would be running around loose is if Vinay is hurt badly, too. So badly that he can't move. Or he's—" She blinks. "His flock must be out there without a shepherd. With all the gold."

Jay runs a hand through his curls. Then he turns to Nimmi and says, "Could someone else have taken Vinay's flock?"

My mouth falls open. I hadn't considered the possibility that bandits might have taken the sheep.

Nimmi's jaw clenches. "You don't think that's occurred to

me? My brother has a wife and two sons. If the smugglers think the gold's been stolen—if it doesn't get delivered to the people who are waiting for it, they'll kill everyone in Vinay's family. They'd kill our entire tribe if they think that one of us knows where the gold is." She bends down and pulls the knot on her bundle tight.

Baby Chullu senses his mother's unease. He starts fussing. She reaches an arm over her shoulder to stroke his neck. He quiets down.

I look at Rekha. She's stopped eating. She looks at her mother, then at the two of us. She senses something's wrong, but I don't know how much of what we're saying she understands.

One of the main reasons I sent Malik to Jaipur was to keep him from falling in with traffickers. Carrying illegal goods tempts many who have heard that there's good money to be made. I'd worried Malik might try trafficking guns, given that a war was on up north. With his enterprising instincts, he might have thought himself too clever to be caught despite the risks. But gold smuggling hadn't even been on my radar.

Silently, I offer thanks to Manu and Kanta for agreeing to give Malik a home, away from all these temptations.

Now I squat next to Nimmi. "How would they—the smugglers—find your brother's home? Your tribe is always on the move."

"We are until we reach our summer destination. All the families have huts up there. Dev's and mine is next to Vinay's, though I wouldn't be surprised to hear another family has since moved in." She reaches around her neck to stroke Chullu again. She must be remembering her husband and the life they had together with their tribe.

With renewed fervor, Nimmi begins rolling the bundle on the floor.

"You really plan to leave tonight? And take the sheep?"

Nimmi says nothing.

I look at Rekha, her eyes large, unblinking. "What about the children?"

Nimmi raises an eyebrow. "We've always traveled the mountains with our children."

"And Malik?" I think about the letters I'll receive from him addressed to her. How much he wants to say to her. How much he *doesn't* say because he knows I'll be the one to read it to her.

Her hands hover over the quilt for a second. "He's not here," she says. Then she cinches the bedroll with jute.

I look helplessly at Jay, who seems to be as lost as I am about what to do. I know that Nimmi shouldn't go alone, with her children and the sheep, to find her brother. It's too dangerous. If any one of them falls ill, is injured or encounters bandits, there'll be no one there to help.

Now Jay squats beside us. "Wait until the morning, Nimmi. Please. Let us think about this, make a plan together."

Nimmi flashes her dark eyes at him. "You won't go to the police?"

He shakes his head. He and I had already talked about this. The police would be inclined to punish and jail a poor shepherd serving as nothing more than a courier. Or they might want the precious metal for themselves and decide Nimmi knows more than she does, in which case, they might threaten her life. When it comes to smuggling contraband goods, it's hard to know whom to trust—even among the police, who are supposed to control the trafficking.

Nimmi looks at her daughter, who has wandered over to the sheep and is petting the animal's head. Without meeting our eyes, Nimmi nods.

Jay and I breathe a collective sigh.

Jay rises and goes to the sheep. He smiles at Rekha. "Can I pet her, too?" he asks.

She whispers in the way small children do—loud enough for all of us to hear. "Her name is Neela."

Gently, Jay lifts the sheep's woolly pelt and inspects the wound. "Hello, Neela," he says. He turns to look at Nimmi. "You did a good job. The wound will heal and she'll be fine. I'm thinking maybe we could use a veterinarian in Shimla."

The look of puzzlement on Nimmi's face makes him smile. "Animal doctor," he says. "We need one."

But in the morning, Nimmi does not show up for work. I go directly to her lodging. No one's there. The children, the sheep, the bolster and the bedroll—gone.

9

MALIK

Jaipur

I'm at my desk just outside Hakeem's office, admiring the new red Ford Maverick in the latest issue of *LIFE* magazine ("The first car of the '70s at 1960 prices!"), when a ledger lands on top of it, barely missing the glass of chai on my desk.

"*Arré!*" I yell. When I look up, I see Hakeem standing on the other side of my desk. He's glowering.

He taps his stubby index finger on the ledger several times. "You made a mistake. Yes!" He is triumphant.

I turn the ledger around so I can read the spine: *Purchasing 1969.*

Hakeem strokes both sides of his mustache with his finger. "Tell me, Abbas. C–M–T. What does it stand for?"

"Cement," I say.

"And B–R–K?"

"Brick."

Hakeem clears his throat. "Correct. So why would you have switched those two figures in the ledger?"

I'm still taking this in when he opens the ledger, then flips back a few pages. "See here? C–M–T? Yes? And here? B–R–K? Yes?"

I nod.

"The sum for bricks and the sum for cement used for the Royal Jewel Cinema is the opposite of what it should be. You have transposed the two."

I look again at the columns. "But, Hakeem Sahib, I double-checked the bills against the ledger."

He flicks his mustache with his finger. "Check them again. Sloppy accounting will not be tolerated here."

"Yes," I say, with a straight face, eliciting another cold glance from the little man.

When he goes back to his office, I look at the numbers in the ledger. I can see his point. There should have been a lot of cement used and very little brick for a project of this size. I've learned that much from the engineers who work for Manu. Manu himself has taken me to different building sites (ignoring the disapproving glare of Hakeem) to teach me about materials and methods employed for different parts of a building.

I'm aware Hakeem resents my presence in his little kingdom. He might think I've been hired to take his place. For all that, I can't believe that he would stoop to jiggering the books to get me into trouble.

I turn the pages of the ledger slowly to see how much has been spent on the cinema house project since the beginning of the year. I add the totals up; the sums surprise me. The amount Singh-Sharma Construction has spent on cement is three times the sum the firm has spent on bricks. So why would the latest invoices show the opposite?

I'm puzzling over this when Hakeem comes out of his office, locks the door behind him and leaves for his lunch hour, dangling his tiffin in one hand, an Agatha Christie novel in the other. Hakeem is passionate about his murder mysteries.

I don't need my watch to tell me that it's one o'clock. As always, he will head to Jaipur's Central Park and claim his favorite bench (Bhagwan forbid that someone else arrives to claim the bench before Hakeem!).

He will return at two o'clock. Not a minute earlier, and not a minute later.

Hakeem's office is a tiny, windowless room set off in one distant corner of this floor, but years of loyal service have earned him this small privilege.

From where I sit, I can see the desks of project managers, draftsmen and overseers. The secretaries who type letters for the office sit closer to me. But at lunch, employees either leave the office or sit quietly behind their desks, eating lunch, reading a newspaper or taking a nap.

I let several minutes pass before I make my way to Hakeem's office door. I was raised on the streets of Jaipur, left to my own devices when I was just two or three years old, which was when Omi gave me a home, even though she had three of her own children to feed. Her husband was absent for long periods, so I helped her out any way I could. I played Parcheesi for food and marbles for money, learned how to cheat well at cards, haggled for things Omi's children needed.

And I excelled at picking locks.

I am inside Hakeem's office in three seconds.

The file cabinet marked Support holds the original invoices from suppliers. At the end of every day, when I've finished inputting the invoice amounts in the ledger, Hakeem snatches the invoices from the box on my desk, double-checks my work and stashes them in this drawer.

I pull the bills for April, looking for the invoices from Chandigarh Ironworks marked Paid. I find both items: one for concrete, one for bricks. Both amounts match what I recorded in the ledger. Were the bricks purchased for another project and inadvertently billed to the cinema house project? I put the two receipts in my pocket and check my watch. It's still lunch hour, so there won't be anyone at the supplier's office if I call.

Back at my desk, I shoo a fly away from my tea, now cold. The sluggish fan overhead does little to cool the room. I may as well step out for a *parantha* and a mango *lassi* before I head over to the offices of Singh-Sharma, just a few streets over, for a chat with Ravi Singh.

"So what's the problem?" Ravi is gazing at me across his immense desk at Singh-Sharma Construction as I stand with the two receipts in my hand.

"The amounts are the opposite of what they should be."

"And?" He sounds impatient, eager for me to leave so he can continue inspecting the blueprints in front of him. The sleeves of his white shirt are rolled up at the cuffs. His elegant linen jacket hangs on a wooden coatrack in the corner.

"The invoices are from Singh-Sharma suppliers. Have they made a mistake? Should I call them or would you like to?"

Ravi narrows his eyes, considering me. He pulls a cigarette from the pack on his desk and offers one to me. He pats his pockets for his gold lighter, the one that's a duplicate of Samir's. He frowns, his head tilted. Then his face clears and a smile plays about his lips.

Inwardly, I roll my eyes. Has he left his lighter at the home of his latest conquest? I pick up the matchbox on his desk and light his cigarette first, then mine. I shake the match to extinguish it.

Ravi takes a drag of his cigarette. "Show me."

I lay the receipts on the desk.

He blows smoke from his nostrils as he examines the invoices.

Unscrewing his fountain pen, he crosses out the total at the bottom of the first invoice and writes in the total from the second. Then he does the same to the other invoice. He hands them both back to me with a broad smile. "There. Not so hard, was it?"

For a moment, I say nothing. What kind of strange accounting is this?

Ravi shrugs. "Look, there's no need to complicate things. Hakeem needs the numbers to match. They'll match. End of story. What are you doing for dinner tonight?"

His habit of abruptly changing subjects always throws me off guard. I'm still trying to make sense of what he's just done to the invoices.

"Why not come out with us tonight? Sheela and I are leaving the kids at home. We're dining at the Rambagh Palace. The *rogan josh* is sublime." To his credit, he doesn't boast about the relationship of the Singhs to the Jaipuri royal family. He doesn't have to; it's a well-known fact; his father has always been a favorite of the court.

Before I have a chance to say anything, Ravi reaches for his phone. "I'll tell Sheela you'll be joining us."

When I lived in this city as a boy, Rambagh Palace used to be the maharajas' personal residence. After independence, when the purses of India's maharajas were dwindling rapidly, His Highness of Jaipur had the bright idea of turning the Rambagh into a hotel to replenish his coffers. It worked. Royalty from around the world, successful businessmen and wealthy globetrotters all frequent the Rambagh.

It's one of the grandest places I've ever been. The waiters are dressed in maroon maharaja coats cinched with orange cummerbunds, orange turbans on their heads. Overhead, multitiered chandeliers hang from the ceiling, their lights bouncing off the gems on the fingers, wrists, necks and ears of diners. I try to store the details in my memory so I can describe them to Nimmi in my next letter.

At dinner, Ravi is the attentive host, ordering for us, making sure our wine glasses are filled, regaling us with amusing stories. He gossips about the polo club (*His Highness is bringing the Bombay polo team here for an* elephant *polo match—that should be charming!*), praises Sheela's progress at tennis (*Mark my words—she will be a regional champ next year!*), and India's cricket team (*We're going to show the Australians a thing or two come November!*). Sheela is in fine form, too, dazzling in an emerald-green chiffon sheath with spaghetti straps, laughing at her husband's jokes, teasing him about his cricket obsession and chatting merrily about their friends at the Jaipur Club. I try to picture Nimmi's granite-dark skin, exposed, glistening, under a dress like Sheela's and feel a blush creeping from my neck to my ears.

After dinner, as Sheela is getting into their car, Ravi tells her he has promised a potential client a late-night drink. The driver will take Sheela home first, then me. Ravi will take a taxi to his appointment.

Sheela's face falls. "But it's almost midnight!"

"And that's when deals get sealed in Jaipur."

"Which deal is this?" There's an edge to Sheela's voice.

I'm in the passenger's seat, next to the driver. I can see Sheela and Ravi in the side-view mirror.

"I need one more piece to come together for the grand opening of the Royal Jewel Cinema. That's the guy I'm meeting."

Seeing that Sheela is starting to pout, Ravi leans close to her and slips a finger under one of her spaghetti straps, sliding it up and down the delicate fabric, grazing her skin. "He's the one who's always ogling you. I can't have that. That's why you're not invited."

The act is so intimate it makes me blush. Are they always like this? I shift my gaze away from the side-view mirror, wondering what their driver, the ever stoic Mathur, is thinking.

Sheela looks at her husband sideways. And smiles.

After a beat, Sheela reaches up a hand to straighten Ravi's tie. "Abbas will have a drink with me, won't you, Abbas? Mathur can take him home afterward."

I turn around to object. I have a lot of work to do for Hakeem tomorrow and a tutorial with one of Manu's engineers. It's late, and I'd rather go to bed.

Ravi's face has darkened. He's staring pointedly at Sheela. She returns his stare, coolly.

He pushes his lips out as if considering the idea. "A little Sheela hospitality. Sounds like a plan." He straightens and pats my shoulder as if the matter is settled.

My acquiescence, it seems, is neither warranted nor necessary.

At Sheela and Ravi's home, the driver parks, then hops out of the car to open Sheela's door. I stay where I am, hoping that the invitation for a drink was only a maneuver to make Ravi jealous.

"You don't mind, do you, Abbas? Spending time with me?"

Quietly, I let out a sigh. She *is* my hostess this evening. I follow her into the house where she hands Anu, her maid, her shawl and purse. Then she leads me to the drawing room—an airy space with a high ceiling and enormous French doors that take up the entire east wall. I imagine, in the daylight, that this room is even more spectacular. It's so quiet at this hour I can hear the hum of the air conditioner.

Two yellow damask sofas facing each other dominate the room. They're separated by a coffee table—long, rectangular—finished in a pale birch. The room is decorated lavishly but sparingly. No clutter. Nothing out of place. My guess is that the furniture, alone, in this one room, cost more than what Dr. Jay earns in a year.

Sheela opens the drawer of a matching side table and removes a packet of Dunhills. "Ravi thinks I don't know where he keeps his stash," she says. When she turns to face me, she's holding a cigarette between her jeweled fingers.

I reach into my pocket for matches, wishing I, too, could offer her a gilded lighter. The yellow matchbox is the one I picked up earlier today from Ravi's desk.

I lean in to light her cigarette. This close, I can smell her orchid perfume, the white wine she drank over dinner, the scent of cigarette smoke on her breath. I can see the small black beauty mark, nestled in the faint lines next to her right eye. Do I think that she's attractive? Yes. She's self-assured, and confident. Well aware of her sexual allure. I remind myself that Sheela Singh was once a girl who wouldn't take a second look at me—was offended, if fact, by the sight of a me—the ragged eight-year-old I was then, when she was fifteen. Has she changed? Have I? Or am I simply tempted by the possibility of something forbidden?

She offers me the pack. I take one. Then she takes a seat on one of the sofas and draws on her cigarette slowly and deeply. She tilts her head back and blows smoke rings at the ceiling, her mouth kissing the air. "One cigarette after dinner is a lovely thing," she says. "After two kids, tennis alone won't help me slip into this." She points to her dress. The chiffon bodice does little to hide the fact that she's not wearing a bra. Her breasts are high and full. The women of Nimmi's tribe don't wear bras. Nimmi's breasts have stretch marks, as does her stomach. (If Sheela ever breastfed, I would be surprised.) I like that Nimmi is comfortable in her body. Even so, that low-cut dress succeeds in making Sheela look salacious.

I can't help but stare, which is exactly what that dress is asking me to do. I notice that my cigarette is still not lit and make a show of lighting it now. I force myself to think of Nimmi—her shy smile, her cinnamon lips, inviting me to go to her. When I undress her, Nimmi counts each hook aloud, softly, as I undo her blouse.

"Ravi keeps the good scotch in the library. Feel free to help yourself." Sheela makes a careless gesture with her cigarette in the direction of the hallway. "Never had a taste for it myself."

I take a seat on the sofa opposite Sheela's. "I'm fine. Thank you."

When Sheela leans forward to tap the ash from her cigarette into the ceramic ashtray on the coffee table, she makes sure that I can see her cleavage. The triangle of shadow between her breasts is sprinkled with gold powder. Despite myself, I'm getting hard. I look away, embarrassed, and shift in my seat.

Nimmi, who at this moment is four hundred miles away, would never think of sprinkling gold dust between her breasts.

"Two months, already, you've been here, Abbas. And we still know nothing about you."

"You assume there's something to know."

"I'm guessing that you have a family."

I don't know how to answer that without involving Auntie-Boss. And it's better Lakshmi's name isn't mentioned in this house. Nor can I tell Sheela about Omi, or my shoeless, shirtless beginnings in the Pink City. I tap the ash from my own cigarette into the ceramic bowl. "Some."

"Hmm." A smile is playing about Sheela's mouth. Her glossy lipstick catches light, competing with the shimmer of gold between her breasts. "You've never told me how you came to know my father-in-law."

I'm assuming Sheela doesn't know that Ravi had a son with Auntie-Boss's younger sister, Radha. Or that Samir made up for Ravi's indiscretions by paying Radha's way through school. Why he paid for mine has always been a mystery to me.

I release a plume of smoke. "I know Samir the same way lots of people do."

"Meaning?"

Ignoring the question, I point to the large portrait in a silver

frame, hanging on one wall—a family portrait of two generation of the Singhs. "Great photo," I say.

The original photo was taken in black and white but then
hand-colored so every person's lips and cheeks are pink, even
Ravi's. In the photo, little Rita is an infant, her eyes lined with
kajal for good luck. She's looking off to one side, gnawing on
her fist. When the photo was taken, Baby hadn't yet been born.

Sheela glances at the photo but says nothing. She adjusts the
large emerald and pearl ring on one of her fingers. "Society
says it's fine for Ravi to have his *women*—and I use the term
loosely." She arches a shapely eyebrow. "But if I did the same,
they'd be outraged."

She flicks ash from her cigarette into the bowl, again leaning
forward, demanding my attention.

I try to keep my eyes on hers.

"It's not as if I've had no offers," she says. "His clients. Our
friends. Men I've known for ages. Some of whom would have gladly
married me when my parents were entertaining proposals. Now
those same men see me as a conquest." She takes another long drag
from her cigarette and releases the smoke from her mouth, slowly.
She pouts and raises one eyebrow. "Why do you think that is?"

Her hair is lustrous, shiny from expensive shampoos, her dark
eyes fixed on me. The ridge of her collarbone reflects the lamp's
light; a lovely glow. I take my time, observing her, letting her see
what I see in her.

"I think you know," I say.

She has the grace to blush.

I lean forward, extinguish my cigarette in the bowl and stand.
I smile at her, apologetically. "I have work tomorrow," I say, and
start to leave the room.

"Before you go…"

I turn around.

She holds her hand out. For a moment, I imagine that she's asking me to hold it. Then I understand.

I take the matchbox from my pocket and put it in her outstretched hand.

I reach the Palace Guest House fifteen minutes later and go directly to my bedroom. I take off my clothes, dropping them onto the floor as I make my way to the shower. I turn the water on, as hot as I can stand, and let the feeling of it soothe me. Even so, I picture Sheela's naked breasts, recall the scent of her perfume. Her dark eyes, taunting, or inviting, me. I take care of my erection, feeling shame and guilt, as if I've actually cheated on Nimmi. But now I'm home, I'm safe. And when I get in bed, I immediately fall asleep.

10

NIMMI

Foothills of Himalayas, Northwest of Shimla

Chullu is strapped to my back, lulled to sleep by the rhythm of
my steps. I'm using my husband's walking stick on the trail up
to the mountains. When I find the rest of Vinay's flock, I'll use
the crook to herd them, the purpose for which it was intended.
My baby's weight, the bedroll and our few possessions steady me.

I've fashioned a smaller walking stick for Rekha from the
branch of a poplar tree, and she's doing her best to keep up.
Every so often, I pause to let my daughter catch up to us on the
path. When she does, I give her water from my goatskin bag.

We've been walking for an hour, climbing gradually through
meadow and scrub. We left at first light when a thin layer of

frost was still on the ground. Old habits die hard: our tribe always starts out early in the morning, when the temperatures are cooler, so we can walk longer distances without tiring. I can no longer see the city of Shimla, now that we're in the forest. Without the children and Neela the sheep, who stops constantly to eat along the way, I would be making better time. But the animal is livelier and faring better since we cleaned her wounds.

From Shimla, I had turned northwest, in the direction the children at the clinic had told me to go. It's the same route our tribe always takes to get to the Kangra Valley, and it makes sense my brother would have chosen this trail. When I arrive at the spot where the children told me they had found the sheep, I stop. I spot the tiny stone temple they told me to look for; it's the size of an armoire. Hindus have erected many such miniature temples throughout the Himalayas. The path I've been on and the one before me are wide enough for ten goats or ten sheep to pass. But directly across from the temple, to my left, is a canyon separating two steep inclines. There, through a small gap, I spot a narrower, rougher trail, lined by boulders and rocks on either side. My instinct tells me that, for his purposes, my brother would have favored this smaller, more secluded trail over the wider, more exposed path. I look for sheep droppings, and when I find them, I poke them with my stick. They are slightly soft, which means the sheep have recently been on this trail. The droppings on the wider path are dry.

Neela bleats. I imagine she's calling to the other sheep in the area. But there's no answer. She starts toward the gap. I'm about to follow her when my ears catch the faint sound of hoofbeats. Sound can travel far in these mountains, and the rider may yet be miles away. Even so, I am a woman alone with my children on a deserted path—not something I'm used to. I know this is more dangerous than when I traveled with my tribe. I gently nudge Rekha forward through the gap, then urge her to move faster once we're on the narrow trail. Chullu wakes up, and I pull a rag wet with my milk from my blouse to quiet him; there's no time for me to nurse him.

Once we're past the first few boulders, I look back. From here, we're partially hidden, and I'm feeling safer. Rekha has gone ahead to keep up with Neela. We continue like this for a while, until I look ahead of me and see Rekha freeze. Her shoulders tense. Has she seen a snake?

I rush to catch up with her. "Rekha!" And then I see what looks like a sack of cloth up ahead. I grab Rekha by the shoulders, turn her round and tell her to stay back. I approach the bundle carefully. Neela follows me, bleating more insistently now.

It's not a bundle. It's a body, lying facedown. A shepherd, dressed like most male shepherds: a wool jacket and pants, his head wrapped in layers of cloth. His left leg juts out at an unnatural angle and there's a large tear in his pants. One foot is bare, the bones flattened as if a giant boulder crushed them. All at once I'm cold and hot.

I squat, feel his neck for a pulse. It's faint, but it's there.

I say a prayer. *Please don't let it be Vinay.*

Then I roll him over, gently, faceup. His nose is broken, caked with blood; there is a deep gash across his forehead. His eyes are swollen closed, his mouth slack.

It's him.

To stop myself from crying out, I slap both hands over my mouth. I can't speak, but the thoughts run through my head: *Vinay! I didn't want to believe it was you carrying the gold! Why? That's the very thing we were taught not to do: smuggle gold and your family will pay the cost. What will become of Arjun and Sai? Who will keep your sons safe now?*

Vinay had always been the dreamer, the one who felt the life he was born to was not the one that he deserved. He always wanted more than he was given. When my father died, as the younger of two brothers he received fewer animals than my older brother, Mahesh. And only sheep; the more expensive goats now belonged to Mahesh. Vinay received less silver, too.

No wonder Vinay always thought life was unfair. When Dev died, and I told my father-in-law that I would stay in Shimla instead of joining our tribe for their migration north, Vinay had uttered something under his breath. I'd pretended not to hear, but his words come back to haunt me now, clear and sharp: *Well, you got away, didn't you?*

Was it my departure that had pushed Vinay to forswear his duty to our tribe? To carry gold for racketeers so he could live a life he felt would be superior to the one our tribe could offer him?

I put my mouth against his ear. "*Bhai*, can you hear me?"

His lips move. Quickly, I untie the sling holding Chullu and lay my son down next to me. I remove the goatskin bag, filled with water, from my waist and hold it up to Vinay's parched lips with one hand. With my other hand, I lift his head carefully so he can drink. He gulps greedily but most of the water drips down the sides his mouth. I wipe it away with my hands.

"Tell me how this happened."

No response.

How long has he been lying here? I'm wondering if I can move him, take him back with me to Shimla and the Lady Bradley Hospital?

Now he's speaking. "Po—t," he says.

I lean in so close I can smell the staleness of his breath. "We need to get you to the clinic. Dr. Kumar will take care of you."

Vinay tries to shake his head, but the movement is too painful. He grimaces. "Poc—poc—t."

I'm trying to think clearly, but my thoughts are jumbled. If his back is broken, I can't carry him; he's far too heavy. With the children, it would take me hours to walk back to Shimla. I can't go on my own and leave the children with Vinay. What should I do?

"Pocket." He says it with more force this time.

With shaking hands, I rifle through his pockets. He's carrying his pouch of tobacco, and a few sharpened twigs to clean his teeth. I'm breathing hard, trying not to cry. "*Bhai*, what am I looking for?"

He tries to point, but he can barely move his arm. "Inside," he manages to say.

I search until I feel the edge of something solid in the inside left pocket. I turn the pocket inside out and see a tiny home-sewn pouch attached to it. I tug and rip the pocket open with my fingernails and find a matchbox. Bright yellow, printed with an image of Lord Ganesh. I turn it over. I recognize the English script imprinted on the back, but I can't read it.

"You wanted matches?" I ask, incredulous.

Before he speaks, he runs his tongue along his chapped lower lip. "The go—gold."

"*Vinay*, I need to get the doctor."

"Shee—p."

I look around, but I see only Neela in the clearing. "I don't see them, Vinay. Where are the sheep?"

"Keep..." he says. He's using every ounce of energy he has left to talk. "My sons..."

His lips are moving, but he makes no sound. His body shudders once, and then again, before his mouth yawns open and the breath escapes.

I press my ear to Vinay's nose, but now there isn't any breath. Still, the air is thick with his spirit. My children feel it. Chullu starts to fuss. Rekha pulls on my sweater. "Maa?"

I pick Chullu up and stand, taking comfort from his body, from its warmth. I cup the back of Rekha's head, and she holds tighter to me. There is no need to shield the child from death;

we do not do that in my tribe. We want our young to understand that death is as natural as life for man and animals alike,
and the sooner they're aware of that, the better.

"You remember your uncle, *bheti*?"

She nods.

"He is no more."

Rekha looks up at me, then back at her uncle's body on the
ground. She puts her thumb in her mouth, a habit she had shaken
a year ago.

Chullu nuzzles my breasts. I should feed him, but first I must
take care of something else. Again, I wet Chullu's rag with my
milk, and he takes it in his mouth and sucks on it. I set him down
on the sling lying on the ground and tell Rekha to watch him.
Then I sit next to Vinay, take his dusty hand in mine. I murmur incantations learned in the womb, long before I entered
this world. I ask our gods to look after my brother in the realm
of spirits, to give him the new life he deserves, to help his soul
maintain harmony with those who came before him and those
who will follow him. I repeat the words until they become one
with the air we're breathing.

The children watch me quietly. They seem mesmerized, as
I once was, by this ritual. I don't know how long we stay this
way, the three of us.

Horse hooves, louder this time, closer. Then a whinny.

I turn to see the sleek head of a chestnut horse being jerked
to a halt by his rider at the entrance to the gorge. I grab Chullu
and snatch Rekha's hand and lead us to the shelter of a nearby
boulder.

"Nimmi!" My name echoes across the ravine.

Cautiously, I go back to the clearing. Across the way, I see
Neela chewing grass. She stops and looks around to see where
the noise is coming from.

It's Lakshmi. The small mountain horse she's riding is the

color of wheat. As she gets closer to us, the horse sees Vinay's mangled body, and rears back, startling Lakshmi. She bends to pat his neck, then dismounts, holding tightly to his reins. She looks over at the body, then at me, her eyebrows raised in a question.

I blink. "It's Vinay," I tell her.

She comes nearer and says, quietly, "I'm so sorry, Nimmi."

Rekha is staring, openmouthed, at Lakshmi, who is wearing a man's wool pants, the legs stuffed inside short boots. Her dark brown wool coat is too large for her frame; she must have borrowed her husband's. She has a woolen shawl wrapped over her head and around her shoulders. I've only ever seen her in saris. I didn't know she could ride a horse. But then I remember the day Dev died and Chullu came into the world. She and Dr. Jay must have ridden horses to reach us in the mountains.

Lakshmi's face is flushed. She had to have been riding fast. She offers a reassuring smile to my daughter, then to my infant son, who has stopped fussing long enough to stare at her. I know that if she turns that steady, consoling gaze on me, I will start to cry. As if she senses this, she walks the horse to the other side of the clearing and ties him to a scrawny tree. Then she steps around me and approaches my brother's body. As she crouches, she studies Vinay's wounds—like I've seen her husband, Dr. Kumar, do.

Now I see that Vinay's fingers have been gnawed on, by some animal, as he lay dying. There are bite marks on his ears. The toes of his exposed foot have been chewed.

I tremble, thinking of it. How much pain did he endure? How alone he was in his suffering!

Lakshmi raises her head and scans the steep slopes to the left and right of us. I follow her gaze.

"How do you think this happened?" she asks.

My mouth is dry. I ponder for a moment, take in the scene.

"He might have stumbled—most likely, fell—and hit his head. This crevice is so rocky. His leg looks broken, and I think his hip might be broken. When I found him, he couldn't move. I'd say he's been here for at least a day or two. It's possible his back is broken, too."

It's one thing to think these thoughts, another to say them out loud.

I wipe a hand across my mouth.

"Could bandits have done this to him?" Lakshmi asks.

Those of us who have grown up in the Himalayas have long known that gold is being carried through the mountains. Our elders always told us gold is the elixir of life for many people, and there is never enough to go around. Our country has so little of it that it has to be brought in from elsewhere—legally or illegally. Bandits and the authorities are always on the lookout for a lone shepherd who might be transporting the precious metal using his goats or sheep. Our people know this. My brother Vinay must have known the risks, which is why he would have taken this trail off the main path.

"The sheep droppings here are fresh," I say, pointing to the ground away from my brother's body to avoid looking at him. Then I see Neela, across the clearing, nibbling at the dry foliage growing between the rocks. "She knows this place. She's been here before." I look up at the ridge again, imagining how the accident would have happened. "See that pile of stones that reaches up to the top of the ridge? It looks like a rough path. Vinay could have been bringing the flock down from there. Or…maybe Neela slipped on that path, fell on her side and skidded all the way down. The gold bars have sharp edges, which would have gouged her skin. The wound on her side was deep."

A memory comes to me, unbidden. Dev sliding down the ravine. I blink back my tears. "Vinay might have come down the slope to get to her. But, after falling, she was probably scared and might have bucked and kicked him. He could have lost his balance, fell and broken his nose along the way. It wouldn't be the first time something like that happened."

Lakshmi must know I'm talking about Dev. I've just described how my husband died last year, trying to save a goat from falling down the mountain. I look away from her, again, to keep from showing her how much this memory upsets me. I take Chullu's milk rag from him and wet it again with my milk. He grins at me, flashing his tiny front teeth. At least he will never suffer a fate like his father's—or his uncle's.

I hear Lakshmi sigh. She stands, walks to the horse and pulls a goatskin bag from the saddlebag. She pulls the drawstring open and holds the bag in front of the horse's mouth while he drinks.

"What will you do now?" she asks.

I don't know how to answer her. I expected to find my brother and return the sheep to him. I hadn't given any thought to what I would do next.

I smooth Chullu's hair. I remember Vinay's final words as if he's standing next to me and realize I must act quickly now. I turn to Lakshmi.

"The flock," I say. "I have to find them. Then I have to see that the gold is delivered to the next relay point." How I'm going to make any of this happen isn't clear to me.

Rekha looks up at me; again, she sucks her thumb. I stroke her hair to reassure her. In my arms, Chullu gurgles.

Lakshmi ties the goatskin bag closed and puts it back in the saddlebag. She's facing away from me, when she says, "Is this about the gold or your brother's family?"

I tighten my hold on Chullu. He squeals and wriggles, trying to get out of my arms. "I don't know what you mean."

She turns to face me. Her gaze is direct, but there is softness in her voice. "You could profit from the gold, couldn't you?"

Does she think I'm doing this so I can *sell* the gold? That all I care about is *me*? "You think I'd take advantage of my brother's death to claim the gold for myself?"

She answers in a gentle tone. "Or for your children. I wouldn't blame you if you did."

"Those *goondas* would do to me what they've done to Vinay." I glance at Vinay's body sprawled a foot away. "My brother made a mistake. He must have been desperate. Our life is not easy. The work is hard and there's no money in it. He wanted to send his sons to school, so they could have a different life, away from herding and shearing—" I have to stop myself from babbling. Tears have blurred my vision.

Lakshmi looks, again, at my brother's body. "What about…" She pauses and lets her words hang in the air. Her expression tells me what she's thinking.

"We burn our dead like all Hindus," I say. "But…"

I look around me, at the rocky landscape. The proper thing to do would be to burn his body where he died. But there's no way to make a platform, or to cut the wood. I have no tools with me. In this moment, I feel an intense longing for my tribe. If we were all together, we could have—would have—made it happen. It's what we always do when someone dies on the trail. It's what we did when Dev died.

If I were with my tribe, we'd have a proper funeral. The village elder would recite the prayers, and the women, all of them, including his wife, Selma, would bathe Vinay, and wrap him carefully, tenderly, in a freshly washed sheet. Tears again fill my eyes. Rekha reaches for my hand.

"Next to the hospital," Lakshmi says, quietly. "There is a crematorium—where we burn those who have died."

I feel as if I've walked a hundred miles. I don't remember ever feeling this exhausted. I no longer try to hide my tears; they spill over my cheeks and down my chin. I've been holding Rekha's hand to comfort myself as much as her. Now I let go and wipe my face with my free hand, pressing my knuckles into the sockets of my eyes until I see stars.

Why did you leave me, Dev? If you were still here, we'd be with our people, up in our summer home. None of this would be happening. And where are you, Malik? Why have you gone away? First Dev, then Malik, now Vinay. Must I lose everybody?

Lakshmi gently eases Chullu from my grasp. She combs his hair away from his forehead with her fingers and smiles at him. She holds her hand out to Rekha, who moves to take it. As if she knows what I'm thinking, Lakshmi says, so softly I think I might have imagined it, "It will be all right, Nimmi."

I heave a sigh. After a moment, I remove the bedroll from my back and set it to one side of the clearing. Lakshmi flattens out the bedroll and sets Chullu down on it. I untie the bundle from my waist to take out a few *chapatti* and an onion. I break off a piece of bread and give it to my son to gnaw on with his baby teeth. The rest I hand to Rekha.

"Sit with Chullu for a bit, okay?" I say to her. My daughter sits next to her brother and feeds him another piece of *chapatti*.

I go over to my brother's body. It hurts to look at him. I can't stop thinking of the hours he was suffering before death relieved him. I start to undress him, thinking that he looks much younger in death than he did in life. Gone are the wrinkles around his eyes, the result of his habitual squinting. I see his cheeks are smoother now. I am embarrassed to look at him in his full nakedness. Our mother would be the one to bathe him if she were still alive, but, now, I'm the only family available to do this.

I untie my goatskin bag. I remove the *chunni* from my head and dampen it with water from the bag. I start with Vinay's face, washing the blood from his nose, then I wipe the sweat from his arms and legs. Silently, I pray for the safety of his wife and sons. I am vaguely aware of Lakshmi, behind me, talking quietly to my children.

When I've finished cleaning Vinay's body, I turn to Lakshmi and nod. She picks up Chullu and sets him to one side of the bedroll. Rekha follows, carrying the food. My children are quiet, watchful, as if they know something sacred is happening.

Lakshmi picks up the padded cloth we sleep on, shakes it off and lays it on the ground closer to Vinay's body. When she grabs hold of my brother's bare legs, I place my hands under his armpits.

"Ake, dho, theen," she counts.

Together, we lift him. The men of our tribe are lean and stringy; they've spent their whole lives walking up and down these mountain trails. But they're strong, and their muscles are surprisingly heavy. We struggle, at first, to balance Vinay's body between us, and, then, to lay him on the bedroll. I should have a clean cotton sheet to wrap him in, but then I didn't expect to be performing his last rites today. We wrap him in the bedroll as best as we can, then carry him to the horse, who prances and raises his head high, his eyes rimmed in white. He's spooked by the dead body. Lakshmi motions to me to lay the body down again. She walks to the chestnut, strokes his muzzle, talking to him softly until he's calm.

We try again to hoist Vinay's body onto the saddle. It takes us several tries, but we manage. I watch as Lakshmi uses a coil of rope to secure the body to the saddle.

She has been quiet throughout this ordeal, leading me tenderly through every step. If she hadn't come along, what would I have done? How could I have handled this—my brother's dead body, my aloneness, my grief, my children—without her? Malik has told me about their time in Jaipur—when Lakshmi was such a sought-after henna artist. I can picture her—taking care of her clients, soothing them, comforting them, as she soothed and comforted me today.

Reluctantly, I pull the yellow matchbox from my skirt pocket and hold it up for her to see. "This has something to do with whatever Vinay was up to. I think that's what he was trying to tell me before he..."

She takes the matchbox from me. "Canara Private Enterprises Limited, Shimla," she reads aloud. She frowns and looks at me, a question in her eyes, but I can only shrug my shoulders in response.

She nods, understanding. "Mind if I keep this?" She puts it in the pocket of her coat, then turns and covers the Vinay's shrouded body with a blanket she pulled out from her saddlebag.

I hoist Chullu into his sling again and position him on my back.

"What's your horse's name?" Much to my surprise, it's Rekha, my quiet girl, talking to Lakshmi.

"Chandra," Lakshmi says.

"Why did you name him that?"

"You see that mark on his forehead? Don't you think it looks like the crescent moon?"

Rekha stares at the horse. "When I get a horse someday, I'll name him Gooddu."

Lakshmi smiles at my daughter. "That's a fine name. How did you come up with it?"

"That's what Malik calls me."

Lakshmi glances at me, smiling. When she turns again to my daughter, she says, "But if you name him Gooddu, how will you know if Malik is calling you or your horse?"

Rekha frowns. Then her face brightens. "Well, I don't have a horse yet, do I?"

Lakshmi's pretty laughter echoes in the narrow crevice.

Gradually, we make our way out of the canyon and down the

trail toward Shimla: Lakshmi leading the horse, Rekha chatting to Lakshmi, me carrying baby Chullu, Neela following behind. I'm heartbroken about Vinay, and I'm glad we found him, but I'm also relieved to be going back home. I hadn't realized how much I'd depended on my people when I'd lived with my tribe. The mountains are no place for a woman—or man—alone. A sunny sky can turn gloomy in an instant; a leopard can gut a goat while your head is turned; a pit viper can paralyze a child in seconds. I reach around to pat Chullu's head, to reassure myself that he's still there.

We've been walking for only twenty minutes when we hear sheep bleating, and the jingle of the bells around their necks. Neela answers them. To our right, in the distance, and above the tree line, we see them: a flock of sheep far up on the mount. Before I can hold her back, Neela bounds up the hill. I follow. When I reach the top, I'm out of breath. I check the ears of one sheep, then the others: the markings on their ears are my brother's. I probe their ribs to see if bars of gold are hidden underneath their fleece. They are. I return to the trail, where Lakshmi and Rekha are waiting, to tell them what I've found.

"Good. We can take the flock into town," Lakshmi says.

I stare at her. "There must be thirty or forty of them. Where would we keep them?"

Lakshmi smiles. "The hill people who come to the Community Clinic. I'm sure one of them would be willing to shepherd a flock for a short while." She surveys the horizon. "We have to move them now or we'll lose the light. It will be much harder to keep track of the flock and protect them from wolves when it's dark."

She's right.

"And the gold bars?" she asks.

"Still with the sheep."

She nods. "Good. First thing tomorrow, we'll start searching." She takes the matchbox from her pocket and examines it again. "Canara Enterprises. Maybe they can tell us something."

Do the furrows on her forehead mean she's worried, or just curious? Is she really so confident, or is she just pretending for my sake? I rest my hand on my son's head again. We're in unfamiliar territory here. Neither of us knows the people Vinay was working for. How many of them there are. What my brother's arrangement with them was.

I look at Vinay's body draped over the horse. And I realize: I'm angry. At Vinay. He has made his responsibility mine—something I never bargained for. Now I'm the one who has to keep my family *and* his from being hurt. Vinay has threatened the lives of everyone in our tribe, too! How could he be so foolish? Why would he put everyone we love in danger?

The more I struggle to control my panic, the angrier I feel. And more confused. I know I shouldn't be resentful when I've sought the same for my children, as Vinay wanted for his. Who am I to judge him when my bond to the tribe is now as fragile as a spiderweb?

I glance at Lakshmi. Her back is straight, one hand holding Chandra's reins, and the other holding Rekha's hand. To look at her you'd think she has this situation under control. She'll make sure Vinay is sent on to his next life as he should be. She's come all this way and taken on a risk that Vinay thrust upon us, when she could have washed her hands of the whole affair.

A month ago, I was still angry with Lakshmi Kumar for telling me what to do, for sending Malik away from me, for being so bloody competent. But now I just feel a sense of relief that someone—anyone—is willing to take charge and help.

If only that someone were Malik.

I walk back up the hill to herd the sheep and bring them to Shimla.

11

LAKSHMI

Foothills of Himalayas, Northwest of Shimla

We're quiet on our way back to Shimla. We stop from time to time to let the sheep graze. I sounded confident enough when I told Nimmi we would find someone to keep the sheep, but now I'm wondering how we'll manage. Sheep need to be moved every few days to find fresh grass. I had to suggest we take the sheep back with us; otherwise, Nimmi might have insisted on staying with the flock overnight and keeping the children with her, waiting until I could return to help her. In these hills, sheep are a valuable commodity. And this herd is carrying gold on their flanks! Leaving Nimmi and the children in the foothills would be far too dangerous.

Rekha walks beside me, alternately speaking when an idea

comes to her, and staying quiet when she's pondering. Earlier, when she'd been watching the white clouds floating overhead, she asked me why we don't just ride the clouds.

"Clouds could get us to Shimla faster, Auntie," she says. "Remember the clouds in that book about the birds?" She's referring to a picture book about Himalayan birds we read last week.

"Clouds are tricky, Rekha," I tell her. "The moment you get close to them, they disappear." She looks up at me, her eyebrows raised, and I explain that while the clouds might look like fuzzy cotton from far away, they're actually made of water—mist. "If we got close enough to them," I tell her, "we would go right through."

Later, she asks, "Could we live inside a rainbow?"

I can't help but wonder if I thought of things like this when I was four years old. I try to find an answer that will satisfy her, and eventually, I say, "We could. But if we were inside them, we wouldn't see them in the sky, would we?"

She blinks several times, taking this in, then shakes her head.

I would sit her on the saddle of my horse if it weren't carrying her uncle's body. With her little legs it's hard for her to keep up. But she seems to have inherited her mother's ability to walk without tiring. She never once complains, never asks for food or water.

"After we finish the monkey story, can we read the one about the elephant? I would like to have an elephant." When we started off from the canyon toward Shimla, she put her tiny hand in mine and left it there, as I've seen her do so often with her mother and with Malik. The gesture touched me.

"Of course, we can," I say.

Both Rekha and her mother seem to enjoy the books we've been reading. At first I worried Nimmi would feel self-conscious, learning alongside her daughter. Maybe even feel as if I were intruding too much into their lives. But she becomes a different person when we're spending time together, reading. She's genuinely curious, and obviously proud of how quickly her daughter learns to read and write.

I stop and turn around to check on Nimmi and Chullu at the back of the flock. Nimmi is grieving for her brother, and her grief is palpable—as if the weight of it is pressing on her, making this hard journey all the harder. She's using a crook to keep the herd together, but her shoulders are slumped, and she moves the sheep forward half-heartedly. The animals sense her listlessness, seizing the opportunity to wander off until she calls them back.

I've covered Vinay's body as best as I can, but it's attracting insects, and I worry about maggots on my horse. So far, Chandra's been only a little skittish, but I need him to stay calm until we get the body to the crematorium.

The town of Shimla is built on a series of hills dotted with pines, cedars, poplars and birch. Anywhere else these hills would be considered mountains, but the craggy Himalayas to the north overshadow these canyons, making them seem puny by comparison, so we refer to them as hills. The Lady Bradley Hospital sits high on a substantial property that extends down into a ravine. When we glimpse the spire of Christ Church, I know the hospital will soon come into view. We take the higher, steeper road, the longer way around to the back entrance of the hospital where the morgue is located.

By late afternoon we're close enough to the hospital that I ask Nimmi to wait up on the hill with the sheep. Then I walk my horse down the slope to the hospital morgue. Prakesh, the attendant, knows me, and I ask him to take the body discreetly to the crematorium. If he's at all surprised by this request, he doesn't let it show; his caste is used to dealing with the dead. I ask him to keep the ashes for me, then I hold on to Chandra's reins as he and another attendant lift Vinay's body from my horse. I ask a third attendant to water Chandra and offer him a rupee for his kindness.

Then I walk over to the Community Clinic. I must look a right mess because, when I enter through the front door, all the patients in the waiting room turn to stare. I realize, too late, I smell of horses, my own sweat and the pine forest up the hill. I go quickly to the exam room and stop at the curtained door.

"Jay?"

I can hear him excuse himself to the patient he's attending to before he parts the curtain. When he sees me, he pulls the curtain closed behind him. "Lakshmi!" he says, taking in my disheveled state. He guides me into the back hallway, so we're out of sight of the reception room. "I've been so worried! First, you didn't show up for clinic. When I sent someone home to see if you were all right, he came back and told me there was no one at the house."

I place the flat of my hand on his chest to calm him. "I took Chandra and went to look for Nimmi. She wasn't at her place when I stopped by this morning, everything she owns was gone."

"And did you—"

"Yes. Everyone's safe. But I need to find a place for forty sheep."

His eyes go wide. "You found the flock?"

"Yes. We only need to keep them for a few days. I promise."

He pulls at his lip, looking down at his feet. "The grounds-keeper at the hospital has been nagging me to have the lawns mowed."

"*Shabash!*" I say. I smile and place a finger on his lips.

He takes my hand and squeezes it. "A few days only, *accha*? Once I'm done with this patient, I'll have a talk with the grounds-keeper."

"Can you handle this afternoon's load without me?"

He nods. "So far today we've only had three patients. So I think we'll manage."

I hand him my coin purse. "For the groundskeeper." Every

favor has a price. "Also, I've left a body at the crematorium. It's Nimmi's brother."

Before he has a chance to ask more questions, I turn and leave.

An hour later, Nimmi is busy corralling the flock onto the lower ravine of the hospital grounds, out of sight of patients and staff.

I'm sitting on a low stone wall opposite the hospital's front entrance where the street vendors gather to sell their *chaat*, homemade *paranthas, paan* and *beedis*. Chullu is a warm bundle on my lap; he's gnawing on a slice of mango while Rekha munches on a sugarcane, sucking up the sweet juice as she goes. Chandra is standing quietly to one side, munching on his bag of oats and flicking his ears every now and then to shoo away the flies.

Nimmi and the children are safe for now; we've found the sheep a temporary home, and I'm planning our next step. I take the yellow matchbox from the pocket of my coat and read the print again: Canara Private Enterprises. I've looked inside the matchbox more than once; there's nothing but matches. It's possible the box means nothing. Maybe Vinay only carried it to light his evening campfires. But then, why would it have been hidden inside a secret pocket?

When I check my watch, I see it's almost 5:00 p.m. The local businesses stay open until six or seven in the evening. I have no idea what I might find at Canara, but I think it's best if I go there alone. I need to find out what, if anything, Nimmi's brother had in common with that place.

Men enjoying their late afternoon *chaat* and *gupshup* at the stalls can't keep from staring at the four of us. I look down at the clothes I'm wearing.

I'm an Indian woman with blue eyes. I'm dressed as a man. Who wouldn't stare?

When Nimmi returns from the lower ravine, I tell her I'm going to go find Canara Enterprises. She wants to come with me. "It's my problem, *Ji. I* should be the one to go."

"No," I tell her. "The children are exhausted. Feed them, put them to bed. We'll talk later."

Her nostrils flare, and I realize I've been too harsh. "Nimmi," I say. *"Please."*

She tilts her head, her way of telling me, *Okay.* She takes the children with her. Rekha turns her head to wave her sugarcane at me.

I rub Chandra's neck. He's been fed and watered by the hospital attendants.

I should go home and make myself presentable, but I decide it's best if I approach the people at Canara as I am. In my jodhpurs and my long coat, I somehow feel less vulnerable. They might be thrown off by the outfit just enough to take me seriously.

Another advantage: horses are the most practical way to get around in this hilly city. When Jay first taught me to ride horses, I was scared of being so high off the ground. I wouldn't have my feet to guide me. Would I lose my way?

"You're used to being in control," Jay told me, smiling. "The very reason you'll love being on a horse. The horse is looking to you for directions. Just order him around the same way you do me."

I'd threatened to throw one of my new boots at him unless he stopped himself from laughing. Slowly, gently, he coaxed me into riding, and it wasn't long before I realized I felt confident on a horse. Later, when he learned that one of his maternity patients wanted to sell her horse, he bought Chandra for me.

Now I pat my lovely chestnut on his glossy neck as we make our way through town. I ask people walking on the street if they've heard of Canara; there is no other way to find a business in Shimla. One person in four will point you in a direction— but not necessarily the right one.

An hour later, after I've made a few wrong turns and observed many arguments between locals, I find myself in a small clearing surrounded by pines. The large yellow sign displaying the company's name hangs askew from a rusty barbed-wire fence. There's a drying yard behind the fence, where bricks are stacked in rows, a clay quarry, and, at the far end of the yard, a kiln that must be forty feet tall. If this is a brick factory, I should be seeing workers mixing clay, preparing molds, taking fresh bricks to the kiln. But there's no one. The yard is quiet, the kiln inactive.

I dismount. To the left of the locked gate I notice a small building. The sign on the front door says Office. I tie Chandra to the fence, walk over to the building and push open the door. The young man behind the counter looks startled. Either he wasn't expecting a customer or he had not expected the customer to be a woman.

The room is tiny. The counter spans the whole width of the narrow interior, neatly dividing the space into two halves. The sole decoration is a calendar hanging on the wall from 1964, advertising Coca-Cola, and a painting of the monkey-god Hanuman. I can see an office through the open door behind the young man. There, an older man—middle-aged with a black beard flecked in gray—is sitting at a desk. He's talking to someone on the office's rotary phone. I understand the language that the man is speaking—it's Punjabi, a language I've come to recognize only since I came to live up north.

He is saying, "*Nahee-nahee.* It will not be a problem. *Hahn.* Yes. It will get done."

The younger man behind the counter says, "What do you need?" His tone is far from friendly.

Without a word, I put the yellow matchbox on the counter.

He looks at it, and then at me. His coal-black eyes are wary, as if he doesn't quite know what to make of me.

My heart is pounding, and I realize I don't know what I'm getting into. Jay has no idea I'm here. Come to think of it, why *am* I here? I could be with my patients at the Community Clinic and my plants in the garden instead of in this room, which is pulsating with an uneasy tension I can't quite identify.

I meet the counterman's gaze, and hold it, without blinking.

He picks up the matchbox and takes it with him into the other room. He waits until the older man gets off the phone. Their voices low, they have a hurried conversation. The older man leans his head to one side, looking past the counterman, so he can get a better look at me. Then he takes the matchbox from the young man and dumps the matches on his desk. Running his fingernail along the inside of the box, he removes a piece of paper.

Neither Nimmi nor I had thought to look underneath the matches! The man pulls a ledger from the middle drawer on the right side of his desk. I watch him run his index finger down the page until he finds the entry that he must be looking for. He looks again at the tiny piece of paper taken from the matchbox, lifts himself out of the chair and walks to the counter. He's larger and taller than his younger companion. His eyebrows come together as he looks at me.

"You don't look like a shepherd," he says in Hindi.

I shrug but offer no excuse or explanation. The fact that he was expecting a shepherd means I've come to the right place. My palms are moist, and I resist the urge to wipe them on my coat.

"You're late," he tells me. "We expected you three days ago."

I arch a brow. If it's gold he's after, what's the difference if it arrives late? He must know that weather, a sick animal or an injury can always stall a shepherd.

His eyes are narrow as he studies me. "We thought you might have kept it for yourself."

I frown at him.

He looks around me, through the open entryway, then turns to me again. "Where is it, then?"

ALKA JOSHI

My underarms are slick with sweat. I don't know what to tell him, but I make a calculated guess at his question. "It's with the sheep."

He rolls his eyes. "I've told your lot before. No sheep shit in my yard. Bring the cargo, not the shit. You understand?"

"Tomorrow," I say. *Hai Bhagwan!* That means we'll have to remove all that gold from the flock tonight and find a way to bring it here.

I take a risk with my question. "No bricks being made today?" I want to keep him talking. Maybe find out where the gold goes next and how it gets there.

He chews on his cheek, lets his gaze linger on me. He thinks I'm being nosy, which I am. "What's it to you?" he says.

I shove my hands into my pockets, meet his stare. Then, as coolly as I can, I turn around and leave the office. The big man follows me, watches as I mount my horse and ride away. He might be thinking a shepherd who can afford to own a horse as fine as Chandra might be more experienced at moving stolen goods than he assumed.

Once I'm several miles away, I let my grip on Chandra's reins relax and slow him to an easy trot. My fingers, stiff from clutching the reins as if my life depended on it, unfurl slowly. Only then do I start breathing normally again.

12

MALIK

Jaipur

On my day off I make a trip to the area of the Pink City bazaar where all the jewelry shops are. Is it because I need to assuage my guilt about lusting after Sheela or because I've been wanting to see my old friend Moti-Lal?

Lal-*ji* is the city's premier jeweler. When I arrive, at two o'clock in the afternoon, Moti-Lal Jewelers is pulsing with activity. A porter in a white uniform brings me a cup of chai while I wait for the big man.

The plump proprietor is beaming at the middle-aged couple sitting across from him as his assistant sets a stack of squat black velvet boxes on his gleaming mahogany desk. "Today," Moti-Lal says, "I am almost as excited as I would be if *I* were the one getting married." His teeth are very white, very straight and very large. "I've put aside something very special for Akshay's big day," he says.

The prospect of the jewels about to be displayed draws the wife forward in her seat, her silk sari rustling.

Sipping my chai, I observe Lal-*ji*, from the railing that separates the more elaborate bridal room from the rest of the store, where minor purchases—birthday bangles or baby's first earrings—are made. No matter how small, or how large, the occasion, it can always be celebrated with a little gold, the universal panacea for what ails us Indians.

In the bridal area, the whisper-soft carpet allows the delicate tinkling of *jhumka* earrings and customers' exclamations of joy to take center stage. The lighting at Moti-Lal Jewelers is brighter than that of the typical shop, the chairs more luxurious, their padded arms inviting shoppers to linger as they ponder the decision of a lifetime. Mothers, grandmothers, aunties, fathers, brides-to-be, sisters and impending grooms sit in front of glass cases in which necklaces, earrings, bangles, anklets and rings glitter and beckon. Customers, carrying purses bulging with cash from the bride's parents, are buying gold that will protect the bride in case of widowhood, sickness or financial calamity. The gold is what ensures her future.

When I was a boy, little more than five or six years old, I came to this store once a week, and sometimes more, to deliver Auntie-Boss's scented clove and geranium body oils and her custom *bawchi* hair oil. Moti-Lal's wife was one of our first customers in Jaipur. She loved the products, and when she raved about them to her husband, he made a practice of presenting a brass container filled with Lakshmi's potions to every bridal client. It was that kind of personal touch that drew Moti-Lal's customers back to him time and time again. It was also a good source of income for Auntie-Boss.

Now a porter steps up onto the dais where Moti-Lal sits and

carefully places three steaming porcelain cups on the desk. Moti-Lal's domain is elevated several feet above the hubbub, in one corner of the store, allowing Lal-*ji* to keep an eye on every customer going in and out.

To a blushing girl, Lal-*ji* might say, "I see you have brought your auntie with you today." Or he might interrupt his inspection of a new shipment of rubies to call out to a matron, "There is nothing that makes me happier than seeing young Seeta with such a good family."

When I first entered the store today, Lal-*ji* acknowledged me with a nod and a smile of recognition to let me know he'll make time for me when he's finished with his other clients. I'm in no hurry. It's much more pleasant to bide my time in the air-conditioned store than to linger outside, in the dry, dusty heat. The smells are nicer in here, too. Better than the reek of cabbage and sweat in the bustling street outside. Inside, all is sandalwood incense, *rath ki rani* perfume and *champaca* cologne. Most important, I have the privilege of watching Moti-Lal at work. He's taught me more than a few things about business.

With deliberation, Moti-Lal opens the first of the velvet boxes for his clients. "Not even Shah Jahan's artisans could surpass this workmanship," he says. Inside the case, glistening against the black satin lining, is a *kundan* necklace, a forehead *tikka* with a gold hook that attaches to the hair, a pair of matching earrings and two bangles.

He points to the necklace, being careful not to smear the gleaming gems with oil from his pinkie finger (something he does on purpose to allow his clients a good look at the four-carat emerald and gold ring he wears on that finger) and says, "Forty-four flat diamonds, twelve good-sized emeralds, twenty-two drops of the whitest pearls from Ceylon." He intones the words with a sort of reverence, as if he were a priest.

He turns the necklace over gingerly. "Such incredible *meena* enamel work on the back. I had one of my Delhi men work on this—his family have been *meenakaris* for generations."

What follows is a pregnant hush as the soon-to-be mother-in-law examines the jewelry, greed apparent in her eyes. Her husband picks up and inspects a bangle, evaluating its craftsmanship, leaving the heavy necklace for his wife to handle. She does, holding the necklace to her neck and admiring it in the wall mirror opposite the desk. No doubt she's remembering her own bridal dowry and how it compares to what she's now selecting for her future daughter-in-law. My guess is *her* jewelry will still come out the winner. In her mind, she's thinking, *The enamel work was so much better in my day. These stones aren't cut near as fine as those in* my *necklace.* Whether the balance of the quality is in her favor or not, she will almost certainly walk away from Moti-Lal Jewelers with a pair of gold bangles for herself. After all, *It's only fair.*

Moti-Lal observes her movements in the mirror. "You see how it sparkles? I sold a similar necklace just last week, but those diamonds were not as large as these." He turns down the corners of his mouth and shakes his head, as if he's embarrassed that another family would have settled for less. "*This* necklace is one your guests will notice from across the room."

Now he looks up, as if he has just noticed me, excuses himself and leaves his assistant in charge. With his cup of chai, he joins me at the railing, facing away from the customers he's just left, as if he is too busy chatting with me to be concerned about their purchase. I've seen him do this time and time again. Of course, that's why there are floor-to-ceiling mirrors everywhere; he can still keep an eye on them. One of many age-old tactics from his bag of tricks.

He's smiling at me, his sleepy eyes almost disappearing in his face, his triple chins a sign of his success: a source of pride. When he speaks, his voice is soft and low. "Do you think Mrs. Prasad is already savoring the jealousy her rival will be sure to feel when she sees her new daughter-in-law wearing such a fine piece?"

I grin at Moti-Lal. "I take it that you know her rival."

"One of my best customers." Moti-Lal laughs and drinks his chai in a single swallow. "*Ake, dho, theen.* I'll be right back."

As large as he is, the jeweler moves as gracefully as a cheetah stalking fresh game. Like the family doctor, an Indian jeweler stays with a family for a long time, becomes a trusted friend and guide to several generations throughout marriages, births and festivals.

I turn around to watch him again. Moti-Lal shows off a few more features of the bridal set to his clients, reminding them that the stones are set perfectly flush within the *kundan* setting, just as Shah Jahan demanded carnelian, lapis lazuli, tiger's-eye and malachite be inlaid in the marble of the Taj Mahal.

The jeweler and his clients exchange a few remarks before it's time to haggle over price. Moti-Lal punches the numbers into his adding machine with a kind of flair that makes the other customers in the store look his way, curious about who's buying what.

Once the show is over, I turn my attention to the non-bridal side of the store, letting my eyes wander across the glass case of necklaces. In the cases are elaborate pendants set with rubies and diamonds as well as gold chains of various thicknesses and heft. I'm bending at the waist to take a closer look at one gold chain when I feel a meaty grip on my shoulder. Lal-*ji* says, "Success, Malik! Look at you, *Burra Sahib*! You are every father-in-law's dream. Come, come!"

The door to his private office is hidden on one mirrored wall. Aside from allowing Lal-*ji* to spy on his customers, the many mirrors invite clients to try on jewelry and admire themselves from every angle. It's startling to see myself reflected in so many mirrors in this small space.

Inside Moti-Lal's cozy chamber, the floor is covered with padded cushions and round bolsters upholstered in white cotton, leaving bare a narrow walkway in the middle of the marble floor. Moti-Lal removes his slippers; I remove my shoes.

"Lace-ups, Malik? Like the *angrezi*?"

"Himalayan winters were brutal on my toes. Had to give up *chappals* altogether. Now I can't wear anything but shoes." I don't tell him that wearing shoes at Bishop Cotton School wasn't an option. Nor was wearing dusty ones to school, which would surely earn you a rap on the knuckles from master and matron alike.

He slaps my back. "How proper! I cannot believe you are the same child I used to know," he says.

The faint fragrance of cherries and sandalwood reminds me of past visits to this room. We sit cross-legged on the cushions, chilled by the air-conditioning. At the center of the room, on the uncovered marble, sits a silver tray with two tall hookahs, a box of matches, a pouch of tobacco, a small statue of Ganesh, an incense cone and a scale for weighing gold. This is where the biggest deals are made. It's also where Lal-*ji* meets with friends.

His servant has put stones and one hot coal into each *chillum*. Moti-Lal pulls strands of tobacco from his pocket pouch, puts them in the bowls and tamps them gently. He moves one hookah closer to me.

"*Accha*, my young friend, what brings you to Jaipur?" As he's speaking, he strikes a match and lights the tobacco on his hookah. Taking the pipe in his mouth, he sucks several times on it, his cheeks puffing out comically. Then he releases a cloud of white smoke and the room fills with a sweet, fruity fragrance.

"I want to thank you, Lal-*ji*, for looking after Omi all these years."

He waves his fleshy hand as if to wave my gratitude away. "*Koi baat nahee hahn*. You sent the money. I made sure it got to Omi. Only that. She hasn't had it easy with that husband." Moti-Lal, who believes in hard work, shakes his head in disgust. "Runs

off to join the circus every year and comes back empty-handed."
He puffs more aggressively on his hookah, as if Omi's husband
has in some way slighted him. "Have you seen her since you've
been in Jaipur? Omi?"

"Only from a distance. I've kept my promise. I just wanted
to make sure she's okay."

Moti-Lal makes a face. "A grown man being jealous of a little
boy—and that's exactly what you were—a little boy who provided for Omi in a way her husband couldn't. And then threat-
ening to kill her if you dared see her again." He shakes his head
again. "What a prince."

I nod. The memory's a painful one.

Omi was an *ayah* of sorts; she looked after the neighborhood
children like me, for a small fee. Mothers like my own cleaned
houses or swept office floors or washed people's laundry. One
day, my mother didn't return from work. I waited and waited,
but she never came back. Omi took me in without a word. She
never treated me any differently than she did her own three
children. I was so grateful to her that I did whatever I could
to bring something home every day. It might be nothing more
than a rotting banana, or a spool of thread I'd pilfered from a
shopkeeper, or *puri* fried in old oil that a vendor was about to
throw away.

I made friends with all the shopkeepers of the bazaar. I shined
their shoes or told them where they could get a bargain on hair-
pins or ran errands for them. In return, they gave me castoffs
for Omi's children, shared their *chapattis* with me, sent me home
with a small bag of rice. Moti-Lal was the most generous of all.
He would always ask me what I'd learned that day. Could I count
to a hundred for him, or name the capital of France? And when
I did, he'd pull a rupee coin out of my ear and give it to me.

This last memory leaves me looking fondly at my old friend.
I tell him, "Uncle. I would like to buy two gold chains."

Moti-Lal arches an eyebrow. "You have a woman?"

I smile at him as I pick up the matchbox and light my hookah, then suck on the pipe to draw smoke. The tobacco—so clean and strong—goes immediately to my head, making me a little dizzy.

He thrusts his chin upward and nods sagely. "Ah," he says. "I see. Two women?"

Now I laugh, blowing out smoke. "One of the chains is for Omi."

He tucks his chin into the folds of his neck. "You know her husband will just sell it."

"I don't expect her to wear it—her husband would just rip it off her neck. But I want her to have something for security, for an emergency. I was hoping you would tell her it's here, waiting for her—if and when she needs it."

Lal-*ji* considers this as he smokes his pipe. He nods. "I will let her know."

"I also want to buy a pair of earrings," I add.

Moti-Lal blows on his *chillum* until the orange glow turns into gray ash. "Also for your woman?"

"No. They're for a little girl."

Moti-Lal stops puffing for an instant and his mouth goes slack. "You have a daughter?"

I laugh, pleased to be able to surprise him. "No. It's not like that."

His shrewd eyes narrow as he takes the pipe again. He blows out more smoke and looks into my eyes. "Then you have a woman with a child."

"Two children. A boy and a girl."

"Widow?"

"Yes."

I should have known that Moti-Lal would figure it out. More than once, he's told me selling gold requires an insight into human nature. He says you must be able to discern the intensity of a customer's desire by looking into their eyes. That will tell you what to show, what to hold back, and how much the customer is willing to part with.

"I saw something out there that I liked." I point to the main room on the other side of the door.

He blows a stream of smoke out of his mouth. *"Bukwas,"* he says. "Tourist stuff." He hoists his large frame upright and goes to the door. He calls out to someone, waits a moment, then returns with two large velvet boxes, which he hands to me. Once he is again settled on his cushion, I open the first box. I see three gold chains inside.

"Pick two," he says, smiling at me, puffing on his *chillum*.

I pull out the slimmest of the chains, pounded flat so it will sit flush against the skin. I can picture it on Nimmi's slim neck, how the gold would glow against her dark complexion. Maybe next time, I think. "Uncle, I can afford only half this gold."

He smiles. "What is this *afford*, Malik? It is my gift. Haven't I told you more than once you are the son I never had?" Now he's frowning, offended that I have mistaken his generosity for a business transaction.

"And what about your son-in-law out there?" I say, to tease him.

He lifts a hand and swats the air. "Mohan is fine. But if you come to work for me, I will die a happy man." He puts the hand on his chest and tilts his head to the side beseechingly.

"Lal-*ji*, you are not going anytime soon. And I know nothing about the jewelry business." I've said these very words to him at least a hundred times.

"Listen carefully," he says, and takes another puff. "Lord Brahma, the creator of our universe, threw a seed from his body into the waters. That seed became a golden egg, an incarnation of the creator himself. This gold, symbol of purity, good fortune and godliness, is what we sell here. Now you know as much as I know." He blows a large smoke ring at me.

I laugh. "I'm in Jaipur only at Auntie Lakshmi's request."

At the mention of my Auntie-Boss, Moti-Lal opens his slit eyes and smiles broadly. "And how is the beautiful Lakshmi Shastri? All of Jaipur misses her. Most of all my wife! Without Lakshmi's hair oil, she'll soon be as bald as a baby monkey!" He lets out a tremendous guffaw and slaps his hand on his thigh.

"It's Mrs. Kumar now. She's married to a doctor."

"*Bahut accha!* I'm happy for her." He points his hookah pipe at me. "You're lucky she offered to take you to Shimla when Omi's husband threw you out."

"*Zaroor.*" As I've often said to Nimmi: I owe Lakshmi my life. Since moving to Shimla, I've sent a portion of my earnings to Lal-*ji* to pass on to Omi (those I don't record in my bank book because I know Boss checks it periodically). It's an arrangement that's lasted twelve years.

"What does Lakshmi want you to do in Jaipur?"

"Learn the building trade. I'm working at the palace under Manu Agarwal."

Moti-Lal raises his eyebrows. "Agarwal's a good man. Honest. That cinema house the palace is building is going to be bloody marvelous! My wife plans to go with our daughter and her husband to the grand opening. I will be here, of course. Although I don't know why I'm bothering. Everyone who's anyone will be at the Royal Jewel Cinema that night."

"Her Highness Latika certainly hopes so."

There's a knock at the door, and Moti-Lal's son-in-law Mohan enters. I stand up to salaam him and he folds his hands in *namaste*. He is a shy man, quiet, ten years older than me.

"The Guptas have arrived," he says to Moti-Lal.

"See that they are seated, *bheta*. I'll be right there." Moti-Lal passes an enormous hand over his face, a gesture of frustration. When the door closes, he rolls his eyes. "Ten years and no children."

When I look questioningly at him, he points to the door, and I understand the comment is directed at his son-in-law. "I'm beginning to think he doesn't have it in him."

I smile. Parents are always anxious for grandchildren. That won't be the case with Auntie-Boss, and I'm glad of it. Whether I have none or ten, it's all the same to her. She likes talking to children; she just never wanted any of her own. I pick up the chain I was admiring earlier and another, heavier gold necklace. Moti-Lal observes me while he smokes. I put both chains aside, open the other box and select a pair of small gold studs that I think little Rekha will like. Her ears were pierced when she was just a few months old; they're fitted with the thinnest silver hoops. I place both chains and the earrings on the scale.

Moti-Lal frowns again and sighs. "*Arré*, Malik, leave it alone."

The scale registers one ounce. The current going price is 321 rupees per ounce, but I ask Moti-Lal if he will take 200 rupees for it.

"I'll let you have it for free if you'll take some advice from me."

I arch an eyebrow, waiting to see what he has to say.

He wags a stubby finger at me. "Never marry a poor widow."

I shake my head and laugh.

Pocketing the necklace for Nimmi and the studs for Rekha, I lay two one-hundred-rupee bills on the scale next to Omi's chain.

"I'll make sure Omi knows, Malik. I'll go to her tomorrow."

The heaviness of my guilt—lusting after Sheela, how little I can do for Omi—has lifted a little.

13

NIMMI

Shimla

Rekha watches me as I pace the floor of our room. In her lap is the book about monkeys Lakshmi-*ji* loaned her. She loves looking at the pictures and sounding out the names of the different kinds of monkeys.

"Do your studies," I tell her. She's read the monkey book so often she has memorized it. "Write the words down exactly as you see them in the book."

"Do it with me, Maa," she says.

Chullu is sitting with Neela the sheep, who is busy munching on a leaf. Chullu pets her, then rolls over her. The sheep has won them over and my children want her to stay home with us, so I brought her here from the lower pasture. Watching the animal now, I think about the gold hidden under her fleece. What, exactly, does it look like? The women of my tribe wear silver, but I've seen gold jewelry on other women. I've never seen a solid brick of gold.

I reach for the *patal* that hangs from my waist belt next to a coil of rope and a goatskin water bag. I test the sharpness of the blade. I use this *patal* to cut vegetables and fruit, branches, wood—anything and everything. I pick Chullu up and set him next to Rekha on the cot, where he tries to cram her monkey book into his mouth.

I approach Neela, gently. She stops chewing and watches me. She bleats, then stands, now wary. I run my hand over her fleece to find the hard mound opposite her injured flank. Then I find the edges of the wool that have been sewn shut and cut the stitches carefully, keeping Neela in place with an elbow. Two bars of gold, each five inches long, two inches wide and half an inch thick fall to the ground with a thud. The sound scares Neela, and she struggles under my grasp. I let her go.

The gold is a dull color. It isn't beautiful, as I'd thought it would be. Someone has written numbers on the bars. They're heavy and surprisingly warm. The silver our tribe wears is cooler to the touch. To think anyone would kill for a lump of dull yellow metal!

A knock on the door startles me. I gather up the gold bars and look for someplace I can hide them. My bedroll is within reach, and I quickly stuff the bars under it before I go to see who's at the door.

It's Lakshmi. She's still in the same clothes she was wearing this morning. She has deep circles under her eyes and her hair is loose around her face; it hasn't been oiled. She looks exhausted. I tell her to come in and close the door behind her.

"Tomorrow, we will deliver the gold to that place," she says. She's speaking in a whisper.

"The place on the matchbox?" I ask.

She nods and rubs her forehead. "But first we must think how to remove the gold from the sheep and carry it from the hospital's lower pasture to Canara."

"Where is it? The business?"

"About four miles from here, just outside the city."

"Which direction?"

Lakshmi points with her chin to the east.

I think I know that area; it's where I go sometimes to pick the mountain flowers that I sell. That gives me an idea. I get up and find my flower basket—the large one I use at my stall. Then I take the gold bars from under the bedroll and put them in the empty basket. When Lakshmi sees the gold, her eyes grow wide. Then she looks at Neela and the patch of fleece that's open on her side.

How much can the basket hold? "We have thirty-eight sheep," I say, "counting Neela, thirty-nine. If each sheep is carrying four bars, two on each side, that would add up to one hundred fifty-six bars. But two are missing, so it's actually one hundred fifty-four." I don't know how to read, or write my numbers, but I do know how to count them in my head.

Lakshmi takes a bar from the basket and weighs it in her hand. She's used to mixing natural remedies, calculating the correct proportion of ingredients. "Each bar is slightly different, but the one I'm holding is about two ounces. It would sell for maybe six, seven hundred rupees."

"So that would mean..." I look at Lakshmi, my hand flying to my chest. I can feel my heart thumping against my palms. Now I know why smugglers take the risk of smuggling. All the bars, together, add up to about a hundred thousand rupees! *Hai Shiva!* It starts to sink in just how serious, how trecherous this business is. Lakshmi tried to tell me all along—how crazy it would be, how foolhardy to return the gold to people who would sooner cut their mother's throat than do without their treasure. I should have listened to her.

"We have to get it out of here," I say. I look at my children, who have heard the panic in my voice and are staring at me with open mouths.

Lakshmi sees my *patal*. "Is that what you used to open the seams?"

"*Hahn.*" I put the sharp tool back in its slot on my belt.

She presses her lips together, frowning, and looks at Neela. I know she's calculating how much time it will take to remove the gold from the sheep. She's good at making plans. She's organized every section of the garden according to what kind of soil the plants need, how much water they require, how much fertilizer. The garden is efficient and well-ordered. Like everything Lakshmi does.

She nods, decisively, as if she has made up her mind. "We have no choice. We have to remove the gold tonight. The grounds-keepers at the hospital will all have gone home."

I notice the tired lines under her eyes. She's done so much already—trekking up and down the mountains, carting my brother's body to Shimla, riding to that business on the out-skirts of town. Now it's dark outside. And cold.

We aren't of her blood. Yet, she's willing to do more.

Lakshmi moves to the door. "Meet me at my house in a half hour. Bring Neela, please."

"*Ji*, when was the last time you ate? I made *chapatti* and *palak subji* tonight. You should have some before you go."

I often hold back the respectful *Ji* with her. I see her soften. She smiles to thank me for my offer but she shakes her head. "I have to figure out how I'm going to explain all this to Jay—Dr. Kumar. I had to tell him what we've found. He's concerned, of course. And I have to work out how we'll bring the gold from the pasture. Chandra is worn out. I'm not sure I could ask him to do any more today."

I nod. "I'll ask the Aroras to look after the children."

She smiles faintly. "Tell them I need you at the hospital tonight. It won't be a lie."

14

LAKSHMI

Shimla

Jay wouldn't let Nimmi and me go alone into the lower pasture in the dead of night to collect the gold. He's already upset with me for going out to Canara Enterprises by myself.

Now he's with us at the edge of the pasture as we call out, softly, to the sheep. We work as quietly as we can, but there is little we can do about their bleating. Nimmi grabs a sheep, I shine the flashlight on it and Jay cuts through the stitches to retrieve the gold bars.

I've stabled Chandra for the night and brought our other horse, a short blond pony. If our calculations are correct, the gold will weigh no more than twenty pounds, less than a small child, and the pony should be able to handle the burden.

The task is difficult because we're working in the dark. We hear night animals around us: marmots and weasels going about their business in the recesses of the surrounding pine forest. Down here, in the lower meadow, the sheep are relatively safe from large predators. If a leopard or Himalayan bear were to attack the flock, it would leave us with fewer gold bars. I tell myself I mustn't worry about what I can't control; even so, my heart is racing and the blood is pounding in my ears. Although the night is cool and my fingers feel like ice, I'm sweating underneath my jacket. I'm still wearing the same clothes from this morning when I went to look for Nimmi up in the mountains.

From time to time we happen upon a sheep we've already worked on; we let her go and find another. Nimmi was smart to count the flock when she brought them to the lower pasture earlier. Once we've reached thirty-nine, we'll know for certain that we've checked them all.

It takes two hours. We know we're done when the total number of gold bars we've collected matches the number we calculated. As we predicted, every animal was carrying four bars. We put the gold in Nimmi's flower basket, then tie the basket on the pony. I use the *rajai* I brought from home to cover our illicit cargo.

Nimmi casts an eye over the flock, the pockets of fleece hanging open on both sides of their bodies. "They should be sheared—*really* sheared. Then I could sell the wool and keep the money for my nephews." Nimmi's voice catches. "That's what Vinay would have done." She turns to me. "I can do it in the mornings little by little before I get to the clinic. I should be done in four days."

I tilt my head. *Of course.*

It's midnight before the three of us and the pony arrive at Nimmi's house. Jay and I wait at a distance with the pony while Nimmi collects her children from the Aroras and brings them down to her lodging, one in each arm, both asleep.

She asks me to come inside with her as she settles Rekha and Chullu on the bedroll.

She whispers, "I won't open my flower stall tomorrow. I'll go with you to Canara instead, *Ji*."

I understand why she doesn't want Jay to hear; he's upset enough at me for going alone today. "We can't both be absent from the clinic for a second day. We've caused enough disruption. I would rather you go to the Healing Garden tomorrow. Pretend everything is normal. Tell the nurses you weren't feeling well today or make some other excuse." In the quiet of the evening, I'm careful not to speak of gold. "They know me now at Canara, so it's better if I take it."

Nimmi looks at me for a long moment, her face covered in shadow. I can see the white orbs of her eyes. It's as if she wants to say something, but then she wags her head and closes the door after me.

I can tell when something's bothering Jay. He stops teasing me. While I stable the pony next to our backyard corral, and give him food and water, Jay carries Nimmi's gold-laden basket into the house.

When I come into the drawing room, he's sitting in an armchair, rolling a glass of Laphroaig between his palms. He's already poured a glass for me and holds it out for me to take.

I take the glass and smooth his hair. "You're worried?"

"Who wouldn't be, Lakshmi? Why would you risk your life—our lives—for someone else's problem?" His voice is low and measured.

I let his words sit for a moment. Then I go to the side table where I keep letters and extract the most recent letter I received from Malik.

I return to Jay and hand him the letter. "Malik sent this to me a week ago." I pick up my glass of scotch and leave him to read the letter alone.

Dear Nimmi and Auntie-Boss,

I'm learning a lot here in Jaipur. Like what materials are best for which type of building. The cost of buying land and the cost of building from the ground up. How foundations are laid. Manu Uncle has been sending me around to different departments within his facilities division so his people can teach me all parts of the business. By now I'm starting to see buildings being constructed in my dreams. (You would love Hakeem, the accountant I work with. He's a funny little man. But I like him. He's been here forever—probably since the Moghul Empire!)

The best part of this experience has been spending time with Nikhil. He's just like Radha—twelve going on twenty! Boss, you would be so impressed with how Kanta Auntie and Manu Uncle have raised him. He's a sweet, funny boy, and—more important, in my book—a phenomenal cricket player! We spend many Sundays batting and bowling. He's almost as good as I am! (I'm sure he would disagree and say I'm pretty good for an old man.) I can't wait until Chullu is old enough for me to put a cricket bat in his hand! Please tell Rekha that I haven't forgotten about the rainbow I'm supposed to bring back for her from Jaipur. She thinks every city has its own rainbow, and I don't have the heart to disappoint her!

Boss, the next part is just for you, so don't read it to Nimmi!

I know you want the best for me. You always have. And for that, I'm grateful. But the longer I'm away from Nimmi, the more I realize how much I care for her. I miss her quiet ways. I admire how hard she works to feed and clothe Rekha and Chullu (both of whom I've come to love as my own). I help her out with a little money now and then, but—Hai Ram!—I have to practically force her to take it.

I realize that you might wish a different woman for me—more learned or more sophisticated—but I'm content with Nimmi. In the eight months I've known her, I've learned about the beauty of the Himalayas and the treasures the mountains hold. I know she's perfectly capable of taking care of herself, but I would ask you for a favor.

Please treat Nimmi as you would a sister, as you've always treated Radha. Nimmi will never ask you for anything, so you might have to thrust your kindness on her. She has such a good, loyal heart. Her loss has been tragic—no one should have to lose a spouse so young. But it has been my gain and brought me much happiness.
Yours,
Malik

Jay finds me in the bath. I'm scrubbing the last of today's grime, horse odor, dust and sweat from my skin. Jay sets the letter on the edge of the tub, puts his hands in his pockets and rattles the loose change he's carrying in them.

"I know you think helping Nimmi is best because of Malik's feelings for her, and you've always done what you thought best. But I'm uneasy."

I stop scrubbing. "Jay, if you could do something to help your family—something that could possibly save their lives—wouldn't you do it?"

"Yes. Of course, I would. But these are *goondas*—*professional racketeers*—you're dealing with! I think that it's too great a risk for you to get any more involved. I've talked to the local police—"

"Why?" I can feel myself getting angry. Talking to the authorities can be risky; you never know who's on the take.

He motions with his hands, a gesture meant to calm me down. "I didn't talk about this instance in particular, but I wanted to know more about the gold running taking place in the Shimla hills."

"And, what did you learn?"

"They're aware that there's activity to the west, around Chandigarh and closer to Pakistan, but they don't seem to think there's any in this area."

"They must have been curious about why you were asking." *Have you tipped them off to what we're doing?*

"*Arré.* I told them only that I'd read the article about smuggling in the paper and was concerned for the safety of my patients." He's jiggling the coins in his pants pocket again, another sign that he's worried.

I press my lips together, trying not to let my irritation show. I learned early that talking to the police has never been a good idea.

After independence, when the British left and government posts needed to be filled, nepotism reigned. The higher-level posts, like police commissioner, went to friends and family, whether or not they were qualified for the job. The result? Incompetence and corruption. There's always a chance that the police are colluding with the gold racketeers, pocketing protection money. And if the police commissioner suspects Jay spoke to them because he has information about the smuggling, he can use that to his advantage or, worse, decide he needs to keep Jay from revealing what he knows to anyone else.

Jay has put himself—and us—in danger. If the authorities were to find those half-shorn sheep at the bottom of the lower pasture, we'd all three of us be implicated.

Which means we have to sheer the sheep completely and as soon as possible. Tomorrow night at the latest. Nimmi's timeline—three days—is now compressed into a single day. And it will take all three of us to make it happen. I'm already so exhausted from riding out to find Nimmi, then spending the evening removing gold from the sheep. I didn't dare let Jay see how badly my knees were shaking.

I put my head underwater, drowning out Jay's voice and my body's protestations.

★ ★ ★

Early the next morning, I ride a rested Chandra the four miles outside Shimla to Canara Private Enterprises. Jay and I have put the gold bars in the saddlebags and covered them with a horse blanket. I've put on a clean pair of jodhpurs and Jay's wool coat. I've wrapped a brown shawl around my head and shoulders. It's a hazy morning, the mist curling lazily around the pine and cedar trees, hesitant to move on.

Convincing Jay to let me go alone was a battle. He wanted to go in my place. I refused because I don't want him more involved than he already is. He has an important position at the hospital. And he has a full load of patients this morning, including two cesareans.

Today, the barbed entrance gate to Canara Enterprises is open. Inside, a lone woman in a sari and sweater blouse squats on the ground, patting clay into a wooden mold and dumping the formed brick onto the ground. She works quickly—probably because she gets paid by the brick—adding another row to a growing layer of bricks drying in the open air.

I dismount and walk Chandra into the clearing, stopping right next to her. She looks up but doesn't stop her work.

I *namaste* her. "You're an expert at this."

Her overbite makes her self-conscious, so she puts her hand in front of her face as she smiles and wags her head from side to side, pleased to be acknowledged.

I notice all the bricks have rectangular indentations in the center. I wonder why. "Who buys these bricks?"

When she looks confused, I try again. "Who are the customers—"

She waves a hand. "I don't know, *Ji*. I see a truck take them away. The driver says he's taking them to Chandigarh."

"*Arré!* What are you doing out here?" It's the young man from yesterday, the one who sits behind the counter. He casts a dark look at the woman, who hastily returns to her brickmaking. To me, he says, "Go to the office."

I try to look apologetic, but I can tell he's suspicious. He watches me until I've led Chandra to the office door. The saddlebags filled with gold are heavy, but I've practiced lifting them so it looks like I know what I'm doing.

I bring in one saddlebag, and then the other, placing them on the counter. The older man from the back office comes to take the bags. He carries them to his desk and closes the inner office door so I can no longer see him.

"How did you get those blue eyes?" the young man says.

I'd been so focused on the boss that I'd forgotten the younger man guarding me. "What?"

"We see eyes like yours in Kashmir."

In Jaipur I'd often been asked about my blue eyes. People thought I might be Anglo-Indian (a group that fell out of favor once the British left the country). Or perhaps I wasn't Indian at all? Might I be Parsi, or Afghani? But I'm not about to get into a conversation with this man about my heritage or tell him that blue eyes have been common in my family for generations. I simply say, "I'm not Kashmiri."

Now he puts his elbows on the counter, leaning forward with a sly smile on his face. "You shepherds never consider yourselves Kashmiri or Punjabi or Rajasthani, do you? It's your tribe that matters. But I've never seen another tribal member with blue eyes." He cocks his head, considering me seriously. Then he says something to me in a dialect that I don't understand.

The fine hairs on my arms rise. He's trying to suss out where I'm really from. I can't respond convincingly in dialect. The risk I'm already taking becomes dangerous if I'm exposed. My best bet is to act embarrassed.

I cast my eyes downward, draw my shawl tighter around my neck. "Please," I say, "I am married."

He turns playful once again. "And your husband lets you do a man's job?"

I think about Vinay, his body splayed on the ground. "Only because he's injured. Badly."

His smile is coy. "You must be needing comfort in that case. And I—"

The inner door swings open and the older man appears. The flimsy bracelet on his wrist is made of colored thread—one strand red, the other gold colored. It's likely that a sister made the amulet for him so he would protect her for the remainder of her life. But when he drops the empty saddlebags onto the scarred wooden surface with a scowl on his face, I realize I can't count on the softness he might show his sister. "You're missing two," he says.

I raise my chin in question.

"There are only one hundred and fifty-four bars. There should be a hundred fifty-six."

I can feel the sweat begin to gather on my upper lip. But I keep my voice firm. "We took two as payment."

"*Kya?* You took payment in gold?" He straightens, frowns. "That wasn't the bargain."

I look at the younger man, open my blue eyes wider, appeal to his softer approach. "It's a dangerous route. My husband fell. Broke his back. We needed a hospital. That's why we're late. We had no money. We used the gold to pay our bill."

Now the older man slams his hand on the counter, making me jump. "That is not a decision you get to make." Spit flies out of his mouth. "What am I to tell the next courier?"

I sense the fear behind his anger. I level a gaze at him. "Tell him the Shimla authorities have heard rumors about the gold running at the edge of town. Tell him two bars is fair payment for carrying gold along the route that the police are watching."

We lock eyes. I'm out of breath and feel as if I'm about to faint.

I turn when I hear a noise behind me. It's the woman from the courtyard who was laying bricks. She says to the men behind the counter, "I'm out of clay. What do you want me to do?"

I choose this moment to grab the empty saddlebags, run to the door and jump on Chandra. In seconds, we are galloping down the winding path through the forest. I hear shouts behind me, but there were no vehicles in the yard, so I know they have no way to follow us as quickly as Chandra and I can travel.

In my ears I hear the rush of wind, the thrum of Chandra's hooves pounding the earth and my own blood coursing through my veins. Would they really harm me for two bars of gold when they have most of the treasure in their possession? I hope not, but I can't be sure. What I do know is that I need to get as far away as I can as quickly as I can.

I've traveled less than a mile when I realize Jay's horse is riding beside mine. I slow Chandra to a canter. Only when I turn to look at Jay do I realize he must have followed me out here to make sure I'd be safe. My eyes fill. Slowly, I let the terror of the last hour drain from my body the way Madho Singh allows his feathers to settle onto his back after he realizes the loud noise that terrified him is no more.

15

NIMMI

Shimla

I run my hands over the smooth porcelain of the bathtub in Lakshmi's guest bathroom. I'm in the bath with Rekha and Chullu. Rekha is fine on her own, but I have to hold on to Chullu with one hand while I soap him down with the other. There are two spouts. Every now and then, I turn the one on the left, as Lakshmi taught me, and more hot water magically appears! I'm used to the rice-bran-and-yak-fat soap our tribe makes, but Lakshmi's soap is heavenly—it makes so many suds when mixed with water! And the scent! I feel as if I'm in the meadow collecting flowers.

When Chullu tries to put the bar of lavender soap in his mouth, I tease it out of his hands.

Rekha slaps her hands on the surface of the water to see how high she can make it jump.

Always before, when I came to Lakshmi's house, I was so obsessed with Malik's letters that I didn't notice anything else. Now I realize every detail of her home has a purpose and a simple beauty. I see no point in comparing this house with my own simple lodging, but I can't help feeling embarrassed, imagining what Malik must think when he visits me at my home. I'm thankful that he's been there only at night, when it's hard to see the cracks between the wooden planks of the walls.

I was watering the plants in the Healing Garden when Lakshmi arrived at the hospital this afternoon, after she'd delivered the gold to Canara. My children were nearby, playing in the dirt. No one else would have guessed she'd been up half the night removing gold bars from sheep. She had bathed and dressed in a sari to work her shift at the afternoon clinic, her hair in a neat bun at the back of her neck. She looked, as usual, alert.

"The whole flock has to be sheared tonight," she said quietly. "The groundskeeper told Jay that the sheep have almost grazed the lower pasture clean. They need to be moved tomorrow. And we can't have people speculating about their half-shorn fleece."

I was wondering how I'd manage by myself when Lakshmi said, "Come to our house tonight. We'll go together."

My *patal* could cut cleanly and quickly, but it wasn't meant for shearing sheep. The blade was too sharp and could nick their skin. I'd sheared sheep in the past, with my tribe, but it was a group activity, with everybody helping. I wasn't sure that Lakshmi and I could do it by ourselves.

"Will Dr. Kumar help us, *Ji*?"

Lakshmi nodded. "He has to. Otherwise we'll never get it done." She gave me a reassuring smile, but I saw the worry in her eyes. "Do you think you can find someone to move the flock?"

That would be the easy part. I nodded. I wanted to ask the question that had been hovering on my lips for the past two days. Lakshmi had separated me from the second man I'd ever loved (the mountains had taken the first), and it had caused me so much pain. I finally asked her, "Why are you helping me?"

She looked surprised, as if she thought I should have known the answer. "You're part of Malik's life, Nimmi, and so you are a part of mine." Then she turned to leave but stopped and spoke to me with her back turned. "Before I met Dr. Jay, Malik and my sister, Radha, were my only family, and both came late into my life. You've met Malik. Someday you'll meet Radha and you'll see how special she is. I would do almost anything—and have done what I can—to keep both of them safe and happy." Finally, she turned to look at me, her gaze direct and unflinching. "As happy and safe as Malik wants to make sure you and the children are."

In her blue, guileless eyes, I saw nothing but concern.

Then she frowned. "*Suno.* The men who've taken the gold are unhappy that two bars of gold are missing. The two bars we never found. I'd be more comfortable if you and the children stay with us for a while."

This took me so much by surprise I wasn't sure I'd understood. "Stay with you?" I asked. "In your house?"

She smiled. "That's the idea."

Looking at her clean sari and matching sweater blouse, I felt ashamed. I had not had time to wash my clothes with so much going on the last few days. I could feel my face grow warm. Rekha and Chullu were no cleaner. After all the work with the sheep the night before, I hadn't had the energy to draw water, heat it, and wash the dirt and sweat off me or my children in our lodgings. Would she want our private grime to soil her home?

"You and the children can stay in Malik's room. He has an adjoining bath."

How is it that she always manages to read my mind?

"And I think it's better, safer that you not sell flowers on the Shimla Mall until we get this sorted."

My pulse quickened. "You think it's that unsafe?"

"I do."

A little while later, I took a break from my work in the Healing Garden and went to the waiting room, where I approached patients who were people of the hills, most likely shepherds—their homespun woolens and darker skin giving them away. One middle-aged man with a cloudy eye and half an ear missing said he could take our sheep to graze with his flock, north of here. I told him I'd let him know tomorrow where to find my brother's sheep and described the notch on their ears so he could keep his sheep separate from my brother's.

He smiled then, showing me his five teeth. "I don't need to mark my sheep," he said. "I know which sheep is which because I know their personalities. And every single one of them is ornery!"

The woman sitting next to him joined his laughter.

So tonight I find myself with Rekha and Chullu in Lakshmi and Dr. Jay's house. I left work early to retrieve our few belongings from the Aroras' so I could to take them to Lakshmi's house. She'd asked me not to tell my landlords where we were going. Better, she said, to be safe. I didn't like keeping things from them; they've been so kind. But Lakshmi has been right about most everything, so I left without saying goodbye to the old couple. It took only one trip; we don't have much. Lakshmi said she'd send our clothes to the *dhobi*. I always wash my own clothes, but I didn't want to say as much to Lakshmi. Perhaps she thinks I don't clean them well enough.

Now the children are up in Malik's bedroom with Lakshmi's housekeeper, Moni. Lakshmi is putting on her boots and Dr. Kumar is buttoning up his wool jacket. Madho Singh is pacing on his perch. Every now and then he squawks, *"The hand that feeds us is in danger of being bitten."*

I can tell by Dr. Kumar's expression that he wishes we weren't doing this. But just as Lakshmi will not put a child at risk, Dr. Kumar will never fail to protect Lakshmi. What choice does he have? She is determined. I want to apologize to him for the danger Vinay put us all in. But the mention of my brother's name would only increase the tension in the room. I say nothing.

It's eight o'clock at night, dusk, and we're in the lower pasture, close to the edge of the forest, with Vinay's flock. The ground has been mowed clean, and the sheep seem eager to be moved. Was it only yesterday we were here, collecting the gold? Then, I was preoccupied with the work to be done, hardly thinking about where we were. Tonight, the woods feel sinister. Tree branches resemble claws. Leaves whisper dark omens. Mulch on the forest floor smells of rot, death.

I show Lakshmi and Dr. Kumar how we shear the sheep.

I take one, turn her on her back and squat on the cloth I've spread on the ground so I can hold the animal between my knees. The sheep are used to being sheared and know they'll feel much better when they've lost their heavy coat, so they lie still. The shepherd at the clinic this morning lent me two long-handled shears. I start by grabbing a handful of the wool on the sheep's stomach and trim it with the shears. Once I've cleared this small area on the sheep's belly, I know how close I can cut without grazing the skin, and the shearing goes much faster.

I keep going until I've sheared all the sheep's fleece from the underside. Then I turn the animal on her side so I can shear the wool there, then I turn her once again to shear the other side. The work of shearing has a rhythm that can be soothing and, at times, hypnotic. It doesn't take me long before I've finished with the body and can shear the legs.

I tell Lakshmi and Dr. Jay, "The best shearers get the fleece off in one piece. They can shear forty sheep in a day and never nick or cut the skin."

When I'm done, I release the animal and gather the wool, showing the others how to twirl it all in a big ball. We'll pack as much of the wool as we can on the horses and leave the rest here, to collect upon our return.

Lakshmi watches the process with fascination. I can tell she's never seen this done. Dr. Kumar seems unfazed. Not only does he work with scalpels: he grew up in Shimla and has long watched shepherds doing this same task. I hand him the other borrowed shears.

But seeing and doing are different things. At first, the sheep are not relaxed in Dr. Kumar's arms; they're just not used to him. Soon enough he gets into a rhythm and is shearing almost as fast as I. Lakshmi finds the work more challenging; she doesn't want to nick the sheep. They sense her hesitation, so they squirm and wiggle out of her grasp. As it grows darker, she decides to take on a different task: she holds two flashlights—one for the doctor and one for me—so we can get the work done as soon as possible.

After three hours, everything—the field and the surrounding forest—is pitch-black, illuminated only by the flashlights Lakshmi is holding.

My arms are fatigued from holding the sheep down, my legs are tired from squatting and my thumbs have blisters on them from handling the shears.

In the light of the flashlights, I can see Dr. Kumar's face and know he's every bit as tired as I am.

I've counted thirty-seven sheep, including Neela. Two more to go.

But the flashlights suddenly go dark.

I'm about to call out to Lakshmi when I feel her hand on my shoulder. That's when I hear the voices. I see lights, like fireflies, blinking in the distance. Men are calling out to one another through the forest to the east. One man is shouting orders; others are answering his commands.

Lakshmi, Dr. Kumar and I stand still as tree trunks. I hold my breath.

Dr. Kumar whispers, "Nimmi, come with me."

I rise from my squat.

"Lakshmi," he whispers, "you stay here."

He takes my hand and leads me away from the flock, toward the men. I don't know what he's up to, and I want to let go of his hand and run the other way, but his grasp is firm, and I have to trust that he knows what he's doing.

We run a hundred yards in the dark. Then Dr. Kumar stops, turns my body so he's facing me. He kisses me. I'm so startled I don't know what I ought to feel. His lips are not as full as Malik's, but they're just as warm.

One of the men shines his torch on us. "Sir!" he calls out.

Another voice, this one with authority, shouts to us, "Stop where you are!"

And then we see him, and the others behind him: it's the police.

The doctor turns, as if he's as surprised as they are. "Captain?" he says. "I… What is this?"

There's a pause, and then the captain moves into the light. He's a gaunt man with a black mustache that only makes his scowl look more severe. Without his uniform he wouldn't look quite so intimidating. His voice uncertain, he says, "Dr. *Kumar*?"

The doctor steps in front of me, as if he means to keep me hidden, or protect me. He lowers his head, doing his best to look ashamed. "What has brought you here?" he says. "You told me you were no longer doing night patrols in Shimla…"

The captain shines his flashlight over both of us. I stay behind the doctor, who now shields his eyes with one hand.

"Is this what I think it is?" the captain says. I hear the sly smile in his voice. The way he says it tells me that he's putting on a show for his men.

"This is awkward," Dr. Kumar says, apologetically. "Not to mention inconvenient." The doctor chuckles.

Now the captain's voice softens. "So *this* is why you asked me about smugglers running gold?"

Before I step out from behind the doctor, I undo a few hooks on the front of my blouse, putting my cleavage on display. I keep my eyes fixed on the ground. "We are sorry, *Ji*," I say, "to trouble you."

A few men snicker. The captain comes a little closer to me, and I'm hoping he's more interested in what I'm showing him than what we might be doing with the sheep.

"I heard a rumor that this woman is living with you. But I didn't believe it."

Dr. Kumar attempts another embarrassed laugh. "News travels fast."

"The mountains have ears, Doctor."

"Ah, then the mountains have also told you that my wife is still living with me, too."

Now the men laugh louder.

"*Chup!*" the captain tells his men, asserting his authority.

I fight the urge to look behind us, at Lakshmi, who must have heard this exchange. After everything she's done for us, she has to listen to this disgusting talk!

Dr. Kumar looks at me, tenderly, as if I am the only thing that brings him joy. "We have to sneak away, you see," he says. "This is the only time we can…"

He reaches into his pocket, pulls out a wad of rupees and insists the captain take them as a "gift." "To make up for the trouble that we've caused you, Sahib."

The captain clears his throat but doesn't hesitate to take the rupees being offered. He dithers only a second before the money disappears inside his jacket pocket.

I pull on the doctor's arm. "What about...you know?"

Dr. Kumar turns to me; one side of his face is lit up by the policeman's flashlight, the other is in darkness. His expression is bewildered, and alarmed. He's taken by surprise and seems to think that I'm about to undo everything he's done to get us out of trouble.

"The gold," I say, "just outside Shimla." I give the captain a shy, apologetic glance. "The doctor doesn't like to get people in trouble, Sahib." I turn to the doctor again. "That business. What is it called? Can—Canra—?"

We're both now looking at the captain. His head is tilted, his interest piqued.

"I remember now," I say as if I've just remembered. "Canara!"

The captain says, "Canara?"

I lower my voice to a whisper. "Where they move the gold. But, Sahib, you must already be knowing about it."

Hastily, the public servant clears his throat, glances at his men. Then he nods, several times. "Of course, of course. But how did *you* find out?"

Dr. Kumar pulls me to him, smiling. I can almost believe that he's in love with me. "The mountains have ears."

Now the doctor looks at the captain, then at me, and hastily puts his hands together in a *namaste*. "But please, Captain. Don't tell my *bibi*. It would break her heart."

"You can rely on me, Doctor. As for my men—" he glances behind him "—I can vouch for them."

Bukwas! By tomorrow morning, the rumor mill will be working overtime at the hospital.

I wonder how Dr. Kumar will be able to hold his head up after this.

16

LAKSHMI

Shimla

We didn't talk about what just happened on our way back from the lower pasture. It was awkward with all three of us present. The only time Nimmi spoke is to tell us she had arranged for a local shepherd to move the sheep tomorrow.

I don't know why, but I felt wary about bringing up the altercation with the police. I couldn't say exactly why but wondered if I might not like his answer. Still, it kept replaying in my head, like a broken film that's stuck in the projector, slapping the machine with every revolution of the reel. I saw the way that Jay reacted when confronted by the captain, pretending—so convincingly—to be having an affair with Nimmi. Even I almost believed him.

I was crouched behind a tree trunk far into the darkness, but I could still make out the silhouettes of Jay and Nimmi. He was holding her in an embrace, *and then he kissed her!*

Did he feel anything? Did *she*?

There are nurses at the hospital and the clinic who have a crush on Jay. They see him as the kind, and bashful, doctor. But I've never felt they were a threat. The jealousy that overwhelmed me when I saw him holding Nimmi was entirely new. And, after all, *I* am the one who insisted Nimmi live with us, for now.

Should I be worried? *No.* A liaison between the two of them is inconceivable. Jay loves me; he's always claimed he fell for me the first time he saw me at Samir Singh's house twelve years ago. I have no reason to believe he hasn't been faithful during our marriage.

As the three of us step onto the front veranda, I can hear the phone ringing inside. I know Moni won't answer the phone—she doesn't trust it. I hurry to unlock the door. The only phone calls we get late at night are from the hospital for Jay. Sometimes Radha calls from Paris, but she's careful about calling, as the charges are exorbitant, and she calls only on her girls' birthdays, and on Diwali.

But the phone call is not from Radha or the hospital. It's Kanta, telling me the Royal Jewel Cinema collapsed tonight.

She quickly assures me that Malik, and her family, are fine, which sets my racing heart at ease.

But she's speaking quickly, and she's crying. I don't catch every word and have to ask her to repeat herself. "I'm so glad we didn't take Nikhil to the cinema tonight," she says. "He was furious with us because he wanted to be in on the excitement. So many of his classmates were going…" She stops herself, and I can hear her sobs. When she manages to calm herself, she says, "Oh, Lakshmi. It was horrible for everyone. People were hurt.

They were crying. The biggest project for the palace so far—the maharani invested all that money to build it! And Manu was in charge of it. He's beside himself! Says he has no idea how it could have happened."

"How many were hurt?" My mind is sprinting through the names of everyone I used to know in Jaipur. *Hai Ram!* Were any of them there? Were they hurt?

"We only know that the actor, Rohit Seth—you must have heard of him—died instantly. He fell to the first floor when his part of the balcony gave way. Many people sitting just below the balcony were injured, too. A child is being treated—we heard his leg was badly crushed. A woman is in critical condition. She may survive, or not. It's touch and go." She blows her nose and takes another moment to control herself. I can picture Kanta with her phone, twisting the black plastic coil around her finger, leaning back against the hallway wall. I can see her shake her head, dramatically, and wring the handkerchief she's soaked with tears.

"They'll try to blame this all on Manu! He's convinced of it. But it *isn't* Manu's fault! You know that he's meticulous about his work! The last to leave the office every day. He checks and double-checks the figures, quantities, the costs of labor and materials. He constantly goes over everything. You should see how carefully he checks our bills at home—I can't even watch him do it. If he finds an error, or an overcharge, he just assumes I haven't paid attention. *Baap re baap!*"

When I had my henna business in Jaipur, Kanta was a client—and among the few who offered me their friendship from the first day we met. She knew I was a fallen Brahmin in the eyes of other matrons because I handled women's feet when I painted their henna. That task, considered to be unclean, was reserved for lower castes; it wasn't respectable for Brahmins to do it.

Then when Radha became pregnant with Ravi's child, Kanta,

who was also pregnant at the time, took her to Shimla, where they could have their babies together, far from prying eyes and wagging tongues. Sadly, Kanta lost her baby because of septic shock and almost lost her own life.

But fate, aided by a bit of nudging on my part, led to the adoption of Radha's son by Kanta and Manu. It was Jay, of course, I had to nudge.

I can hear Kanta wailing at the other end of the phone. I make my voice as creamy as *rasmalai*. "But Singh-Sharma is responsible for the construction—not Manu. I'm sure there'll be an inquiry. They'll find out what caused it, Kanta. Brand-new buildings don't just fall to pieces every day." I pause. "In your most recent letter, you said they were hurrying the project to complete it on time. Could somebody have cut corners?"

She makes a small choking sound. "But Manu signed off on everything! His name is everywhere, on all the palace paperwork!" Now she's worked herself into a frenzy, and that can't be good for Niki or her *saas*, both of whom are probably listening.

"Listen to me, Kanta. It will all work out. The maharanis are fair. They're smart. They won't accuse Manu. It will be handled." As I'm saying this, I'm thinking that I need to talk to Malik to get a fuller picture of the cinema's collapse. I say, "Where is Malik now?"

"At the cinema house with Manu and Samir. They're helping with the rescue effort. Will be for hours. I wanted to come home, to see that Niki's safe. He is. Was that bad of me? There were other mothers there whose children had been hurt, and I couldn't think of anything but Niki. I kept thinking, what if it was *my* child who was injured?" Now she's speaking in a whisper. "I'm going to keep Niki home from school for a few days. I don't know how his classmates will react, or what they'll say to him. Many of his friends were at the cinema with their parents.

If some of them were injured… Oh, Lakshmi! I'm not thinking clearly… I don't know what I ought to do!"

If Kanta's right, and the accident isn't Manu's fault, everything will, eventually, be okay. But for the moment, fingers will be pointing at him; he will be blamed. If he's forced to leave his job, it will be difficult for him to get another—anywhere. Palace scandals spread, and quickly, and if the scandal's big—as this one is—no one can contain it. A scandal in which lives are lost will never be forgotten. Or forgiven.

Kanta is falling apart. My friend needs me the way I needed her all those years ago. I realize I must go to Jaipur; I can catch the first train in the morning. I tell Kanta. Immediately, she begins to calm down. After a few more words of reassurance, I hang up.

I hear Nimmi ask, "What's happening? Is Malik okay?"

I turn around; she's standing behind me. While I've been on the phone, I realize Moni, our housekeeper, must have left, and Nimmi has come back downstairs after looking in on the children. She must have heard some of my conversation. Her wild-eyed look reminds me of how the sheep greeted us tonight when we came to shear them. She is nervously rubbing her palms along the sides of her skirt.

"He's fine." My legs are shaking, and I take a seat on the couch.

Jay comes into the drawing room, bringing Nimmi a glass of scotch, but she doesn't acknowledge it, or him. He sets it down on the credenza next to her. Next, he hands me my glass. I sip my drink, feeling the golden liquid snake its way to my belly. Jay sits opposite me.

After a breath, I tell them what Kanta told me.

I turn to Jay. "Tomorrow I'll take the early train to Jaipur. Kanta needs me right now—"

Nimmi steps between us. Her face is a knot of anxiety. "I

knew Malik shouldn't have gone to Jaipur. I knew something awful would happen. Just like with Dev."

I reach for Nimmi's arm to calm her. "Malik is not hurt, Nimmi."

She pulls her arm away. "He didn't want to go. You know he didn't want to go! You *made* him go...*you* did that. *You* put him in danger. He wouldn't have gone if you hadn't asked him. Don't you see? He does everything you tell him."

Nimmi towers above me, gesturing wildly. "I know you want to decide who he should be with, too. And I don't fit, do I? You want him to be with someone *padha-likha*. Someone who wears silk saris and speaks *angrezi*." Her body is vibrating with energy. "Why is it so important for anyone to read-write when all you need to survive is air and mountains and apples off the trees and pine nuts and the sweet milk of goats? I've survived on that all my life!" She throws her arms up in the air. "Malik isn't even yours, is he? He's someone else's child. If you wanted children so badly, why didn't you have them yourself?"

She's blaming me for wanting the best for Malik? She thinks I smother him? I sit there, numb, my glass of scotch like a prop in my hand. How am I supposed to comfort her? The woman who was kissing my husband an hour ago? Do I defend myself? After I've risked my own life to keep her and her children safe from the danger her brother put them in?

Nimmi plops herself down on the sofa next to me, surprising me and upsetting my drink. She seizes my free hand with her strong, hot fingers. Her face is just inches from mine and her dark eyes are blazing. "He—he does things you want him to be-cause he's good. Malik is good. And he owes you so much. He's told me. He doesn't know where he would be without you. But he needs to live his own life now. He deserves to make his own way in the world. It's time for you to let him go. He needs to hear it from you. Please. He'll let go if you let go. Mrs. Kumar, you have to let him go. You *have* to."

She opens her mouth to say more, but nothing comes. She merely stares into my eyes, as if she wants to reach the part of me that I don't allow anyone to see.

Her gaze is so penetrating that I have to look away.

Is she right? Do I use my hold on Malik in a way that doesn't serve him? Am I using my influence to lead him toward a life that will make him unhappy? I've never thought of Malik as a son, more as a younger brother. But he's more than that, isn't he? He's a part of my past, a part of me. He has known me at my best and my worst. At my happiest. And my most despondent. He's known me longer than anyone in my life—longer than Jay—or Radha, who came into my life when she was already thirteen years old. If I ceased to look after Malik, would I feel the loss, like a limb I'd mislaid? Or would it be a relief to know I no longer had to be responsible for his well-being? Is Malik even expecting me to look after him that way? Or does he just humor me, allow me to direct him, because he knows it makes me feel useful?

I feel hollow—like a reed before the henna paste fills its core. I don't know what to say, or what to think. I can neither speak, nor move.

Jay sets his glass on the table. He takes Nimmi by the shoulders, eases her off the sofa, and leads her out of the room and up the stairs.

My hand, where her fingers had just been, feels like it's burning.

I finish my drink in my bath, then set the glass on the soap basket. Even now, after washing off the memory of the day— the pungent sweat smell of the men at Canara, the rough wool of the sheep on my palms, the humiliation of seeing my husband kiss another woman, the unsettling questions Nimmi has planted in my mind—I don't know what to feel.

When the water has, at last, gone cold, I step out of the tub, and Jay comes into the bathroom to stand before me. He wraps me in a towel and rubs it gently on my back, looking at me all the while, never taking his eyes off mine. He still smells of the outdoors, the scent of pine needles on the forest floor, the musty odor of the wool we'd sheared.

Then he lets the towel drop to the floor. He puts his forehead against mine and leaves it there. Is he sympathizing with me? About what Nimmi said? Or maybe he feels the same way she does. Perhaps he's asking for forgiveness for kissing her? Is there anything to forgive? The rational part of me knows he acted in *our* best interest tonight when the police showed up. It's ridiculous to think that he has been carrying on with Nimmi. Even so, I want to hear him say it. I know how long he waited for me, how long he wanted me before I realized I wanted him, too. But there are times—like now, when I'm at my lowest—that I need to hear the words.

Water from my breasts is soaking through his shirt. He slides his hands down my arms and lets them rest on my hips. He kneels.

The warm touch of his lips in the triangle between my breasts makes me draw a sharp breath. His lips travel lower—down to my navel—and lower still. My buttocks tense and every nerve in my body vibrates with anticipation.

I put my hands on either side of his head and press his lips to the space between my trembling legs. He squeezes my buttocks, pulls them apart, pushes them together. Then his tongue finds the spot that makes me tingle inside and out; it licks and sucks and darts until I feel that I'm about to faint. When I come, I let out a loud groan, not thinking of, or worrying about, the other woman in the house, in Malik's room. Jay stops moving.

We stay like that until I am no longer shaking. Then he turns his head to one side, wraps his arms around my legs and says, "You, Lakshmi."

For a long time, we stay that way.

Finally, Jay says, pleadingly, "My knees." And then he's laughing. I feel his lovely eyelashes brush against my belly, and I release him.

Not long after, I will fall into the deepest slumber of my life, my arms around my husband.

THE COLLAPSE

17

MALIK

Jaipur

We're still in the lobby, making our way back to our seats after the refreshment break, when we hear the crash. Followed by shrieks and groans, the plaintive cries for help. All at once, people are stampeding—into and out of the Royal Jewel Cinema. They're pushing one another to get to the lobby doors or running inside the theater to tend to the injured. For a split second, our group—Kanta, Manu, me, the Singhs—stands frozen, in the middle of the lobby, as desperate people dash frantically around us. Baby is now awake and screaming.

Then Samir is fighting to get inside the ground floor of the theater. Manu is right behind him. I can hear Samir yelling at everyone to evacuate the theater immediately.

He calls for Ravi, who is nowhere to be found. I run toward the lobby, shouting at the ushers to open the doors and pleading with the crowd to quickly go outside. The exodus is a tidal wave, but there's also an opposing force—people fighting to get in to rescue loved ones who remained in their seats during the intermission.

While Samir disappears inside the theater, I tell Sheela to take her children and Parvati and Kanta outside. But she shakes her head, hands the baby to her mother-in-law, and tells her and Kanta to go home. Then she runs inside the theater. I follow her.

Groups of men and women are lifting the mound of rubble off the injured. Sheela and I join them. We can hear pleas for help underneath the chunks of concrete, rebar and bricks.

I spot Samir talking to the theater manager, a man I know only as Mr. Reddy, whom Samir hired from a smaller movie house in Bombay.

Hakeem is standing next to Mr. Reddy. That's strange. I'd expected to see the accountant earlier with his wife and daughters up on the balcony. Hakeem is nervously swiping at his mustache as if he's wiping away the memory of the accident that's just occurred. Samir is barking orders. Mr. Reddy wipes the sweat from his brow and snaps into action. Hakeem runs after him.

Manu looks as if he's in shock; he keeps asking Samir how this could have happened.

The police arrive in short order, and for the next hour, about a hundred moviegoers who escaped from the building without injury help them rescue the wounded buried under the debris, lifting steel and concrete off the people underneath and making bandages from shirts and *dhotis*. I see Sheela rip her fine silk sari with her teeth and quickly fashion a tourniquet to stanch the bleeding of a crushed leg. By the time we get the injured to the lobby, a ragtag convoy of cars, trucks, scooters, cycle rickshaws, motor rickshaws and *tongas* are waiting to transport them to nearby hospitals. Sheela is efficiently directing who goes where. The few ambulances in Jaipur are privately owned and come only when called.

When I glance at my watch, I see that it's now 1:00 a.m. For the past three hours, I haven't stopped to think; I've been engrossed in what needed to be done. My arms ache from the effort of lifting bodies. I rub the back of my neck to ease the headache that I've just become aware of. My throat feels parched—from thirst, or from the dust of the debris? I go inside the theater, again, to see what I can do. One side of the theater is almost completely destroyed. That's where a good part of the balcony collapsed. The theater's other half appears to be intact. But no one knows, yet, why the structure in the one area failed, and so we can't assume the rest of it won't. Better we clear the building just in case the worst happens.

Samir is standing, arms akimbo, in the middle of the wreckage. The theater is almost empty. He's speaking again to Mr. Reddy, whose face, and Nehru jacket, are covered in plaster dust. The man's perspiring; he looks dazed. Mr. Reddy removes a handkerchief from a pocket, blows his nose, then wipes his eyes. He nods to Samir, walks around him, goes past me and heads through the corridor that leads to the back of the stage.

Now Samir stands alone, his back to me; I'm not sure he knows I'm watching him. His silk coat's torn neatly down the center back seam and across one shoulder. His hair and clothes are covered with mortar dust. He cocks his head; something on the floor seems to have caught his attention. He leans down to pick up a broken piece of cement concrete. He examines it, turning it over in his hand.

I survey the rubble, too. I look up at the innards of the balcony, the skeleton of rebar and cement mortar. Three seats, still securely bolted to the now exposed balcony floor, lean precariously toward the gap, as if, at any minute, they, too, might let go. I can see that two columns supporting the balcony gave way, sending several rows—maybe fifteen, twenty seats—to the ground floor. These are the seats that landed on the audience sitting directly below.

I study the torn carpet, littered with chunks of building material, broken seats lying askew, covered in plaster and mortar dust. All at once, I feel pity for Ravi Singh—a thing I never thought possible. All the work that went into this building. All the hours. And the money, and the talent. He had planned this grand opening down to the last detail.

I kick one piece of broken brick, and it rolls over. I can tell by the indentation on one side that it was a decorative brick. *Strange.* I squat and pick up another piece. Also a decorative brick. Manu once showed me that one side of each decorative brick is stamped with the manufacturer's logo. Suppliers take pride in their work.

But the bricks I'm looking at have no factory stamp—just a shallow indentation where the logo would usually be. I spot another brick without a logo. Then another. These, too, have the same rectangular well in the center. Why are there so many decorative bricks? I look around the theater. Bricks weren't used to adorn either the walls or the balcony facade. I think about those invoices I've been logging in. Every invoice for bricks came from the same place: *Chandigarh Ironworks.* So where's their stamp?

I weigh the brick in my hand. It feels lighter and looks more porous than the bricks Manu showed me. If I were to pour a glass of water on any one of them, I'm pretty sure the water would flow through and saturate the brick in record time.

"Abbas?"

I raise my head to see Samir standing next to me. Dust has settled in the grooves of his forehead and the crevices around his mouth as if he were a stage actor made to look older than his years. I stand up, a piece of brick still in my hand. Samir looks at it, too.

"I told everyone to go home. Tomorrow morning, my people will start cleaning up." He takes the brick fragment out of my hand. "After that's done, we'll sort out who's doing what, and when."

"But, Uncle. How could this have happened? So many people worked on this. The building was inspected many times—"

He holds up a hand. "I know no more than you do, Malik. But, for now, take Sheela home. She'll be exhausted." He looks directly into my eyes as he says this: "Ravi must have escorted the actress back to her hotel. He may not be aware of what's happened."

Is he guessing that's the case, or is he telling me? It doesn't matter. I'm too tired to argue, much less disagree.

Sheela and I are quiet in the car. We're sitting in the back seat, as far away from each other as possible. Mathur's driving. It's almost 2:00 a.m. When we finally arrive at Sheela's house, every light in is on. She looks at me.

"You'll stay for a little while?" she asks. There's a tremor in her voice.

I hesitate because of how it was the last time I was here, alone with her. I'm not impervious to her charms. Tonight, though, she and I have been through a catastrophe we could never have imagined, and I'm sympathetic to her need to talk to someone, someone who experienced what she experienced tonight.

When she says, "Please," I ask Mathur to wait in the drive until I return.

Asha opens the front door and cries out, "Oh, MemSahib, please come inside. Samir Sahib called Mrs. Singh to let her know you are all right. It must have been so terrible! Mrs. Singh said she would keep the children tonight so you can rest. I was to wait for you, then go back to her house so I can take care of Rita and Baby in the morning."

Sheela nods faintly. Her sari is in tatters. Her hair is disheveled. The *ayah* hesitates. "*Ji*, there is blood on your arm. Shall I get a plaster?"

Sheela looks at her arm as if seeing it for the first time. "It's someone else's blood," she says.

The *ayah*'s eyes go wide, but she says nothing more about it. "I will serve the food," she says. She locks the front door and steps around us to head to the kitchen, barely giving me a glance.

Sheela looks at me, as if to see if I want dinner. I shake my head.

"Asha," she says, "we're not hungry. You can go."

The maid turns, her expression puzzled. Sheela shakes her head again. Then, with a quick glance at me, Asha heads down the hallway, to the back door where she'll leave this house and walk the hundred yards to Samir Singh's.

Sheela steps into the library. At the mirrored cocktail cabinet, she fills two glasses with Laphroaig. I'm still standing in the foyer when she holds out a glass to me. After everything that happened at the movie house, the frenzy and the chaos of it all, my body is too tired to move.

"Come," she says.

I step into the room. "Thought you couldn't stand the stuff."

"Don't believe everything you hear," she says.

I take the glass from her. We sip the whiskey; this is not a night for offering a toast.

Now she smiles. "You're a right mess."

"Look who's talking," I reply.

I turn her by the shoulder so she can see her own face in the mirror over the fireplace. She looks at her reflection: face covered in dust, her blouse torn at the shoulder, her tattered sari, a tendril of hair that seems to be standing at attention while the hair on the other side of her head looks flattened. She takes a deep breath in, then lets out a whoop of laughter.

Her laughter takes me by surprise, and hearing it is a relief. *This* Sheela, this disheveled girl who's laughing at herself, is a reprieve from everything that happened earlier tonight. It almost makes me happy. At fifteen, a privileged girl with rosy cheeks who thought herself a queen, she was too good to tolerate my presence. But at this very moment, I can almost believe I'm seeing the real Sheela, the one without polish, without pretense.

With her glass of scotch, Sheela gestures to my pants, ripped at the knees and covered in grime. We do look a mess: a pair of ruffians, or beggars. She covers her mouth with her hand to keep from spitting out her liquor. Then she starts to hiccup, and it's one more thing we find hilarious. Now we're doubled over, giggling. We're in tears, because we're giddy and exhausted. And we're still alive, despite the mangled bodies, and the blood, and the tears and pain. It's hard to believe it really happened, even if we saw the chaos for ourselves, the people suffering and people helping others, even when they couldn't know if more was coming—more destruction, more suffering, more death.

When we finally stop laughing, Sheela wipes her eyes. Her *kajal* has smudged her face so that the area beneath her lower lids looks bruised. She studies her ruined makeup in the mirror, suddenly serious. Then she takes another gulp of scotch and glances at me.

"People died," she says.

"Only one," I say. *So far.*

She raises one eyebrow. "And that's supposed to be a comfort?" She goes over to the cabinet to fill her glass again. "I saw that boy—the one whose tibia was smashed. He's Rita's age. And that actor, who plays everybody's favorite grandpa—

Rohit Seth. Millions of his fans will miss him…" She takes another sip of her drink. "How many injured? Forty? Fifty? This calamity will… There will be consequences. None of this will go away."

Sheela has that look I'd seen on the faces of Omi's children when they were feeling hurt and didn't know what to do about it. The feeling of betrayal, when things went wrong, or didn't happen in the way they expected. Tonight was supposed to be Ravi's triumph. And she had stayed to help knowing full well that her husband was with another woman, oblivious to what's happened. She must know that the others in their circle—the tennis club, golf club, the polo club—know about it, too.

When one of Omi's children was confused, or sad, I'd sing a song and rub their back until they fell asleep. I can't do that with Sheela, but I think of the remedy Auntie-Boss taught me years ago.

"Come," I say, and take her elbow. "Do you have lavender oil?"

She frowns at me as, not sure why I'm asking. "Ye-es?"

"Good." But in my head, I hear warning bells: *Bevakoopf! Her husband isn't home. Remember the last time you were alone with her? Can you trust yourself?* I answer my own questions: she's spent, traumatized, she needs comfort. I'm doing nothing more than drawing her a bath.

She's a little unsteady and lets me lead her, drink in hand, upstairs. She points to their bedroom. I gently sit her down on the bed, covered in white satin. Then I remove my jacket, roll up my shirtsleeves and go into her bathroom, where I turn on the faucet to fill the bathtub.

I'm not surprised to see the bathroom's made for comfort. Samir designed it, after all. The claw-foot tub is generously sized. It's made of porcelain and occupies at least a quarter of the room. White Carrara marble he must have imported from Italy covers the floor and the walls.

In the cupboard, I find a box of English bath salts and an indigo bottle of lavender oil; I dump a handful of salts into the steamy water, and a capful of the oil, then I go back to the bedroom. Sheela hasn't moved. She's sitting, staring at the Persian carpet; her glass of scotch now empty.

I put my hands on my knees and bend at the waist so we're looking at each other eye to eye, the way I might approach a child. "Let's get you in the tub."

She stares at me, uncomprehending. I help her to stand and point her to the bathroom. Then I pick up my jacket, *salaam* her and leave the room.

I'm at the bottom of the stairs before a chilling thought occurs to me: since we arrived, she's put away two healthy glasses of the scotch, and she's been drinking on an empty stomach. If no one else is with her, might she drown?

I run back up the stairs and into her bedroom, throwing my jacket on the empty bed. The voices in my head are screaming now: *Bevakoopf! Mat karo!* The bathroom door is open, and I step inside. Sheela's hands are holding on to the sides of the tub, but the rest of her, including her head, is under water.

"Sheela!" I run to the tub, grab her under her arms and haul her up.

"What?" she says. She sounds annoyed. She can see from my expression that I'm panicked, and it makes her chuckle. "I was only wetting my hair. In any case, you're just in time to shampoo it." She's slurring her words.

I'm looking at her naked body, when I wonder what I'm doing here, and back away as if I've just been scalded. The cuffs of my shirt and suit coat are soaked, and my hands are dripping water on the sari, blouse and petticoat she was wearing tonight, lying next to the tub.

She raises her eyebrows and points. "Abbas," she says, "shampoo!" Now she is the girl with the cut-glass surface: imperious and spoiled. But then she looks at me, offers me a playful smile and says, politely, *"Please."* She points me to the shelf above the sink, where I can see the shampoo bottle. It's as if the Sheela that I'm dealing with tonight has two sides: the first haughty, used to giving orders to the help, and the second needy, wanting company and consolation.

"And if Sahib comes home?"

"He won't," she says. "He has a thing for actresses."

She sinks under the water again as if to put an end to any conversation about Ravi. When she comes back up, she wipes her face with her palms.

I've spent a lifetime serving others. I'm good at it, and always have been. But only so long as it serves me, too. I do it gladly, willingly, when I can see the benefit. When the benefit is questionable, or when there might be consequences, I weigh the two. Usually, the end result is a zero sum. *What's the harm?* I ask myself. It doesn't make me lesser if I'm helping someone who's in need of a simple service I can provide.

I sigh, take off my jacket again—now mostly wet—and roll up my shirtsleeves again. I take the shampoo bottle from the shelf and stand behind her, squeezing a generous amount of shampoo onto her scalp.

"Where'd you learn how to make a tourniquet?" I ask. A question I've been pondering all evening; how she knew just what to do, despite the chaos.

"Maharani Latika taught us at the Maharani School for Girls. She taught us Western dancing, how to set a table for ten guests and how to save a life in an emergency."

Sheela cleans under her fingernails while I massage her scalp. "She'd boarded in Switzerland for school, and guess where the Red Cross started?"

She turns her head to look at me.

"Close your eyes," I tell her, "or I'll get shampoo in them."

She closes her eyes and faces front again like an obedient child. "I was good at all the medical stuff. I could have been a doctor."

"What stopped you?"

She sighs. "My father wanted me to marry Ravi so his business could be merged with Singh Architects. And I *wanted* to marry Ravi."

She takes gardenia soap from the tray attached to the tub. It takes two tries because the alcohol has slowed her down. Now she's using it to soap her arms.

"He was such a prize, Abbas. Every girl I knew was hoping to land Ravi as her husband. But I was determined to win. The marriage was arranged when I was fifteen, but his family sent him off to England and we had to wait until he finished his degree."

My ears are burning, now, with indignation. *They sent their son to England to conceal his dalliance with Radha and the son he fathered with her.* I'd like to say it, but I don't. I don't want anyone to know that Niki's illegitimate. It's better that he's with the Agarwals than with the Singhs. Of that, I've always been sure.

Sheela rinses the soap off her arms. "Abbas? What will happen now?" The tremor is back in her voice.

I don't know any more than she does. I've seen rickshaw drivers get a leg smashed by a passing motorist. I've seen drunks fall off the second story of the Pink City bazaar. But I've never seen anything like tonight's catastrophe. "Close your eyes," I tell her.

"Yes, Sahib."

"Lean forward." I open both the bathtub taps and fill the steel container that was sitting on the floor with warm water. I pour the water on her head and watch the suds fill up the tub. The fact that I no longer see her breasts, or the dark triangle of hair between her thighs, is a relief. I realize the feeling that I've been having is guilt—as if to look at Sheila's naked body is to cheat on Nimmi. But now that feeling starts to ease.

"It isn't Ravi's fault, you know," she says.

I rinse the remainder of the soap from her hair. "What's not?"

"The cinema. Tonight." She turns to face me, the water from her wet hair splashing my face. "I want to show you something." And before I know what's happening, she climbs out of the tub, grabs a thick white towel from the rack and wraps it around herself. She runs into her bedroom, still a little unsteady on her feet.

When I open the drain to let the water empty from the tub, the vision of her rising from the water—supple buttocks, slim waist, caramel-colored legs—is seared into my brain. I can hear her in her bedroom, rummaging through her dresser drawers.

"Here it is!" I hear her say. Just as suddenly, she's standing next to me, her scented body, her warm, damp skin, the water dripping from her hair. She's pointing to a piece of paper that she's holding.

It's a transcript from Ravi's final year at Oxford. "See? He's very good in math and material sciences. He understands how buildings work, and how to make them strong. There's no way he'd have anything to do with the disaster we went through tonight. He *couldn't* have. He *didn't*."

Her eyes are begging me to agree with her. I know she wants me to absolve her husband. But I can't stop thinking of those bricks I saw at the cinema house tonight. Why were they there? If they came from somewhere other than Chandigarh Ironworks, how did they end up in the Royal Jewel Cinema? There's something off there. I just don't know what it is. And there's no way I can confide in Sheela. She loves her husband—I can see that plainly—and will do anything he asks of her. I also see the question behind her question—*What if he has done something wrong?* I don't know. And the answer, when it comes, could hurt those who are dear to me. I'm thinking about Manu and Kanta. And Niki.

"I have to go," I tell her, gathering my jacket and walking to the door.

She calls out to me and I stop to listen but don't turn around.

"Thank you," she says.

As I descend the marble stairs, I'm rolling down the cuffs of my shirtsleeves. Ravi rushes in through the front door and runs directly into the drawing room. He calls out, "I heard about the—"

He comes back out of the drawing room and sees me coming down the stairs. "What are you doing here?"

The sight of him—disheveled, frightened, in a panic—fills me with disgust. Where was he when we were taking care of people injured in the building he built, the project he's been boasting about?

"Taking care of your wife." I button the sodden cuffs of my shirt as I come near him. "You can take over now."

His mouth twists into an ugly frown. "You! You stay away from Sheela," he says. "Think I haven't seen how you look at her?"

Now I'm standing right in front of him, putting on my damp coat. Ravi smells of alcohol and cigarettes. His eyes are bloodshot. His hair, usually slicked back with Brylcreem, falls in tendrils across his forehead.

I take the cotton handkerchief from my pants pocket and dab the wet patches on my coat. I take my time, letting him wonder why my coat is damp. Then I raise my chin. He's taller than I am, but that doesn't stop me looking him in the eye.

"*You* should look at her more often, Ravi." I push his chest lightly.

He stumbles back, as if I've slapped him.

I step around him. When I reach the front door, I turn.

"Sheela helped a lot of people at the cinema tonight. Now it's your turn."

The sedan is waiting for me when I walk outside. When I step inside the car, I realize I've brought the scent of Sheela's gardenia soap with me.

AFTER THE COLLAPSE

All India Radio Bulletin

May 13, 1969

Last night, a balcony at the newly constructed Royal Jewel Cinema in Jaipur collapsed, killing two and injuring forty-three others. Over a thousand people were in attendance for the grand opening of the much-anticipated building, a wholly modern theater with a screen to rival Mumbai's biggest cinema house and surround-sound technology straight from the United States. In the opening remarks, Maharani Latika of Jaipur, who initiated the four-thousand-lakh project built by the renowned Singh-Sharma Construction, called the Royal Jewel Cinema "an historic occasion for Jaipur, home to world-renowned architecture, dazzling textiles and jewels, and, of course, Rajasthani dal batti." Rumors of cost overruns and construction delays have been circulating for the past year. The palace expressed tremendous sadness at the loss of lives, one of whom was beloved veteran actor Rohit Seth. Mourners have laid flowers for him at the site of the tragedy. The other victim has yet to be identified. A formal statement is expected from the Jaipur Palace later today about possible reasons for the catastrophe and anticipated remedies. The actors

ALKA JOSHI

Dev Anand and Vyjayanthimala, who were present for the showing of
Jewel Thief, *the first film to premiere at the cinema, were unharmed,*
having left at the beginning of intermission. It's not clear how soon the
Royal Jewel Cinema will reopen for business. We will bring you further
developments throughout the day.

18

MALIK

Jaipur

It's the morning after the Royal Jewel Cinema tragedy; the street sweepers have not yet started swiping at the dust with their long-whiskered *jharus*. After only a half hour of exhausted, numbing sleep, I wake with a start, the images of horror that I'd witnessed coming back to me: a man's leg bent in an unnatural angle; the fleshy arm of a matron pierced with rebar, gushing blood; a gaping wound on a child's forehead. In the night, I got up several times to pace my room, drink another glass of water, look out the window at the street—deserted but for stray dogs settling to sleep in the cool night dust.

Then the images of Sheela Singh's naked hip, her brown nipple, float through my mind. What will Ravi say the next time he sees me? Will he tell Manu I was trying to seduce his wife? It isn't true, but Ravi wouldn't hesitate to stir up trouble—for Manu or for me—if it took the heat off him. Another thought: Does she know something about Ravi's role in the construction? Is that why she was defending him to me? Or was she pardoning him for something he'd done?

It's six o'clock, but what's the use of trying to sleep in when sleep won't come? I've been home three hours. I meant to call Auntie-Boss to tell her I'm all right, but the guesthouse has no phone. I'm sure Kanta would have called Lakshmi the moment she got home last night. I worry about Nimmi. She can't read the *Hindustani Times*, but she'll surely hear about what happened from the Aroras or from vendors at Shimla Mall, or from Lakshmi the moment Auntie-Boss finds out.

I bathe, then head off to the office just before eight. Employees usually traipse in between nine and nine thirty, but today, almost all of them are at their desks when I arrive.

Last night was a big occasion for the palace, and most of the facilities staff were present at the event. As I pass through, I nod to colleagues here and there. Engineers and secretaries huddle in clusters, talking quietly among themselves. The mood is somber, thick with uncertainty. Like me, they're probably assuming Manu will call for an all-hands meeting about last night's events to find out what went so wrong that the balcony could fail. Will there be an investigation, or an inquiry? Who pays for the injuries? Who among us is responsible in some way or another for the accident?

I settle at my desk and ask the operator to dial Auntie-Boss. It's long-distance, but I don't think Hakeem or Manu would object. I let the phone ring several times, but no one answers. So I call Kanta Auntie, who picks up at the first ring. She sounds drained, as if she, too, has not slept well, but she's relieved to hear from me. She tells me that she spoke to Lakshmi last night, who promised to take the first train out from Shimla. I'm to pick her up at the train station this evening.

The news that Auntie-Boss is coming down floods me with relief. She's someone I can always count on to keep a level head during a crisis.

As Kanta chatters on, I see the Maharani Latika leaving the conference room on the far side of the floor. Her eyebrows are drawn in a frown. On either side of her are gentlemen in suits. My guess is they're her lawyers. Her Highness's face is slightly flushed, as if she's angry. Samir Singh and Ravi, shoulders slumped, follow her out of the conference room, and after them come Manu and two of his engineers. I interrupt Kanta to tell her I'll stop by later and hang up.

Neither of the Singhs looks my way, which is just as well; I'm still irritated by Ravi's late appearance last night and his callous disregard of Sheela's feelings. He must have known she'd figure out where he'd been. Did he even bother to make up some excuse or just ask for her forgiveness?

At the front doors of the facilities offices, Her Highness stops and turns to shake the hand of everybody behind her. She's as tall as every man, and her presence is commanding. A turbaned attendant dressed in white holds open the double doors while she goes through; he must be from the palace. Manu and his engineers watch everybody leave, then Manu says a few words to them before releasing them to return to their desks. When he catches my eye, he gestures with a pointed finger toward his office.

I step outside the office to buy two small glasses of tea from the chai-*walla* across the street. Then I bring the tea to Manu's office as he's draping his suit on a coatrack in the corner.

"Close the door," he says.

I set the chai on his desk and do as he says.

It's eighty-five degrees outside, but Manu is warming his

hands on the steaming glass when I sit down opposite him. His skin is sallow. There's a fresh cut on his cheek where he must have nicked himself shaving. He looks like a man being sent to his funeral pyre before his time. Does he think what happened yesterday is his fault?

He is staring at his tea as he says, "Last night was a tragedy no one could have anticipated. Kanta called Lakshmi to let her know what happened and that you were okay."

I nod.

"Mr. Reddy confessed to selling far more tickets than the balcony could support. He'd been instructed to limit the number, but so many people wanted a glimpse of the actors onstage that he…" Manu throws up his hands as if he were the theater manager giving up on the situation. "Singh-Sharma will pay for a new balcony—time and materials—and replace anything else that was damaged, and the palace will pay the medical bills for the injured. They'll also look at compensation for families of the deceased. Nevertheless…"

He downs his tea in one gulp, then sets his glass carefully on his desk as if he doesn't want to mar the mahogany finish. Finally, he meets my eyes. "Everything is settled. We will make a formal announcement about who will pay for what. Reporters called my house last night for comment, but I had to clear what we'd say publicly with Her Highness." He attempts a smile.

I can tell he feels enormous guilt. "It wasn't your fault, Uncle. It sounds like the theater manager is to blame."

Manu clears his throat and fiddles with the pens on his desk. He doesn't look at me. "Well, the maharani is beside herself. And with good reason." He scratches the top of his head delicately, with one finger, where a bald spot is growing. "Two casualties. One woman. And Rohit Seth—the actor. His fans are in an uproar. Can't blame them. This shouldn't have happened, Malik."

Manu picks up the glass again, realizes it's empty and sets it down. I haven't taken a sip from mine, so I push it toward him. He clutches it as if it's a lifeline.

"Uncle…" I pause delicately. "Wasn't Mr. Reddy recommended by Singh-Sharma? If he let more people into the theater than was safe, why aren't they paying the medical costs, as well?"

He shrugs. "We share the burden—that's business." He finishes the second cup of chai and pushes himself away from his desk, as if we're finished. "Now go help Hakeem. He has work for you."

"But…what about the bricks?"

He blinks and rubs his chin roughly. "What about them?"

"I noticed all these bricks in the debris after the collapse. What happened to the cement that was invoiced? And the bricks— they're different than the ones your engineers recommended on the specs. The bricks I saw last night were lighter weight—more porous. With no logos stamped on them. Could the supplier be held accountable for delivering the wrong material?"

Manu frowns, waves his hand as if what I've said is of no consequence. "They are a small player in all of this. Even if we hold their feet to the fire, they won't be able to compensate us for so much damage and injury." He straightens some papers on his desk. "There will be an official inquiry, which could answer some questions. But nothing for you to worry about. Go work with Hakeem now." He stands up.

As I turn to leave, he says, his voice shaky, "I hate what this is going to do to Kanta. To Niki. They've been so proud of me. Now…everywhere they go…people will ask them about what happened. The shame… I don't want them to have to explain or apologize." He wipes his forehead, sweaty from the tea, with the flat of his hand.

I want to comfort this gentle man who has always been kind to me, to Auntie-Boss and to Radha. But I'm twenty to his forty. It would be unseemly for me to pat his shoulder or tell him everything will be all right when I know so little about this business. Still, I'm touched that he's treating me like a member of the family, entrusting me with his deepest fears.

"Kanta Auntie will manage. And given your son's batting, I'd say Niki can more than take care of himself. Besides, you've got me on your team—don't forget!" I chuckle lightly.

His smile is faint, but it's there.

I pick up the tea glasses to return them to the chai-*walla*. My heart is heavy with Manu's burden—the pain of the injured, the disappointment of the maharani.

I also realize I'm angry at the injustice of it all. Manu's signature is on everything. He'll be held responsible for the greatest calamity Jaipur has known in decades. The Singhs will walk away with only a portion of the blame. And Manu is right: Kanta and Niki will pay the price, too. Auntie-Boss always says gossip-eaters have sharp teeth. They will chew on this tragedy for years to come.

Manu has the air of a defeated man; he's already given up. It doesn't seem fair. Surely there's something I can do to help.

Thank Bhagwan Auntie-Boss will be here tonight. I can talk all this over with her.

On the way to my desk, I knock on Hakeem's office door.

"Uncle," I say, "you're in early."

The accountant looks up from his ledger, the overhead light glinting off his eyeglasses. "Mr. Agarwal asked me to come in before regular hours. After last night, we have much to do." He takes off his glasses to polish them with his spotless white handkerchief. "Such a tragedy! My daughters had nightmares last night."

I hadn't remembered seeing Hakeem with anyone but Mr. Reddy.

"Everyone got home safely, I trust?"

"Barely. Every rickshaw, motor, *tonga*—all were taken. So many people trying to escape! Fights were breaking out. I was afraid I'd lose one of my girls. We held hands and had to muscle our way through the crowds. It took us the better part of three hours."

I lean against the door frame. "What do you think caused it?"

Hakeem runs a finger under his mustache. "Mr. Agarwal tells me there were too many people on the balcony. Yes?"

Now I come into the room, stand in front of his desk. "But how could such a collapse happen because of the weight of a few extra people, Hakeem Sahib?"

"I'm told it was more than a few. More like a hundred extra."

I take a moment to digest this. "Still, don't the engineers *over-build*...just in case? To compensate for human folly? Aren't there standards that have to be met for the overbuild?"

Hakeem shrugs his rounded shoulders. "Who knows? We are accountants, not detectives. We need to put together a report on the building expenses associated with the damage, post-haste. Yes? We are to make a list of all the materials used and the suppliers we paid and how much we spent. You'll work on the seats, carpets, decorative materials that will have to be replaced. Singh Sahib asked me to work on the cost of the construction materials for the repair and rebuild."

"You mean Manu Sahib?"

"No, young Abbas. Ravi Sahib gave the order. Mr. Agarwal is in charge of all palace facilities, but since the larger building projects are often contracted out to Singh-Sharma, it feels like we work for them, too."

Does Manu know Ravi gives orders to his staff? Isn't that a conflict of interest? If Mr. Sharma hadn't had a stroke and both Singhs weren't in charge, I wonder if protocols would have been different. "So we'll be estimating all the materials costs for replacement purposes?"

He shoots a glance at me as if I'm simple. "Yes."

I clear my throat. "You're so busy, Uncle," I say. "I can help you with your estimates if you'd like."

"Mr. Ravi asked me especially, yes? And you, Abbas, have your own assignment. Go." He waves his hand at me, as if he is shooing a fly.

"But...couldn't the collapse have been caused by something other than overcapacity? Substandard materials, for instance? A compromised structure?"

Hakeem frowns at me, sets down his fountain pen and leans forward on his elbows. "Think about what you're saying, Abbas. Singh-Sharma is a very trusted contractor. The palace has been working with them for decades. And they've used the same materials suppliers for years. Trusted companies, reliable companies. There is no need to cast aspersions on them."

"Surely there have been some changes in suppliers over the years?"

He sighs. "Abbas, did I mention I have four daughters? The oldest will be ready for marriage soon. The rest will follow. Yes? How will I be able to afford their dowries unless I'm sitting behind this desk, adding up the numbers Mr. Singh wants me to?"

I ignore his frustration. I know what I saw, and none of it makes sense. I need to tread carefully in case Hakeem thinks I'm blaming him for sloppy paperwork or casting doubt on Manu's ability to manage the project. "Maybe Singh-Sharma used a new supplier, and they delivered materials different from the design specs—by accident. Have we added or changed any suppliers in the last year?"

Hakeem glares at me over his glasses. "You have much to learn, young man."

I give him my most charming smile. "What if I agree to marry your eldest *without* asking for a dowry?"

His lips twitch. I've made the little accountant *almost* smile!

He narrows his eyes, shakes his head. He reaches for his Rolodex and flips through the cards. He stops at one. "Let's see…this one's new. Yes. We added Chandigarh Ironworks thirteen months ago. They beat out our former supplier by twenty percent."

I whistle. "Twenty percent is a steep discount."

He raises his brows, taps the card. "Hmm. It is."

"They supply iron rebar?"

He shakes his head. "Used to. These days they supply us with bricks and cement."

I don't ask to see the contract with Chandigarh Ironworks. Hakeem wouldn't show them to me; he's already wary of my questions. Naturally, I wait until he leaves for the day and then I slip inside his office. I don't have to collect Auntie-Boss from the train station for another hour and a half.

It's fortunate for me that Hakeem is an organized accountant: everything is neatly labeled, all receipts are kept. I find the contracts cabinet and open the top drawer. Each contract is filed under the vendor name, which is listed in alphabetical order. I find the folder labeled Chandigarh Ironworks and pull it out. Inside I find an invoice that indicates they are indeed located in Chandigarh, in the state directly north of Rajasthan.

Hakeem told me this was a new contract, so I want to compare the terms with the previous supplier, but I don't know the name of the previous supplier. One way to find the company name is to look at paid invoices from thirteen months ago or beyond. But invoices don't always list the name of the project, and there are so many overlapping projects in which the palace is involved. Until I started working for Manu, I didn't know about the various renovations to the Rambagh Hotel, the Jaipur Palace and the Maharanis' Palace or that the royal family was buying smaller estates (from Rajputs who could no longer afford to keep up their properties) and turning them into boutique hotels. And, of course, the design and build of the Royal Jewel Cinema was an extensive construction project three years in the making.

The better option, I decide, is to look through the individual folders of suppliers. I sigh and get busy. I start by looking for suppliers whose names indicate they might sell bricks instead of electrical or plumbing or interior furnishings. There are many names ending in "building supply" or "materials," so I review the contracts in each folder to see whether they're still an active source for one of the palace's projects.

An hour later, I run across the folder for Shree Building Materials in Jaipur. The contract, which was for supplying class 1 bricks, ended the day the Chandigarh Ironworks contract went into effect. I understand why the palace would insist on top-of-the-line materials free from cracks, chips, stones and other flaws. The Chandigarh Ironworks contract likewise promised to supply class 1 bricks.

I lean back in Hakeem's chair and think about this. I don't understand how Chandigarh Ironworks could deliver the same quality as the previous supplier for *less* cost when they would have to add in transportation fees. Chandigarh is, after all, five hundred miles away!

And something else that's puzzling: the bricks from the cinema house—the ones I picked up and examined—weren't construction quality. They can't support load-bearing structures like the balcony. So who authorized their use?

I examine the signatures on both contracts—Shree Building, and Chandigarh. Manu Agarwal and Samir Singh on the previous contract; Manu Agarwal and Ravi Singh on the current contract. It is palace policy to sign off on all contracts for their building projects and keep the original for auditing purposes. Singh-Sharma would have a copy in their files also.

But the bigger question is why brick was even being used.

From the palace engineers I'd learned that cement concrete reinforced with rebar—a far stronger material—is preferred for load-bearing columns. Bricks are used only in conjunction with cement concrete. Was inferior cement the problem? If I asked Ravi, would he just manufacture false invoices—like he did before? I dare not ask Samir, who would be quick to cover Ravi's tracks if he thought his son had done anything untoward. Now I remember that Samir made no comment about the bricks when he and I talked at the cinema house last night.

I realize I need to find and take another look at those receipts for the bricks and cement—the ones Hakeem thought I'd entered incorrectly earlier. The same ones I'd then taken to Ravi, who merely crossed out one figure and inserted another. I get up from the desk and go to the ledger where I recorded the invoices weeks ago. Then I look around for the cabinet where paid invoices are kept in chronological order. I spot it and search by date, grateful for once to Hakeem for his annoying meticulousness. For there, attached to the invoice for that time period, are the receipts in question, the ones I need. Here is the receipt from Chandigarh Ironworks for the purchase of bricks and cement. Except...these receipts are clean, unmarked. These aren't the ones on which Ravi had transposed the quantities with his fountain pen.

Quantities... I double-check them. They've been switched! These receipts show more cement being purchased than bricks, the opposite of what I'd noted previously. That should mean the ledger won't agree. But am I right? I run to Hakeem's desk and check the open ledger. The amounts there match those on the receipts in my hand. How could that be?

I lower Hakeem's gooseneck desk lamp to take a closer look at the ledger. Hakeem's penmanship is so precise the numbers look like they were typewritten instead of formed in ink (Hakeem, of course, has a special fountain pen specifically for this

227

purpose, which he forbids anyone else to use—yes!). Someone has carefully scraped off the old entry with a fine razor blade and inserted the new figures. I recognize this old trick from my time at Bishop Cotton. It's how certain boys changed their test scores when the masters weren't looking.

But why in the world have the entries and the receipts been changed? And who changed them?

I can think of only two explanations: the original receipts were incorrect and had to be updated. *Or*—and this one makes the hair on my arm stand up—someone has doctored the information to match what *should* have happened—that more cement concrete should have been used to shore up the balcony. If the right amount had been used, there would have been no collapse.

I drum my fingers on Hakeem's desk. Manu said Mr. Reddy had admitted that he sold too many tickets, and the balcony was overcapacity. There had been more weight on the balcony than it could support.

So, was the theater manager telling the truth or had the receipts been in error?

I'm so lost in thought I don't hear his footsteps.

"Abbas?"

I look up, startled, from the ledger. Hakeem is standing in the open doorway to his office.

"Yes, Sahib?" I keep my voice calm, as if what I'm doing is entirely normal.

"What are you doing here?"

"I'm sorry, *Ji*. I've fallen behind in my estimate of the cinema house reconstruction. I found your door unlatched and thought that instead of carrying ledgers back and forth to my desk, I would do the work here. *Maaf kar dijiye*." I pull both my earlobes in apology.

He glances at the doorknob—*had he not shut the door properly?*—and brushes his mustache, frowning.

"Sahib, what are *you* doing here?" I'd learned this tactic long ago, when I was caught swiping a comb for Omi or candy for one of her kids from a stall at the Pink City bazaar. When under attack, it's best to counterattack.

"I left my umbrella here, yes? I was just at dinner with a friend who said it's supposed to rain tomorrow, and I don't like to catch a chill when it's wet."

"Good thinking. Yes." I pray he doesn't come any closer to examine the contracts, receipts and ledgers I've spread on his desk. I fight the urge to cover the paperwork with my hands.

He gathers his umbrella, which is leaning by the door. "Don't stay up too late. The work will always be there, young man. Yes?"

He gives me an indulgent smile. For now, at least, I'm his hardworking protégé.

"You're right, *Ji. Zaroor.*" I nod reassuringly at him and begin stacking the ledgers and papers.

As soon as I hear the front door click close, I drop my head in my hands. Will Hakeem tell Manu about my being in his office? I doubt it. Hakeem knows I'm at the palace offices as a special favor to Manu Uncle and it might be politically imprudent to call me out. But Hakeem might wonder if I've been telling him the truth.

And, if not, why.

I check my watch. Lakshmi's train should be arriving soon.

19

LAKSHMI

Jaipur

At the Jaipur train station, I look for the Agarwals' black Ambassador sedan. It's early evening, and I've been traveling for nearly eleven hours. But instead of their driver, Baju, Malik steps out of the driver's seat. I'm so happy to see him I feel like crying. I've missed him. He's wearing a crisp white shirt, sleeves rolled up to his elbows, and black trousers.

"I thought Kanta was sending Baju to pick me up," I say.

Malik offers me a strained smile. "Would I let you ride alone with that lech?" He's keeping his tone light, but I can sense he's holding something back. The whole of the Pink City must be buzzing with news of the cinema tragedy. I can only imagine the toll it's taking on the Agarwal family, the palace, the families of the injured.

Malik lifts my suitcase into the trunk of the stately sedan, which Kanta's father upgrades every five years on their wedding anniversary. This must be their third Ambassador. Her family has money, whereas Manu comes from humble beginnings. The palace provides Manu a driver and a Jeep for work, so Kanta and her mother-in-law can always have this sedan at their disposal.

After Malik helps me into the passenger's seat, I say, "Now, before you tell me what's going on, let me assure you that Nimmi misses you terribly, Rekha asks after you constantly, Chullu has started to speak and Jay is fine. Oh, he asks about you all the time, too."

He chuckles. That's better. I'm not going to tell him about Nimmi's outburst last night. I left the house early enough this morning that I didn't see her. (Was I trying to avoid her?) Either way, I had time on the train to think about what she said and whether there was any truth in it. Do I feel possessive about Malik? Yes, I do. I feel about him the same way I feel about my sister, Radha. I want both of them to do well, to develop their skills and use those skills in whatever way they wish. How could that be wrong? Why should I feel guilty for helping them along their path?

With Radha, I think I fell short. She met Pierre Fontaine at the Shimla Mall in her last year at Auckland House School. Pierre was twenty-eight—ten years older than Radha—and absolutely smitten with her. He knew nothing about her past, the baby she gave up for adoption at thirteen. He came to ask me for my blessing, which warmed me to him. He was thoughtful, kind. And French, of course.

Radha had studied French at Auckland and fallen in love, first with the language and then with Pierre. I would rather she had enrolled at college in nearby Chandigarh instead of marrying, but by then I knew how headstrong she can be; the more I fight her on an issue, the deeper she digs in. (I've often thought she's like the Himalayan balsam, a deceptively delicate flowering plant that's hard to tame.)

In the end, I gave Radha and Pierre my blessing. It seems to have worked out well. Radha trained at a fragrance house and became a perfumer. She was always good at mixing my henna paste, and testing the mixture with different oils, lemon juice and sugar to create the right silky consistency. And the scent of it was heavenly.

Radha has what she always wanted: a family. She sends me photos of her two adorable daughters—Asha, now two, and Shanti, four years old.

Malik slides in behind the steering wheel. "Nikhil has a cricket game tonight, so Kanta Auntie asked me to drive you there first. *Accha*, Boss?"

I tap his arm to reassure myself he's really here. *"Accha."*

Malik eases the Ambassador through the clog of cycle rickshaws, taxis and pedestrians. "Can't tell you how glad I am to see you. I called this morning but got no answer."

"Jay had probably left for work." I'm looking out the window, enjoying the choreographed chaos of the city: a lipsticked *hijra* on her way to the market, slim hips swaying; a wagon drawn by a bony laborer carrying old tractor tires; children flicking marbles on a dusty street corner—what Malik liked to do once upon a time in Jaipur.

Malik slows for a family of six balanced precariously on a motor scooter. "I want to thank you for taking Nimmi under your wing."

"Koi baat nahee. She's a hard worker. And I'm enjoy teaching Rekha how to read."

"I bet she learns fast, my little monkey." There is so much affection in his tone that it makes me smile. "Permission to talk frankly, Auntie-Boss?"

I turn to him and nod.

"I'm trying to piece together what happened at the cinema house the other night, and why. But every time I find something that doesn't look right to me, I get shut down. Samir, Hakeem and even Manu don't want me to pry any further."

"Well, it's not your job, is it, Malik? To investigate? Shouldn't you be concentrating on what Manu's teaching you?" For half a second, I wonder if Malik did something that got Manu in trouble. Not deliberately, but by accident.

"That's exactly what I *am* doing." Malik taps his horn at a woman carrying a basket of beans on her head. She moves to the side of the road. "After the collapse, I found these...chunks of bricks in the debris. Lots of them."

My ears perk up. He goes on to describe bricks similar to the ones I saw at Canara Enterprises.

"The project specifies cement mortar—not bricks—for the columns. I've examined the contracts. I'm *not* wrong. But no one wants to listen to me."

I'm listening. And what Malik's saying makes my heart race. He describes the ledgers where he enters figures; how the purchase receipts for bricks and cement were altered by Ravi right in front of Malik's eyes and then replaced in the files; how the numbers in the ledgers have been altered, too.

By the time he finishes, my palms are sweating and ideas are buzzing in my head like bees. I'm trying to connect the threads, but they come and go before I can make sense of them. I moisten my lips, realizing, only then, I'm parched, as if I haven't had a drink of water in days.

The car comes to a stop, and Malik turns off the ignition. When I look around, I see we're at the cricket grounds. A group of boys in cricket whites are milling about the field. It's dusk and the park lights have come on. A man with a whistle stands on the sidelines, refereeing the game. Malik reaches behind the front seat and grabs a thermos. He unscrews the top and fills it with steaming chai; the scent of cardamom, cinnamon and cloves fills the car. He hands me the cup, and I sip from it. The chai's delicious and sweetened just the way I like.

"May you live a thousand years," I say, *"and may every year have fifty thousand days."* I bless his thoughtfulness by placing my hand on his head.

He grins. "Okay if we just watch from the car? I think it's not a good idea to have you standing in public next to Niki with fifty of the Agarwals' closest friends." Of course, he's right. Indians with eyes the color of the ocean are unusual, and Niki's eyes are like mine, and like my sister's. The gossip-eaters would take notice.

We watch the game for a few minutes while I finish my tea. I'm thinking about what Malik has told me. I don't want him worrying about Nimmi, but I need to tell him some of what's been going on in Shimla.

"Baat suno," I say.

I tell him that two children found a sheep wandering the hills; how Nimmi recognized it as belonging to her brother's flock; that we found the flock—and her brother—and discovered that the sheep were carrying gold; how we brought Vinay's body on horseback to be cremated in town; and how we then delivered the gold to the next courier.

At each new piece of information, Malik's eyes widen and his breathing quickens.

"But… Nimmi's all right, isn't she? And Rekha and Chullu?"

Naturally, he's concerned for his *priya*. "For the moment, Nimmi and the children are staying with us. They're sleeping in your room. Jay is making sure they're safe."

Malik releases a long breath.

"The bricks you found in the rubble?" I say. "I saw a woman in Shimla making bricks that look like that," I tell him.

"Where?"

"At a small factory called Canara Private Enterprises—the place where I had to deliver the gold." I raise my eyebrows as if to ask, *Does that fit with what you know?*

Malik shakes his head. "Singh-Sharma buys their bricks from Chandigarh."

"From *Chandigarh*?" My heartbeat quickens.

"*Hahn.* Why?"

"The woman making the bricks told me that the truck that comes to pick them up goes to Chandigarh."

Malik drums his fingers on the steering wheel. "The bricks are made in Shimla, then taken to Chandigarh? That makes no sense," he says. "Chandigarh Ironworks is a huge company, with at least four brick kilns. They wouldn't need more bricks from a smaller supplier in Shimla."

Malik turns to face me. "Something else that I don't understand, Boss. Why would any large company working with Singh-Sharma sell them inferior materials? Contracts from a construction firm like Singh-Sharma are so lucrative. Any company that tried to skimp on quality would be shooting themselves in the foot."

Malik's right; cheating the company that fills your coffers makes no sense. "Is it possible this Canara Enterprises makes a kind of brick that can't be made in Chandigarh?"

"You mean they're using a special clay or some other material?"

He shrugs.

A tap on my window makes us both jump, and the tea from the thermos cup spills onto my sari.

"Sorry, sorry!" Kanta says, opening the passenger door. "You look like you've just seen a ghost!"

"I have!" I tell her. *"You."*

She laughs delightedly. Vivacious Kanta! How I've missed her! Aside from Jay, I haven't grown as close to anybody else in Shimla. But even as she's laughing, I can see anxiety etched in the wrinkles across her forehead. Her red lipstick contrasts vividly with her anemic complexion.

Malik grabs a towel from the trunk of the car and hands it to me so I can dab the damp spots on my sari. I step out of the car to hug Kanta. Over her shoulder, I see a boy in cricket whites, his cheeks flushed, smiling shyly, looking at me with his green-blue eyes. He is beautiful.

Kanta takes him by the elbow. He's nearly as tall as she is, and on his way to being taller.

"Lakshmi," Kanta says, "this is my son, Nikhil. Niki, meet the famous Lakshmi!" She beams at me. "He's heard so much about you, growing up, and now you get to meet!"

I laugh, approvingly. "Lovely to meet you, Niki. I've only had the pleasure of seeing you in photos."

The boy blushes and bends down to touch my feet. His movements are graceful, almost balletic. *Oh, Radha*, I think, *how you would love to know this boy.*

I can't stop staring at him. When I saw him last, he was an infant, and I couldn't have envisioned what he'd look like as he aged. The photos of the family that Kanta regularly sends me in no way do him justice. His ink-black hair, which he keeps brushing back, falls over those mesmerizing eyes. In his cricket uniform, standing with his legs apart (knee pads on), and his arms behind his back, he reminds me of the athletes featured in the pages of the *Hindustani Times*. The polo-playing, tiger-shooting Maharaja of Jaipur used to stand this way.

And just like that, I've traveled back to Jaipur, where I'm sitting on a raw-silk sofa in the palace of the dowager maharani, signing an agreement for this baby, Niki, to be adopted by the royal family as the crown prince.

Only it never happened.

When he was born, Radha—then just thirteen—refused to let him go. She'd never meant to give him up.

Soon enough, she realized she couldn't care for him—she was a child herself—and she asked Kanta and Manu to adopt him. I blink to keep my tears at bay. How close we came to losing Radha's son to the palace instead of seeing him here, now, basking in the warm embrace of loving parents, dear Kanta and Manu.

Kanta breaks my reverie. "Shall we go home and get you settled in, Lakshmi? Baju has been making lots of treats for you. He's hoping he can best the ones you used to make for me, the jealous sod!"

I let Kanta sit in the front with Malik so I can sit in the back with Niki and get to know my nephew.

Kanta's husband, Manu, greets us at the door to their trim, government-issued bungalow. I'm shocked at the change in him. Always a mild-mannered, pleasant fellow, he now looks beleaguered, harried. He has dark pouches under his eyes, which makes me think he hasn't slept in days. He settles his thick black-framed eyeglasses on the bridge of his nose before he asks after my health.

I drop my chin and assume a serious expression. "I hope Malik hasn't caused you too much trouble. I know that he can be a handful."

That, at least, elicits something resembling a smile.

"He's a joy to have around. He learns quickly. My staff have taken to him, as have I."

Catching sight of Niki behind us, Manu lights up. He calls his son to him and cups the back of his head. "How was your bowling today, Niki? Did you pitch some zingers to your competition?"

Niki laughs. "*Yar.* I did what Malik Uncle showed me. Sonny couldn't bat one of my burners today!"

Kanta tells Niki to take a shower and suggests her husband make Malik comfortable while she shows me to my room. We'll be having dinner in an hour.

In the guest bedroom, as I'm unpacking, Kanta drops the cheerfulness as quickly as if she were casting off a veil. "Oh, Lakshmi," she says, "I'm so glad you've come. Manu's worried, and I don't know how to help him." She suddenly looks ten years older. "He's never had a black mark on his work. Now he does, and it's a big one. I know he's innocent, but even I've wondered how he could have overlooked a detail so important."

"What exactly are they telling Manu? At the palace?"

She tugs at the fringe on the *rajai* covering the bed. "The maharani's lawyers questioned him for hours this afternoon about documents that bear his signature. They told him those documents confirm that he bears full responsibility. That his errors caused the accident, the loss of life. They seem to be insinuating he was cheating the palace by replacing quality materials with lesser ones and pocketing the difference in cost. The maharani has asked him not to return to work until the inquiry is complete." The *rajai* is coming undone as Kanta pulls on a thread. "Manu is devastated. Where are they getting all this information? It's as if someone is sabotaging him." She smiles sadly. "Saasuji is praying triple-time at her *puja* for him to be released from all this bad karma."

I sit on the bed next to her as she describes how quickly the news about Manu's alleged wrongdoing is spreading. "This evening, at cricket, the mothers I usually talk to didn't show. They probably thought that was kinder than ignoring me in person."

She wipes a tear with the end of her sari. "I worry about Niki. Some of the boys on the field tonight were saying things to him. I couldn't hear them, but I knew by the expression on his face that Niki was angry. I'm afraid it's only going to get worse. Soon they might start being openly hostile.

"I can't imagine what's going to happen at his convent school. He's been with those same classmates since he was this high." She holds a hand, palm down, three feet off the ground. "That's why I'm keeping him home from school. This is a small city with a lot of powerful people. And reputations can be ruined just like that." She snaps her fingers together.

I reach for her hand to comfort her. On the train, I had hours to think of possible ways to clear Manu's name, and an idea had occurred to me. "Kanta, do you think the maharani would still remember me?"

She raises her eyebrows. "How could she not remember you? You helped her through the worst depression of her life. She was so grateful she gave Radha that full scholarship to the Maharani School for Girls."

I make a face. "But we let that opportunity slip through our fingers. My sister only lasted one term. Once she got pregnant, she left. I've always felt bad about that."

"But don't forget! We got Niki as a result." She gives my hand a squeeze.

I smile. "And he's so lovely. You've raised him well. *Shabash*."

Kanta looks down at our hands, entwined now. "I don't know what we'd do without him. He's the light of our lives. Even Baju's. Remember how Baju and my *saas* used to make me drink rose milk before I lost my baby? Well, now he has Niki to feed rose milk to! Saasuji swears that's what gives Niki those rosy cheeks of his!" She laughs softly.

Now she flips my hands over so she can inspect my palms. I applied the henna to my palms a few days ago; the cinnamon color is still vibrant. I show her the monkey frolicking in his apple tree on one palm and the crocodile swimming in the water on the other.

"I've been teaching old folk tales to the daughter of a friend of Malik's. Recognize this one?"

"The monkey and the crocodile!"

"*Hahn.* I'm also teaching the little girl to write in Hindi. She can almost write *bundar* but so far she's helpless with *magaramaccha.*" I'm picturing her small fingers holding the chalk, trying her hardest to spell crocodile.

"Big word for a little girl!" Kanta grins. "Oh, Lakshmi, I do miss you and your henna! The hours we spent together talking and laughing. The babies you drew on my stomach when I wanted to get pregnant."

It had finally worked. Perhaps it was the sweet yam *laddus* I fed her to encourage the production of her eggs. Or maybe it was her belief that the paintings of babies on her belly would encourage a real baby to grow inside her. Sadly, in the end, she lost that baby and was never able to conceive another.

Kanta traces the pattern on my palms. "You will find Maharani Latika changed. You left for Shimla right after the maharaja sent their son to boarding school in England. Well, the boy never forgave his father for taking the title of crown prince away from him. Whenever they fought, Her Highness took her son's side and relations between the maharani and maharaja were never the same. They grew further and further apart until they were barely talking to each other. When the maharaja died, their son refused to come home for the funeral."

Kanta releases my hands. "Remember how Her Highness used to drive her Bentley round the city, wearing those fabulous sunglasses, tooting at people? No driver for her, no, thank you." She smiles at the memory as she pulls at the thread on the quilt again. "She's nowhere near as carefree as she used to be, Lakshmi. So serious now. No more *joie de vivre*." She shakes her head.

We're quiet for a while.

"Did Malik tell you that the actor Rohit Seth died in the collapse? All India Radio has been covering the tragedy all day long. How many people were injured. How Seth's fans feel. How Bollywood is reacting. I tried to confiscate the radio, but Manu grabbed it first and took it in his office. Been listening to it all day. Torturing himself." She tilts her head to one side and lets out a sigh. "I don't know how we're going to survive this."

"I know what the dowager maharani would recommend—stiff G&Ts all round!"

Kanta gives me a half-hearted smile.

"Lakshmi, has Malik told you...about Samir?"

I must look puzzled, because she continues. "I've seen Samir at the cricket grounds, watching Nikhil. I think he knows, Lakshmi. I don't know how, but I'm pretty sure Samir knows we're raising his grandson."

Twelve years ago, when Radha first found out she was pregnant by Ravi, she was so in love she was sure he would marry her. My sister believed he loved her as much as she loved him. She had no way of knowing that I had already arranged the marriage between Ravi and Sheela, that I was the matchmaker who facilitated the merging of two prominent Jaipur families—the Singhs and the Sharmas.

Both Samir and Parvati made it clear that they wanted nothing to do with their son's illegitimate child. After Ravi's engagement to Sheela, they couldn't hustle their son to England quickly enough, and Radha's baby became solely my responsibility. I reasoned that with the Singhs' relation to the royal family, if the baby were a boy, he could be considered for adoption by the palace as the new crown prince. I worked hard to arrange that adoption only to realize later how determined Radha was to keep her baby. But with the help of Jay—Dr. Kumar, as I knew him then—we changed the paperwork; the baby's heartbeat became an issue, and the palace adoption became null and void. The Singhs never knew that their grandchild ended up living only a few miles from their house.

As I'm mulling over this uncomfortable history, I feel a headache coming on. It's been a long day; I'm exhausted from the long train ride. I rub my temple. "But, Kanta," I say, "you know just as well as I do that the Singhs refused any claim to the baby. Why would Samir have a sudden interest in a child that he's ignored these past twelve years?"

"I don't know, but… I worry. Could he take Niki away from us?"

After years of trying for a baby, having several miscarriages and one stillbirth, Kanta had been so excited to become a mother. If I had to fight Shiva to keep Nikhil with the Agarwals, I would. "*Bukwas*. You adopted that baby legitimately. You have the papers to prove it."

A tear escapes the corner of Kanta's eye. "Papers based on false information."

I place my hands on Kanta's bony shoulders and turn her toward me, gently. "You mustn't think that way. Niki has the best parents, and the best home, any child could hope for. He's had more love from you and Manu than he ever could have had from the nannies and governesses at the palace. I will never let *anyone* take him away from you."

Her face crumples. She falls against my shoulder, sobbing.

Once again, I find myself promising something I'm not sure I can deliver.

20

MALIK

The next morning the area in front of the Royal Jewel Cinema is crowded. Female laborers in bright cotton saris, their bare feet covered in dust, are emerging from the building. The baskets on their heads are filled with rubble from the collapse. One by one, they dump their loads on the open end of a truck waiting at the front curb, then go back inside the cinema house for more. Men in *dhotis* are mixing dry cement and water in a wheelbarrow. Others are bringing damaged seats outside to be inspected. Can they be repaired, or do they need to be replaced with new ones? Can the mohair be resewn? Through the open lobby doors, I see a team of laborers erecting bamboo scaffolding so they can start work on the damaged balcony. Plasterers, painters, electricians and plumbers are milling about, their supervisors shouting orders. Women are using *jharus* to sweep the plaster and dust into containers of all shapes and sizes.

I see Ravi Singh with Mr. Reddy. Ravi, his face pinched, is pointing at the theater manager as Mr. Reddy holds his hands placatingly in a *namaste*, begging Ravi's patience or forgiveness. I move out of Ravi's sight line and quietly approach a woman who's just coming out of the cinema, balancing a basket filled with cement fragments, plaster, broken chunks of brick on her head.

"*Behenji*," I say softly. I call women close to my age "sister." The woman slows to look at me, uncertain.

"May I check your basket before you put the rubble on the truck?" I remove a rupee from my pocket and hold it out to her.

She wags her head yes. In the time it takes her to lower the basket to the ground, I put the coin in her hand; it swiftly disappears in her blouse.

Sifting through her basket, I pick a piece of indented brick with no logo that's three-quarters intact. I also pocket a chunk of cement; it's also too porous, which suggests the ratio of water to cement powder was incorrect. Manu's staff has told me more than once that they have to be vigilant with inexperienced laborers who might mix in too much water, which weakens the cement. I put my evidence in the cloth bag I've brought with me. Before I left the office, I stuffed the bag with engineering books, a clipboard and a sweater from the office, and use them now to hide the fragments I'm collecting. I help the woman put the basket back on her head, and as I do, I see Ravi coming toward me. I salaam him.

"Don't do that. You're interfering with her job and slowing her down." I can see he's furious. Is he still sore that I took Sheela home in the early hours of the morning after the collapse? He looks like he wants to punch me in the face.

I smile to show I intend no offense. "Apologies. I thought *be-henji* was about to drop the basket."

His eyes narrow. "What brings you here?"

"I'm putting estimates together for those theater seats that have to be repaired or replaced." I casually hang the cloth bag over my right shoulder.

He glances at the bag but makes no comment. "Haven't the palace engineers given you a list?"

"They have, but I thought it better to come here and see for myself. This is an important project. I want to get it right." I'm trying to sound earnest, helpful. Otherwise, I won't get the results I want.

His expression softens, slightly. Now he tries to strike a milder, friendly tone. "Look, old chap, why not come to dinner tonight? It's been too long. We can talk about this..." He indicates the scene around us. Is he trying not to call it the tragedy and disaster it actually is? "All will be made right in the end. You'll see. My father knows a lot of people."

No doubt his father has been busy, on the phone, talking to the palace lawyers, the media and his vendors, doing what he can to mitigate the damage to the reputation of his firm. Now that Samir is picking up the pieces, Ravi can assume a more relaxed attitude.

"What time?" I have no intention of staying for dinner, but at least I'll have an opportunity to talk to Samir.

"Eight o'clock. Mummi schedules dinner at the same time every night."

I check my watch; I've got time to finish what I need to do.

Back at the palace facilities office, I spend my lunchtime talking to one of Manu's engineers. He's single, about ten years older than me, and we often walk to the local street vendors to eat lunch together. After we've dug into our *palak paneer* and *chole*, I show him the materials I picked up from the Royal Jewel Cinema site.

He looks puzzled. "These are not to the specifications I saw in the documents for the construction of the cinema." He takes a bite of his *aloo parantha* and shrugs. "So many of us worked on that project. Maybe the specs changed when I was no longer involved. One of the other engineers may know more."

But I can't find one engineer who knows how the specs changed.

At the office, in the final hour of the day, Hakeem keeps me busy. I enter new invoices into the ledgers and reconcile accounts until my head is spinning. By the time the motor rickshaw drops me off at Samir's house, I barely have the energy to socialize. And there's every chance I might run into Sheela—something I'd prefer to avoid. (Even though Sheela won her battle for a house of her own upon her marriage, she agreed to the nightly dinner at her in-laws'.)

I've no sooner stepped inside the door when Sheela comes out of the drawing room, looking peeved. Her daughter Rita, in a yellow tutu this time, follows her.

"Did Ravi not come home with you?" Sheela makes it sound as if I'm Ravi's designated minder and have managed to lose him just to spite her. It's as if the tender moment we shared right after the collapse never happened. The Sheela standing right in front of me, her hand on one hip, is a stranger. Has she forgotten that I helped her take a bath two days ago when she was fragile and alone?

I shake my head in answer to her question.

Tonight, she's wearing a *salwar kameez* in a soft moss green that sets off the pink glow in her cheeks. A white *chunni*, embroidered with tiny green beads, falls gracefully across her shoulders. The fine cotton *kameez* hugs her breasts and hips and accentuates her flat stomach. The memory of her naked body rising from the bathtub makes me blush. She notices—a smile, or smirk, appears at the corner of her mouth.

I turn my attention to Sheela's daughter. I squat down until we're eye to eye. "Who is that, Rita?" I point to the plastic doll she's holding, upside down, in her fist.

The girl takes cover behind her mother. With some impatience, Sheela tells her to answer when a grown-up is talking to her. Rita sneaks a peek at me from behind her mother and holds her arm out so that I can see her doll—a full-figured woman, about eight inches tall, with blond hair. The doll is naked.

I look up at Sheela, who rolls her eyes. "Ravi's brother doesn't have a clue about what to give a little girl. So he sent his niece what *he* thought was an American Barbie doll. It's not. It's a Tessie doll."

Now Rita grins at me. A dimple appears on her chin. She looks much like her mother, but that chin is Ravi's. "You push her tummy and her hair gets big. See?" Rita pushes her tiny finger on the doll's stomach and, sure enough, the blond hair lengthens three inches.

When I hear the front door opening, I stand up and turn around. Samir comes in and hands his suit coat and his briefcase to the servant waiting to receive them. He smiles at his granddaughter.

"Rita," he says, "your doll is going to need a lot more than hair to cover herself."

The little girl examines her doll, turns her around and offers her to Samir. He chuckles and picks Rita up to kiss her cheek.

Sheela has both arms crossed against her chest. "Papaji," she says, "you can't keep Ravi at the office such long hours. His children hardly ever see him!"

Samir looks vexed, and then, just as quickly, smiles at her. He gives me a knowing look, as if he and I are coconspirators, and says, "But, Sheela, who will pay for tennis lessons and your club membership and Rita's ballet lessons?" He jiggles Rita, making her laugh. "Hah, *bheti*?"

Sheela presses her lips together, as if she's holding back a retort. She takes Rita from Samir, gives us both a look and stomps off to the dining room.

Samir beckons me to follow him. He leads us to his library and shuts the door. I remember being in this room when I was a boy. The built-in bookshelves, crammed with English, Hindi and Latin tomes. Red-leather armchairs. A hearth, always blazing with a fire in winter, is empty on this warm May evening.

I sit down in one of the two armchairs. Samir removes his gold cuff links and rolls his shirtsleeves to his elbows. "Ravi told me you'd be coming by. The tragedy at the cinema isn't quite what Manu had in store for your internship at the palace. A little too much excitement, wouldn't you say?" He opens a cocktail cabinet, unscrews a bottle of Glenfiddich and pours us each a measure of single-malt scotch.

"As they used to say at Bishop Cotton, *there's nothing quite like baptism by fire.*" I take the glass of scotch from him.

"Right-o," he says, holding up his glass as if to toast my wit, before he takes a healthy sip of scotch. Then he sits in the other armchair and rests his glass decisively on the arm as if he's come to a decision.

"Before we merged Singh Architects with Sharma Construction, we were a small firm that employed five draftsmen. Ten years later, we have fifteen architects and almost a hundred employees. As you know, when Mr. Sharma had a stroke, I took over all his duties. I do far less design now, and a great deal more management. Which is to say, I'm not so much involved in day-to-day decisions. Of course, I oversee the projects, but the...details..."

The scotch burns my throat but when I swallow it goes down

like honey. I can feel my jaw relax, and then the muscles in my neck. In Shimla, Dr. Kumar and I share a glass of scotch from time to time—Laphroaig's his brand, and I enjoy it—but I always have, and always will, prefer a good, cold beer.

Samir continues. "After Oxford, Ravi graduated from architecture school at Yale. He came back full of new and bold ideas about design. About construction. He's a natural, and people know it. Clients like him. So do our employees. And he manages his projects well."

Samir drains his glass and straightens in his chair.

I take another sip of scotch.

He smiles and points a finger at me. "Listening is the most important trait in business. I can tell you're good at it."

I'm also good at waiting. At first, I followed Auntie-Boss around the city until she noticed me. Eventually she started paying me to carry her supplies. Then I'd go with her to Jaipur's grandest houses, sitting on their lawns outside until she finished painting henna on the fancy ladies like Parvati Singh. Later, still, at the prestigious Bishop Cotton School for Boys, I waited patiently for classmates to accept my less desirable pedigree. It was hard at first, the hazing. A school-issued shoe stuffed with a garden snake. A toothbrush filled with sheep's wool. A school tie wound around my ankles while I slept. I didn't retaliate. Instead, I made myself useful. I knew Nariman liked American cigarettes; I got him some. Ansari preferred photos of naked women. Modi was into rare stamps. For me, it wasn't hard to find these items, as I'd once found Jaipur's best pistachios—the ones the palace chef preferred—all those many years ago. Overnight, I became valuable to the biggest bullies, and they stopped harassing me.

Now I swallow what's left in my glass and hold it up for Samir to refill. He seems relieved to have a task, something to distract him from his thoughts. He can't quite bring himself to tell me what he wants to tell me. I can see it's hard for him.

As he returns my replenished glass, he says, "Did Ravi tell you that he finished his two most recent projects well ahead of time? He did the ballroom and restaurant remodel of the Rambagh Hotel and, after that, developed that old Rajput estate on Civil Lines Road into a world-class boutique hotel."

I nod.

Samir sits down and takes a deep breath. "All of that is hard to do. So many variables, so many things to track—the weather, or materials that don't arrive on time. Days when workers don't show up. All sorts of things."

He reaches for the pack of Dunhill cigarettes on the table next to him. He shakes one free, then holds out the box for me. I take a cigarette. Back when I lived in Jaipur, he used to smoke Red and Whites, a less expensive brand. I make a note of the upgrade. As I've made a note of the nicer cars in his driveway.

He takes a gold lighter from his shirt pocket and lights our cigarettes. Once he's had his first, deep drag, he starts talking again.

"Accidents can happen," he says. "It's the law of nature. What happened at the cinema house is devastating, but…" He lets out a stream of smoke, taps his glass on the chair arm. "It's my name on the company, Malik." With his free hand, he points to his chest. "I don't allow gross errors on my projects. Not in judgment, not in code compliance, *never* in materials."

He leans forward now, his elbows on his thighs. "With the cinema project, I gave Ravi freedom to do things his way. Didn't want him thinking I didn't trust him to make the right decisions."

He locks his eyes on mine. "After the accident, I asked him to go through the books, the process, everything we did, what part the palace played. He did exactly that. And, honestly, I can't find any reason he would be at fault. He did it by the book. Every single thing. And yet…" He leans back against the leather armchair. "From what I hear, you're doubting him. And me. You're doubting my professional ability." Now his voice has taken on an edge. He sucks his cigarette, blows out a steady stream of smoke.

The liquor is worming its way into my brain. I take another look around the room. A rich man's room. The leather-bound books. The gilded clock. A rich man in a rich suit who wants me to protect his son. Now I understand why Ravi wanted me to come. It wasn't so we could make peace. It was to warn me.

I set my glass of scotch on his desk. "What is it I'm supposed to have done, Uncle?"

"Hakeem told me he found you in his office yesterday, snooping around. Ravi saw you lurking around the reconstruction site doing Bhagwan knows what. And—" he points his finger at me accusingly "—you've been asking questions of the palace engineers. Oh, don't look so surprised. I'd be a lousy businessman if I didn't keep my ears to the ground."

The hair on the back of my neck tingles. All at once, I'm back at Bishop Cotton, at the swimming pool, three upper-form boys forcing my head underwater. How did he find out I've been talking to the engineers at the palace facilities office? Has Hakeem been spying on me? Does everyone I've talked to go directly to Samir? Are *all* of them in his pocket?

I'm careful with my words. "All those years ago, you're the one who helped Lakshmi gain an introduction to the palace. You of all people know how she helped the maharani through a rough patch. Since that time, I've always felt a strong connection to the maharanis. I'm honored to be working on their behalf at the facilities office with Mr. Agarwal. I simply want to make sure that we're putting together a good and thorough estimate for reconstruction. That's all." I open my arms wide, palms up.

He taps the ash from his cigarette into the large brass ashtray on his desk, his voice buttery again when he says, "I completely understand. But any questions you may have about what you turn up should come to Ravi or to me. We can clarify important details you're unsure about. No need to waste your time talking to the palace engineers. They're too busy with their own construction projects to waste much time on ours." He shows me his most charming grin. "And besides, you and I, we're old friends. Surely you don't doubt me?"

In this rich man's room, I know only one thing for sure: a father and a son are bound by blood. Samir and Ravi have no kinship to me. I'm the odd man out. Samir would like me to believe he has my back, but I know better.

I return his smile, keeping my gaze steady on his face. "Let me understand something. I'm here tonight because you wanted to remind me of our friendship? The very friendship that forced Lakshmi out of Jaipur?"

Now his face becomes a slab of marble—grayish white. He manages a chuckle, as if I've told him an amusing joke. Once again he reverts to being the benevolent, good-humored Samir Uncle. "Nonsense!" he says. "You're here because I want you to experience the Singh hospitality."

I stub out my cigarette in the ashtray. "Thank you, but I'm afraid I have a prior engagement."

There's a sharp rap on the door. The knob turns and the door bursts open. Parvati steps inside the room, and I stand politely.

"There you are, Samir!" she says. "I didn't hear you come in." When she looks at me, her expression hardens. This is not the friendly face she put on for me when I was here for dinner just a month ago. Have Ravi and Samir told her I've been asking questions? She scans the room, taking in the scotch, the cigarettes. *Before* dinner?"

She stares at Samir until, reluctantly, he rises from his armchair. Then he goes to her until he stops, just inches from her face. She does not budge. He smiles and lightly gathers the *pallu* of her sari from behind and drapes it over her shoulder so it covers her like a shawl. It's a lover's caress, and I see her face soften.

"Lead on, MemSahib," he says.

The corners of her mouth turn up, but only slightly. She executes a graceful turn and exits through the open door.

When I turn to leave, Samir takes hold of my right elbow. In a voice I have to strain to hear, he says, "As far as Sheela is concerned, Ravi's always working late. *Accha?*"

I give him a cold stare. Like father, like son.

21

LAKSHMI

Jaipur

Back when I used to tend to the Maharani Latika's depression, my appointments at the palace were set by the older maharani's secretary. Malik and I would check in at the guard station at the entrance to the Maharanis' Palace before we were allowed inside. It was Samir Singh who helped secure my first audience with the Dowager Maharani Indira; she found my subsequent visits to the younger queen to be critical to Latika's recuperation.

But it's no longer possible for me to ask Samir to help me gain admittance to the palace. We've neither seen each other nor spoken in twelve years. Not to mention that the thing I've come to talk about with the Maharani Latika involves his firm.

This morning, I'm dressed in an ivory silk sari edged in a

wide emerald-green border and threaded with gold. My hair is perfumed with jasmine flowers and arranged in a low chignon at my neck. Other than my dark red lipstick, I have no makeup on. My jewelry is simple: a double-strand pearl necklace at my throat. My lobes are bare. I wear a watch with a black braided rope bracelet and no other jewelry on my arms or fingers. Long ago, I learned it's better, when you're sharing space with royalty, to affect a simple elegance, and never to upstage them.

The gray-mustachioed guard at the station might be the same one who was here a dozen years ago. It's hard to tell. All the palace guards, and all of the attendants, look alike: they wear the same red turbans, their white jackets tied at the waist with red cummerbunds, and white leggings. The younger guards are clean-shaven. All the older, seasoned ones have beards and mustaches.

This guard recognizes me. "Good morning, *Ji*," he says. "It has been a while. You are here to see the elder or younger maharani?"

I didn't know the dowager queen was back in Jaipur. The last I heard, she had taken up residence in Paris once Maharani Latika was well again and able to resume her official duties. It's not proper for me to ask the guard why the elder Maharani Indira has returned, so I hold my tongue. I'm sure to find out soon enough.

"Maharani Latika," I say, speaking confidently, as if she is expecting me. With no invitation, I can only fool the guard this once; the next time I come without an appointment, the guard will recognize me and refuse me entry.

Through the high iron gates, I see the younger maharani's Bentley. As usual for this time of day, it's parked in the circular driveway, its polished body gleaming in the sun, ready to be taken out for the day.

The guard looks at my hands, then cocks his head to look

behind me, probably expecting Malik to be carrying the tif-
fins that contained my supplies: my henna paste, treats for the
maharani, and a variety of lotions meant to soothe and calm.
Seeing none, he looks at me as if about to ask a question, then,
instead, he waves his arm, and a young attendant steps forward
to accompany me. I know my way around this palace from my
frequent visits here twelve years ago. Even so, protocol dictates
that an attendant lead me in and out of it.

This bearer takes me through the once familiar hallways decorated with mosaic floors, Victorian mirrors, and paintings of
past and present maharajas and maharanis on tiger hunts, seated
on their thrones or surrounded by their families. It feels like a
lifetime ago that I used to attend to the maharani here. I was a
different person then, more focused on what I could earn from
my henna applications than on whether I was doing my life's
work—healing others—as my *saas* had taught me.

The black-and-white photographs on the walls show maharanis with dignitaries like Jacqueline Kennedy, Queen Elizabeth
and Helen Keller. The most striking are moody compositions
of the Maharani Latika, taken in her drawing room as she gazes
out a window or on her terrace, the wind gracefully ruffling
her georgette sari.

I would have thought that each successive maharani would
leave her aesthetic fingerprints on the decor. Yet, along the hallways I see the same mahogany tables inlaid with ivory. Each
table holds a cut glass vase with mounds of pink roses, blue hya-
cinths and purple foxglove, freshly cut from the palace garden.
I wonder if the queens are allowed to put their touch only on
their personal living quarters.

Finally, I see the tall brass doors of the drawing room where
I used to meet the dowager Maharani Indira. The attendant politely asks me to wait on the chaise longue beside the door while
he goes in and introduces me. I notice that the chaise has been

reupholstered in crimson satin since I was last here. Maharani Latika's choice, perhaps? The wait is longer than it used to be, and I fear the maharani has refused to see me, but eventually the bearer reappears and invites me to enter.

I drape my *pallu* over my hair, respectfully, before entering, smiling at how often Malik needed to remind me that this necessary courtesy was critical in the beginning of my service to the maharanis; I was usually so nervous I'd forget. Now I'm surprised that my heart no longer flutters with anticipation at the prospect of being in the presence of royalty.

I can see the three Victorian sofas in this elegant room have been reupholstered, too. The silk damask's a different color—a rich, deep rose—but other than the couches, the room looks just the same. The sofas flank an enormous mahogany coffee table. The elaborately painted ceiling, high above us, depicts the courtship of Lord Ram and his consort Sita from the epic Ramayana.

In one corner of the room, Maharani Latika sits behind a desk of ebony with ivory and pearl inlay. She looks up and smiles when I come in. "Lakshmi!" she says. "How lovely to see you. I understand you're living, now, in Shimla. Please." She gestures to the sitting area. "I'm in the middle of a correspondence, so I'll be just a minute."

Aside from the trilling of the English clock on the marble mantel, the room's so quiet I can hear Her Highness's pen scratching the surface of the paper. I remember the first time I entered this room and met Madho Singh. He was shouting *Namaste! Bonjour! Welcome!* from the safety of his cage. His constant muttering and squawking made this room so lively when the dowager queen occupied it.

"There." The maharani holds out her envelopes and an attendant suddenly appears, as if by magic. The bearers stand so still I never even notice that they're in the room until they spring to action. This one will now be replaced by another; the maharani is never without service.

I stand up to touch her feet as she walks to me and settles on a sofa. "Now then," she says. "Tea?"

She is as beautiful as I remembered. Older, yes. I think she must be in her late forties now. A little older than me. Her eyes are the color and size of areca nuts, long lashed. The wrinkles at the corners weren't there the last time I saw her. There's a shrewdness in those brown eyes now that seems to assess, calculate, evaluate. Her brows are tweezed into an arch that makes her appear more commanding than ever (she is!).

"As you wish, Your Highness."

"On second thought, I think a glass of *nimbu pani* might be more refreshing."

She looks up and the second attendant comes forward, bows and leaves the room.

"So tell me about Shimla. It's so lovely there this time of year when the heat is upon us in Jaipur like a winter cloak." She wears a cool georgette sari printed in blue hydrangeas. Her blouse matches the blue of the flowers perfectly. Large diamond drops grace her earlobes, a heavy gold chain her neck, and diamond and sapphire rings on her fingers complete the ensemble.

"Coming back to Jaipur—and its heat—*was* something of a shock after living in the mountains all these years," I laugh.

"You're married now, I hear. It must suit you. You look well."

"Thank you, Your Highness. You look the picture of health."

She waves her fingers as if to dismiss my compliment. "I have too much work to do. I'm not getting the sleep I need. And I have less time to spend with the girls at the school."

She's referring to the classes in etiquette, tennis and Western dance she teaches at the Maharani School for Girls she established decades ago and which Radha attended for one term.

"And your son, Your Highness. How does he fare?"

There is a pause. When she speaks, her voice is hard. "He fares in Paris. I believe he's well-known at all the drinking establishments. But you will have heard that already."

I'm surprised by the news, and it must show in my face. From Kanta I know that her son hasn't set foot in India recently, not even for his father's funeral. But I thought he might come once in a while to visit his own mother.

She gives me an ironic smile. "So they don't know all our business in Shimla...yet?"

The attendant has returned with our glasses of sugared lime water. Unlike the *nimbu pani* the street vendors serve, this batch has had all the pulp removed so that the brilliance of the yellow-green liquid is on display inside the crystal tumblers. I wait until she picks up her glass to lift mine. The taste is sublime. A little tart, a little sweet, a little salty, a burst of coolness all the way down my throat.

There is something more formal than I remember about the woman sitting across from me, something cold. She used to be light as a breeze, swirling in and out of activity. I know the forced separation from her son when he was eight was devastating, but his response to it has been far more catastrophic. From what Kanta tells me and what I'm also inferring in her presence, her son must blame his mother for not fighting harder on his behalf. He must feel that if she had, he would now be the maharaja of Jaipur. Perhaps he doesn't visit Jaipur because he doesn't want to come face-to-face with his replacement, the adopted crown prince. Niki could have had that title, too, if we'd allowed his palace adoption to go forward.

I clear my throat. "Do you have much to do with the current crown prince, Your Highness?"

She takes another sip of her drink. "He's only twelve. A little young for anything but waving to the crowds. Luckily, I'm not expected to act as his mother, only as his guardian. Much the same way the dowager was guardian to my husband when he was waiting to come of age and assume the duties of the maharaja of Jaipur." She levels a steely gaze at me. "But you haven't come to chitchat."

I set my glass on the silver tray and clasp my hands together. "No, Your Highness. I come firstly to express my sorrow over the cinema accident. I understand a few moviegoers lost their lives and many more were injured?"

She squints, takes a deep breath. "It is a most unfortunate event. No one can have foreseen it. My heart goes out to those who suffered harm. At this point, the best we can do for them is to pay for and treat their injuries." She drops her gaze to the coffee table. "Words cannot express how terrible I feel about Rohit Seth—a dear old friend—and the young woman, both of whom had their lives cut short." She takes another sip of her drink. "But commiseration is also not the reason you've come to me today."

I rub the back of one hand with the palm of the other and study my trimmed nails. "It has come to my attention, Your Highness, that Mr. Manu Agarwal may be suspended from employment at the facilities office."

She arches one fine eyebrow. *And?*

"Mr. Agarwal and his wife Kanta are good friends of mine. I do not wish to deceive you on that point. But I have information that exonerates Mr. Agarwal. He was not made aware of certain material inconsistencies during construction. If Your Highness will allow, may I introduce the deception of which he has become the target?"

"Why is Manu not presenting this information to me himself?"

"He is not yet aware of it."

She ducks her chin. "And you are?" She sounds incredulous.

"Forgive my impertinence, Your Highness. May I speak plainly?"

"Always, Lakshmi."

"I don't know if you remember my young helper from my time in Jaipur. His name is Malik. Through a fortunate circumstance, he was able to come with me to Shimla and attend the Bishop Cotton School for Boys. Malik is now twenty, and as a favor to me, Mr. Agarwal agreed to take him on as a student-apprentice on his facilities staff. Malik has been helping out on the Royal Jewel Cinema project, mostly in accounting."

I've got her full attention now. Her gaze is penetrating.

"During the performance of his duties, Malik has inadvertently come across receipts for substandard materials being applied to the cinema project."

"May I see these receipts?"

I close my eyes in frustration and shake my head. "That's just it, Your Highness. He didn't realize what he'd seen at first. When he went back to retrieve the receipts, they'd been replaced with...different documents."

She regards me for a long moment. "I see."

She twirls the drink in her glass and takes a sip. "From the palace's position, the development of the Royal Jewel Cinema was under Mr. Agarwal's purview, and his alone. If these receipts cannot be found to prove his innocence, how am I to absolve him of responsibility? If the inquiry finds him culpable, he will be terminated."

I see now that in the interest of settling this matter to the public's satisfaction, a scapegoat must be sacrificed. Manu is that scapegoat. And he has not one shred of evidence in his possession to prove he shouldn't be.

"If Mr. Agarwal is accused of something he didn't do, it would ruin a good man's reputation forever," I say. "He has served this palace for fifteen years honorably. He has devoted his life to making sure the royal family's name remains above reproach." I tap a finger on my lips. "If I—if we could bring proof of actual culpability to you, would you be willing to consider it? Might you put Mr. Agarwal's future on hold until then?"

She runs a hand through her hair. "Mr. Seth's fan club and the movie industry are putting a lot of pressure on us, Lakshmi. This may be a private palace project, but we are always beholden to the public for our reputation. We have to take swift action."

"Your Highness, please. I hope you remember me as someone who keeps my word." Obviously, she trusts me or I would not have been allowed in her private quarters without an appointment. "If I promise to bring you something credible, posthaste, will that satisfy you?"

"How much time do you need?"

"A few weeks?"

"You have three days. I'm sorry. After that, I will have to announce his suspension and possible termination." It's worse than I thought! And her tone tells me that she does not hold out much hope for my success.

She sets her glass on the tray and stands. It's my signal to leave.

I reach for her feet again. "Thank you, Your Highness."

As I turn toward the door, she says, "How's your sister, my former student, doing? Radha, I believe her name is? She showed promise if I remember correctly."

I laugh lightly. "She came to that promise late, I'm afraid. She now lives in Paris with her French husband, who is an architect. They have two daughters. She works with perfumes."

Maharani Latika seems pleasantly surprised. "But that's marvelous! I may drop in and see her the next time I'm in Paris. You'll have to tell me where I can find her."

"The House of Chanel. She started at another fragrance house and found not only did she enjoy mixing elements—she has a nose for scents."

"Well, well. Give her my regards, will you?"

I *namaste* her and leave.

Malik and I have just three days to save Manu Agarwal. Three days to make sure neither Niki's life nor his father's is destroyed by this calamity.

Back at the Agarwals', I call Jay in Shimla. It's late morning. He must be at the hospital.

He answers on the first ring.

"Miss me yet?"

He laughs lightly. "*You may lock up a cock, but the sun will still rise.* You're not in Shimla, but that doesn't mean I don't imagine you doing the crossword in the drawing room or coming out of your bath smelling of lavender or giving the nurses hell at the clinic."

I laugh. "I do no such thing!" I tell him about my day so far, what the maharani said, how I've never seen Manu so depressed and how it's affecting the family. "Malik has some things he's following up on." I pause. "How are Nimmi and the children?"

"Lakshmi, you must know she didn't mean the things she said to you. She's scared right now. She has no idea what Vinay has gotten us all into."

It's hard to be understanding when Nimmi's rage was so palpable. In a few minutes, she dispelled the goodwill we'd built between us. I murmur something noncommittal.

He can hear my reluctance. He sighs.

"What about the sheep?"

"Nimmi's paid the local shepherd to continue moving the flock every few days. He's happy to do it because he has to move his own flock, and he herds them both together."

"What about the wool we sheared?"

"Still in the pantry. Making it impossible to access Madho Singh's food."

"That's why I hired that woman to cook for you."

"*Hahn*. And now the bird has developed a taste for *chapattis*! Don't be surprised if Madho refuses to eat seeds anymore." He chuckles. "How long will you stay in Jaipur?"

"Maharani Latika has given us three days from today to provide evidence that Manu is innocent of wrongdoing. If we don't produce it, Manu will be fired for the good of the palace's public image."

We're both quiet for a moment.

Then Jay says, "*The thief that is not caught is a king.* You're going to find the evidence, Lakshmi. Don't let my old friend Samir get away with being the king here."

"I wasn't planning on it."

22

MALIK

Jaipur

The clerk on the other end of the phone at Chandigarh Ironworks sounds like he's about my age. When I introduce myself as the assistant to the accountant of the Jaipur Palace, I can almost hear him sit up straighter.

"*Bhai,*" I say, "I'm hoping you can help me."

I clear my throat as if I am reluctant to begin. "This is my first important job, you see, and I'm embarrassed to admit that I have misplaced several documents."

I follow this up with a nervous laugh.

He seems to be an agreeable sort of fellow. He chuckles. "I've done the same myself." I imagine him as conscientious, understanding, popular among his friends.

ALKA JOSHI

I exaggerate my sigh to make sure he understands how grateful I am. "The palace has so many projects going on, and what
I need I've probably filed in the wrong drawer." I'm giving him
my hail-fellow-well-met act—a holdover from Bishop Cotton.
"Without your assistance, it could take me hours to find those
documents. But, *bhai*, think we could keep this between ourselves?"

"No bother." He lowers his voice. "Which documents exactly? I'll mail a copy of them out to you."

Mail from Chandigarh might take a week. Maharani Latika
has given us three days. "So very kind of you," I say. "Alas, my
boss…he needs them right away, you see. He will have my head
on a platter and serve it to the maharani unless I get them to
him within the hour."

"But you're calling from Jaipur. How can I get them to you
in an hour?"

"I only need the numbers. Maybe you could send them to
me in a telegram?"

Now I hear him falter. "I would have to justify the expense,
bhai. Telegrams are expensive."

I chuckle. "Send it collect, and the palace will pay! I can always find a place to bury the expense. Accounting always has a
way to work around these things, *hahn-nah*?" That gets an ap-
preciative laugh out of him.

I tell him to send the telegram to the Jaipur post office and
give him all the necessary details. Then I get up and grab some
random invoices from my desk, so that when I pass Hakeem's
office, it looks as if I'm taking care of some official, necessary
work.

"Abbas?"

I had not expected him to stop me. I turn my head, but not
my body, as if I'm in a hurry. "Yes, Sahib?"

"The theater floor reconstruction? I still haven't seen the estimate."

I hold up the papers in my hand. "One last thing to verify. I've not yet received the cost of the seating. I think Singh-Sharma hasn't figured out what needs to be replaced, and what can be repaired."

He stares at me, trying to look stern, and glides his fingers under his mustache. "Make sure it's done by end of day."

I nod. Then I head out the front doors and make my way to the Jaipur post office. Now that I know he tattled about me to Samir Singh, I'm giving Hakeem a wide berth. Apparently, he's not as dull as I thought, but neither is he the diligent accountant I've assumed him to be. Why would Hakeem do the Singhs' bidding? Is Samir paying him to be his spy within the palace organization?

On my way to the post office, I'm thinking about Auntie-Boss telling me the bricks she saw in Shimla are similar to the ones I've seen here at the site of the balcony collapse. I knew, then, that I needed to find out if the two are related and how.

I'm also thinking of the argument I witnessed yesterday at the Agarwal house between Auntie-Boss and Manu.

Kanta and Niki had gone to the sweetshop to get dessert. Manu, Lakshmi and I were in the Agarwal drawing room. When Lakshmi told Manu what I'd found, and that she'd gone, on his behalf, to visit the Maharani Latika, he exploded. "You went behind my back? Her Highness will think I have no spine. That I have to send a—a—"

"A woman?" Auntie-Boss was speaking in her calm voice, the one she always used when placating her more difficult henna clients.

Manu said, "Don't you see how it looks? It's like you've cut my legs out from under me! All of Jaipur will know Manu Agarwal is a coward, not to mention an embezzler of the highest order!"

He turned to look at me in the armchair. "And *you*, Malik! I took you on in good faith, and you're trying to dig up—dirty laundry? You're talking about this project to all and sundry without my knowledge?"

I had never seen Uncle so angry. I didn't think he was capable of it. I watched him pace round and round his drawing room, his arms flailing, his hair flying about as if it, too, was gesticulating. If I hadn't known him since I was a child, I'd think he was about to have a nervous breakdown, just as my English master at Bishop Cotton did when he found out his wife was cheating on him with the math tutor.

Boss's soothing tone never wavered. "I'd never want Niki to hear his father called either of those things," she said. "That's why I went to see Her Highness."

The mention of his son's name stopped him in his tracks. When he looked at her, Manu's face was contorted in anguish.

Auntie-Boss patted the sofa cushion next to her. "Come sit, Manu-*ji*. Please. You're making me dizzy." He pushed his glasses farther up the bridge of his nose and did as he was told, suddenly contrite.

"What Malik found is nothing you would ever have discovered yourself. You're an overseer. It's not your job to scrutinize details such as receipts and invoices. Your people report to you. They come to you with summaries of what they've done. You listen, question and discuss, then sign off on what they've recommended."

"Are you saying that my people—my handpicked staff—could have been lying?"

She had put her hand on his shoulder, as if she were talking to a younger brother. "Your employees have been with you a long time. Naturally, you trust them to do the right thing. Perhaps their recommendations in this instance were based on information that was incorrect? And, having worked with Singh-

Sharma so long, you've come to trust them, too. Nothing you were aware of would have made you think that they were doing anything...untoward."

Manu was staring at the Persian rug beneath his feet. He puffed up his cheeks and blew out air, as if letting go of something. He turned to Lakshmi.

"This—alleged—conspiracy. Tell me that isn't just your way of getting back at Samir Singh for that business between Radha and Ravi. Retaliation for the way he left you in a lurch."

I could tell that Auntie-Boss hadn't seen this accusation coming, but she didn't hesitate to answer. "Don't even think it, *bhai*. All of that is in the past. I never waste a minute dwelling on it. But the past *does* color my impression of that family and the things they're capable of. If you look at what Malik has found, you might conclude they bear some measure of responsibility for all that's happened."

Manu looked conflicted. He frowned at me. "Samir paid for your education at Bishop Cotton. Don't you owe him any loyalty? How could you accuse his company of fraud and recklessness when Samir opened doors for you?"

Manu looked so lost; I wished that I had words to help him. He was no longer in control of what was happening around him. He'd been raised to never question his superiors. Since he'd always been an honest broker, he couldn't imagine that others might not be the same. For fifteen years, the royal family had employed him. He'd sooner cut his arm off than question their decisions or blame them for anything inappropriate.

"I would never make such a charge lightly, Uncle," I said as gently as I could. "But I know what I saw, and it's wrong for the palace to terminate you for something you didn't do. The Singhs may buy a lot of favors, but I don't consider myself one of their purchases. Samir Singh paid for my education to make amends for the heartache his family caused Auntie-Boss. What happened twelve years ago forced her to leave Jaipur and abandon her successful henna business. I never asked Samir to pay for anything. And I won't be indebted to him because he chose to do that. My only loyalty is to you, to Kanta Auntie, to Auntie-Boss and to Nikhil."

Manu looked chastened. I could see we were starting to get through to him. He stood up and started pacing the room again, this time more slowly. He was pulling at his lip, deep in thought.

Auntie-Boss sent me a look. *Just wait.*

Finally, Manu said, "I can't condone what you're doing. I still have a code of ethics to honor. But as long as I'm not aware of how you go about making your case, I promise not to get in the way. *Theek hai?*"

I go straight from the post office to the Agarwals' to show the telegram to Auntie-Boss.

Lakshmi looks over the telegram, before she says, "So Chandigarh Ironworks supplied class four bricks when they were supposed to supply class one. What's the difference in quality?"

"Class four are used for decorative purposes. Not for load bearing. Never should have been used on the cinema project."

She reads the telegram again. "And the quantities noted here—for bricks and cement—they were reversed in the ledger?"

"Also on the doctored receipts."

She sets the telegram on the Agarwals' coffee table.

"The more I think about it, Malik, the less I think Samir initiated the fraud. He's involved in it, but I think it started with someone else. It didn't take a great deal of effort for you to identify the discrepancy. Samir has been in business a long time, and he has a lot to lose. He's not an amateur. The palace is not his only client. His company has taken on several contracts outside of Rajasthan. Why would he risk ruining his reputation?"

I agree. I think back to Ravi telling me how his father is

THE SECRET KEEPER OF JAIPUR

old-school. Ravi has grander plans for his future. He told me he doesn't want to keep doing things the same way his father has always done them. What does he consider to be a more innovative way of doing business? Substituting inferior materials but charging full price and pocketing the difference? The palace pays well, but Ravi isn't satisfied? He already lives in a mansion. He has a beautiful, clever wife who adores him. What more could he want?

Lakshmi sighs. "Let me take it from here." I hear the resignation in her voice when she says, "Can you get word to Samir that I need to see him? As soon as possible."

23

LAKSHMI

Jaipur

I'm standing in front of my old house in Jaipur—the one I built with money I earned from thousands of henna applications, my herbal lotions and healing oils. Parvati Singh bought my house from me when I left Jaipur—an apology of sorts for destroying my livelihood.

The hibiscus bushes that line the edge of the property are neatly trimmed, the grass in the tiny front yard freshly mowed and dewy. The windows sparkle in the evening light as if they've recently been washed. Parvati might have let the house to renters, but somehow I think not. It has a cared-for look—like a museum piece, ready to be displayed before admiring eyes.

Earlier today, Samir sent a messenger to the Agarwals asking me to meet him here. He wouldn't have had time, since then, to make the house presentable, or spruce it, and so I wonder who's been taking care of it. The tiny, single-story building is nothing special on the outside. It's what's inside that matters; that's what persuaded Parvati to buy the house from me.

"So glad you've come."

I turn at the sound of a woman's voice.

"I know you planned on meeting Samir, but it's me you really want to talk to," Parvati says, brushing past me to the side corridor that leads to the threshold.

I'm so stunned to see her, here, that I can't move.

Parvati has the front door unlocked now and turns to me. "Come," she says.

I dumbly follow Samir's wife inside. She goes around the room, turning on overhead lights and table lamps. I didn't have the money, when I owned the house, to pay for electricity. To the left of the front door I see the entrance to a privy—the Western bathroom that I'd wanted but couldn't afford.

Now that the lights are on, my handiwork, my crowning achievement, shines: the *mandala* on the floor, made of terrazzo, a fusion of Indian, Moroccan, Persian, Afghani and Egyptian henna designs that mean as much to me, today, as they did then. The Ashoka lion, symbol of my ambition—an ambition that led me from the village of my birth to the heights of Jaipur society, where I used my henna reed to help wealthy women realize their desires. And there!—baskets of saffron flowers, a sterile plant and symbol of my choice to remain childless. Jay and I talked about it, well before we married. We both love what we do, and given our long hours at the hospital, the clinic and the Healing Garden, we have little time for our own children. We've nurtured them in other ways: tended to their cuts, soothed their hurts, brought them into this world or coaxed them back to health.

Hidden in the *mandala* among the swirls, and loops, and whorls is also my name. I'm looking at it now. Does Parvati know it's there?

"I've taken good care of your masterpiece," she says, and gestures to the floor. "I hope you approve."

I keep my expression blank and brace myself for what's coming. I'm never sure what Parvati has in store for me.

Since I saw her last, a dozen years ago, she's put on weight; the sleeves of her coral blouse are tight around her arms and upper back, the flesh squeezed out, like toothpaste coming from a tube. She'll need to have the seams taken out. Again.

But the elaborate gold *pallu* of her sari cascades gracefully from her shoulder down her back. She's still a handsome woman with distinctive features, like her full lips, painted a bright pink to offset her royal blue sari. The kohl around her black eyes makes them appear to be wider, more appealing, more alert. Her cheeks have filled out and there's the hint of a double chin, but these things are her birthright; symbols of a well-tended Indian woman of a certain age.

"I heard you married Jay Kumar. Quite a catch." She's smiling, but she sounds annoyed. "Still, it seems you just can't stay away from Samir, can you?"

She's alluding to a single night of passion years ago between Samir and me. Brief enough, but long in coming. Samir and I had danced around our attraction for ten years. I knew it would destroy my reputation if I ever acted on it, but Samir was patient. Eventually a night came when everything around me crumbled, and I needed to be comforted, desired and loved.

Parvati found out soon enough, and then the life I'd built in Jaipur, the financial independence I'd gained, fell apart.

Strange enough, remembering all of this, I find my voice. "You won't like what I'm about to tell you, Parvati."

The fact that I've dropped the respectful *Ji* is not lost on her.

She blinks. "Try me."

"It's about the Royal Jewel Cinema."

She waves a hand, dismissive. "An accident. Unfortunate, but unforeseeable."

Exactly what the newspapers and radio are calling it. It isn't true, and I'm tired of it. "It could have been avoided."

Now she rolls her eyes. "*Every* accident can be avoided, Lakshmi. That's why we call them accidents. If everything had gone as planned, there would have been no mishap."

"Except this 'mishap' is the consequence of something Samir's company appears to have set in motion."

Her mouth is set in a firm line. "What does any of this have to do with you? I understood that you are now a garden tender somewhere up there in the Himalayas. I can only guess that you want to bring our family down. Exactly like your sister."

The mention of my sister makes me bristle, but I keep myself in check. "It isn't personal, Parvati. An honest man is being falsely accused for what Singh-Sharma should have known about and could have prevented. I won't let that happen. Manu Agarwal shouldn't lose his job and his reputation for something he didn't do."

In the center of the terrazzo floor are four comfortable chairs upholstered in cream raw silk. In the middle of the grouping there's a table set for four. A deck of cards lies on the table.

Parvati pulls one chair out and takes a seat. "My bridge group meets here. Samir never even enters this house." She shoots a pointed look at me, as if I'm the one to blame for that.

She waves at the chair opposite, an invitation, or command, for me to sit. I go over to the chair and sit in it, wondering if Samir has seen my note asking him to meet me here, or if he knows Parvati has come in his place.

Now she leans forward and picks up the deck of cards. "You mentioned Manu Agarwal. He's the head of all building projects for the palace, and, as such, he is responsible for anything that happens to the royal properties." She meets my eyes. "That's exactly what I told Latika. If Manu isn't held responsible, she'll never hear the end of it. The press, the magistrates, the lawyers—they all need someone they can hold accountable. She needs to fire someone or else she'll be the one skewered."

I should have known Parvati would have gone to see the Maharani Latika even before I did! She's distantly related to Jaipur royalty, which gives her access to the palace and allows her to talk to Her Highnesses as a close friend and adviser—even to call them by their first names.

"Parvati, I have proof. Singh-Sharma bought and accepted materials for the cinema project that didn't meet the engineering specs. How can Mr. Agarwal be held responsible for that? He would have nothing to gain by sabotaging a palace project."

"How do you know this?"

"Contracts and receipts that were altered."

"And I suppose you know who did what in all this? You have evidence?"

"Convincing enough to take to the maharani."

She divides the deck of cards in two and shuffles them, a thing she must have done a thousand times before. "But you don't have any proof that Samir authorized any of it, do you?"

I hesitate. "The doctored receipts were submitted by Singh-Sharma. Samir is ultimately responsible for the actions of his company."

She divides the deck in half again and puts them on the table. With a manicured fingernail, she taps one stack. "On the one hand," she says, "the head of Palace Facilities is responsible for the projects initiated by the palace." Now she taps the other deck. "On the other hand, the head of the construction company bears full responsibility."

She stares at me. "Who's to say Samir can't prove that Mr.

Agarwal made bad decisions? Decisions that resulted in the injuries incurred by all those people? Why would you think you
get to decide this matter?"

"Why not let the courts decide? We should ask the maharani
to leave the matter to the legal system."

Her pained expression tells me she thinks I'm a simpleton.
One too dull to understand her logic.

"That isn't how these things are done. The settlement's been
made. Samir's company will pay for reconstruction, plus materials. The palace has agreed to pay the costs for injuries incurred." She moves both piles of cards together, shuffling them
and merging them into a single deck. "If it's a good reference
Manu is looking for, I'll talk to Latika. I'm sure she would have
no objections. It's out of your hands." Her dark eyes regard me.
"Your interference is neither needed nor wanted."

I decide to take a different approach. "Is Ravi happy working for his father?"

The change of subject jars her just enough to still her hands.
"What business is that of yours?" She gently sets the deck back
on the table.

"It's what I would have asked Samir if he'd come to this meeting." Then it hits me: *Did Samir send his wife to confront me? Is he
that much of a coward?*

"Ravi has a great life and a great future," she says. "Once
Samir retires, he'll take over the company."

"Samir is healthy. What if he decides not to retire? At least
not soon? Would Ravi enjoy working *under* his father for a few
more years? Or decades?"

Parvati crosses her arms over her chest.

I continue. "Ravi's lived abroad. He's known a lot of freedom.
Now he's back, virtually living with his family again, working
on whatever projects his father gives him. Have you ever asked
him if this is the life he wants?"

She looks at me with a grimace. "We aren't nomads. We don't wander, looking for a way to make a living, begging help from other people. We're not at the mercy of any *ara-garra-nathu-kara*. Not like your lot." She spits this last bit out; she might as well have called us good-for-nothings.

When I saw her last, she came to this house—*my* house—to offer me a bribe. I could have taken the money she was offering if I swore to her I'd never sleep with Samir again. I had no intention of repeating that mistake, and I refused the money— money that I needed, money that might have saved my ruined business. *Back then, who was begging who, Parvati?*

But I say nothing. I know this woman well. Parvati has the right to be high-handed just so long as she hides behind a curtain of wealth and privilege. I've seen her as few others have— when she was powerless—confronted with the sad reality of the philanderer she married and the reckless son she bore. She didn't have the will to criticize me then.

But I'm not here to open old wounds. The only thing I want is that Manu and Kanta survive this scandal unscathed.

Now Parvati leans across the table, close enough for me to smell the betel nut she's fond of chewing. Her eyes are blazing. "*We* have important destinies. *We* are the ones who make or break this country. My family has responsibilities to make sure people like you have food to eat, a roof over your head. Now you'll leave my family alone, or you'll have bigger things to deal with—more significant than whether Manu Agarwal is about to lose his job. And you won't go spreading lies about my son."

She pushes her chair back from the table and stands up. "Lock the door behind you."

With a final scowl at me, she leaves. Through the room's front window, I watch her driver hold the back door of the Bentley open for her, then get behind the wheel and ease the car out onto the street.

THE SECRET KEEPER OF JAIPUR

★ ★ ★

As I take a *tonga* to the Agarwals', I ponder Parvati's certainty; the might, and right, to be imperious is hers, and hers alone. An attitude I thought I had become inured to years ago.

Once I'm inside the Agarwals' house, Kanta hands me a cup of tea and a lavender-scented envelope. She says, "Hand delivered from the palace."

I recognize the elaborate handwriting and slide the envelope's flap open.

Dear Mrs. Shastri (or should I say Mrs. Kumar?):
I was so pleased to hear about your marriage to Shimla's eminent physician, Dr. Jay Kumar. How lovely it must be to enjoy cool breezes while we, in Jaipur, swelter.

Latika told me that you came to see her. Am I not worthy of a visit, too, my dear? I am old and not as agile as I used to be. Truth be told, the Parisian doctors tell me I have cancer of the uterus. (Ironic, isn't it? Considering my husband wouldn't allow me to make use of my uterus even once!)

I decided I would rather pass my remaining years in the country of my birth than in a country where the coffee is divine, but where the cheeses offend my sensitive nose.

Do let me know when you might have a moment free to pay a visit to this old woman and offer me the kindness of a chat and news of Malik and that old rascal Madho Singh.
Warmly,
Her Highness Maharani Indira of Jaipur

24

MALIK

Jaipur

At lunchtime, I slip out of the office to go see the Agarwals. I want to know what Samir Singh told Auntie-Boss. But when Lakshmi arrives, she tells us that Parvati showed up for the meeting.

Baju brings the tea tray into the drawing room. Kanta tells him to take a cup to Manu, who has sequestered himself in his study; he's made it clear he doesn't want to hear our conversation. Niki's in his room, doing homework; Kanta is still keeping him from school. Saasuji is napping.

Lakshmi says, "Parvati is confident Samir was not involved in this."

Kanta's adding sugar to her chai. "Well, of course, she would be. She has generations of a family reputation to protect." She stirs her tea. "I think she believes the Singhs are indispensable to Jaipur. That their family, alone, is keeping the economy afloat. But how would anything get built without the women and men who work as laborers on their sites?" She shakes her head. *"It takes two*—or hundreds, really—*to tango."*

"Do you know I believe her when she talks about Samir?" Auntie-Boss insists. "Where his work's concerned, he's honest. Samir would compromise neither his reputation nor his integrity." She and I trade a look. "His home life is another matter altogether."

I don't like to think about how many mistresses Samir has taken over the years. As a boy, I crisscrossed this city delivering the contraceptive sachets that Auntie-Boss sold to him and his friends for their paramours.

Lakshmi continues, "Ravi, however, is different. You should have seen Parvati's face when I brought up his name. *Bilkul* rattled. What if Ravi is the one behind this fiasco? What if he's the one who's been cutting corners for reasons of his own? Malik has noticed some interesting discrepancies."

I shake my head. "I still can't work out why Ravi would risk it. He's got everything—a comfortable present *and* an even better future." I can't help thinking about Sheela. I've tried, and failed, to wipe the images from my mind: her clingy green dress; dark hair, wet from her bath; her seductive smile; the gold powder glittering on her cleavage.

And suddenly—like a ninety-mile-an-hour cricket ball—an idea hurtles through my brain.

In the inner sanctum of Moti-Lal Jewelers, I set the broken pieces of bricks in front of the big man. He's seated, cross-legged, on his padded cushion while he smokes his hookah. Auntie-Boss is sitting next to me.

Lal-*ji* had been so pleased to see her, when we first came in, he had almost tripped when he hurried from behind his desk to greet her. She'd brought a gift for him—the hair oil that his wife used to buy from her. (Lakshmi always carries several bottles with her, just in case.)

Now the jeweler picks up a brick fragment and examines it before he puts it down, and then he does the same with all the others. When he's set aside the final piece, he drums his fingers on his thigh. Today he's clad in an expensive linen *kurta pyjama*. The large emerald ring on his pinkie finger catches, and reflects, the lights from the ceiling. He stops and looks at me—and keeps me in his gaze at least a minute. Then he picks up the receiver of the phone beside him and mumbles a few words—he's speaking softly and the only words I hear are *sona* and *dibba*—then he puts the receiver back in place. Boss and I exchange a look.

His son-in-law, Mohan, comes in carrying two glossy rosewood boxes. He nods and smiles at me, then sits down next to Moti-Lal, who pulls out the long gold chain he wears around his neck. Several small keys are attached to the chain's end. He uses a key to unlock the first box. Inside are several pristine bars of solid gold. About ten of them. They're identical, same size, same shape, same markings: weight (one ounce), the manufacturer's logo and, in the center, the numbers 999.9.

He instructs Mohan to unlock the second box. The gold bars in this box are uneven, unstamped, and slightly different in weight from one another.

In this brightly lit room, where Lal-*ji* examines jewels and stones, the glow from the gold bars is dazzling.

Moti-Lal points to the first box. "Legal." Then, to the second. "Not legal."

He takes a bar from the first box and sets it in the indentation of the broken brick. It's a little too big to fit in the space. He does the same with the illegal gold, and this time the bar fills the space, not perfectly, but well enough. Next, he puts an-other fragment of brick on top and leaves it there. The gold is now concealed. He looks at us and grins.

"And that, young Malik, is how some gold is transported." He guffaws, his balloon belly jiggling.

"But why hide it?" I ask him. "Why not just bring it through proper channels?"

The jeweler and his son-in-law trade a look. "Any jeweler will tell you that he buys very little gold through legitimate sources. Why? Last year's Gold Act. It limits the amount of gold a jew-eler like me can hold in my possession. But Mrs. Patel and Mrs. Chandralal and Mrs. Zameer want a lot more for their daugh-ters' bridal trousseaus than I'm allowed to carry." Lal-*ji* raises his eyebrows at Boss. "Am I right, Mrs. Kumar?"

Lakshmi shuts her eyes for half a second. *Yes.*

He continues, "Also, the Indo-China War depleted our coun-try's gold reserves. Mrs. Patel, Mrs. Chandralal and Mrs. Zameer did their bit by donating their gold for the war effort. Well, the war is over and the ladies want their gold back. Only…it's gone. It was used to purchase munitions from other countries. So where can suppliers replenish the gold customers want? Africa. Brazil. Wherever they can smuggle it from, they're doing it."

Moti-Lal rubs the back of his neck with his fleshy palm. "I'm doing the same thing every other jeweler's doing. If I can buy gold being smuggled into India—gold I won't declare to the authorities—why wouldn't I? Otherwise, my shelves would be completely empty! *Samaj-jao?*"

I nod my understanding. But it still boggles the mind. Here we live in a country where the demand for gold is staggering. Yet, almost none of it is mined here. No wonder the illegal im-port business is thriving.

"Surely the government must have known what would hap-pen when they passed the Gold Act."

The jeweler laughs and rubs his hands together. "I'm sure they did. They understand human nature. Squeeze the mango from the bottom and the pulp comes out through the hole you've made at the top! No matter what obstacles you set before an Indian, he'll find a way to get around it. People have to eat. The world keeps turning. But the government has to set limits. Otherwise, who knows how out of control the gold racket would get?"

Moti-Lal has taken up his hookah once again. He observes us through the smoke. That delicious scent of cherries and cloves fills the small room. He sees me looking and hands me the other hookah but not before he asks Lakshmi, "MemSahib is not bothered?"

She shakes her head.

I take a puff of *chillum* and a feeling of light-headedness comes over me. I start to wonder if I ought to reconsider Moti-Lal's offer to work in his shop and learn the jewelry trade. What would it be like to sit here with him, scrutinizing gold bullion like that in front of us, the *kundan* necklaces, uncut rubies and emeralds, and bangles studded with pearls out in the main showroom—all while smoking this exquisite tobacco? To chat up beautiful brides-to-be about their wedding trousseaus? How seductive, tantalizing…dangerous!

Pointing to the bricks, Lal-*ji* asks, "Want to tell me where you found these?"

I blink, uncertain how much to reveal. I steal a glance at Auntie-Boss. She tilts her head ever so slightly.

Finally, I answer, "A construction site."

Lal-*ji* runs his tongue over his large, wolflike teeth and looks at Mohan. The younger man immediately understands this signal. He removes the bar of gold Moti-Lal had placed inside the brick, places it in the second rosewood box and locks both boxes with his own set of keys. I realize that when Lal-*ji* suggested he would hire me and let Mohan go, he didn't really mean it. The two men are a team. They work well together, seem to speak a silent language all their own.

Mohan gathers the boxes and stands, but before he leaves the room, Lal-*ji* calls out to him, "Make sure Mrs. Gupta buys the ruby and diamond *kundan* set, not the inferior one her cheapskate husband wants to buy."

His son-in-law wags his head to indicate agreement, nods a respectful farewell to us and leaves the room.

Now that Mohan's gone, Lali-*ji* says, "You told me you were working with the palace facilities office. Which means Singh-Sharma was most likely the contractor on the construction site."

I keep my eyes on his, but don't respond.

"The project that's been in the news is the Royal Jewel Cinema." He stops, inspects the bricks again. "So...you found these bricks after the..." Lal-*ji*'s brows draw together. "You know my wife and daughter and Mohan went to opening night at the cinema? They could have been killed." The jeweler's blood pressure is rising; his cheeks are an irritated red. "*Hai Bhagwan!* If the Singhs did something that caused that balcony to collapse, I'll never let Parvati Singh darken my door again. She will buy no more from Moti-Lal Jewelers!"

It's hot in the room, and not because the air-conditioning has been turned off. Lal-*ji*'s anger is generating the heat. He wipes his face with his palm. "There have been rumors. I heard one maybe a year ago. Another gold route being created. New supplier. Contraband, of course. The supplier was well financed. They could get gold—lots of it—guaranteed. I didn't take the bait, though. I have my supplier and I'm happy. But I was curious and looked into it."

He puffs a few scented clouds into the room. "Now, you must never say this information came from me. It could be false." He studies Auntie-Boss again, as if he's weighing whether to proceed.

She understands his hesitation, because, when she speaks to

him, she uses her persuasive voice. "Lal-*ji*, I would never choose to bring you into this. But a dear friend will be blamed for something he didn't do if we don't find out more. And this relationship between the gold and these bricks may be at the heart of why he is being framed."

Lal-*ji* looks pained. "You already know the players. People involved with the palace."

Is he talking about Manu? Is Manu guilty after all, of misappropriating funds so he can traffic gold across India? I almost don't want to know the rest. I feel dizzy and my mouth feels dry. Is it the tobacco or the idea that I've misjudged someone I trust?

I set the hookah aside. "Just tell us, Uncle," I say. "Please."

"They're saying it's Ravi Singh. That he's set up his own operation, his own route. But that has to be *bukwas*. Why would a man from one of the wealthiest families in Jaipur want to get into that kind of treacherous business? I'm several steps removed from smugglers, so my involvement is a lot safer. I'm not out there crossing mountains and deserts, hiring *goondas* to get things done. If I get caught with more gold than I should have, a little *baksheesh* and a little more tax paid to the city coffers takes care of it. But a transporter—" he shakes his head "—has to take all kinds of risks."

I pick up my pipe, take a drag and think. Could it be that the Singhs are not as wealthy as everyone assumes? I realize that at the facilities office no one wants to talk badly about the maharani's favorite contractor, Singh-Sharma. And I've been there only a few months, not long enough to know the full scope of the project and its trajectory these last three years. Manu is too much of a professional to share gossip about what, if anything, wasn't up to snuff on the project.

"What else have you heard?" Auntie-Boss asks Lal-*ji* quietly.

The jeweler frowns, concentrating. "I remember someone telling me the project was considerably overbudget. Far more money being spent than what the maharani had intended. That same person said that duplicating the design of a fancy cinema in Amreeka was to blame. The construction of the project took far more time than they had bargained for." He shook his head. "But, again, that's only rumor. And I don't know any more than that." Lal-*ji* takes a few more puffs of his hookah. "What will happen to the cinema?"

I say, "They plan to reopen it as soon as the damage is repaired. The maharani's losing money every day it stays closed, and she wants Singh-Sharma to step up the rebuild."

The big man nods, understanding, as he does, the ways of commerce and the people who must make the hard decisions.

Boss takes an auto rickshaw to see the Maharani Indira at the palace while I go back to my desk at the palace facilities office. When Hakeem quits for the day, I follow him home. I'm convinced he knows more than he lets on.

I expected a man who has four daughters to rent a house, but Hakeem appears to be renting an apartment in a run-down area of Jaipur, near GulabNagar, the Pleasure District. This is surprising. After all his years of service, does he earn so little? I watch him mount the stairs to the first-floor terrace of an apartment building and make a note of the door he enters.

I give him enough time to change out of his work clothes. I want him to be relaxed when I show up at his door.

Fifteen minutes later, I'm knocking at his door. It opens a crack. Hakeem peers out, guarding the entrance in a half-sleeve undershirt and a white *dhoti*. But his relaxed expression changes to astonishment when he sees me. He rubs the underside of his mustache.

"But...why are you here, Malik? Has something happened?"

I smile and salaam him. "Nothing like that, Uncle. I wanted

to talk to you away from the office. May I?" Without waiting for an answer, I push open the door and enter the narrow room.

There's a cot on one side of the room, with a tiny washbasin in the corner. Someone has left the newspaper folded open to the crossword puzzle on the cot. On the other side of the room is a table with two chairs and a tall bookshelf. Next to that, on a small cabinet sits a two-burner stove, two metal plates, two glasses and two bowls. A frying pan and a stainless steel pan sit on the burners. The bottom portion of the cabinet is covered with a rough striped curtain, no doubt hiding the rice, lentils, tea and other sundries.

Everything in the room is neat, if a little shabby. The two sunken pillows on the cot have a defeated look, as does the cotton quilt, the threads of which are coming loose. There are no photos, no female clothing, jewelry or hair products in sight.

The scent of cardamom, peppercorns and ginger wafts from the pan. Tea, I assume. There is a cauliflower, two potatoes, a tomato and a knife beside a cutting board on the table. Just then, I hear a toilet flush. A door at the far end of the room opens and a thin man in a sleeveless bush-shirt and *dhoti* emerges from the bathroom.

I don't know who is more surprised: me or the Royal Jewel Cinema theater manager who still has one hand on the doorknob of the bathroom. He is frozen in place. He glances at Hakeem, whose eyes behind his thick black glasses have grown as big as saucers. The look that passes between them is one of fear—and something akin to guilt? Embarrassment?

I recover more quickly. "Mr. Reddy, isn't it? I don't believe we've met. I'm Abbas Malik. I work with Hakeem Sahib."

Hakeem clears his throat. "Mr. Reddy boards with me, yes? Until—until he can find a place. He is new in Jaipur."

"But, Sahib. Your wife and daughters. Where are they?" I'm genuinely puzzled.

The accountant looks to his right and left and then at Mr. Reddy, who is still clutching the bathroom doorknob. "My family is in Bombay. My job is here, yes? I send them money every month."

"I thought you said they were with you on the opening night of the cinema house. You said something about how all of you had to hold hands to get home."

"They were here for the opening. Then they left."

I look around the room. It's plausible. It's just that this apartment feels like it's never seen the inside of a woman's suitcase.

Mr. Reddy is watching our exchange as if he's watching a tense cricket match. He looks tired and a little sad.

I pull a chair from the table and sit down. "Bombay? Isn't that where you're from, Mr. Reddy?"

"Yes." It comes out as a croak, so he tries again. "Yes."

"Is that a coincidence or...?"

"No, it is not," the theater manager says as he lets go of the doorknob and stands with his hands clasped in front of him, like a naughty child.

"I met Mr. Reddy in Bombay at the cinema, yes?" Hakeem says. "I thought he might like to apply for the job of theater manager here for when the new cinema opened. I talked to Ravi Sahib about it. And he put a word in Mr. Agarwal's ear—"

The tea starts boiling over, and Hakeem rushes to take the pot off the burner. But the metal handle is too hot and he cries out. He drops the saucepan on top of the frying pan. Immediately, Mr. Reddy rushes to examine his hand. He puts an arm around Hakeem and guides him gently to the small washbasin tucked in the corner of the room. Turning on the tap, he moves Hakeem's hand in a circle so the cold water will soothe the reddened skin. He pulls the threadbare towel off the rack and wraps it around Hakeem's hand. Then he reaches inside the tiny cabinet above the washbasin and extracts a jar of ointment and a roll of gauze. Mr. Reddy rubs a little ointment tenderly on the burn, then wraps the gauze around Hakeem's hand.

The theater manager places an arm on Hakeem's lower back. "I'm always telling you, Hakeem. Leave the cooking to me. You're too distracted."

This is not an admonishment. It sounds like a lover's correction.

I'm embarrassed, witnessing the intimacy between them.

As if Hakeem realizes my discomfort, he pushes away roughly from the other man and turns to me. "Why have you come to invade the privacy of my home? Why can you not just leave things alone? What business is it of yours? What business is it of anybody's? I take care of my family back home. Isn't that enough?"

He sounds more broken than angry, more defeated than indignant. It takes only one step for him to drop his sturdy frame on the cot. His head is bent low, playing with the gauze around his hand. He hasn't noticed that his ample rump is now seated on the *Times of India* crossword puzzle.

Mr. Reddy, who is still standing at the washbasin, looks at Hakeem and sighs. After a beat, he walks to the table and begins cutting the vegetables with slow, measured movements of the knife. "We met in Bombay when Hakeem was visiting his family one year and took them to the cinema house. We saw each other and just knew. And we found a way to be together in Jaipur when the theater manager job came up." His eyes are wet when he looks up from the cutting board. "This was the best way of saving his family from the embarrassment and still making sure they're taken care of. Hakeem's job at the palace is so good. He'll never find another like it in Bombay. And we get to be alone. We don't bother anybody." He stops to pull a handkerchief from his *dhoti* and blows his nose.

I'm puzzling it out. I point to Mr. Reddy. "When did you start working for the cinema house?"

"Three months ago. They needed to decide on ticket prices, organize putting up the flyers, coordinate the films to be shown. Oh, and the actors."

I point to Hakeem, who is studying his bare feet. "The Singhs found out about the two of you?"

"It was Mr. Ravi," Mr. Reddy says. "He saw us together one day in Central Park. Having lunch. You had a cold that day, Hakeem, remember? I brought you extra chilies for your *dal*."

The two men exchange a look. Hakeem is the first to look away.

A memory comes to me. Omi beseeching her husband, home during a hiatus. He was a handler for the *mahoots*, the men who trained the elephants in a traveling circus. She had fallen at his feet, begging him to divorce her. "Let me marry someone else! Let me lie with a man as other women do."

I hadn't understood what I'd heard that day; I was then only a boy. I've been in the world many more years since then, and I've learned a few things. There were passions beyond our control, beyond what we had been taught to believe were normal.

I rub my eyes with the flat of my hands. "Look, I'm not interested in your private life. My intention is to clear Manu Agarwal's name. I know those receipts for supplies were doctored, Hakeem Sahib. And there's only one person who could have manipulated them."

Hakeem picks at the bandage on his hand. He nods. "I got rid of the original receipts. If you look carefully, you'll notice the ones I replaced them with are on a different paper. I had no choice."

He looks at his lover, who comes to sit beside him on the cot.

Mr. Reddy gives me an imploring look. "It didn't help in the end. They got me to say that I let too many people into the balcony. The palace is firing me."

He covers Hakeem's hand with his own. "We will find another way to stay together."

"But your job is guaranteed, Uncle?"

The accountant nods. "That was the deal."

"Are you willing to tell your story to the maharani?"

He shakes his head. "No, young Abbas, I will not. I cannot. My family needs to be protected. I cannot let my daughters' lives be ruined by my failings. If word got out about what I am, they will never be able to marry. No one will have them. I will never confess any of this to Her Highness or to Manu Sahib or I will lose my job. In disgrace. I can't afford that." He looks directly into my eyes. "You would have to kill me first."

His companion gasps and turns to him sharply.

Hakeem turns moist eyes to him. "Not even for you could I do this, BK, I'm sorry to say. My daughters are young. They have their whole lives ahead of them. Lives that won't survive the scandal of our relationship." He squeezes Mr. Reddy's hand.

"What if I can guarantee discretion?" I have no idea if I can, but I have to try.

Hakeem scoffed. "You can't. No one can." He shook his head. "No, Abbas Malik. There is no solution here. I'm sorry for the families of the injured, but there is nothing I can do to change the outcome."

His eyes are hard. I can see his mind is made up. Mr. Reddy looks at me hopefully, as if I had a prepared response that would make all this better. I hadn't.

Of the three days Maharani Latika gave us to provide evidence of malfeasance, we've almost used up two. We have one more day to find enough evidence to clear Manu. I check my watch. It's nine o'clock in the evening. The Singh family will have had their dinner by now. The *chowkidar* is used to me (I always share a cigarette with him when I visit), and he lets me in without alerting the family.

The house servant greets me at the front door. I tell her I want to see Samir. She takes me to the library door, then knocks.

"Come in," I hear Samir say. The servant opens the door for me and leaves.

Samir is seated behind his desk. He's marking blueprints. When he looks up and sees me, the surprise in his face is evident. "Cinema house again?"

I nod.

"You're like a bad *anna*. I thought we were done with that." He waves at the drawings in front of him. "There's another project on the horizon. Everyone's moved on."

"Manu Agarwal hasn't. He can't."

Samir throws his mechanical pencil across the desk. It bounces off the blueprints and lands at my feet. I pick it up and step up to his desk. I place the pencil on his blueprints, gently. Samir is angry, and I can see why, but I won't let that deter me.

"When employees make tragic mistakes, they lose their jobs. It happens every day, Malik."

"You've worked with him. He's hired you for some of the palace's largest projects. You know he's above reproach. How can you let him take the fall for this?"

"This has nothing to do with you. Malik, if you keep badgering me, I may have to bar you from this house." He's looking at me with a charming smile, but he sounds annoyed.

I take a piece of brick and a chunk of cement out of my coat pockets and set them on the blueprints. I take out the telegram from Chandigarh and set it there also.

Samir looks down at my offering. Without raising his head, he lifts his eyes to mine. "What am I to do with these?"

I put my hands in my pockets. "They're pieces of a puzzle I'm trying to put together, but I'm missing a piece." I begin pacing the area in front of his desk.

"On the Royal Jewel Cinema project, decorative bricks like this were substituted for the bricks specified in the original contract. The invoices show that the palace paid for class one bricks, not these less expensive ones. If the palace was charged full price, did Singh-Sharma pocket the difference?

"Now, as for this cement. It's too porous to be used on the balcony of the cinema house. Wrong ratio of sand to water. That can happen when unskilled labor is used. But I thought Singh-Sharma has a reputation for using only the most qualified labor. The palace certainly pays top rates for your labor costs. So once again, if the palace was charged full price, did Singh-Sharma pocket the difference?"

"Sit, Malik. You're making me dizzy."

"You again?"

I turn around. It's Ravi.

He walks into the room, rolling his eyes at his father as if to say *Malik is pagal.*

Ravi throws up his hands. "Abbas, is this another flimsy excuse to catch a glimpse of Sheela?"

What? The confusion must show in my face.

"With or without her sari?" He tosses a chin at his father. "Papaji knows all about it."

I turn to Samir, who has put a hand over his mouth, as if hiding a smile.

"My wife is a stunner, *hahn-nah*?" Ravi smiles. "She told me how you'd tried to get her clothes off the night of the cinema house collapse."

The image of Sheela, fresh from the bath, appears unbidden in my mind. I feel my face flush. What did Sheela tell Ravi? Why would she say such a thing?

Now Samir chuckles. "You do look guilty, you know."

"It wasn't like that!" I say.

"Let's ask her, shall we?" He walks to the door and calls her name. She appears with Baby on her shoulder and a cloth diaper.

"Where is Asha when I need her?" Sheela sounds irritated. She stops midstride when she sees me. Ravi places his hands on her shoulders and guides her to stand in front of me.

"Now, *priya*, did this man not ogle your naked body the night of the collapse?"

Her mouth forms an O and her eyes widen in surprise. "No, not like that. He helped me with my bath. But—not in that way. I... I was drunk—and tired." She turns to Ravi. "I didn't say he tried anything, did I?" She pivots to face Samir, waiting behind his desk. "Papaji, I wouldn't. I love Ravi! I've never—"

Samir holds up his hand, nodding his head. "Enough, *bheti. Theek hai*. Go. Go take care of Baby."

Stricken, Sheela throws a bewildered look at me, shaking her head. *You must believe me, Abbas! I never said that!* Ravi escorts her out of the library and returns with a grin on his face. I know that look. When you think you're about to win the match.

But the game isn't over yet.

Without a word, I pull the last item from my pants pocket. One of the unmarked gold bars I borrowed from Moti-Lal. I set it on the desk next to the other items.

Samir inches forward in his seat, staring at the bar. The light from his banker's lamp shines directly on the gold, making it glow. I lift the gold and place it neatly in the recessed area of the brick. It fits.

For a moment no one speaks.

Ravi comes forward. "Party tricks, Abbas? Papaji, he'll say anything—"

Samir silences him with a warning look.

To me, he says, "What's your point?"

"I think these bricks are used to smuggle gold into Jaipur. The bullion is removed and the bricks are mixed with all the other class one bricks Singh-Sharma uses in construction." I point to the brick on Samir's desk. "These can't be traced to Chandigarh Ironworks, your supplier, because they don't have a manufacturer's stamp on them. They do, however, have an indentation deep enough to hold a gold bullion."

I turn my gaze on Ravi, who is looking at me with a bemused expression. But I notice the sheen of sweat on his brow. "What could be easier than mixing up the two kinds of bricks during construction and covering them with mortar cement or plaster? I believe the money Sharma-Singh saves by using cheaper, substandard materials is financing the purchase of contraband gold. Which is then sold on the black market, where there's a demand for it."

Samir smiles warily and leans back in his chair. "Abbas, you could have picked up these pieces of brick and cement from anywhere. How do I know they're from the Royal Jewel Cinema?"

He's got a point. I shrug. "Because I saw you looking at these, too, the night of the collapse. And I have no reason to lie to you."

Ravi makes a face. "Yes, you do. If Agarwal loses his job, so do you."

"I don't need this job, Ravi. I never needed it. I only came because—"

I stop, look at Samir. I was about to say I'm here because of Lakshmi, and I've brought this to Samir's attention because I owe him that much; he paid for my education. There are so many secrets in our world, aren't there? Ones we keep, ones we reveal, but only at the right moments. I know now that I should not have said yes to Jaipur, yes to Auntie-Boss. I've been happy in Shimla. The air is cooler, the breezes cleaner. I can think in the mountains. And Nimmi is there. How could I have left her there when she begged me not to? When I was just getting to know Chullu and Rekha?

"Because why?" Ravi challenges me.

I say nothing.

Ravi turns to his father. "Papaji, who is this boy to you?"

The room is so quiet that I can hear the second hand of the English clock on the mantel advancing. *Tick-tock. Tick-tock.*

Ravi is watching his father, who is ignoring him.

Samir picks up the mechanical pencil. He screws and unscrews it so the lead moves in and out of its casing. "You said a part of this puzzle was missing, Abbas. So what part is that?"

I glance at father, then at the son.

"What I don't know is whether you knew anything about this, Samir Sahib, or if it is a one-man operation. *You don't need a mirror to see the wound on your palm.*"

I remembered this saying as one of Samir's favorites.

It's obvious who is moving all the parts, isn't it? I'm looking openly at Ravi. He stands just a few inches from his father's desk, tall, upright, with his broad chest. He's flexing his powerful hands.

Samir looks at him, too. His voice is calm; it's hard for me to know what he's thinking.

"Ravi, do you have anything to contribute?" Samir says to his son.

"Only that it's a good story, as stories go. A bit like Scheherazade, our Abbas. Keep spinning the tale every which way so he can keep the king awake. Look, it's embarrassing to have to admit that I inadvertently accepted a bad shipment of bricks, but that's all it was. And I—we—our company, Singh-Sharma—is paying the price for the reconstruction. It's costing us plenty, I can tell you that."

Ravi takes step toward me. "But why am I having to justify anything to you anyway? Who are you, Abbas? Why do you feel you can just come here anytime you please and make accusations?"

He turns to his father. "Papaji, you and I have talked about his obsession with Sheela. It's insulting! We should bar him from entering our house ever again."

"I thought we were all playing Parcheesi after dinner." It's Parvati. How long has she been standing at the threshold to the room? Her eyes take in the scene. Me, standing in front of Samir's desk, frowning at Ravi. The gold bar glowing inside the brick cavity. Her son clenching his jaw, looking as if he'd like to slit my throat. Samir, his mouth in a grim line, sliding the lead up and down his mechanical pencil.

It's never a good idea to underestimate Parvati. She's as sharp as the *patal* Nimmi carries for cutting her flowers and stems. She enters the room.

When she is standing next to Samir, she looks down at the desk, sees the gold, scans the telegram. Samir looks up at her and some sort of understanding passes between them. The clock on the mantel trills: it's nine thirty.

Finally, she turns to me. Her smile is more of a grimace. "I've finally figured out why you look so familiar, Abbas Malik. You're the runt who used to run after Lakshmi, carrying her supplies like the good little servant you are."

She scans my clothes, my shoes, my watch. I meet her gaze. "And look at the *Pukkah Sahib* now. Did Lakshmi buy you those things? Is she still your minder? Looking after her minions?" If I respected her more, her words might have the power to hurt.

She looks sideways at Samir. "One thing's for sure. She certainly knows how to stir up trouble."

Parvati smiles at me, sweetly this time, and I almost believe it's genuine until she says, "You tell Lakshmi that jealousy is not an admirable quality. She shouldn't send her boy around here to get what she wants. Now, take your toys and go. You are not welcome here. Again. Ever."

Should I explain my theory of the puzzle and the missing

piece to Parvati? I steal a glance at Samir, who appears absorbed in his pencil. He looks—mortified? Embarrassed? It's hard to say, but he won't meet my eye.

I scoop up my discoveries, tuck them into my pockets and head out the door.

As I do, I hear Ravi's voice. "Mummi, this is pure speculation! He's trying to cause—"

I feel the force of the slap as if it had been directed at my cheek instead of Ravi's.

25

NIMMI

Shimla

Yesterday and today, Dr. Kumar insisted on driving us to and from the Community Clinic. I'm used to walking there with Chullu on my back and Rekha at my side, but the doctor is afraid the traffickers might have heard about the tribal woman who walked into town with forty sheep a few days ago. It's not a common sight. Men are usually the ones who do the herding, and it's bound to have stirred up the gossip-eaters—careful as Lakshmi and I had been in choosing the route we took to the hospital grounds. Today, the sheep are in the custody of the old shepherd I hired to graze the flock west of here. And the sheared wool is safely stored in the Kumar pantry.

Once we're at the hospital, surrounded by staff, Dr. Kumar

breathes easier. He gives the sisters and nurses strict instructions not to let anyone through who is not a patient of the clinic. Then he heads over to the hospital to do his rounds while Rekha, Chullu and I walk out the back doors of the clinic into the Healing Garden.

I was relieved to find Lakshmi gone when the children and I awoke yesterday morning; Dr. Kumar had already taken her to the Shimla train station. I wouldn't have known what to say to her after my outburst the night before. I know I shouldn't blame her for the tragedy in Jaipur; she had no way of knowing what would happen. I'm just so scared that I'm going to lose Malik the way I lost Dev. Surely she must understand that.

Then, when I brought the children downstairs for breakfast, I saw that Lakshmi had set out saris and blouses for me to wear on the hospital grounds and in town so I wouldn't draw attention to myself. That simple kindness, her concern for my safety, unsettled me. Was it shame I felt for not acknowledging the many things she has done for us since Malik left? For being disrespectful to my elder the way I would never have been to a woman of my tribe? For protecting us from the danger Vinay has put us in? How can I be both angry at her and grateful?

Now I cover my head with Lakshmi's sari, shielding my face and my tattoo. I keep close watch on the children because Rekha tends to wander and Chullu waddles after her. He's started walking only in the last month, but once he starts, he can get pretty far away before I notice.

I give the Healing Garden an appraising glance. Malik would be impressed. In the spots of the garden that used to be bare, I've planted herbs and flowers that Lakshmi and I agreed upon. The garden looks fuller now, with new shoots popping up in different places. I need to fertilize and water and make sure I remove dead leaves and any insects feeding on the plants. Lakshmi's collection of herbs is impressive; I know some of them, but most are new to me. She's trying to grow varieties from Rajasthan, but they're not thriving at this altitude. If she asked for my opinion, I would tell her not to waste her time.

At the end of his workday, Dr. Kumar and the kids and I go back to his house, where we eat the dinner a local woman has made for us. (It seems that Lakshmi has seen to everything.) Last night, after dinner, Dr. Kumar helped Rekha and me with our reading and writing. Lakshmi left a stack of books for us, and he is diligently following her instructions.

A few times, when he's handing me a book, our hands touch, and we both recoil as if we'd touched a flame. The taste of his lips on mine that one night in the fields has stayed with me. I sometimes touch my fingers to my lips, remembering where his lips had touched my own. It reminds me of Malik and how much I miss his touch.

I miss his letters, too. But with all the turmoil around the collapse, I don't expect he will write.

Lakshmi's been gone two days, and I know the doctor misses her. He told me this morning that he'll call her when he returns from work tonight.

Madho Singh is also missing her. He complains when he's in his cage, which is much of the day. When I leave the door to the cage open, he often stays inside instead of perching on the back of the sofa, as he does when Lakshmi is home. At random times, he shouts out proverbs that the maharani taught him. *A drowning man catches at a straw. Squawk! Two swords do not fit in one scabbard. Squawk!* Lakshmi and the doctor are fond of quoting him.

He'll come out of his cage to greet the doctor when he comes home or anytime he happens to see Rekha. She talks to him as if he's just another child her age. He always answers. His answers often make no sense, but Rekha makes up interesting conversations that don't make any sense to *me*. She pretends to read to him from different children's books (she knows the stories by heart now, and she likes to point out the illustrations to Madho Singh). It always seems to soothe him, and he's usually asleep on his perch before the story's ended.

Tonight, the doctor is working late. He dropped us off at the house and went back to the hospital. I'm in bed with the children on the second floor, in Malik's room. There isn't much of Malik in it, however. It's a comfortable room with a warm wool blanket on the bed, a window where I can look out on the horse pasture, and a poster of four *gore* called the Beatles. Malik told me they're musicians, and amazing. That, a year ago, they came to India to see their guru, which seems strange. The elders of our tribe are skeptical of gurus, whom they think of as false prophets.

Rekha and I are looking at a picture book that shows the different flowers of the Himalayas. Chullu has fallen asleep on his stomach, nestled against my side.

Squawk! "*Namaste, bonjour,* welcome!" *Squawk!*

I hear Madho Singh flapping his wings around the house, landing on a perch, screeching, then taking off again. This is not the way the parakeet greets visitors, so something has set him off. But what? An animal? A weasel or a monkey?

I try to remember if I locked the doors and windows, as the doctor is always telling me to do. (At the Aroras', there *was* no lock on the door of the little room where we were staying.) Here on the second floor, we can leave the windows open for fresh air, but downstairs, we must lock every door and window tight. The neighboring houses are few and far between and tucked amid the pines, which means bandits are concealed from sight. Calling for help would be futile.

Dr. Kumar showed me how to use the phone to call the police or the hospital. I was too embarrassed to tell him I've never used a phone. And I certainly didn't tell him that the police are the last people I would call. Our tribal elders never trusted the authorities, who are quick to push us off our grazing land the moment anyone complains. And, now that the police are under the impression the doctor and I are intimate with each other, they might see me as an easy woman, someone they can bed without much effort.

I'm wondering what to do about the parakeet's squawking when Rekha jumps off the bed and runs out the door, calling to Madho Singh.

"Rekha!" I yell. I prop pillows around Chullu to make sure he doesn't fall off the bed while he's sleeping. Then I scramble after Rekha.

When I reach the bottom of the stairs, Rekha is running around the drawing room, following Madho Singh on his flight from armchair to lamp to fireplace mantel. The only light is from the moon outside. I pull the curtain back to see if anyone is there.

There is. A figure in the shadows, standing on the veranda.

My heart begins to pound. I try to see through the darkness.

It's the shepherd who's been looking after my flock!

I take in a deep breath and let out a sigh of relief. I call to him through the window. "What is it, *bhai*?"

He turns to face my window. I can't see his features. Nor can he see mine.

"What should I do with the flock? They've grazed the area I was paid to clear. They were very hungry!" His laugh is high and shaky.

"I'll pay you to keep them for a few more days. Are there other places they can graze?"

"Theek hai," he says. "I will take them farther north." When he turns to go, I remember I still have his shears.

I call out: "Wait!"

I run upstairs to get them, taking another moment to pick up a few coins from my week's pay. When I get back to the drawing room, it's quiet. Madho Singh is back in his cage, mumbling. But where is Rekha?

Then I see the open front door, and I hurry out to the veranda. Rekha's there, talking to the shepherd.

"Why do sheep have tails?" she asks him.

I pull her back behind me. "Silly girl!" I say. I return the shepherd's shears to him and put the coins in his hand.

He looks confused by the panic that's so apparent in my voice and my expression. He drops the coins into his vest pocket and turns to go but then he stops and turns around.

"*Behenji,*" he says, "earlier today, when I was moving the sheep, a man came up to me and asked if they were mine."

My heart, again, begins to race. Rekha starts to squirm before I realize I've dug my fingers into her shoulders. I make an effort to relax them.

"What did you tell him?"

The old man lifts his chin and draws himself up to his full height. "What business is it of his?" he says. "*That's* what I told him!"

He grins, and the moonlight glows on the few teeth he still has left.

I nod. "How did *you* know where to find me?"

He scratches the back of his neck. "Word gets around," he says.

Then he steps off the veranda and disappears into the darkness.

I close the door and lock it. I pick Rekha up and hug her tightly. "What have I told you? You mustn't open the door for anybody. Not even old men."

"I know, Maa, but Madho Singh likes him."

"Madho Singh doesn't even know him!"

I feel Rekha's steady heartbeat, as I'm sure that she feels mine. When I was with my tribe, I never felt unsafe, the way I'm feeling now. If a shepherd can find me so easily, how long will it be before the smugglers find me, too?

An hour later, I'm huddled with the children on the drawing room sofa. They're both asleep when I hear Dr. Kumar's car in the driveway. I open the front door and go out on the veranda to wait for him. When he sees me, he rushes over.

"*Kya ho gya?*" he asks me. He ushers me inside the house and locks the door.

"It's just that… I don't think we're safe here, either." I tell him what the shepherd told me, how he'd found me. "If *he* found me here, then other people can find us."

"Did he threaten you?"

"No. Nothing like that. I want to take the children somewhere, but, unless we're with my tribe, we won't be safe. Not even in the mountains. Now that people know I live here with you…" I realize I'm wiping my sweaty palms against my skirt again and try to still them.

He sits down in his armchair, opens his briefcase and takes out a notebook. After he's turned a few pages, he picks up the phone and dials. It's ten o'clock at night. Who could he be calling so late?

A minute later, he hangs up.

"Collect your things," he says. "We're going to move you tomorrow morning to a place where it will be difficult for anyone to find you or the children. Outside the city."

"But what about the garden? Who will tend to it? I have to water the young plants—"

Dr. Kumar shakes his head. "For now, your safety has to take priority. Mrs. Kumar will take care of things when she returns. *Chinta mat karo.*"

Don't worry? Worrying is all I've done since Malik left.

306

26

LAKSHMI

Jaipur

This morning marks the third day I've been away from Jay. Malik comes to the Agarwals' early to tell me about his visit to the Singhs. Kanta and Niki have already gone out for a walk with Saasuji. Manu has barricaded himself in his study, far from the drawing room where we're sitting.

Malik says Samir seemed genuinely shocked when he showed him how the gold bar fits into the brick. We agree it's unlikely that Samir would put his firm in jeopardy for the promise of more money. What he really wants, we decide, is to believe his son has made the honest mistake of accepting damaged goods. But neither Malik nor I believe that Ravi's error is an innocent one. Based on how smoothly he seduced my sister twelve years ago and shrugged off the consequences, we know how disingenuous Ravi can be.

Malik also summarizes his visit to Hakeem, the facilities accountant.

That puzzles me. "And Hakeem won't come forward to say that he switched the receipts? Why? Who is he protecting?"

Malik hesitates. He never lies to me, but I know he won't share things that might hurt me or hurt others. I wait.

"Hakeem...lives with Mr. Reddy."

"The theater manager?"

Malik nods. "They share lodgings here in Jaipur. And Hakeem has a wife and four daughters in Bombay. He doesn't want them to know about Mr. Reddy. It would destroy their lives."

I'm trying to put the pieces together when it comes to me. *"Accha."* Who am I to judge the accountant? I'm a woman who deserted a marriage and slept with another woman's husband. People find love where they find it. "And the Singhs know... about the relationship?"

"Ravi Singh found out. Mr. Reddy will sacrifice his job. Hakeem will keep his. He has a large family to support."

"So Reddy agreed to say he let more people onto the balcony than he was supposed to. Even though that's a lie?"

"Right."

Samir certainly won't turn his own son in for fraud and misappropriation. Parvati will keep pressing Maharani Latika to fire Manu. And, as appalling as it is to me, Maharani Latika isn't interested in an investigation; she wants the problem to go away and for the cinema to open again as quickly as possible. I understand. The tarnish on the royal reputation increases every day the situation is in limbo.

I'd promised Kanta that the maharanis were fair, but now I'm realizing how foolhardy that was of me. We have just one day to convince Her Highness not to let Manu go.

THE SECRET KEEPER OF JAIPUR

The pressure of being labeled a thief is getting to Manu. Instead of returning to work, he stays locked in his study, listening to the radio or reading poetry. At mealtimes, Kanta brings him his food on a tray instead of having Baju deliver it so she can sit with her husband while Niki, Saasuji and I eat in the dining room. Kanta says he takes only a few bites, claims to be full and asks her to leave. He hasn't shaved in days, so when he does make a rare appearance to walk from the study to the bathroom, he looks more and more like the holy men of the Ganges. His unwashed hair hangs over his brow. He's been sleeping in the same shirt and trousers for three days.

Niki is also reacting to this shift in his father. Even if Kanta allowed him to go back to school, her son wouldn't go. Bad news travels even faster than good news, it seems. Niki's friends have called to tell him some of his fellow students are calling his father a cheat and an embezzler. Niki knows his father isn't capable of such deception, but neither is he capable of defending a father who isn't even trying to defend himself.

Kanta spends time with Niki going over the lessons his teacher drops off. Reading novels, which they both love to do, keeps them busy, too. I stop by Niki's door sometimes, listening to them discuss *Slaughterhouse-Five* and *Travels with My Aunt*. It reminds me of the way Radha used to lose herself in her *Jane Eyre* and *Wuthering Heights*.

Manu's despair is affecting Saasuji and Baju, as well. Manu's mother finds fault with everything the old servant does (he didn't salt the *dal* or he let the *parantha* burn or he didn't roast the cumin long enough), and Baju is grumpy as a result, clanging pots and pans in the kitchen and grumbling to himself. It almost makes me wish Madho Singh were here.

What a relief it is to leave the Agarwal house for my next appointment.

★ ★ ★

This time when I arrive at the Maharanis' Palace, the guard gives me a warm smile. "Elder or younger?" he asks.

"Elder," I reply.

He tilts his head ever so slightly to show his surprise. But he nods and beckons an attendant forward. The immaculately uniformed bearer leads me up a set of marble stairs, the centers of which are grooved from the weight of thousands of feet over two centuries. The stairs lead to a terrace overlooking the lush garden in the center of the palace. I've never been to the upper terrace of the palace before. I stop to admire the scene below; it's like the fairy tale of *The Three Princes* I was reading to Rekha the other day. Bushes trimmed to look like giraffes or hippopotami or elephants (Rekha would love those!). Waterfalls and fountains. Pink-faced monkeys, often seen around the Pink City and royal buildings, hop from guava to pomegranate to banana trees, taking their meal where they find it. Live peacocks cry out in full display. Sunbirds flit from one flower to another, gorging themselves on nectar.

Finally, I'm shown into a large bedroom off the terrace. White gauze curtains are drawn across the latticed windows, leaving the room in shadows. Two attendants stand at the doorway, beyond which is a large four-poster bed. I assume the doors are left open so the maharani can enjoy the watching the macaques scurrying across the high walls of the palace from her bed.

Several ladies-in-waiting are sitting on settees or armchairs. One is embroidering, one is fanning the maharani with a large sandalwood fan and the third is reading.

I find the Maharani Indira much changed. Her hair, without my signature *bawchi* oil, has thinned. It's more salt than pepper now. I used to meet her in the drawing room—the same place I met with Maharani Latika only two days ago. Now the dowager maharani lies in the mahogany bed amid satin pillows stuffed with goose feathers. The table next to her bed contains many jars of ointment and bottles of pills. Vases of sea hibiscus, magenta roses and sunset *champak* do little to disguise the medicinal odor.

The old queen is smaller, shrunken, her cheeks are hollow. Before, she seemed to fill the room with her bawdy jokes and gin-infused laughter. Now she lies quietly with her eyes closed.

"Wait a little while and she will wake up," the nearest lady-in-waiting says to me. I study the dowager's face. The skin around her mouth and cheeks, so used to stretching into a smile or a laugh, has gathered into folds, making her appear older than her seventy years.

One thing that has stayed constant is her love of jewelry. Her neckline is adorned with a *kundan* choker, its teardrop-shaped diamonds and cabochon rubies reflecting the light from the open doorway. Her matching earrings also feature teardrop diamonds surrounding a center ruby. Pearl and ruby bangles, now too large for her thin arms, threaten to slide off her wrists.

Another noblewoman indicates an armchair by the maharani's bedside, and so I sit, setting my carrier on the floor beside me. I think back to the day Her Highness first received me and changed my life forever.

Twelve years ago, after the dowager hired me to cure the Maharani Latika of her depression, rumors spread—as rapidly as the macaques jumping from tree to tree—of my incredible powers to heal royalty. Everyone wanted a piece of me then. My business grew to the point Malik and I worked from dawn till sundown to fill orders for henna applications, custom oils and healing lotions. If not for the generosity of this woman, all of that may never have happened.

The maharani opens her eyes, still sharp and filled with mischief as they once were. "Lakshmi, you're thinking so loudly, my dear. You woke me up."

Her face is gaunt, but her smile is radiant.

She offers me her hands and I take them. The many ruby, emerald and pearl rings are loose on her fingers.

"Your Highness, I am surprised to learn you've returned to Jaipur. The charms of Paris aren't enough for you?" I tease.

"The men certainly are." She releases one of her spicy laughs. "And the food is divine. But after a while, I missed our turmeric, coriander and cumin. I longed for the scents of ripe mangos. Those whitest of white *rath ki rani*."

She rubs her thumbs over the henna design on my hands. "And this." She pulls my hands closer to her nose and inhales the plant's lasting aroma as well as the geranium oil I use to moisten my skin.

"The scents of my India." She closes her eyes.

Has she drifted off to sleep? Slowly, I start to remove my hands from hers. Then her eyes pop open. "Tell me, my dear, what have you been up to since we last met? And catch me up on news of my young friend Malik."

I open my mouth to speak, but she interrupts me by lifting her hand. She twirls her gnarled index finger in a circle. "Let me see."

Her eccentricities make me smile. I lift the *pallu*, which I had respectfully covered my hair with, and let it fall over my shoulder. Then I turn my head in one direction and then the other.

"Excellent, my dear. Still a well-shaped head. The mark of a good entrance into the world. Excellent."

From my previous dealings with her, I know the Maharani Indira feels that if a person's birth had been easy, if they've left the birth canal unscathed, their karma is good and that karma will follow them into their present life. Whether or not this is true doesn't matter. She is headstrong in her beliefs and contradicting her is futile.

"Thank you, Your Highness. I've brought my henna supplies

with me. If you will permit me, I would like to decorate your hands while we talk."

She raises her splendid brows in surprise. "Well, now." She glances at the nearest lady-in-waiting. "I think that can be accommodated." The other woman gestures to an attendant, who brings a table for me to set my supplies.

I remove her rings and hand them to the nearest noblewoman. Then I open a bottle of clove oil from my carrier to warm her hands and massage them. My fingers, of course, are naked. My hands are too often immersed in soil or applying poultices to wounds to warrant decoration.

Her skin is like a *peepal*-leaf skeleton: dry but pliable. She watches as I pull her fingers one by one, smoothing the crevices between them. I roll my thumb over the fleshy part of her palm. When was the last time anyone touched her in this way? I wonder. As a royal, she has the power to allow intimacies; but no one may take that liberty without permission.

"Any special requests?" I ask.

"I trust you to do what you think best, my dear."

She closes her eyes as I start drawing with the henna paste I brought with me from Shimla. I tell her about my work at the Healing Garden in Shimla, my marriage to Jay—

"Ah, that explains the lovely red *bindi* on your forehead. So you married that doctor, the one we appointed as royal physician in Shimla for the adoption that never was? My dear, you do astound me!"

My heart flutters in my chest. The dowager is a clever woman. Did she ever consider that we deliberately sabotaged Niki's adoption? All these years we've let her think he was born unhealthy and, therefore, unfit to be adopted as the Crown Prince of Jaipur. If only she could see the robust cricket-obsessed boy Niki is now.

Some lies are best kept secret.

I tell her how Jay offered me the opportunity to work at the

Community Clinic he founded; how he's worked hard to treat the local people in the holistic manner that's most comfortable for them.

"He sounds like an honorable man," she says. Her voice is fainter now. She is beginning to sound drowsy.

I finish the palm of one hand and nod to the lady-in-waiting to hold it open so the damp henna paste will not smear before it has a chance to dry.

I keep talking. I believe it's the rhythm of my voice along with my continual, consistent touch that is lulling her to sleep. I tell her about Malik and his schooling. No use conning her into believing he did well there, when he didn't. But he did graduate with a degree and his natural intelligence. She has a soft spot for Malik, whom she found immensely charming as a boy. I think I see the ghost of a smile on her lips, but perhaps I'm imagining things.

"He's now, what? Twenty?"

Once again, she's surprised me with her memory. *"Hahn-ji."*

"And what of his love life? Surely he has one?"

She lifts her lids, glancing at me slyly from the corners of her eyes.

I'm making a design on her palm when she asks this. My hand stops moving.

She moves her head slightly so she can look directly at me. "You don't approve?"

Despite her illness, her intuition is as sharp as ever. Nimmi had also accused me of not approving of her.

I resume painting the henna on her fragile skin.

"It's not that. I want Malik to see more of the world before he settles down. The young woman he is fond of has two children from her first marriage. She's a widow. It's a lot for a twenty-year-old to handle when he hasn't a proper way to earn a living."

She is thoughtful. "Yes...I imagine. Though he is a resourceful young man." She grins. "I have the feeling that he could've taken on the whole Indian army even at the age of eight." She chuckles.

She holds her palms up to inspect them. The skin on her forearms is loose on her bones. "Saffron flowers? Lions? Whatever have you painted, Lakshmi?"

"I seek your forgiveness if I've been too bold. However, I know you to be a woman who has far more ambition than it was seemly for you to display. The lion is a symbol of that ambition. A long time ago, you told me your late husband prevented you from experiencing motherhood. I drew the saffron plant because it's unable to reproduce without human assistance."

What I'd actually painted on the Maharani Indira's palms is a copy of the terrazzo *mandala* I'd designed for my Jaipur house. Until I started drawing on her hands, I hadn't realized how much she and I actually had in common. "And here, Your Highness—" I point with my henna reed to a spot on her upper palm "—is your name hidden in the design."

"Too clever." Her voice is full of wonder. "Thank you, Lakshmi. They must give me a shot now and heaven knows what else to make me more comfortable. Will you please join me in my greenhouse in a half hour?"

I walk around the hothouse where Her Highness tends to her orchids. It's off the terrace, a few doors down from her bedroom. Fortunately, the attendant who brought me to this nursery with its glass roof and glass walls also supplied me with a tall *aam panna* to cool me down. Still, tiny beads of perspiration line my brow and dampen my underarms.

The room is cheerful. Full of light and packed with well-tended plants. Some of the names I forget since I'm not an expert on these varieties, but I recognize a few of her favorites: the lost lady's slipper with an unusual yellow flower that resembles a butterfly, and clusters of blue vanda, which strike me as more purple than blue. I remember this nursery to be Maharani Indira's shelter, the place where she loves and nurtures freely. It smells of life and rich soil and damp and heat.

I've almost finished my cool mango drink when one of her attendants wheels the dowager maharani into the hothouse and stops in the center of the room where there is a metal settee. Her Highness is holding her hands aloft, careful not to smear the henna paste. I sit on the settee and test the henna paste; it's mostly dry. I warm my hands with geranium oil from my carrier before I rub her hands, until the dried paste has completely flaked off onto the towel I placed on my lap.

She praises the finished design, admiring the renewed silkiness of her skin.

With the barest turn of her wrist, the Maharani Indira instructs the attendant to leave us alone. He exits and stands just outside the closed hothouse door as he awaits her next command.

She curls her index finger, now bright red with henna, and flicks it behind her. I suppose this is my signal to wheel her around. I station myself behind her chair and we begin moving. She inspects a few plants, exclaiming satisfaction or disapproval at the state of their health.

"Now, what's this I hear about the Royal Jewel Cinema, *hmm?*"

I've been wondering how to bring up the subject, so I'm a little taken aback by her forthrightness.

"Some sort of shenanigans about building materials and whatnot?" She's making it sound as if she's only slightly familiar with the cinema fiasco, but I get the feeling that she's well-informed.

"Your Highness, I'm sure you'll recall Mr. Agarwal, the palace's director of facilities. He is being accused of having authorized poor quality construction materials that may have caused the accident at the cinema house."

THE SECRET KEEPER OF JAIPUR

"But you think otherwise, I take it?"

"The Maharani Latika has talked to you?"

"We keep a joint counsel."

We come to the end of one row of plants. There is a low cabinet in front of us.

"Open that cabinet if you would," she says.

I do. It's an icebox. Inside is a covered glass pitcher of clear liquid and two glasses.

"Pour us each a glass, my dear."

Now I remember. The gin and tonic the maharani is so fond of—and which she firmly believes is the secret to orchid health. After I hand her a glass, she toasts mine. "To everlasting health." She laughs at her own joke and takes a sip. "Aah. So cool and crisp. Let's keep moving, shall we?"

I wheel her down another row.

"I believe the reason for the cheap materials has nothing to do with Mr. Agarwal," I say.

"I understand Manu Agarwal lives beyond his means," she says. "The palace does not pay him enough for that expensive sedan and the silks his wife wears."

I try not to show my surprise at how much she knows. "His wife comes from money, Your Highness. Kanta Agarwal is related to the writer-poet Rabindranath Tagore. She's originally from Calcutta."

"Ah. Well, that does explain things." She dribbles a little of her drink on the base of a droopy orchid. She looks at my glass, which I've barely touched. "Drink up, my dear."

I take a sip. It's refreshing. Lighter and sweeter than the Laphroaig that Jay and I drink in the evenings.

Her smile is ironic. "You never used to touch the stuff."

"Times change, Your Highness. My husband favors scotch and I find I like the smoky flavor."

"Next time we'll be sure to accommodate you."

She's speaking as if she'll live forever, and what good would it do to refuse her? I smile back.

"Your Highness, Mr. Agarwal's integrity has never been in question."

"So let's hear your theory."

I hesitate, look into my glass. "You won't like it."

I've irritated her. "Do not presume to know what I think, my dear."

"Gold is being concealed within building materials and couriered to construction sites here in Jaipur, specifically in bricks designed for that purpose. The gold is then sold to jewelers and the bricks are used in construction. Only problem is that those bricks aren't strong enough for load impact—forgive me for the technical explanation. Malik has been teaching me a lot of engineering terms over the last few days."

At the mention of Malik's name, the Maharani Indira breaks into a smile. "Malik is an engineer now?"

"He's recently graduated from private school in Shimla and is here in Jaipur spending some time learning from Mr. Agarwal and the palace facilities engineers. At my request."

"Yes, it's hard to turn you down, Lakshmi. I've noticed that." She arches an eyebrow at me. "Go on."

"Those bricks are substandard. They don't meet current building codes. Couple that with inexperienced laborers mixing the cement mortar that covers the bricks, and you have the makings of a disaster."

She holds up a hand to stop me moving her wheelchair. Then she crooks her index finger for me to come around and face her. I look around for another chair so I won't be peering down at her. There's a bamboo one at the end of the row. I bring it over and place it in front of her wheelchair.

Her Highness waves a gnarled hand as if she's wiping a window. "In your scenario, who is doing what?"

I swallow. This will be tricky because Samir Singh is a favorite of hers. She adores him. "I think Samir Singh's son Ravi has become involved in the couriering of gold from the Himalayas."

As I anticipated, she appears shocked and distressed. "What on earth does Samir's son have to gain from couriering gold? He already comes from one of the wealthiest families in Jaipur—and probably the whole of Rajasthan."

"I've been asking myself the same question, Your Highness. But the evidence clearly points to Singh-Sharma. I can't imagine Samir would risk his reputation and that of his company for money. All I can gather is that Ravi wants to strike out on his own. As you said, he comes from a wealthy family, but none of the wealth belongs to him, per se. Perhaps he wants something all his own. A separate income? Something only he has control over."

I search her face to see if any of this has sunk in or if I've managed to alienate her. If I were her, I might think I've lost my hold on sanity to accuse such prominent members of society. The hothouse feels very warm now. I can feel a trickle of sweat running down my temple.

She's thinking. She sips more of her drink. "What proof have you of any of this?"

"We have extracted sample materials from the disaster site. And we have evidence of falsified receipts."

"Who is *we*, my dear?"

"Malik and I."

"Ah, so we come to Malik again. Cheeky little devil."

"Mr. Agarwal had assigned Malik to work with the facilities accountant. It was Malik who first noticed the discrepancies."

"He would. That boy has the eyes of a goat!" She cackles. "Is there anyone who will attest to their part in this—scheme?"

I let out a slow exhale. "No, Your Highness. They are too frightened of repercussions."

Finally, she wags her command finger. I push the chair out of the way and we continue our perambulation. She sprinkles a little more G&T on the plants.

"Tell me, Lakshmi. Why are you so wedded to the idea that Mr. Agarwal bears no responsibility in this scheme? Could he not be the one who is pocketing the extra monies?"

"I don't believe so. I know Mr. Agarwal well. He is totally and utterly devastated by the accusation. He comes from humble stock, and he's devoted to his wife and son. He takes his position at the Palace Facilities very seriously and feels enormously blessed to have it. He would never do something to jeopardize how far he's come. It would be tantamount to chopping off his own arm."

This might be the last time I am allowed an audience with Her Highness. I come around and kneel in front of her.

"He has a son—Nikhil—who is just turning twelve. A lovely boy. Such a disgrace upon the father would ruin that boy's life forever. You know it as well as I do. On the other hand, if Ravi Singh is found to be guilty of this scheme—and I'm sure he's culpable—he can survive the scandal unscathed. His life will continue as before elsewhere—England, Australia or the States. Samir and Parvati can and will ensure that for him and his family."

I look into her eyes—alarmed, bewildered—a little while longer. Have I completely destroyed any credibility I'd built up over the years with her?

Then I rise and begin pushing the wheelchair again.

"Lakshmi, what's your solution to all this? How do we prove the guilt or innocence of the parties involved?"

Malik and I had talked about what our next step should be. "We go to the scene of the accident. The Royal Jewel Cinema," I say. "We see what materials were used where. Much of the debris has already been removed, but we can test other areas that weren't destroyed in the collapse. Ask questions of all the parties present."

She sighs. She looks worn out. I experience a pang of guilt to be the cause of it.

"Leave me be, Lakshmi. I will think on this." She takes the last sip of her gin and tonic. "I can think better alone in the heat."

She raises her glass at me in farewell.

I take my glass and set it on the icebox cabinet. Then I pick up my carrier.

What a relief to step out of the orchid nursery! My blouse is soaked through. Under my sari, perspiration is running down my legs. I swallow large gulps of air. Fight the urge to run. It's as if I've narrowly escaped being buried alive.

Back at the Agarwals', I'm sitting down with Kanta at teatime when Jay calls.

"Now, I don't want you or Malik to worry, but I've moved Nimmi and the children."

I hear the effort Jay is making to break the news to me calmly over the phone. I take a deep breath. "What's happened?"

Across the drawing room table, Kanta looks up at me sharply.

"It's too easy for people to find our house, Lakshmi, and especially with you gone, she and the children are vulnerable when I'm not here. Last night I was called back to the hospital…"

He's distracted. I can picture him looking around the room, his cautious gaze alighting on the windows, the door, back to the windows, ears sensitive to foreign noises. *Did he remember to lock up?*

"Are you all right, Jay?"

"I'm fine. I keep hearing noises. The old shepherd—the one she hired to look after the flock—came to the door. She'd never told him where we live. If he can find her so easily…"

"Of course. Where did you take them?"

"My aunt, the one who raised me, used to spend a month every year at a nearby convent. She wasn't religious, she just found comfort in their silent ways. She'd help them with gardening and cooking, mending. Always came back refreshed. I talked to their mother superior and she agreed to house Nimmi and the children for a week until the heat dies down."

He pauses.

"And the police?"

"So far, nothing. But I imagine Canara will shut down their operation for a while."

I think of the brickmaker in her sari, slapping the mud mixture into the wooden forms. How will she earn her living now?

"Can you give Malik the phone number of the convent, Lakshmi? I think Nimmi would like to hear from him."

27

MALIK

Jaipur

I had a feeling that if anyone could convince the palace to take a second look at what happened at the Royal Jewel Cinema, it would be Auntie-Boss. She has that ability. She speaks to people in a way that encourages them to listen.

What I didn't know was that, after her visit, the dowager queen would come to our rescue.

We are standing at the site now: Samir, Ravi, Mr. Reddy, Manu, two Singh-Sharma foremen, a few palace engineers, Auntie-Boss and me.

To my surprise, Sheela is here as well, standing a few feet from Ravi. She's not in a dress but a proper sari—a red-violet silk—perhaps out of respect for the occasion. With her dark sunglasses,

Sheela's affect is cool and somewhat haughty in an old familiar way. Her chin is lifted as if in defiance of something. She says nothing, speaks to no one.

I have no idea what she said to Ravi about us or if Ravi made up the insinuations. I'd like to think the few moments Sheela and I shared that felt real, intimate, were just that, but I don't know anymore. Was she only playing up to me to give Ravi ammunition?

In anticipation of the Maharani Latika's arrival, a narrow strip of red carpet has been laid from the hardscape of the courtyard to the foyer and straight into the theater. The reconstruction seems to be in hiatus. The women and men who carry debris or mix cement are nowhere in sight. The area has been swept clean. The remnants of the accident—bricks, pebbles, dust, cement chunks—all gone. It's hard to imagine that only four days ago this was the site of the worst disaster Jaipur had seen in years.

Has everything inside also been cleaned up? Without any of the original materials to examine, how will we convince the palace a fraud has been perpetrated?

Samir looks calm. Ravi looks nonplussed. They're talking quietly together.

As he listens to Samir, Ravi keeps digging his heel in the mosaic tile of the courtyard. Manu stands closer to Mr. Reddy, Lakshmi and me. It's as if we've all chosen sides.

I see Samir glancing at Lakshmi now and then, but Auntie-Boss seems determined not to make eye contact with him.

Kanta must have made Manu shave, bathe and cut his hair for this meeting. He looks thinner, but a lot more presentable than he has since the collapse. He even has a hopeful air about him, a child waiting to see if he will be granted a present for Diwali.

Maharani Latika's Bentley arrives. Her Highness is behind the wheel. To my surprise, the dowager maharani is in the passenger's seat. A lady-in-waiting sits in the back. The Bentley is followed by another sedan from which two attendants emerge to assist the older queen. One unfolds a wheelchair; the other lifts the dowager out of the seat and settles her carefully into the chair. Maharani Latika walks slowly beside the wheelchair as one of the attendants pushes the elder maharani.

The dowager's face lights up when she spots me. "Malik! My boy. Come here, young man."

The old queen is the only one who has not been instructed to call me Abbas. Automatically, I glance at Sheela. She removes her sunglasses and stares at me, as if she's hearing Auntie-Boss calling my name all those years ago. Does she finally recognize me as the boy she spurned? I turn away.

I catch a glimpse of Ravi's frown. He looks at his father as if to ask how I could possibly know the queens of Jaipur so well. It's a small satisfaction, and I feel a deep pleasure as I approach Her Highness.

Auntie-Boss has prepared me for the diminished state of the cancer-ridden queen, but it is still a shock to hear her robust voice coming from that shriveled frame. I hurry to touch her feet. As I straighten, the older queen puts her hands on either side of my face and peers into my eyes. Her smile is wide and joyous. She looks at Auntie-Boss and says, *"Shabash!"* I can tell Boss is pleased with the queen's assessment, if a trifle embarrassed. For my part, I'm touched—and impressed—that she recognizes me from a past when I paid more attention to her talking parakeet than I did to Her Highness. When I was eight, Madho Singh fascinated me far more than royalty. At twenty, I'm honored to be in the dowager's presence.

Everyone else in our party takes their turns touching the feet of both queens. The younger queen greets Sheela, who was a first-rate student at her private school, warmly. The elder queen fawns over Samir and Ravi, telling the father how absolutely

ALKA JOSHI

his handsome son takes after him, chastising them both for not paying her a visit. She smiles graciously throughout.

Now the younger queen casts a critical eye over the assembly. "Let's be clear about what we are here to accomplish today. We've been hearing rumors about low-grade materials being used for the construction of the collapsed balcony columns. We need to verify if that is the case. If we can verify it, we will determine how or why they were purchased or used. What matters most to the palace is the trust of the public. We built this structure for public enjoyment. It's important that their trust in us is warranted and we can guarantee their future safety. I understand all parties have agreed to cooperate?"

There are a few nodding heads. Ravi's eyes are focused on the carpet below his feet.

"Malik," says the dowager. She crooks a finger at me and then behind her. Evidently, I am to push her.

When I place a hand on the back of her wheelchair, she reaches behind with her clawlike hand and pats it. I see now that Auntie-Boss had decorated it beautifully with henna.

"What fun!" I hear her say. It's as if she's treating this meeting as a Sunday outing. Chances are she hasn't had many of those recently.

The maharanis and I lead the procession on the red carpet. Everyone else follows us into the lobby and then the theater itself. I hear Auntie-Boss exclaim in awe at the lobby's grandeur, which has remained intact; the destruction was to the theater space inside.

I want to turn and say to Boss, "Isn't it exactly as I described it to you in my letters?"

And, as I often have on other occasions, I think of how wide Nimmi's eyes would grow taking in all this finery. But for the first time, I also think: Would she be comfortable amid all this glamour?

The engineers and foremen form a tunnel through which the maharanis travel. They're directing us to the far entrance doors where the theater shows no signs of destruction. They all bow as the maharanis go past.

"My, my!" The dowager says when she sees the size of the cinema screen, the graceful fall of the theater curtains and how the orchestra seats angle down as we get closer to the stage so everyone has a good view of the movie. With her illness, I doubt she's had a chance see the cinema house before today.

She glances at Ravi. "A touch of the Pantages, eh?"

He blushes, pleased that she recognized the architectural reference.

I push the wheelchair farther down the aisle to the stage and then turn it around so we can examine the ruined balcony. Everyone follows except Samir, Ravi and Sheela, who remain standing at the theater entrance.

Something's wrong. Everything has been replaced. The balcony has been returned to its original state. The columns have been replastered. The mohair seats in the balcony and down below are in mint condition. So is the carpet. It's as if the accident never happened.

Samir is running his thumb across his lips, his eyes downcast, as if in apology. "We weren't aware that you would want to see the column in its original state. We've been following an aggressive reconstruction schedule. The final plaster went up yesterday." He looks at the younger maharani. "Your Highness had instructed us to get the cinema house up and running as quickly as possible."

He holds his arms out. "I'm sorry if there's nothing to see."

I leave the wheelchair and walk up to the column that had collapsed. I rub my palm on the cool plaster. Turning toward the group, I look at Auntie-Boss, who looks as surprised as I feel. Manu and Mr. Reddy also wear the same dumfounded expression. While we were still putting the damage estimates together at the facilities office, Singh-Sharma must have been working day and night to repair the damage. Or did they accomplish all this since yesterday evening, when they learned the maharanis were coming to inspect the premises?

It's the dowager queen who speaks as if nothing is amiss. "What a marvelous job you've done, Samir. Every detail. So elegant. So appropriate. Don't you think, Latika?" Her voice echoes in the empty theater.

The Maharani Latika nods her assent. She opens her mouth to speak but the dowager interrupts her. The older woman turns her gaze on Samir.

"Do you think, my dear, that you could tear down one of the other columns?"

Auntie-Boss and I exchange a look: *What is the dowager up to?*

"The other columns?" Samir frowns.

"Um. Just so we can see how they were constructed? I would assume they were all built the same way originally?"

I've never known the elder maharani to be agreeable (indeed, she always prided herself in being a contrarian), but she is speaking in such soft, sweet tones to Samir.

The Maharani Latika is looking at her as if she has lost her mind.

Samir is half smiling, half frowning, his glance alternating between the two maharanis. "You want us to tear down one of the other columns? The ones that are fine?"

"Oh, I know it's a bother. But just so we can stop all this fussing."

"I don't wish to be petty, Your Highnesses, but who will pay for the time spent on the demolition and reconstruction of the column that has nothing wrong with it?"

He sounds incredulous. He looks to the younger queen for support. But her face is inscrutable. In private, the two queens may at times disagree, but in public, the queens show a united front.

The dowager smiles graciously, "We will, won't we, Latika? You see, it's the only way to solve this disagreement. And I don't like disagreements, do you?"

Ravi steps forward. He clears his throat. "But, Your High-nesses, it will mean the cinema house won't open for another week or two! That's a lot of ticket sales the palace will lose. And the film's been rented for only a month. The rental fee will also be lost."

"Pity." That's all the dowager says.

An understanding passes between the queens. While the dowager is in residence at the palace, she controls the purse. Maharani Latika signals her acquiescence with a nod to Samir. He and Ravi exchange a look. They are not pleased.

"Let's hope it's all tickety-boo," the older queen says. "If it's not, we may have to take the whole building apart. And we really don't want to have to do that, do we?"

As if the matter is now firmly settled, Maharani Indira beckons me with that commanding finger. The next thing I know, I'm escorting her wheelchair out of the theater. We are almost at the lobby exit when she says, her voice much weaker now, "Tell my attendant to come here, will you, dear boy?"

I lean to one side to look at her. She has slunk down in the chair and she's fighting to keep her eyelids open. She's not quite as spry as she would like for the assembly to believe; she's been putting on a brave face.

I notice Auntie-Boss has joined us at the entrance now. She has taken one of the maharani's hands and is massaging those pulse points, as she calls them.

I whistle at the attendants, who are waiting right there by the car. They come running. The first lifts her from the chair effortlessly, as if she's as light as a bird; the other collapses the wheelchair and off they go. They put her in the back seat of the second sedan that accompanied the Bentley. The lady-in-waiting climbs out of the Bentley and joins the maharani in the back of the sedan. I watch as she removes a syringe from a medical bag and plunges it into the old queen's arm. She bundles the old woman in blankets and the sedan speeds away.

The whole scene, so quickly carried out, has filled me with sorrow. I look behind me, inside the dark lobby. The younger maharani is in a huddle with Samir, Manu and Ravi, probably discussing the timeline for knocking down one of the undamaged columns. The balcony will have to be supported while the column is removed and rebuilt. Mr. Reddy and Sheela stand off to the side, as do the engineers and foremen.

We won a victory, of sorts, today. If the other columns have been constructed with substandard materials, we will get what we came for. We may save Manu's job yet.

But the dowager queen, who once gave me her precious Madho Singh and always appeared delighted to see me when I was a boy and now, today, clearly will not live out this year. And that depresses me in a way nothing has in a long time. It makes me long for Nimmi and the way she looks at me when she knows I need the comfort of her arms.

Last night, when I visited the Agarwals, Boss gave me the number to the convent. When I asked to speak to Nimmi, the novice said she would ask the mother superior. I waited for what seemed like eternity. Then I heard the phone being picked up.

"Please identify yourself," commanded a sonorous voice. The mother superior. I told her who I was, that I was the former ward of Dr. Jay and Lakshmi Kumar. I gave her the Shimla address where we lived.

"What are the children's names?" she asked.

"Chullu and Rekha."

She asked me to wait a moment. I heard shuffling in the background, the murmur of voices and then a long inhale.

"Nimmi?" No answer. I tried again. "Hello?"

"Hahn?"

It was her! My heart sped up. *"Theek hai?"*

"Hahn." Then, silence.

"Is something wrong?"

Her voice dropped to a whisper. "I've never used a phone before! Am I doing it right?"

I smiled to myself, charmed. *"Zaroor!* Lakshmi told me you've been having quite an adventure."

"The doctor has been so good to us, Malik. Now we are with the nuns. It's nice. Peaceful. I work on their garden. Rekha and Chullu like it here, too." At the mention of her name, I heard Rekha mumble something. "She wants to talk to you. She watches the nuns use the phone, and she's been dying to try it out," Nimmi says.

When Rekha came on, she asked, "Are you bringing me a rainbow? When? Will it be soon? Auntie Lakshmi told me if we live inside the rainbow, we won't be able to see how pretty it is. Is that true?"

Before I had a chance to decide which question to answer first, Nimmi took the phone from her. "Are you coming home soon?"

"I need to talk to Boss about that."

"I see." She sounded resigned. We've talked about it before. Nimmi feels that Lakshmi gets too much of me while she doesn't get enough. I've tried to humor her out of her jealousy, but that only seems to infuriate her. "I've been thinking, Malik, how much safer I was with my tribe. Perhaps I was wrong to leave them, to think life in town would be better. It has only gotten worse for us."

This sounded like a different Nimmi, not the one Lakshmi had described. That Nimmi had followed the trail of her brother's sheep into the mountains; she had brought her brother's dead body back; she had sheared his flock. That Nimmi had made a life for herself in Shimla, using her knowledge of Himalayan plants, her intelligence and sheer will. She had left behind everything she had known—her tribal ways, her native tongue, people she loved. She had kept her children healthy and well-fed. Yet, how utterly alone she was—*akelee*.

"I love you," I blurted out. I hadn't realized until then how strongly I felt about her. But the moment I said it, I knew I needed to tell her; she needed to hear it.

For a moment, neither of us said anything.

"We will be together, Nimmi. You must trust me."

28

LAKSHMI

Jaipur

I watch Niki's cricket game from the front seat of the Agarwals' car. On the sidelines of the cricket patch, Malik stands next to Kanta, cheering Niki on. I watch my nephew as he cleverly skirts the second spin bowl to cross the pitch. He's good at this game. Jay is the cricket fan in our house, but I'm thinking I could learn to love this game, too.

After the maharanis visited the Royal Jewel Cinema yesterday, Manu told us that Maharani Latika has given Singh-Sharma Construction three days to shore up the balcony and open up *all* the columns for inspection, even the ones they recently rebuilt and plastered. Almost immediately, Manu lost his look of defeat, growing hopeful that he would be vindicated. He's returned to work. The tension in the Agarwal household has dissipated. Niki will be returning to school tomorrow.

It's early evening and the sun has eased its relentless assault, giving way to a sweet breeze. Once again, Malik has settled me in the car with a thermos of creamy chai.

Earlier today, I called Jay with the update. He had news of his own. Yesterday, he'd called up his alma mater, Bishop Cotton, and asked if there were any high-ranking police commissioners among the alumni. Turns out there is one in Chandigarh. Jay called to tell him about the gold we'd found on the sheep. The deputy commissioner said they'd been hoping for a break like this because they'd been looking for a link to Chandigarh Ironworks, which they'd been watching for a while. Within a day, the commissioner had arranged for the Canara offices to be raided. They were able to seize a shipment of gold. But they weren't able to get the names of the traffickers.

"Would that include Ravi Singh?" I asked.

"Yes, but the paper trail is not clean. They won't be able to make it stick."

"At least Nimmi is safe now, *hahn-nah?*"

He said yes. Nimmi had returned to working in the Healing Garden but her children were still staying at the convent during the day, and all three of them were sleeping there at night, at least until I came home.

What a relief that had been. When I told Malik, he bent down to touch my feet, which made me laugh! Jay is the real hero here, though. I think of that one unruly lock of hair that never behaves, the one I love to push back into place.

I'm so absorbed in my thoughts that I don't hear the back door of the car opening and closing.

"Like father, like son."

Samir's voice in my ear almost makes me upend the cup of chai in my hands. My heart is hammering in my chest, my fingers shaking. I crane my neck around to see him perched on the back seat, his elbows now resting on the top of the front seat. His face is inches from mine.

He's smiling at me with those marble-brown eyes of his, amused by my confusion. The scent of his cigarettes, the cardamom seeds he chews and his sweet aftershave fill the car. I haven't been this close to Samir in twelve years. I sensed his eyes on me when we were at the Royal Jewel Cinema with the maharanis, but I refused to look at him. His family has once again tried to damage those I love.

But Samir has a palpable energy that's hard to ignore when he's this close. Is my heart beating this wildly from fear or excitement? I used to wonder what it would be like to kiss those brown lips, the lower lip exposing a crescent of pink inside. And then, one day, I found out.

"Why are you here?" I manage to ask when I've found my voice.

"Same reason you are." He lifts a finger to point to the game. "Did you know I never missed one of Ravi's games at Mayo? I taught both my boys in the backyard. Ravi had the same natural confidence as Niki. In a split second, he knew if the ball was worth hitting or missing. And sometimes, even when he knew he should give it a miss, he'd strike. And, would you believe it, Lakshmi, he'd hit it dead-on. Score a point or two."

Snap! A roar goes up from the crowd on the sidelines. I turn around to look at the field. Niki has scored. I see Malik put two fingers in his mouth to whistle. Kanta's arms are raised above her head in a clap.

Samir is speaking again. "*The apple doesn't fall far from the tree.* Ralph Waldo Emerson said that in 1839. But I think it's been true since time immemorial, don't you? Niki Agarwal has Ravi's build. He's the same height as Ravi was at that age. And the way he runs! It's almost like watching Ravi lope across the field."

So Kanta had not imagined Samir watching Niki play at the cricket grounds. He's worked it out. He knows Niki is Ravi's son. Is Radha's son.

If we hadn't lied to the palace and to Samir about the baby's heartbeat, Niki would now be the crown prince and the next maharaja of Jaipur. But telling them his heartbeat was too slow was the only way we could nullify the palace adoption and Radha could keep her baby.

How had Samir found out about my lie?

"When did you learn?" I say it slowly, so I don't betray my nervousness.

My gaze is still focused on the game, but from the corner of my eye, I see his chin rest on his closed fist. His stance is so relaxed we could be talking about the weather.

"I stopped by last summer. Happened to see him playing. I was feeling nostalgic for my old life. Before my boys were full grown. When Ravi used to play cricket here. Back when I was just an architect designing the buildings I wanted to build. Before I got into the big business of construction. Before you suggested the Singhs marry into the Sharma family." He turns his head ever so slightly so that I can now feel his breath on my cheek.

I shift in my seat, leaning against the passenger door now, so I can see him better. Or perhaps to get away from the nearness of him. "You seemed happy enough to make the business and personal connection, if I remember correctly." I'm relieved to be off the topic of Niki.

"Oh, I was. I just didn't know then what it would ultimately lead to."

"Meaning?"

"I thought what a great opportunity it was to expand," Samir says now. "So my sons could join my business as architects, builders, engineers—whatever they wanted. I'd planned for Govind to join us when he finished his schooling in the States. I could leave the boys my business as a legacy." He sounds wistful.

"Well, isn't that what's happened? Ravi works with you. And Govind—when is he coming back from America?" I can no longer hear the game. It's as if every cell of my being is tuned only to Samir's voice.

Instead of answering, he reaches in his pants pocket. I think he's going to show me photos of his younger son, but he shows me a battered illustration of Ganesh-*ji*, the elephant god. The paper is heavy card stock, about the size of a playing card. It's obviously been handled a lot. "Last time I had my horoscope done, I was twelve. I didn't want to believe the chart that my parents had done at my birth, so I went to a Brahmin *pandit* here in the Pink City."

He turns the card over. There's a circle in the middle filled with a grid of sorts and triangles on every corner. Each space has a number written on it. "Of course, only the *pandit* knows what all these numbers mean, but I still remember what he said."

He stops.

"What?"

"He said I would travel abroad. I would accomplish great things. I would make a lot of money. But I would never be able to hold on to it." He looks into my eyes. "It was the same prediction as my baby horoscope."

"You were disappointed?"

"Well, I went abroad—to Oxford. True. I started my own firm, then grew it with Sharma. True. I've made piles of money. True. And I'm about to lose it all."

Samir slips the card back into his pants pocket.

"Last night, I asked Ravi what we'll find if we open up the other columns underneath the balcony. He said that we'll find cheap bricks and badly mixed cement mortar. I said, 'You lied to me?' He said I didn't go into the Indian army like my father, so why should he go into the same business as me? Said he wanted to prove he could succeed at something on his own."

He sighs. "I think you know the rest, don't you?" He lays his cheek on his hand, turning his head toward me.

I should feel triumphant, but I only feel sadness. "He bought cheaper materials for the Royal Jewel Cinema and forged the invoices to show higher amounts, didn't he? Then he used the money he saved to finance a gold route to Jaipur. And he used those cheap bricks to transport the gold."

Samir wags his head.

"But how did he fool the inspectors?"

Samir rubs his thumb and two fingers of his free hand together. *Baksheesh.*

A bee flies into the car from the open window. It lands on Samir's shirtsleeve. For the first time I notice that Samir's shirt, while clean, is rumpled, which is unusual for him. His tie, which he's never without, has been carelessly stuffed inside his shirt pocket. I smell something else on him: scotch. I remember how much he enjoyed playing cards and having a drink or two at the pleasure houses. Is that where he's been?

Samir watches the bee walking around in a circle on his arm and carefully flicks it in the direction of the window. It flies out.

"Are the columns of the balcony the only part of the cinema house that are compromised?"

He shakes his head, pushing away from the front seat. He slouches in the back, surveys the roof of the car. "We will have to take that place apart. Salvage what we can. But we have to rebuild it pretty much from scratch." His gaze comes back to me. "It will ruin the business, but I want to leave with my reputation intact. Ravi will not destroy that. In fact, whatever he made selling that gold is going back into rebuilding the Royal Jewel Cinema."

"You're going to fold Singh-Sharma?"

"No choice. MemSahib has spoken. Parvati—of course she was there when Ravi confessed—says we stop operation after the cinema house is rebuilt and go to America. She's heard from friends that there is a great retirement community in Los Angeles."

"Retirement? But you're only—"

"Fifty-two. Don't remind me. She's got it all figured out."

"Why does that not surprise me?"

"We're going to go into real estate." He scratches the bristles on his chin. "I can't be an architect in America without getting licensed there, and I'm too old to go back to school. So real estate it is."

"What about Ravi? Govind?"

He inches forward and leans his arms on the top of the front seat again. "Govind has already told us he is going into finance in New York, not engineering. He has an American girlfriend. Doesn't want to come back for an arranged marriage. And Ravi...well, he'll probably do real estate with me in Los Angeles." He gives me a lopsided smile. "Looks like Sheela will be living in a joint family whether she wants to or not."

I take a deep breath and turn my body so I'm facing forward again. It looks like the game is winding down. We watch it for a while.

"You owe Manu Agarwal an apology," I say.

There's a pause.

"I've told the Maharani Latika what Ravi said. She's disappointed, naturally, and upset that, no matter what, the disaster will be remembered as the fault of the palace. But Manu's job is safe."

Samir is not going to personally apologize to Manu. Had I really expected him to? Do the Singhs ever apologize to anyone? At least the maharanis know Manu was not to blame.

I feel Samir's finger graze my cheek. I tilt my head away from him.

"Marriage to Jay suits you. I miss his friendship, but you can't be friends when you're in love with the same woman."

My mouth falls open. Blood pounds in my ears. But I don't dare turn around.

Twelve years ago, I would have welcomed those words. To know that he cared this much. Not today.

I can't be having this conversation. I love my husband. I could have loved Samir, but Parvati staked her claim on him a long time ago. She makes the key decisions in their lives. And he lets her. Does that make him weak? Has he always been the less powerful Singh and I just never noticed? Or is he more percep-tive than I give him credit for? After all, isn't Parvati the one who always manages the disasters in the family?

I clear my throat. "Don't try to contact Nikhil. Ever."

From the back seat, I hear rustling. He's opening a fresh pack of cigarettes. "Moving to America will help with that."

I hear the flicking of the gold lighter. A stream of cigarette smoke fills the front of the car when he exhales.

Out on the cricket field, the game is over. The players are shaking hands with one another. Private-school etiquette. In the distance, Malik and Kanta are all smiles waiting for Niki to join them.

I hear the back door open. In the side mirror, I see Samir get out of the car and come to stand by my window.

"Samir?"

"Um?"

"If Manu is any indication of what Niki will grow up to be, Ralph Waldo Emerson was right. *The apple doesn't fall far from the tree.*"

I look up at him. He's smiling at me. He gives me an army salute and ambles away.

29

MALIK

Jaipur

Once we all learn that Singh-Sharma is going make the Royal
Jewel Cinema whole again and that Manu has been reinstated
as director of Palace Facilities, we decide to celebrate with a
feast. Saasuji has made her special *chole subji* and Niki's favorite cake. Baju makes *dal*, rice, an okra *subji* and potato *pakoras*.
Manu brings back *besan laddus, cashew burfi* and *kheer* with pistachios from the sweetshop. Neither Auntie-Boss nor I have had
a chance to write letters back home this whole time, so we call
Jay at home.

I hear Jay tell Boss that Nimmi and the kids are back home
now because the heat is off; his commissioner chum has elimi-
nated the danger.

I ask to speak to Nimmi.

"Today is Rekha's birthday." Nimmi sounds happy. In the background, I hear Rekha singing "Happy Birthday" to herself. "Dr. Jay and I have made a cake. And guess what?"

With a pang, I realize how much I'm missing not being in Shimla. "What?"

"I wrote Rekha's name on it. In Hindi!" She laughs that lovely deep laugh of hers.

"You should see it! It's so pretty!" Rekha has grabbed the phone from her mother. I laugh and tell her I have a present for her birthday. "A present?" she says before Nimmi takes the phone back.

"Please, Malik, no more crickets! We can't find the one Rekha let out of the cage!"

I hear the smile in her voice and find myself grinning, imagining her face when I put the gold chain around her neck. Through the phone I hear Madho Singh exclaim, *Namaste! Bonjour!* Welcome!" He must know they're talking to me.

I hand the phone back to Auntie-Boss so she can say goodbye to her husband. She tells him, "We're coming home tomorrow."

As she hangs up, I say, "You said *we*."

"I did."

"I thought you wanted me to stay and learn with Manu Uncle?"

She laughs and takes my arm, leading me away from the family to the Agarwals' front veranda. "Malik, why did I want you to come to Jaipur?"

"To learn the building trade."

She lowers herself on the veranda porch swing and pats the seat next to her. I sit down. "Did you succeed?"

"Yes."

She nods. "In your time here you learned enough about the

business to know when something isn't right. Why else did I want you to come?"

"To keep me from getting involved with...certain types of people."

"Did you succeed?"

I narrow my eyes, not sure what she wants me to say. "Well, I know I don't want to be involved with the likes of Ravi Singh. But I knew that way back when he first got involved with Radha."

She smiles at me faintly. "So there's no need for you to be here anymore. I don't think there ever was. Nimmi asked me to let you go. She said you only do things because you feel an obligation to me."

I'm about to object, but she places a hand on my arm to stop me. "I've been giving it a lot of thought, and she's right, Malik. You are your own man now. Have been for a long time. I think I overstepped. *Maaf kar dijiye?*"

"Why do you need to be forgiven, Auntie-Boss? If we hadn't been here in Jaipur, think what might have happened to Manu. And Niki. I'm glad we came."

She looks skeptical, as if she doesn't quite believe me but wants to.

"But it is time to go home. I agree."

Now her face breaks into a smile.

"Besides," I say, "I've helped Niki become a star cricket player. I'm counting on him to help us make our millions." We share a laugh.

Birds are twittering in the courtyard of the Agarwals'. In the evening twilight, the headlights of scooters and cars scissor between the spikes of the iron fence beyond. We listen to the honks of *tongas*, the twinkle of bicycle bells and the shouts of rickshaw drivers looking for passengers.

"What *will* you do when we're back in Shimla, Malik?"

I've been giving this some thought. "Something Nimmi and

I can do together." I lean forward, my elbows on my knees, hands clasped. "Boss, I'd like to marry her. She's exactly who she says she is. She has no pretensions." Of course, I'm thinking of Sheela when I say this. As tempting as that attraction had been, I knew it wasn't right for me. It would have made me miserable.

I turn my head sideways to look at my mentor. "I'm a non-practicing Muslim with no caste status. I have no idea where my mother went after she abandoned me at Omi's. And I never knew my father. Omi and her children were the closest I had to family, but her husband hasn't allowed me to see any of them in years." I look down at my hands. "Nimmi and I are alike. She's Hindu but also has no caste. She's no longer with her people, her tribe. The two of us—we understand what it is to be unmoored."

"Unmoored? But, Malik, you're a part of our family. Jay and Radha and me. And now Radha's husband, Pierre, and their daughters—"

I put my hand on hers to calm her. "Nimmi and I don't belong. Not truly. To one set of beliefs, one set of traditions. But we can create our own traditions. Observe those we like, abandon those we don't."

I can see from the tension around her eyes that she's distressed. She's still the handsome woman I started following around Jaipur when she was around Nimmi's age. But now her temples are silver, and she has fine lines around her eyes and mouth.

"I don't mean that I want to separate from you or Dr. Jay or Radha—not at all! I don't know what I'd do without you. But I'm ready for my own family now, Auntie-Boss. I'm ready."

She blinks. Looks out into the deepening night.

"I know you'd rather I married an educated woman. Someone posh. Grand. But that's not who I am. Nimmi and I—we're good together. We understand each other. And I love her children. And now that you've started her reading and writing in Hindi, who knows how far she can go?"

We sit through the pause, both of us thinking things we're not saying.

"There's something else I want to talk to you about."

It takes her a moment, but she returns my gaze. I turn my body so I'm facing her.

"What if we turned your Healing Garden into a teaching center for other herbalists? What if we created a greenhouse for propagating the plants you've already grown and sell them to other herbal practitioners in India? I know something about business and can figure out the rest as I go. And—" I stand and start to pace the veranda. "I've learned enough about building to manage the construction of a greenhouse. Radha's husband could help us design it. The hospital has land that we could build on. Nimmi can continue to help you with the garden and the greenhouse."

I'm walking faster now, trying to keep up with my thoughts. "Your name is already well-known in herbal medicine circles. Once we begin teaching other practitioners and selling our own products, we can use the money we make to help expand the Community Clinic."

Lakshmi's eyes have grown large. "That's a tall order, Malik. Where would we get the money for building the greenhouse?"

"That's the easy part."

I think of Moti-Lal. I think of Maharani Indira and Maharani Latika. I think of Kanta Auntie. How hard would it be to raise the initial investment? The hospital must have a capital fund that may kick in the rest—I'll have to talk to Dr. Jay. I know how to source the best materials. Where to find the engineers. And Pierre is an accomplished architect. It can be done.

I stop pacing and stand in front of her. I bend at the waist to look directly into her blue-green eyes. "Remember how much you wanted to set up a business selling your lavender creams and the *bawchi* hair oil and the vetiver cooling water when we still lived in Jaipur? Well, we can make it happen. I want to make it happen for you. For me. For Nimmi. And Jay will get to expand his clinic."

The face I know so well is alight with possibilities. Those bright eyes of hers are jumping—right, left, up, down—in their sockets as she tries to focus on one thought before another presents itself. It takes her a while, but she parts her lips in that smile that says I've made her happy.

"Let's talk to Jay the moment we get home to Shimla," she says.

We hire a *tonga* to take us to the Maharanis' Palace, the way we used to so the guards wouldn't mistake us for *ara-garra-nathu-karas* who couldn't afford a horse-drawn carriage. We're stopping here on our way to the Jaipur railway station to take the train home. The Agarwals wanted to take us in their car, but Auntie-Boss and I decided we needed to do this alone. One thing is for sure: we won't wait another twelve years to see Manu, Kanta and Niki again.

When the carriage arrives at the entrance to the Maharanis' Palace, we ask the driver to wait with our luggage. I help Auntie-Boss off the *tonga* and we carry our package to the guard station. The guard greets Auntie-Boss warmly—she's been here several times already in the last few days. But, as he used to in the old days, he casts a baleful eye at me—more out of habit than because I appear unpresentable (which I don't). I offer him a nod.

"Well, well. I have the pleasure of seeing you three days in a row. That's something!" says the dowager maharani when we reach her rooms. Even though she is nestled in bed, she appears alert and ready to receive visitors in a vermillion silk sari and layers of pearl necklaces.

"We came to say goodbye, Your Highness," Auntie-Boss says

as she reaches for the queen's feet and pulls the energy upward. I follow suit.

"Jaipur doesn't have enough charms to hold you two for another day or two? And who will do my henna now?" She holds up her decorated hands for us to admire.

"Shimla awaits. We must get back to work."

The old queen focuses her shrewd gaze on us. "Let me see. Lakshmi will be tending to the sick and to her plants. And you, Malik, will go back to your beloved. She must be waiting."

I wonder how the dowager knew. I glance at Auntie-Boss but she makes a face to show me she has no idea. She may be imprisoned by her illness, but the maharani keeps herself apprised of all goings-on.

"We have brought Your Highness something to remember us by." I give the beautifully wrapped package to her closest lady-in-waiting, who hands it to the maharani.

An attendant comes forward, no doubt to check the contents, but the queen waves him away with a slight gesture. She tears open the wrapping with gusto, handing the scented gardenia at the top to one of her ladies.

When she sees the elegant wooden box, she cries out with delight. Her arthritic fingers cannot open the lid of the box easily so the lady-in-waiting does it for her.

"Beefeater Gin! My dears, this is marvelous! Although my doctors won't agree." She instructs her bearer to bring three glasses, Indian tonic water and ice.

While her lady-in-waiting mixes the cocktails, the Maharani Indira says, "Did you know they used to throw patients headfirst into juniper bushes, thinking that malaria would magically disappear the moment their bodies brushed against the branches? Those English! So eccentric! Much better to drink the stuff!"

Auntie-Boss and I trade a private smile as we clink our glasses in a toast.

Her Highness closes her eyes in appreciation of her first sip. "Aah. Samir Singh—how I adore that man! He has come to see Latika and me. I am sorry the outcome does not favor him." She takes another drink. "And you, my dear, have you achieved the resolution you were hoping for with the Royal Jewel Cinema?"

Auntie-Boss looks off to the side, as if she's composing her thoughts. Then she says, "The ideal outcome is always the preservation of integrity. It's painful when the consequence of the outcome is so severe. I understand that the Royal Jewel Cinema will have to be completely rebuilt. But it will stand as a reminder to thousands of people who cross its threshold that the right thing is worth doing."

The old maharani grins, and a hundred wrinkles form at the corners of her lipsticked mouth as her hollowed cheeks lift, making her almost beautiful.

"A born politician. That's what you are, Mrs. Kumar. If you'd been born into our family, you'd be in Parliament by now, my dear!"

Today, the dowager queen's laugh is rich and strong. It fills up the room, floats through the door to the outside terrace and the maharanis' garden below, forcing the tiny monkeys to look up from their half-eaten guavas and the sunbirds to scatter into the cloudless sky above.

EPILOGUE
LAKSHMI

July 1969
Shimla

I'm at my kitchen window, admiring the charming tableau on the back lawn. It's dusk. Earlier today, Radha helped Jay and me light hundreds of *diyas* around our back garden for the wedding ceremony. The tiny flames flicker, making sequins and gold threads sparkle on the elegant clothes of the wedding guests.

It's not every day that a Hindu and a Muslim get married; Malik and Nimmi decided to have a civil ceremony much as Jay and I did six years ago. The magistrate who officiated has already come and gone, and now the family and guests are celebrating and waiting for the feast.

Nimmi chose to wear her tribal finery as a way of honoring

her heritage. The gold necklace Malik bought from Moti-Lal in Jaipur is around her neck. When I was preparing to apply her henna yesterday, Nimmi showed me that she'd added the amulet of Shiva to the chain. "It was Dev's," she told me, smiling, as if the memory now brings her joy instead of sorrow. I knew then that I would paint the image of the blue god—both a creator and a destroyer—on her left palm and, on the other, the word *om*, similar to the one on Shiva's right hand.

As soon as she saw what I'd painted, Nimmi said, "I will take good care of Malik." I straightened up then and looked her in the eye. There was a time I might have doubted this union, but that time had passed. I cupped her cheek in my free palm, and she'd leaned against it.

Two novices from the convent have come for the celebration. Nimmi is showing them the sandalwood sapling I've been try-ing to grow here in the cooler Himalayan climate. No doubt she's explaining to them how she uprooted it from the Healing Garden and transplanted it in this sunnier spot at the edge of my backyard garden. The sapling is faring better here; the slight increase in temperature seems to have given it new life. When it's old enough to produce its red seeds, Nimmi and I will grind them, mix them with clove oil, and use them to soothe boils and inflammations for the patients at the Community Clinic.

These young nuns have grown fond of Nimmi and now visit the Healing Garden once a week to learn how to grow the same plants at their convent. They are the first herbal practitioners we've taught in our new business!

Nimmi looks up at my kitchen window just then, as if she knows I'm watching. She flashes a brilliant smile at me. I return it.

Malik, handsome in the charcoal-gray suit he's had tailored for the occasion, is holding baby Chullu and laughing at some-thing my brother-in-law Pierre is telling him. Radha is with them, under the Himalayan pear tree; they make a pretty threesome. My sister, always crazy for babies, reaches for Chullu, and Malik hands him over. The boy tries to snatch the cluster of red primula from Radha's topknot, but she quickly grabs his hand and pretends to gnaw it. Chullu cackles with delight.

This morning, when Radha and I were walking with her daughters, Asha and Shanti, I pulled Kanta's latest letter from my pocket and showed the envelope to her. I raised my eyebrows to form the silent question I ask every time I see Radha. The crease between her brows told me she's not ready.

I patted her arm and returned the letter to my pocket. Someday, when the time is right, she'll let me know she wants to see the photos of Nikhil—the ones that Kanta sends me regularly and that I have been saving. Radha made a decision some time ago that was right for her and for Niki, the only one she *could* make at the time. But to deal with the immense loss she felt from giving up her baby boy, she had to cut all ties. She hasn't seen Nikhil since he was four months old, the night she came to me, heartbroken. Having finally realized that as much as she loved him, she couldn't care for him on her own and decided to allow Kanta and Manu, still yearning for a child, to adopt him.

My *saas* used to say: *If it doesn't bend as a sapling, will it bend as a tree?* But I hold out hope. I know the day will come when Radha realizes that her heart can now survive the pain. She's still only twenty-five; there's time yet.

I take a tray of glasses filled with *aam panna* from the kitchen out onto the lawn and set them on the outdoor table with the other dishes we've prepared. Chicken *tikka masala. Lauki ki subji, palak paneer. Baingan bharta. Aloo gobi subji.* There's cashew pilaf, *puri* and *aloo parantha.* For dessert, we have *semai ki kheer* and *gulab jamun.*

Rekha and Shanti run up to me. Rekha is wearing the little gold studs Malik gave her. The girls are both four years old and have been inseparable since they met yesterday, when Radha's family arrived for the wedding from France. The girls tell me they've been trying to coax Madho Singh, who is muttering in his cage, to join us for the celebration.

"*Tante*, can you help, *s'il te plaît*?" Shanti asks. Radha's daughters transition easily between English, French and Hindi. My sister has been speaking Hindi to them since before they were born.

Shanti has yellow-brown eyes like Pierre, but her willfulness is all Radha. Every few months, my sister will phone to tell me she's doing battle with Shanti. I can only smile, remembering all the challenges Radha presented me when she was thirteen. Shanti is only four, which means Radha has many battles ahead of her!

I should call the guests to the table, but I decide to indulge the girls. "Why don't you ask your father to give you both a helicopter ride?" I say to Shanti now.

The girls turn to each other, eager with anticipation. They squeal delightedly and bound like rabbits toward their target at the far end of the garden. Shanti runs into Pierre from behind, almost knocking him over. I watch the girls delivering their demands as Pierre listens. Then he puts a question to them. Reluctantly, Shanti points to Rekha. Pierre picks up Rekha, then walks to the center of the lawn. Holding on to her hands, he spins her around, twirling her faster and faster. Her hair lifts and falls, lifts and falls. Bubbles of laughter fill the air.

"My turn!" Shanti shouts, raising her arms. Pierre sets Rekha down, takes hold of Shanti's hands, then lifts her into the air.

I catch Malik gazing lovingly at Nimmi. As if he'd sent a silent signal, she turns to him, offering a private smile.

I walk to Jay, who is holding Radha's younger daughter, Asha. At two years old she is besotted with him, and he with her. Whenever he sees her waddling toward him on her chunky legs, the lines around his eyes crinkle with pleasure.

My husband kisses my forehead. I wrap my arms around both him and little Asha. She tries to throw off my embrace, wanting all of Jay's attention for herself. I poke her little belly, which, as always, makes her giggle.

I look around the garden, lush and magical, and see all I've nurtured: Malik and Radha, as dear to me as my own life. Their spouses and their children. Two generations of possibilities, of hope, surrounded by the blue evening, surrounded by us.

★ ★ ★ ★ ★

ACKNOWLEDGMENTS

If it weren't for readers, there would be no writers. After the publication of *The Henna Artist*, I was incredibly moved by passionate readers around the world who wrote to tell me how and why the book resonated with them, or that it inspired them to change something in their lives. They fell in love with Lakshmi, whose character was inspired by my amazing mother, Sudha Latika Joshi, and with Malik, whom they wanted to know more about. This story, then, is for them.

My agent, Margaret Sutherland Brown at Folio Literary Management, always has my back. Even during the pandemic, she found ways to stay positive and imbue our conversations with light and hope. Kathy Sagan, my editor at MIRA Books, is such a joy to work with, turning good manuscripts into better ones; her suggestions are always spot-on! And where would I be without the support of the rest of the HarperCollins team who make sure everyone falls in love with my stories: Loriana Sacilotto, Margaret Marbury, Nicole Brebner, Heather Foy, Leo MacDonald, Amy Jones, Randy Chan, Ashley MacDonald, Linette Kim, Erin Craig, Karen Ma, Kaitlyn Vincent and Lindsey Reeder?

A big, bright message of gratitude also goes to Reese Witherspoon, whose Hello Sunshine Book Club promotes female authors writing stories about strong female characters. Thank you, Heather Connor, Laura Gianino, Roxanne Jones and Cindy Ma of the HarperCollins publicity team for helping to make this incredible connection.

My father, Dr. Ramesh Chandra Joshi, whose encyclopedic knowledge of India (and almost everything else!) comes in handy when I'm writing about India and her people, contributed to the engineering details of the Royal Jewel Cinema. Any misrepresentations thereof are down to me.

Ever supportive and encouraging, my brothers Madhup and Piyush Joshi read drafts of this story and provided helpful comments, as did friends Gratia Plante Trout, Lanny Udell, Christopher Ridenour, Ritika Kumar and David Armagnac.

For this book, I researched India's gold industry and the myriad ways the metal is smuggled into the country. For Nimmi's character, I read about various nomadic tribes of the Himalayas, some of whom herd buffaloes, others who shepherd goats and sheep—all of whom live hard lives. Their knowledge of herbal cures and remedies is essential to their survival in the mountains. A nomadic lifestyle makes it difficult for their children to get a formal education unless they move to town, which many have been forced to do because local laws make it difficult for them to get grazing permits.

I always save the best for last. Years ago, my husband, Bradley Jay Owens, saw something in me that led him to believe I could be a writer. And here I am. With both my profession and my partner in life, how did I get so lucky?

GLOSSARY OF TERMS

accha: okay, all right

ake, dho, theen: one, two, three

akelee: alone

aloo gobi subji: potato-cauliflower curried vegetable

aloo parantha: potato-filled flatbread

aloo tikki: fried potato patty

Amreeka: America, pronounced in Indian-English

angrezi: English

anna: small coin, like a penny

ara-garra-nathu-kara: a nobody

arré: Hey! Come on!

ayah: nanny

baat suno: Listen!

bahut accha: Very good!

baingan bharta: eggplant and onion vegetable

baksheesh: bribe

basmati: a type of rice

beedis: cheap Indian cigarettes

behenji: sister, respectful address for older female

besan laddus: chickpea-flour sweets

bevakoopf: fool, idiot

Bhagwan: God

bhai: brother, friendly term for a male friend

bheta/bheti: son/daughter

bibi: wife

bonjour: hello in French

brahmi: plant used in Ayurvedic medicine

building-*walla*: person who builds

bukwas: nonsense

burfi: cooked sweet made from milk

bush-shirt: T-shirt

chaat: general term for fried snack food

chai: Indian tea

chai-*walla*: person who sells chai

champaca: sweet-smelling flower

chapatti: whole wheat flatbread

chappals: sandals

chemali: tropical flower

chillum: a hookah, for smoking tobacco

chinta mat karo: don't worry

chole subji: garbanzo curried vegetable

chowkidar: gateman

chunni: woman's fabric head covering

cousin-sister or cousin-brother: someone not related by blood but close to you

dal: spicy lentil dish

dhobi: man who washes clothes for a living

dhoti: 4 to 7 yards of white cotton wrapped into a loose pant for men

dibba: box

doctrini: female doctor

ghee: clarified butter

goondas: bad men, gangsters

gore: white people

gulab jamun: dessert made with deep-fried paneer in a sugar syrup

gupshup: gossip

hahn-nah: Right? Isn't that so?

Hai Ram: My God!

jharus: long-whiskered broom

jhumka: bell-like earrings

Ji: respectful address for women and men

joie de vivre: zest for life

kachori: deep-fried bread

kajal: black eyeliner

kheer: rice cooked in milk/cream dessert

khus-khus: handheld fan made of vetiver grass

koi baat nahee: It's no big deal

kundan: type of jewelry with uncut gems

kurta: long-sleeved loose cotton top

lakin: but, except

lassi: cool buttermilk drink, sometimes sweetened with mango

lauki: type of squash

Maa: mother

maaf kar dijiye: please forgive me

mahoot: elephant trainer

mandala: circular design created for ceremonies

masala lauki: spicy zucchini squash curry

meena: type of jewelry with enameling

meenakaris: artisans who create enameled jewelry

MemSahib: madam

moong dal: type of lentil

Mummi: mother (anglicized version)

nag kesar: a type of tree in the Himalayas

nahee-nahee: no

namaste: hello and goodbye

nazar: evil eye, jinx

nimbu pani: sweet lemon–lime water

om: the universal vibration, a symbol of peace and harmony

paan: snack for adults with sweet masala and tobacco

padha-likha: educated (literally "read–write")

pagal: crazy

paise: coins

pakoras: vegetables dipped in chickpea batter and fried

palak paneer: spinach and cheese vegetable

pallu: decorated end of a sari usually draped over the shoulder

pandit: priest

panipuri: a savory snack

parantha: stuffed whole wheat flatbread

patal: sharp knife used by shepherds

peepal: type of tree with large, flat leaves

pritam, priya: lover (male), lover (female)

puri: fried whole wheat flatbread

pyjama: the bottom half of a traditional man's kurta-pyjama outfit

Pukkah Sahib: gentleman

rajai: quilt

rasmalai: a sweet milky dessert

rath ki rani: queen-of-the-night flower, gives off scent only at night

rickshaw-*walla*: one who pedals a rickshaw

rogan josh: a lamb curry

roti: whole wheat flatbread

saas: mother-in-law

Sahib: sir, mister

salwar kameez: woman's tunic and loose pants

samaj-jao: Understand?

samosa: a fried snack with a spicy potato/pea filling

sari: woman's clothing, five yards long

semai ki kheer: sweet milk dessert made with vermicelli noodles

sev puri: type of fried snack food

shabash: Bravo!

sik: tribal dish served to pregnant women

s'il te plait: please (informal, in French)

sona: gold

suno: Listen!

tante: aunt (in French)

theek hai: that's fine

tickety-boo: fine, in good order

tikka: forehead jewelry

tonga: horse-drawn carriage

topa: close-fitting head covering

trousseau: what a bride collects for her marriage (in French)

tumara naam batao: tell them your name

waa: Wow!

yar: yes

zaroor: absolutely

INDIAN GOLD: A WOMAN'S RETIREMENT FUND

People wonder why gold is so important to Indians. In a country where less than 10 percent of the gold that's sold is currently mined there, the scarcity makes it more valuable. Perhaps it's also because that metal can't be destroyed. It can be melted, sure, but destroyed? Never. Which means it has the cachet of lasting forever. It's easy for artisans to work with the soft metal. And, of course, pure 22- or 24-karat gold contrasts beautifully with olive complexions.

At some point, it is customary in Indian culture for a groom's family to gift the bride with gold jewelry (her family provides a cash or land dowry to the groom's family as a way of paying for her upkeep throughout the marriage). Her gold is meant to be sold only in times of hardship. For example, if the husband dies or if the family is in dire financial straits.

Styles of Indian jewelry are as varied as the precious stones used to adorn them. The influence of six centuries of Moghul rule in refining the art of jewelry-making and upscaling the intricacy of the designs cannot be overstated. The most popular style for weddings and special occasions is kundan. Everyday wear includes a pure gold chain and gold hoops or other small gold earrings.

Kundan Style

Kundan is the oldest style of jewelry worn in India. Unlike the "claw" settings for gems in the West, the Indian jeweler sets uncut diamonds, sapphires, rubies and other precious gems flush in the hollow spaces he creates on a solid gold base.

Meenakari Style

Meena means enamel in Hindi. Meenakari is unlike the enameling work in France, England and Turkey. Indian artisans—under the influence of the Moghuls—decorated gold jewelry with detailed enamel patterns into the depressions they created in the metal. My mother was gifted with a complete set of meenakari jewelry for her wedding, including armbands, by my father's family. Each piece has her name in enamel.

Seed Pearls

This delicate style was a particular favorite of my mother's. Film stars in the late '50s and '60s started wearing pearls, eschewing gold jewelry, which seemed old-fashioned to them. And my mother chose sets with lots of tiny, tiny seed pearls sewn together to create delicate earrings, necklaces and bracelets. I love them, too!

Calcutta Jewelry (Calcutta was renamed Kolkata)

Artisans take a piece of yellow gold, flatten it, then hammer and detail it to make very intricate but lightweight, delicate jewelry. No stones, pearls or enamel are ever added to the design.

Silver

Like many women of her generation, my mother wasn't a big fan of silver. Silver is the metal of Rajasthani village women, who often wear multiple silver bangles, silver belts and thick silver anklets. The more silver a woman wore, the richer her family's status in the village.

My mother was gifted a large amount of silver jewelry by her in-laws, who came from a Rajasthani village.

TAKING INSPIRATION
FROM INDIAN FOOD

Aloo gobi. Parantha. Dal chawal. Gulab jamun. Palak paneer. Lassi.
These were the foods of my childhood in Rajasthan. Long after
my family left India and settled in America, my brothers and I
continued to ask my mother—again and again—for those same
dishes. Even now, when my family gets together, our meals include chapatti, subji and raita. When I first started writing this
trilogy, I knew the intricate relationship that Indian people have
with their food would be an important part of the story.

In the centuries before Marco Polo came to India in search of
spices, Indians harvested black and green peppercorns, pressed
oil from cloves, and ground mustard seeds to flavor foods, tan-
talize the senses, and heal the body. The flavors of cilantro,
turmeric, garam masala and cumin are as much a part of my

heritage, and my identity, as are the blue-green eyes I inherited from my mother, Sudha.

Even as I write this, I'm sipping chai infused with cardamom seeds, a stick of cinnamon and whole peppercorns. These overlapping flavors bring the India of my childhood alive again in my imagination, with all its chaotic, phantasmagoric glory.

Making Indian dishes takes time: multiple ingredients must be cut, peeled or diced; preparation must take place in stages; flavor is enhanced only by adding spices (as many as eight) at just the right time. Indian food is bold, colorful, bursting with aromas and flavors. What better way to enrich a plot and show character development than to infuse a story with one of the boldest, most beloved cuisines on earth?

ALOO GOBI MATAR SUBJI

(POTATO-CAULIFLOWER-PEA CURRIED VEGETABLE)

———◆———

My mother made this curried vegetable often. It's easy and fast as well as healthy and delicious. Indian cooks keep plenty of potatoes, onions, garlic, chilies and coriander on hand because they are common ingredients in almost every vegetable dish.

In North India, aloo gobi matar subji is usually eaten with chapatti, nan or roti. Some people prefer basmati rice with their veggies. Another curried vegetable such as okra or eggplant or garbanzo beans might be served alongside it. A bowl of yogurt seasoned with cumin powder and salt would not go amiss. And, of course, a spicy mango or lemon chutney would be an excellent touch for those who want a little more kick to their meal.

INGREDIENTS:

2 russet potatoes (*aloo*), peeled and cubed
1 small cauliflower (*gobi*), florets separated

1 cup fresh or frozen green peas (*matar*)

1 yellow or white onion, finely chopped

4 cloves garlic (or more, if preferred), finely chopped

1/2 cup canola or sunflower or safflower oil

2 tsp cumin seeds

2 tbsp turmeric powder

2 tsp cumin powder

1 tbsp garam masala

1 tsp ginger, finely chopped

2 tbsp coriander powder (if not available, use more coriander leaves)

2 tsp red chili powder or 1 hot chili pepper chopped fine

2–3 tsp salt (or to taste)

1/4 cup water

1 cup coriander leaves

DIRECTIONS:

1. Heat oil in deep skillet or large saucepan with heavy bottom. Add cumin seeds until they begin to sizzle.

2. Add onions and sauté on high heat until they're translucent.

3. Turn down heat to medium. Add turmeric, cumin powder, garam masala, coriander powder, chili powder and salt and stir for three to four minutes.

4. Add garlic and ginger. Stir. Add peas and stir.

5. Add potatoes and cauliflower. Stir until all ingredients are coated well with spices.

6. The mixture will start to sizzle. Add water so as not to burn the vegetables. You have an option here to add more water if you

want a soupy curry. But my father preferred a drier version, as do many North Indians, so my mother didn't add a lot of water to her recipe.

7. Turn down heat and cover the pot. Cook for another 10–12 minutes, taking care not to overcook the cauliflower. You want to leave a little crunch in the florets.

8. Garnish with coriander leaves.

9. Eat!

THE MAHARANI
COCKTAIL

During the winter holidays, my brothers and I used to look forward to coming home from our various colleges. My mother would call my older brother, Madhup, ahead of time to ask which cocktail he wanted to make for the family—he chose a different cocktail every year—so she could have the ingredients ready for our arrival. She rarely drank, but she made an exception when we were all together, savoring the limited time with her three children. Madhup would mix the cocktails and we'd stay up late into the night sipping, trading stories, laughing and teasing one another.

Because the dowager queen is a fan of gin and tonics, I asked Madhup to create a cocktail just for her. Enjoy it with a samosa, pakora or any other savories Lakshmi has on offer.

INGREDIENTS:

1.5 oz gin
Pinch of freshly ground cardamom
4 strands saffron

DIRECTIONS:

1. Combine and let stand for 5 minutes until flavors are infused in the gin.

2. Strain.

3. Then add:

3 oz tonic water
3 drops Patrón orange liqueur
Ice

Cheers! Sláinte! Prost! Na zdravi! Cin-cin! Salud!

THE SECRET KEEPER OF JAIPUR

ALKA JOSHI

Reader's Guide

mira

QUESTIONS FOR DISCUSSION

1. Do you think Lakshmi does the right thing by asking Malik to go to Jaipur and learn the construction trade? Could she have found another way to keep Malik out of trouble?

2. What makes Malik such a likable character? What three things do you think a great book character needs to make readers fall in love with them?

3. In what ways has Malik transformed from the street urchin he used to be? Has he changed from the outside or the inside, or both?

4. Could Nimmi have done something to keep Malik from leaving Shimla? Ultimately, do you think it was good for them to be apart? Does Nimmi learn anything about herself as a result of their separation?

5. How are Nimmi and Lakshmi different? How are they similar?

6. What do you think Malik learns about himself and his place in the world of the Singhs? What are the class differences between him and the Singhs? How do those differences manifest themselves?

7. What secrets is Malik privy to? What makes him keep those secrets to himself?

8. How does Lakshmi use her influence with the Maharanis to help Manu? Do you feel she's manipulating a volatile situation or strategically deflecting it?

9. What kind of power do the Maharanis wield? What are the limitations to their power?

10. Is Sheela making a play for Malik or is she merely flirting? What is her motive for either? Does she betray him on purpose or inadvertently?

11. Lakshmi and Jay trade proverbs playfully. Do they resonate with you or remind you of sayings from your own upbringing?

12. What do you learn about the significance of gold in Indian culture, especially as it relates to married women? In your own family, what do gold or precious metals signify?

13. The book is set in the late 1960s. What does it showcase about life at that time of India's history? Does it reinforce or change any of your assumptions about India?

14. In the end, Ravi is not penalized for his part in a criminal endeavor. What does that signal to you as a reader? Do the wealthy ever pay for their transgressions?

15. Why does Radha refuse to learn anything about Niki's life? Do you think there will be a time when she's ready to know more?

What inspired you to write this novel?

Before I became a writer, I was an avid reader, and I used to marvel at how writers could make characters come to life on the page. I could picture each in the gown or slacks the author had described, moving about a scene, talking to the other characters. And I would wonder: Did the characters feel as real to the author as they do to me?

Fast forward fifty years. I'm sitting -at my laptop, creating a scene between two characters, when Malik, the enterprising servant boy I created in The Henna Artist, starts to tell me he'd like to share his story. He's no longer eight years old; he's twenty. I ignore him for a while, but he's persistent—and persuasive. An extremely likable and loyal character, Malik has captured the hearts of thousands of readers around the world. So I finally set aside the project I was working on and let Malik tell me his story. It came pouring forth. True to his character, Malik's story is full of adventure and danger, and his love interest is a woman of unique character—not unlike Lakshmi.

And the answer to the question I used to wonder about? Yes, characters do come to life for authors as much as they do for readers. And when they do, you have to listen!

What are you working on now?

I'm currently researching the third book in the trilogy. Little did I know when I started writing The Henna Artist ten years ago that I'd end up writing three books, each focusing on one major character. The third book centers on Lakshmi's sister, Radha, as an assistant perfumer in Paris, where she lives with her French husband and two daughters. She's created the family she's always wanted and surprised herself with an ambition she hadn't known she harbored: to become a master perfumer, a difficult accomplishment for a woman in 1974. She's on the cusp of developing a scent using an Indian ingredient unknown to the French when a visitor from the past upends her future.

It's utterly fascinating—the hundreds of ingredients that go into fragrances Radha works with, the mystery of perfume houses like Chanel, Dior and Guerlain, the musky base notes that kiss the skin long after the spicy top notes have dissipated, and the lengths to which perfumers will go to create the perfect scent.

I'm so eager to return to the world of Radha, Lakshmi, Malik, Kanta and the Singhs as their stories develop over the decades. Who knows? Perhaps even the Maharanis of Jaipur will make an appearance in book three?

What inspired you to write this novel?

Before I became a writer, I was an avid reader, and I used to marvel at how writers could make characters come to life on the page. I could picture each in the gown or slacks the author had described, moving about a scene, talking to the other characters. And I would wonder: Did the characters feel as real to the author as they do to me?

Fast forward fifty years. I'm sitting -at my laptop, creating a scene between two characters, when Malik, the enterprising servant boy I created in The Henna Artist, *starts to tell me he'd like to share his story. He's no longer eight years old; he's twenty. I ignore him for a while, but he's persistent—and persuasive. An extremely likable and loyal character, Malik has captured the hearts of thousands of readers around the world. So I finally set aside the project I was working on and let Malik tell me his story. It came pouring forth. True to his character, Malik's story is full of adventure and danger, and his love interest is a woman of unique character—not unlike Lakshmi.*

And the answer to the question I used to wonder about? Yes, characters do come to life for authors as much as they do for readers. And when they do, you have to listen!

What are you working on now?

I'm currently researching the third book in the trilogy. Little did I know when I started writing The Henna Artist ten years ago that I'd end up writing three books, each focusing on one major character. The third book centers on Lakshmi's sister, Radha, as an assistant perfumer in Paris, where she lives with her French husband and two daughters. She's created the family she's always wanted and surprised herself with an ambition she hadn't known she harbored: to become a master perfumer, a difficult accomplishment for a woman in 1974. She's on the cusp of developing a scent using an Indian ingredient unknown to the French when a visitor from the past upends her future.

It's utterly fascinating—the hundreds of ingredients that go into fragrances Radha works with, the mystery of perfume houses like Chanel, Dior and Guerlain, the musky base notes that kiss the skin long after the spicy top notes have dissipated, and the lengths to which perfumers will go to create the perfect scent.

I'm so eager to return to the world of Radha, Lakshmi, Malik, Kanta and the Singhs as their stories develop over the decades. Who knows? Perhaps even the Maharanis of Jaipur will make an appearance in book three?